ACPL, Laramie, WY   02/   P9-DWJ-781
39092062152071
Preston, Douglas J.
Tyrannosaur Canyon
Wyman Ford ;1
Pieces: 1

This book
is in
memory
of

ADELE RUSSIN

TYRANNOSAUR CANYON

Also by Douglas Preston
in Large Print:

The Codex

Also by Douglas Preston
*   and Lincoln Child*
in Large Print:

Brimstone
Still Life with Crows
The Ice Limit

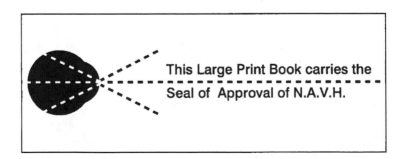

This Large Print Book carries the
Seal of Approval of N.A.V.H.

TYRANNOSAUR CANYON

Douglas Preston

Thorndike Press • Waterville, Maine

Copyright © 2005 by Splendide Mendax, Inc.

All rights reserved.

This is a work of fiction. All the characters and events portrayed in this novel are either fictitious or are used fictitiously.

Published in 2005 by arrangement with
St. Martin's Press, LLC.

Thorndike Press® Large Print Core.

The tree indicium is a trademark of Thorndike Press.

The text of this Large Print edition is unabridged.
Other aspects of the book may vary from the original edition.

Set in 16 pt. Plantin by Ramona Watson.

Printed in the United States on permanent paper.

Library of Congress Cataloging-in-Publication Data

Preston, Douglas J.
    Tyrannosaur Canyon / by Douglas Preston.
        p. cm. — (Thorndike Press large print core)
    ISBN 0-7862-8189-8 (lg. print : hc : alk. paper)
    1. New Mexico — Fiction.   2. Large type books.
I. Title.   II. Thorndike Press large print core series.
PS3566.R3982T97 2005b
    813'.54—dc22   2005023589

For my son,
Isaac

As the Founder/CEO of NAVH, the only national health agency solely devoted to those who, although not totally blind, have an eye disease which could lead to serious visual impairment, I am pleased to recognize Thorndike Press★ as one of the leading publishers in the large print field.

Founded in 1954 in San Francisco to prepare large print textbooks for partially seeing children, NAVH became the pioneer and standard setting agency in the preparation of large type.

Today, those publishers who meet our standards carry the prestigious "Seal of Approval" indicating high quality large print. We are delighted that Thorndike Press is one of the publishers whose titles meet these standards. We are also pleased to recognize the significant contribution Thorndike Press is making in this important and growing field.

Lorraine H. Marchi, L.H.D.
Founder/CEO
NAVH

★ Thorndike Press encompasses the following imprints: Thorndike, Wheeler, Walker and Large Print Press.

PROLOGUE

December 1972
Taurus-Littrow Valley
Mare Serenitatis
The Moon

On December 11, 1972, the last manned Apollo mission to the moon touched down at the Taurus-Littrow landing site, a spectacular, mountain-ringed valley at the edge of the Sea of Serenity. The area promised to be a geological wonderland of hills, mountains, craters, debris fields, and landslides. Of particular interest were several curious impact craters that had punched deep holes in the valley floor, spraying breccia and glass across the valley. The mission had high hopes of returning with a treasure trove of lunar samples.

Eugene Cernan was the commander of the Lunar Module and Harrison "Jack" Schmitt its pilot. Both men were ideally suited for the Apollo 17 mission. Cernan was a seasoned veteran of two prior missions, Gemini IX and Apollo 10; while Schmitt was a brilliant geologist with a

Ph.D. from Harvard who had been involved in planning earlier Apollo missions. For three days Cernan and Schmitt explored Taurus-Littrow with the help of the Lunar Rover. On their first venture across the lunar landscape, it became obvious to all that they had hit the jackpot, geologically speaking. One of the most exciting discoveries of the mission, and one that led indirectly to the mysterious find at Van Serg Crater, occurred on the second day at a small, deep crater known as Shorty. As Schmitt got out of the Rover to explore the rim of Shorty, he was astonished to see that his boots were kicking through the gray lunar dust to expose a layer of bright orange soil underneath. Cernan was so startled that he lifted his orange reflective visor to make sure it wasn't an optical illusion. Schmitt dug a quick trench and discovered that the orange soil graded down to a brilliant red.

The "Backroom" at Houston excitedly debated the source and meaning of this strangely colored soil, and they asked the two men to take a double-core sample to bring back to Earth. After Schmitt took the core, the two men hiked to the rim of Shorty crater, where they saw that the impactor had blasted through the same orange layer, which lay exposed along the sides of the crater.

Houston wanted to get samples of the orange soil from a second location. For that reason, they placed on the exploring itinerary a small unnamed crater close to Shorty, to be explored on Day 3, which they hoped would have an exposure of the same orange layer. Schmitt christened it Van Serg Crater, after a geology professor he had known at Harvard who wrote humorous pieces under the pen-name of "Professor Van Serg."

Day 3 turned out to be long and grueling. Dust fouled their equipment and hampered their work. That morning, Cernan and Schmitt had driven the Lunar Rover to the base of the mountains ringing Taurus-Littrow to examine a gigantic split boulder named Tracy's Rock, which had evidently rolled out of the mountains eons ago, leaving a trail in the soil. From there the two men explored an area called the Sculptured Hills, finding little of interest. With great difficulty Cernan and Schmitt hiked partway up one of the hills to inspect an odd-looking boulder, only to discover it was a scientific dud, nothing more than a "shocked piece of old lunar crust," which had been thrown onto the hillside by an ancient impact. The two astronauts descended the steep, powdery hillside leaping like kangaroos, Schmitt making noises as he jumped from side to side, pretending he was skiing moguls, joking, "Can't keep my edges. Shhhoomp. Shhhoomp. Little hard to get good hip rotation."* Cernan took a spectacular, low-gravity tumble, landing unhurt in the deep, powdery soil.

By the time they reached Van Serg Crater, both men were exhausted. As Cernan and Schmitt approached, they had to drive the Lunar Rover through a field of football-sized rocks blasted out of the crater. Schmitt, the geologist, thought the rocks looked odd.

"I'm not sure what's happened here, yet," he said. Everything was coated in a thick layer of dust. There was no sign of the orange layer they were after.

They parked the Rover and picked their way through the debris field to stand on the rim, Schmitt arriving first. He described it for Houston: "This is at least a large, blocky rim crater. But even it has the mantle dust material covering the rim, partially burying the rocks. And it's down on the floor, as near as I can tell, and on the walls. The crater itself has a central mound

*All conversations quoted above are from the original transcripts of the Apollo 17 mission, edited by *Apollo Lunar Surface Journal* editor Eric M. Jones. Copyright © 1995 by Eric M. Jones.

of blocks that's probably fifty meters in diameter — that's a little high — thirty meters in diameter."

Cernan arrived. "Holy Smoley!" he said as he gazed into the visually striking crater.

Schmitt went on. "The rocks are intensely shattered in that area, as are the ones that are on the walls." But as he looked around for orange soil, he saw none, just a lot of gray lunar rock, much of it in shatter-cones caused by the force of the impact. It appeared to be an ordinary crater, no more than sixty or seventy million years old. Mission control was disappointed. Nevertheless, Schmitt and Cernan began collecting samples and putting them in numbered specimen bags.

"These are very intensely fractured rocks," Schmitt said, handling a specimen. "And it comes off in small flakes. Let's get this one, because this will be the best oriented one for documentation. Plus, why don't you get that one you've got inside there?"

Cernan took a sample and Schmitt picked up another rock in his scoop. "Got a bag?"

"Bag 568."

"That's a corner, I think, off the block that Gene documented here."

Schmitt held out another empty bag. "We'll get another sample that'll be from inside the block."

"I can get it with the tongs real easy," Cernan replied.

Schmitt cast his eye about and saw another sample that he wanted — a curious-looking rock about ten inches long, shaped like a tablet. "We ought to take that just as is," he told Cernan, even though it was almost too big for a single sample bag. They picked it up with the tongs.

"Let me hold this end," said Cernan as they tried to maneuver the specimen into the bag. "Let me hold it, and you put the bag on." Then he paused, looking closely. "Well, see that? See the white fragments in there?" He pointed to a number of white fragments embedded within the rock.

"Yeah," said Schmitt, examining the spots closely. "You know, it might be that these might be pieces of the projectile. I don't know. 'Cause it doesn't look like . . . It's not subfloor. Okay. Pin it down."

When the rock was safely bagged, Schmitt asked, "What's the number?"

"It's 480," responded Cernan, reading out the number printed on the side.

Meanwhile, Houston had became impatient with the time being wasted at Van Serg, now that they had determined there wasn't any orange soil there. They asked Cernan to quit the crater and take some 500mm photographs of North Massif, while Schmitt did a "radial survey" of the ejecta blanket surrounding Van Serg. By this time, Schmitt and Cernan had been out exploring for nearly five hours. Schmitt worked slowly, and during the survey his scoop broke — dust problems again. Houston told him to forget the rest of the radial survey and prepare to close out the site. Back at the Rover, they took one last gravimetric meeting and a final soil sample, did the closeout, and returned to the Lunar Module. The next day, Cernan and Schmitt lifted out of the Taurus-Littrow Valley, becoming the last human beings (at least for now) to walk on the moon. Apollo 17 returned to Earth with a splashdown on December 19, 1972.

Lunar Sample 480 joined 842 pounds of other lunar rocks from the Apollo missions at the Lunar Receiving Laboratory at the Johnson Space Center in Houston, Texas. Eight months later, with the end of the Apollo program, the Lunar Receiving Laboratory was closed and its contents were transferred to a newly built, super-high-tech facility at the Johnson Space Center, called the Sample Storage and Processing Laboratory or SSPL for short.

Sometime during that eight-month period, before the transfer of the moon rocks to the new SSPL, the rock known as Lunar Sample 480 vanished. Around the same time, all entries related to its discovery disappeared from the computer catalog and hard-copy card files.

Today, if you go to the SSPL and make a query to the Lunar Sample Registry Database under the entry LS480, you will receive the following error message:

QUERY: LS480
?> ILLEGAL NUMBER/NO SUCH
  NUMBER
PLEASE CHECK LUNAR SAMPLE
  NUMBER AND TRY AGAIN

PART ONE

THE MAZE

1

Stem Weathers scrambled to the top of the Mesa de los Viejos, tied his burro to a dead juniper, and settled himself down on a dusty boulder. Catching his breath, he mopped the sweat off his neck with a bandanna. A steady wind blowing across the mesa top plucked at his beard, cooling him after the hot dead air of the canyons.

He blew his nose and stuffed the bandanna back into his pocket. Studying the familiar landmarks, he silently recited the names — Daggett Canyon, Sundown Rocks, Navajo Rim, Orphan Mesa, Mesa del Yeso, Dead Eye Canyon, Blue Earth, La Cuchilla, the Echo Badlands, the White Place, the Red Place, and Tyrannosaur Canyon. The closet artist in him saw a fantastical realm painted in gold, rose, and purple; but the geologist in him saw a set of Upper Cretaceous fault-block plateaus, tilted, split, stripped, and scoured by time, as if infinity had laid waste to the earth, leaving behind a wreckage of garish rock.

Weathers slipped a packet of Bull Durham out of a greasy vest pocket and rolled a smoke with gnarled, dirt-blackened hands, his fingernails cracked and yellow. Striking a wooden match on his pant leg, he fired up the quirly and took in a long drag. For the past two weeks he had restricted his tobacco ration, but now he could splurge.

All his life had been a prologue to this thrilling week.

His life would change in a heartbeat. He'd patch things up with his daughter, Robbie, bring her here and show her his find. She would forgive him his obsessions, his unsettled life, his endless absences. The find would redeem him. He had never been able to give Robbie the things that other fathers lavished on their daughters — money for college, a car, help with the rent. Now he'd free her from waiting tables at Red Lobster and finance the art studio and gallery she dreamed of.

Weathers squinted up at the sun. Two hours off the horizon. If he didn't get moving he wouldn't reach the Chama River before dark. Salt, his burro, hadn't had a drink since morning and Weathers didn't want a dead animal on his hands. He watched the animal dozing in the shade, its ears flattened back and lips twitching, dreaming some evil dream. Weathers almost felt affection for the vicious old brute.

Weathers stubbed out his cigarette and slipped the dead butt into his pocket. He took a swig from his canteen, poured a little out onto his bandanna, and mopped his face and neck with the cooling water. He slung the canteen over his shoulder and untied the burro, leading him eastward across the barren sandstone mesa. A quarter mile distant, the vertiginous opening of Joaquin Canyon cut a spectacular ravine in the Mesa de los Viejos, the Mesa of the Ancients. Falling away into a complex web of canyons known as the Maze, it wound all the way to the Chama River.

Weathers peered down. The canyon floor lay in blue shadow, almost as if it were underwater. Where the canyon turned and ran west — with Orphan Mesa on one side and Dog Mesa on the other — he spied, five miles away, the broad opening to the Maze. The sun was just striking the tilted spires and hoodoo rock formations marking its entrance.

He scouted the rim until he found the faint, sloping trail leading to the bottom. A treacherous descent, it had landslided out in various places, forcing the traveler to navigate thousand-foot drop-offs. The only route from the Chama River into the high mesa country eastward, it discouraged all but the bravest souls.

For that, Weathers was grateful.

He picked his way down, careful with himself and the burro, relieved when they approached the dry wash along the bottom. Joaquin Wash would take him past the entrance to the Maze and from there to the Chama River. At Chama Bend there was a natural campsite where the river made a tight turn, with a sandbar where one could swim. A swim . . . now there was a thought. By tomorrow afternoon he would be in Abiquiú. First thing he'd phone Harry Dearborn (the battery on his satphone had died some days back) just to let him know . . . Weathers tingled at the thought of breaking the news.

The trail finally reached the bottom. Weathers glanced up. The canyon face was dark, but the late-afternoon sun blazed on the rimrock. He froze. A thousand feet above, a man, silhouetted on the rim, stared down at him.

He swore under his breath. It was the same man who had followed him up from Santa Fe into the Chama wilderness two weeks ago. People like that knew of Weathers's unique skill, people who were too lazy or stupid to do their own prospecting and hoped to jump his claim. He recalled the man: a scraggy type on a Harley, some biker wannabe. The man had trailed him through Espanola, past Abiquiú and Ghost Ranch, hanging two hundred yards back, making no effort at deception. He'd seen the same joker at the beginning of his hike into the wilderness. Still wearing the biker head scarf, he followed him on foot up Joaquin Wash from the Chama River. Weathers had lost his pursuer in the Maze and reached the top of the Mesa of the Ancients before the biker found his way out.

Two weeks later, here he was again — a persistent little bastard.

Stem Weathers studied first the lazy curves of Joaquin Wash, then the rock spires marking the mouth of the Maze. He would lose him in the Maze again. And maybe this time the son of a bitch would remain lost.

He continued scrambling down the canyon, periodically checking his back trail. Instead of following, however, the man had disappeared. Perhaps the pursuer thought he knew a quicker way down.

Weathers smiled, because there was no other way down.

After an hour of hiking down Joaquin Wash he felt his anger and anxiety subside. The man was an amateur. It wasn't the first time a fool had followed him out into the desert only to find himself lost. They all wanted to be like Stem, but they weren't. He'd been doing this all his life, and he had a sixth sense — it was inexplicable. He hadn't learned it in a textbook or studied it in graduate school, nor could all those Ph.D.s master it with their geological maps and synthetic aperture C-Band radar surveys. He succeeded where they failed, using nothing more than a donkey and a homemade ground-penetrating radar unit built on the back of an old IBM 286. No wonder they hated him.

Weathers's ebullient mood returned. That bastard wasn't going to spoil the greatest week of his life. The burro balked and Weathers stopped to pour some water into his hat, letting the animal drink, then cursed him forward. The Maze lay just ahead, and he'd enter there. Deep in the Maze, near Two Rocks, was a rare source of water — a rock ledge covered with maidenhair ferns, which dripped water into an ancient basin carved in the sandstone by prehistoric Indians. Weathers decided to camp there instead of at Chama Bend, where he'd be an open target. Better safe than sorry.

He rounded the great rock pillar marking the entrance. Thousand-foot canyon walls of aeolian sandstone soared above him, the majestic Entrada Formation, the compacted remains of a Jurassic desert. The canyon had a cool, hushed feeling, like the interior of a Gothic cathedral. He breathed deeply the redolent air, perfumed by salt cedar. Above, the light in the hoodoo rock formations had turned from electrum to gold as the sun sank toward the horizon.

He continued into the warren of canyons, approaching where Hanging Canyon merged with Mexican Canyon — the first of many such branches. Not even a map would help you in the Maze. And the great depth of the canyons made GPS and satellite phones useless.

The first round struck Weathers in the shoulder from behind, and it felt more like a hard punch than a bullet. He landed on his hands and knees, his mind blank with astonishment. It was only when the report cracked and echoed through the canyons that he realized he'd been shot. There was no pain yet, just a buzzing numbness, but he saw that shattered bone protruded from a torn shirt, and pumping blood was splattering on the sand.

Jesus God.

He staggered back to his feet as the second shot kicked up the sand next to him. The shots were coming from the rim above him and to his right. He had to return to the canyon two hundred yards away — to the lee of the rock pillar. It was the only cover. He ran for all he was worth.

The third shot kicked up sand in front of him. Weathers ran, seeing that he still had a chance. The attacker had ambushed him from the rim above and it would take the man several hours to descend. If Weathers could reach that stone pillar, he might escape. He might actually live. He zigzagged, his lungs screaming with pain. Fifty yards, forty, thirty —

He heard the shot only after he felt the bullet slam into his lower back and saw his own entrails empty onto the sand in front of him, the inertia pitching him facedown. He tried to rise, sobbing and clawing, furious that someone would steal his find. He writhed, howling, clutching his pocket notebook, hoping to throw it, lose it, destroy it, to keep it from his killer — but there was no place to conceal it, and then, as if in a dream, he could not think, could not move . . .

2

Tom Broadbent reined in his horse. Four shots had rolled down Joaquin Wash from the great walled canyons east of the river. He wondered what it meant. It wasn't hunting season and nobody in his right mind would be out in those canyons target shooting.

He checked his watch. Eight o'clock. The sun had just sunk below the horizon. The echoes seemed to have come from the cluster of hoodoo rocks at the mouth of the Maze. It would be a fifteen-minute ride, no more. He had time to make a quick detour. The full moon would rise before long and his wife, Sally, wasn't expecting him before midnight anyway.

He turned his horse Knock up the wash and toward the canyon mouth, following the fresh tracks of a man and burro. Rounding a turn, a dark shape sprawled in front of him: a man lying facedown.

He rode over, swung off, and knelt, his heart hammering. The man, shot in the back and shoulder, still oozed blood into the sand. He felt the carotid artery:

nothing. He turned him over, the rest of the man's entrails emptying onto the sand.

Working swiftly, he wiped the sand out of the man's mouth and gave him mouth-to-mouth resuscitation. Leaning over the man, he administered heart massage, pressing on his rib cage, almost cracking the ribs, once, twice, then another breath. Air bubbled out of the wound. Tom continued with CPR, then checked the pulse.

Incredibly, the heart had restarted.

Suddenly the man's eyes opened, revealing a pair of bright blue eyes that stared at Tom from a dusty, sunburnt face. He drew in a shallow breath, the air rattling in his throat. His lips parted.

"No . . . You bastard . . ." The eyes opened wide, the lips flecked with blood.

"Wait," said Tom. "I'm not the man who shot you."

The eyes peered at him closely, the terror subsiding — replaced by something else. Hope. The man's eyes glanced down at his hand, as if indicating something.

Tom followed the man's gaze and saw he was clutching a small, leather-bound notebook.

"Take . . ." the man rasped.

"Don't try to talk."

"Take it . . ."

Tom took the notebook. The cover was sticky with blood.

"It's for Robbie . . ." he gasped, his lips twisting with the effort to speak. "My daughter . . . Promise to give it to her . . . She'll know how to find it . . ."

"It?"

". . . the treasure . . ."

"Don't think about that now. We're going to get you out of here. Just hang in —"

The man violently clutched at Tom's shirt with a trembling hand.

"It's for her . . . Robbie . . . No one else . . . For God's sake not the police . . . You must . . . *promise*." His hand twisted the shirt with shocking force, a last spasm of strength from the dying man.

"I promise."

"Tell Robbie . . . I . . . love . . ."

His eyes defocused. The hand relaxed and slid down. Tom realized he had also stopped breathing.

Tom recommenced CPR. Nothing. After ten futile minutes he untied the man's bandanna and laid it over his face.

That's when it dawned on him: *The man's killer must still be around.* His eyes searched the rimrock and the surrounding scree. The silence was so profound it seemed that the rocks themselves held vigil. *Where is the killer?* There were no other tracks around, just those of the treasure hunter and his burro. A hundred yards off stood the burro itself, still packed, sleeping on its feet. The murderer had a rifle and the high ground. Broadbent might be in his sights even now.

Get out now. He rose, caught his horse's reins, swung up, and dug in his heels. The horse set off down the canyon at a gallop, rounding the opening to the Maze. Only when he was halfway down Joaquin Wash did Tom slow him to a trot. A great buttery moon was rising in the east, illuminating the sandy wash.

If he really pushed his horse, he could make Abiquiú in two hours.

3

Jimson "Weed" Maddox hiked along the canyon floor, whistling "Saturday Night Fever," feeling on top of the world. The .223 AR-15 had been field-stripped, wiped clean, and carefully secreted in a crevice blocked with stones.

The desert canyon took a turn, then another. Weathers, attempting the same ploy twice, had tried to lose him in the Maze. The old bastard might fool Jimson A. Maddox once. Never twice.

He strode down the wash, his lanky legs eating up the ground. Even with a map and a GPS he had spent the better part of a week tramping around lost in the Maze. It hadn't been a waste of time: now he knew the Maze and quite a bit of the mesa country beyond. He had had plenty of time to plan his ambush of Weathers — and he had pulled it off perfectly.

He inhaled the faintly perfumed air of the canyon. This was not so different from Iraq, where he had done a stint as a gunnery sergeant during Desert Storm. If there was a place the opposite of prison, this was it — nobody to crowd you, nobody in your face, no faggots, spics, or niggers to spoil the peace. Dry, empty, and silent.

He rounded the sandstone pillar at the entrance to the Maze. The man he had shot lay on the ground, a dark shape in the twilight.

He halted. Fresh hoofprints in the sand headed to and from the body.

He broke into a run.

The body lay on its back, arms by its side, bandanna carefully spread over its face. Someone had been here. The person might even have been a *witness*. He was on horseback and would be heading straight to the cops.

Maddox forced himself to calm down. Even on a horse, it would take the man a couple of hours to ride back to Abiquiú and at least several more hours to get the police and return. Even if they called a chopper it would have to fly up from Santa Fe, eighty miles to the south. He had at least three hours to get the notebook, hide the body, and get the hell out.

Maddox searched the body, turning out the pockets and rifling the man's day pack. His fist enclosed over a rock in the man's pocket and he pulled it out and examined it by flashlight. It was definitely a sample, something Corvus had pointedly asked for.

Now the notebook. Oblivious to the

blood and entrails, he searched the body again, turned it over, searched the other side, kicked it in frustration. He looked around. The man's burro stood a hundred yards off, still packed, dozing.

Maddox undid the diamond hitch, pulled off the packsaddle. Yanking off the manty, he unhooked the canvas panniers and emptied them into the sand. Everything fell out: a jury-rigged piece of electronic equipment, hammers, chisels, U.S.G.S. maps, a handheld GPS unit, coffeepot, frying pan, empty food sacks, a pair of hobbles, dirty underwear, old batteries, and a folded-up piece of parchment.

Maddox seized the parchment. It was a crude map covered with clumsily drawn peaks, rivers, rocks, dotted lines, old-time Spanish lettering — and there, in the middle, had been inked a heavy, Spanish-style X.

An honest-to-God treasure map.

Strange that Corvus hadn't mentioned it.

He refolded the greasy parchment and stuffed it into his shirt pocket, then resumed his search for the notebook. Scrabbling around on the ground on his hands and knees, combing through the spilled equipment and supplies, he found everything a prospector might need — except the notebook.

He studied the electronic device again. A

homemade piece of shit, a dented metal box with some switches, dials, and a small LED screen. Corvus hadn't mentioned it but it looked important. He better take that, too.

He went back through the stuff, opening up the canvas sacks, shaking out flour and dried beans, probing the panniers for a hidden compartment, ripping away the packsaddle's fleece lining. Still no notebook. Returning to the dead body, Maddox searched the blood-soaked clothes a third time, feeling for a rectangular lump. But all he found was a greasy pencil stub in the man's right pocket.

He sat back, his head throbbing. Had the man on horseback taken the notebook? Was it coincidence the man had showed up — or something else? A terrible idea came to him: the man on horseback was a rival. He was doing just what Maddox had been doing, trailing Weathers and hoping to cash in on his discovery. Maybe he'd gotten his hands on the notebook.

Well, Maddox had found the map. And it seemed to him that the map would be as important as the notebook, if not more so.

Maddox looked around at the scene, the dead body, the blood, the burro, the scattered mess. The cops were coming. With a great force of will, Maddox controlled his breathing, controlled his heart, calling up the meditation techniques he had taught himself in prison. He exhaled, inhaled, quelling the battering in his chest down to a gentle pulsing. Calm gradually returned. He still had plenty of time. He removed the rock sample from his pocket, and turned it over in the moonlight, then took out the map. He had those and the machine, which should more than satisfy Corvus.

In the meantime he had a body to bury.

4

Detective Lieutenant Jimmie Willer sat in the back of the police chopper, tired as hell, feeling the thudding of the rotors in every bone. He glanced down at the ghostly nightscape slipping by underneath them. The chopper pilot was following the course of the Chama River, every bend shimmering like the blade of a scimitar. They passed small villages along the banks, little more than clusters of lights — San Juan Pueblo, Medanales, Abiquiú. Here and there a lonely car crawled along Highway 84, throwing a tiny yellow beam into the great darkness. North of Abiquiú reservoir all lights ceased; beyond lay the mountains and canyons of the Chama wilderness and the vast high mesa country, uninhabited to the Colorado border.

Willer shook his head. It was a hell of a place to get murdered.

He fingered the pack of Marlboros in his shirt pocket. He was annoyed at being roused out of his bed at midnight, annoyed at getting Santa Fe's lone police chopper aloft, annoyed that they couldn't find the

M.E., annoyed that his own deputy was out at the Cities of Gold Casino, blowing his miserable paycheck on the tables, cell phone turned off. On top of that it cost six hundred dollars an hour to run the chopper, an expense that came straight out of his budget. And this was only the first trip. There would have to be a second with the M.E. and the scene-of-crime team before they could move the body and collect evidence. Then there would be the publicity . . . Perhaps, thought Willer hopefully, it was just another drug murder and wouldn't garner more than a day's story in the *New Mexican.*

Yeah, please make it a drug murder.

"There. Joaquin Wash. Head east," said Broadbent to the pilot. Willer shot a glance at the man who'd spoiled his evening. He was tall, rangy, wearing a pair of worn-out cowboy boots, one bound together with duct tape.

The chopper banked away from the river.

"Can you fly lower?"

The chopper descended, slowing down at the same time, and Willer could see the canyon rims awash in the moonlight, their depths like bottomless cracks in the earth. Spooky damn country.

"The Maze is right down there," Broadbent said. "The body was just inside

35

the mouth where the Maze joins Joaquin Canyon."

The chopper slowed more, came back around. The moon was almost directly overhead, illuminating most of the canyon bottom. Willer saw nothing but silvery sand.

"Put it down in that open area."

"Sure thing."

The pilot went into a hover and began the descent, the chopper whipping up a whirlwind of dust from the dry wash before touching down. In a moment they had come to rest, dust clouds billowing away, the thudding whistle of the rotors powering down.

"I'll stay with the chopper," said the pilot. "You do your thing."

"Thanks, Freddy."

Broadbent piled out and Willer followed, keeping low, his eyes covered against the flying dust, jogging until he was beyond the backwash. Then he stopped, straightened up, slid the pack out of his pocket, and fired one up.

Broadbent walked ahead. Willer switched on his Maglite and shined it around. "Don't step on any tracks," he called to Broadbent. "I don't want the forensic guys on my case." He shined the Mag up the mouth of the canyon. There was nothing but a flat bed of sand between two walls of sandstone.

"What's up there?"

"That's the Maze," said Broadbent.

"Where's it go to?"

"A whole lot of canyons running up into Mesa de los Viejos. Easy to get lost in there, Detective."

"Right." He swept the light back and forth. "I don't see any tracks."

"Neither do I. But they have to be around here somewhere."

"Lead the way."

He followed Broadbent, walking slowly. The flashlight was hardly necessary in the bright moonlight, and in fact it was more of a hindrance. He switched it off.

"I still don't see any tracks." He looked ahead. The canyon was bathed from wall to wall in moonlight, and it looked empty — not a rock or a bush, a footprint or a body as far as the eye could see.

Broadbent hesitated, looking around.

Willer started to get a bad feeling.

"The body was right in this area. And the tracks of my horse should be plainly visible over there . . ."

Willer said nothing. He bent down, snubbed his cigarette out in the sand, put the butt in his pocket.

"The body was right in this area. I'm sure of it."

Willer switched on the light, shined it around. Nothing. He switched it off, took another drag.

"The burro was over there," Broadbent continued, "about a hundred yards off."

There were no tracks, no body, no burro, nothing but an empty canyon in the moonlight. "You sure this is the right place?" Willer asked.

"Positive."

Willer hooked his thumbs into his belt and watched Broadbent walk around and examine the ground. He was a tall, easy-moving type. In town they said he was Croesus — but up close he sure didn't look rich, with those crappy old boots and Salvation Army shirt.

Willer hawked up a piece of phlegm. There must be a thousand canyons out here, it was the middle of the night — Broadbent had taken them to the wrong canyon.

"Sure this is the place?"

"It was right here, at the mouth of this canyon."

"Another canyon, maybe?"

"No way."

Willer could see with his own damn eyes that the canyon was wall-to-wall empty. The moonlight was so bright it was like noon.

"Well it isn't here now. They're no tracks, no body, no blood — nothing."

"There was a body here, Detective."

"Time to call it a night, Mr. Broadbent."

"You're just going to give up?"

Willer took a long, slow breath. "All I'm saying is, we should come back in the morning when things look more familiar." He wasn't going to lose his patience with this guy.

"Come over here," said Broadbent, "looks like the sand's been smoothed."

Willer looked at the guy. Who the hell was he to tell him what to do?

"I see no evidence of a crime here. That chopper is costing my department six hundred dollars an hour. We'll return tomorrow with maps, a GPS unit — and find the right canyon."

"I don't believe you heard me, Detective. I am not going anywhere until I've solved this problem."

"Suit yourself. You know the way out." Willer turned, walked back to the chopper, climbed in.

"We're out of here."

The pilot took off his earphones. "And him?"

"He knows the way out."

"He's signaling you."

Willer swore under his breath, looked out at the dark figure a few hundred yards off. Waving, gesturing.

"Looks like he found something," the pilot said.

"Christ Almighty." Willer heaved himself

out of the chopper, hiked over. Broadbent had scuffed away a dry patch of sand, exposing a black, wet, sticky layer underneath.

Willer swallowed, unhooked his flashlight, clicked it on.

"Oh, Jesus," he said, taking a step back. "Oh, Jesus."

5

Weed Maddox bought a blue silk jacket, silk boxer shorts, and a pair of gray slacks from Seligman's on Thirty-fourth Street, along with a white T-shirt, silk socks, and Italian shoes — and put them all on in the dressing room. He paid for it with his own American Express card — his first legitimate one, printed right there on the front, Jimson A. Maddox, member since 2005 — and stepped out into the street. The clothes drove off some of the nervousness he'd been feeling about his upcoming meeting with Corvus. Funny how a fresh set of clothes could make you feel like a new man. He flexed the muscles of his back, felt the rippling and stretching of the material. Better, much better.

He caught a cab, gave the address, and was whisked uptown.

Ten minutes later he was being ushered into the paneled office of Dr. Iain Corvus. It was grand. A blocked-up fireplace in pink marble graced one corner, and a row of windows looked out over Central Park. The young Brit was standing at the side of his desk, restlessly sorting through some papers.

Maddox halted in the door, hands clasped in front, waiting to be acknowledged. Corvus was as wound up as ever, his non-existent lips tight as a vise, his chin jutting out like the bow of a boat, his black hair combed straight back, which Maddox guessed was the latest style in London. He wore a well-cut charcoal suit and a crisp Turnbull and Asser shirt — collar buttoned down — set off by a bloodred silk tie.

Now here was a guy, Maddox thought, who could benefit from meditation.

Corvus paused in his sorting and peered over the tops of his glasses. "Well, well, if it isn't Jimson Maddox, back from the front." His British accent seemed plummier than ever. Corvus was about his own age, mid-thirties, but the two men couldn't be more different, from different planets even. Strange to think that a tattoo had brought them together.

Corvus held out his hand and Maddox took it, experiencing the crisp shake that was neither too long nor too short, neither limp nor aggressive. Maddox suppressed a welling of emotion.

This was the man who got him out of Pelican Bay.

Corvus took Maddox's elbow and guided him into a chair in the little sitting area at the far end of the office, in front of the useless fireplace. Corvus went to his office door, said something to his secretary, shut and locked it, and then sat down opposite him, restlessly crossing and uncrossing his legs until he seemed to get it right. He leaned forward, his face dividing the air as cleanly as a cleaver, his eyes shining. "Cigar?"

"Gave 'em up."

"Smart fellow. You mind?"

"Hell no."

Corvus took one from a humidor, clipped the end, lit it. He took a moment to draw a good red tip on it, then lowered it and looked at Maddox through a turning veil of smoke.

"Good to see you, Jim."

Maddox liked the way Corvus always gave him his full attention, speaking to him like an equal, like the stand-up guy he was. Corvus had moved heaven and earth to free him from prison; and with one phone call he could put him back in. Those two facts aroused intense, conflicting feelings that Maddox hadn't yet sorted out.

"Well," said Corvus, sitting back and re-leasing a stream of smoke.

Something about Corvus always made him nervous. He withdrew the map from his pocket and held it out.

"I found this in the guy's pack."

Corvus took it with a frown, unfolded it. Maddox waited for the congratulations. Instead, Corvus's face reddened. With a brusque motion he flipped the map onto the table. Maddox leaned over to pick it up.

"Don't bother," came the sharp reply. "It's worthless. Where's the notebook?"

Maddox didn't answer directly. "It was like this . . . I followed Weathers into the high mesas, but he shook me. I waited two weeks for him to come back out. When he did, I ambushed him, killed him."

There was an electric silence.

"You *killed* him?"

"Yeah. You want the guy running around to the cops, telling everyone you jumped his claim or whatever you call it? Look, trust me, the guy had to die."

A long silence. "And the notebook?"

"That's the thing. I didn't find a notebook. Just the map. And this." He took the metal box with the switches and LED screen out of the bag he was carrying and laid it on the table.

Corvus didn't even look at it. "You didn't find the notebook?"

Maddox swallowed. "Nope. Never found it."

"He *had* to have had it on him."

"He didn't. I shot him from the top of a canyon and had to hike five miles to get to the bottom. Almost two hours. By the time I reached him someone had gotten there first, another prospector, hoping to cash in. A guy on horseback, his tracks were all over. I searched the dead man and his donkey, turned everything inside out. There was no notebook. I took everything of value, swept the site clean, and buried him."

Corvus looked away.

"After burying Weathers, I tried to follow this other guy's tracks, but lost him. Luckily the guy's name was in the papers the next day. He lives on a ranch north of Abiquiú, supposedly a horse vet by profession, name of Broadbent." He paused.

"Broadbent took the notebook," Corvus said in a monotone.

"That's what I think, and that's why I looked into his background. He's married, spends a lot of time riding around the back country. Everybody knows him. They say he's rich — although you'd never know it from looking at him."

Corvus locked his eyes on Maddox.

"I'll get that notebook for you, Dr. Corvus. But what about the map? I mean — ?"

"The map's a fake."

Another agonizing silence.

"And the metal box?" Maddox said, pointing to the object he had retrieved

45

from Weathers's burro. "It looks to me like there's a computer in there. Maybe on the hard disk —"

"That's the central unit of Weathers's homemade ground-penetrating radar unit. It has no hard disk — the data's in the *notebook.* That's why I wanted the *notebook* — not a worthless map."

Maddox turned his eyes away from Corvus's stare, slipped his hand into his pocket, and retrieved the chunk of rock, putting it down on the glass table. "Weathers also had this in his pocket."

Corvus stared at it, his whole expression changing. He reached out with a spidery hand and plucked it gently from the table. He retrieved a loupe from his desk and examined it more closely. A long minute ticked by, and then another. Finally he looked up. Maddox was surprised to see the transformation that had taken place on his face. Gone was the tightness, the glittering eyes. His face had become almost human.

"This is . . . *very* good." Corvus rose, went to his desk, slipped a Ziploc bag out of a drawer, and placed the rock inside with the utmost care, as if it were a jewel.

"It's a sample, right?" Maddox asked.

Corvus leaned over, unlocked a drawer, and removed an inch-thick stack of hundred-dollar bills bound in a block with rubber bands.

"You don't need to do that, Dr. Corvus. I've still got money left over —"

The man's thin lips gave a twitch. "For any unexpected expenses." He pressed the book of notes into Maddox's hand. "You know what to do."

Maddox parked the money in his jacket.

"Good-bye, Mr. Maddox."

Maddox turned and walked stiffly toward the door Corvus had unlocked and was holding open for him. Maddox felt a burning sensation prickling the back of his neck as he passed. A moment later Corvus arrested him with a firm hand on his shoulder, a squeeze that was just a little too sharp to be affectionate. He felt the man bending over his shoulder, whispering into his ear, overpronouncing each syllable.

"The note book."

His shoulder was released and Maddox heard the door close softly. He walked through the now empty secretary's office into the vast, echoing corridors beyond.

Broadbent. He'd take care of that son of a bitch.

6

Tom sat at the kitchen table, leaning back in his chair, waiting for the coffee grounds to settle in the tin pot on the stove. A June breeze rustled the cottonwood leaves outside, stripping the trees of their cotton, which drifted past in snowy wisps. Across the yard Tom could see the horses in their pens, nosing the timothy grass Sally had pitched them that morning.

Sally came in, still wearing her night-gown. She passed before the sliding-glass doors, backlit by the rising sun. They had been married less than a year and every-thing was still new. He watched her pick up the tin coffeepot on the stove, look into it, make a face, and put it back down.

"I can't believe you make coffee that way."

Tom watched her, smiling. "You look bewitching this morning."

She glanced up, swept her golden hair out of her face.

"I've decided to let Shane handle the clinic today," Tom said. "The only thing on the docket is a colicky horse down in Espanola."

He propped his boots on the stool and watched Sally prepare her own elaborate coffee, foaming the milk, adding a teaspoon of honey, then topping it off with a dash of powdered dark chocolate from a shaker. It was her morning ritual and Tom never got tired of watching it.

"Shane'll understand. I was up most of the night with that . . . business up in the Maze."

"The police have no theories?"

"None. No body, no motive, no missing person — just a few buckets of blood-soaked sand."

Sally winced. "So what *are* you going to do today?" she asked.

He sat forward and brought his chair back down on its four legs with a thump, reached into his pocket, removed the battered notebook. He placed it on the table. "I'm going to find Robbie, wherever she is, and give her this."

Sally frowned. "Tom, I still think you should have given that to the police."

"I made a promise."

"It's irresponsible to keep evidence from the police."

"He made me promise *not* to give it to the police."

"He was probably up to something illegal."

"Maybe, but I made a promise to a dying man. And besides, I just couldn't bring myself to hand it over to that detective, Willer. He didn't strike me as being the sharpest knife in the drawer."

"You made that promise under duress. It shouldn't count."

"If you'd seen the look of desperation on that man's face, you'd understand."

Sally sighed. "So how are you going to find this mysterious daughter?"

"I thought I'd start up at the Sunset Mart, see if he stopped in to buy gas or groceries. Maybe explore some of those forest roads back up in there, looking for his car."

"With a horse trailer attached."

"Exactly."

Unbidden, the memory of the dying man once again came into his mind. It was an image he would never shake; it reminded him of his own father's death, that desperate effort to cling to life even during those final seconds of pain and fear when all hope is lost. Some people could not let go of life.

"I might also go see Ben Peek," Tom said. "He spent years prospecting in those canyons. He might have an idea who the guy was or what this treasure was he was looking for."

"Now there's an idea. There's nothing in that notebook?"

"Nothing except numbers. No name or address, just sixty pages of numbers — and a pair of gigantic exclamation marks at the end."

"You think he really found a treasure?"

"I could see it in his eyes."

The man's desperate plea still rang in his ears. It had affected him deeply, perhaps because his father's death was still fresh in his mind. His father, the great and terrible Maxwell Broadbent, had also been a prospector of sorts — a tomb robber, collector, and dealer in artifacts. While he had been a difficult father, his death had left a huge hole in Tom's psyche. The dying prospector, with his beard and piercing blue eyes, had even reminded him of his father. It was crazy to make the association, but for whatever reason he felt the promise he had made to the unknown man was inviolate.

"Tom?"

Tom blinked.

"You've got that lost look again."

"Sorry."

Sally finished her coffee, got up, and rinsed her cup in the sink. "Do you realize that we found this place exactly one year ago today?"

"I'd forgotten."

"You still like it?"

"It's everything I always wanted."

Together, in the wild country of Abiquiú

at the foot of Pedernal Peak, they had found the life they had dreamed of: a small ranch with horses, a garden, a riding stable for children, and Tom's vet practice — a rural life without the hassles of the city, pollution, or long commutes in traffic. His vet business was going well. Even the crusty old ranchers had begun calling him. The work was mostly outdoors, the people were great, and he loved horses.

It was a little quiet, he had to admit.

He turned his attention back to the treasure hunter. He and his notebook were more interesting than forcing a gallon of mineral oil down the recalcitrant throat of some ewe-necked, rat-tailed bucket of guts down at Gilderhus's Dude Ranch in Espanola, a man legendary for the ugliness of both his horses and his temper. One of the perks of being the boss was delegating the scut work to your employee. He didn't often do it, and so he felt no guilt. Or maybe only a little . . .

He examined the notebook again. It was evidently written in some kind of code, laid out on each page in rows and columns in a fanatically neat hand. There were no erasures or rewrites, no mistakes, no scribbles — as if it had been copied from something else, number by number.

Sally stood up and put an arm around him. Her hair swung down over his face and he inhaled the fragrance of it, fresh shampoo and her own warm biscuit smell.

"Promise me one thing," she said.

"What?"

"Be careful. Whatever treasure that man found, it was worth killing for."

7

Melodie Crookshank, Technical Specialist First Grade, kicked back and cracked a Coke. She took a sip, gazing pensively around her basement lab. When she had gone to graduate school at Columbia in geophysical chemistry, she had imagined a very different career path for herself — trekking through the rain forest of Quintana Roo mapping the crater of Chicxulub; or camping at the legendary Flaming Cliffs in the Gobi Desert excavating dinosaur nests; or giving a paper in flawless French before a rapt audience at the Musée d'Histoire Naturelle in Paris. Instead, she had found herself in this windowless basement lab, doing dull laboratory research for uninspired scientists who couldn't even be bothered to remember her name, many of whom had an I.Q. half of her own. She'd taken the job while still in graduate school, telling herself that it was a temporary stop-gap until she finished her dissertation and landed a tenure-track position. But she had received her doctorate five years ago, and in the years since had sent out hundreds —

thousands — of C.V.s, and gotten no offers in return. It was a brutal market, where every year sixty freshly minted graduate students chased half a dozen openings, a game of musical chairs in which, when the music stopped, most were left standing. It was a sad state of affairs when she found herself turning to the obituary column of *Mineralogy Quarterly*, and getting a thrill of hope from reading that a tenured professor, occupant of an endowed chair, beloved of his students, holder of awards and honors, a true pioneer in his field, had been tragically stricken before his time. *Right on.*

On the other hand, Melodie was an incorrigible optimist, and she felt, deep down, that she was destined for something greater, and so she continued to send out C.V.s by the hundreds and continued to apply for any and all positions that came up. In the meantime, the present was tolerable: the lab was quiet, she was in charge, and all she had to do to escape was close her eyes and step into the future, that vast and wonderful country where she could have adventures, make wonderful discoveries, accept accolades, and have tenure.

Melodie opened her eyes once again to the mundane presence of the cinder block–walled lab, with its faint hum of fluorescent lighting and steady hiss of the forced-air system, the shelves loaded with reference books, the cabinets packed with mineral samples. Even the million-dollar equipment that had once thrilled her had long grown stale. Her eyes roved restlessly over the monster JEOL JXA-733 Superprobe Electron Probe X-ray Microanalyzer, the Epsilon 5 X-ray Analysis System with three-dimensional, polarizing optical geometry, together with a 600W Gd-anode X-ray tube and 100kV generator, the Watson 55 transmission electron microscope, the Power Mac G5 with the dual 2.5 gigahertz water-cooled CPUs, two Petrographic research microscopes, a Meiji polarizing microscope, digital camera setups, a complete sample preparation facility including diamond wafering blades, lap-wheel units, automatic polishers, carbon coaters —

What good was it if all they gave you was boring crap to analyze?

Melodie's reverie was interrupted by a low buzz, which indicated someone had entered her empty laboratory. No doubt another curatorial assistant with a request to analyze some gray rock for a research paper that no one would read. She waited, feet on the desk, Coke in hand, for the intruder to come around the corner.

Soon she heard the confident click of wing tips on the linoleum floor, and a slender, elegant man appeared, rustling along in a snazzy blue suit — Dr. Iain Corvus.

She swiftly removed her feet from the table, accidentally allowing her chair to come down with a loud clunk. She brushed her hair out of her reddening face. Curators almost never came to the lab, preferring not to lower their dignity by associating with the technical staff. But here, against all probability, was Corvus himself, who cut quite a figure in his Savile Row suits and handmade Williams and Croft shoes — handsome too, in a creepy kind of Jeremy Irons way.

"Melodie Crookshank?"

She was amazed he even knew her name. She looked into his lean, smiling face, beautiful teeth, hair black as night. His suit rustled lightly as he moved.

"Right," she finally said, trying to keep her voice easy. "That's me, Melodie Crookshank."

"I'm so glad I found you, Melodie. Am I disturbing you?"

"No, no, not at all. Just sitting here." She collected herself, blushing and feeling like an idiot.

"I wonder if I could interrupt your busy day with a sample that needs analyzing." He held a Ziploc bag up and let it swing back and forth, his teeth dazzling.

"Of course."

"I have a little, ah, *challenge* for you. Are you game?"

"Well, sure." Corvus had a reputation for aloofness, even arrogance, but now he seemed almost playful.

"Something just between us."

Melodie paused, then said carefully, "What do you mean?"

He handed her the sample and she looked at it. There was a label slid into the bag, handwritten, which said: *New Mexico, specimen #1.*

"I'd like you to analyze the sample in here without any preconceived notions about where it came from or what it might be. A complete mineralogical, crystallographical, chemical, and structural analysis."

"No problem."

"Here's the rub. I'd like to keep this secret. Don't write anything down or store anything on a hard drive. When you run tests on it, download the data onto CDs and hard-delete the data from the system. Keep the CDs locked up in your specimen cabinet at all times. Don't tell anyone what you're doing or discuss your findings with anyone. Report to me directly." He gave her another brilliant smile. "Are you game?"

Crookshank felt a tingle of excitement at the intrigue of it and the fact that Corvus had chosen to take her into his confidence.

"I don't know. Why so hush-hush?"

Corvus leaned forward. She caught the faint scent of cigars and tweed. "That, my dear Melodie, you shall know — *after* you've done your analysis. As I said, I don't want to give you any preconceived notions."

The idea intrigued her — thrilled her, even. Corvus was one of those men who radiated power, who looked like he could have anything he wanted just by taking it. At the same time, he was a little feared and disliked in the museum by many of the other curators, and all this false friendliness only confirmed in her own mind that he was a bit of a rogue — albeit a handsome, charming one.

He placed a gentle hand on her shoulder. "What do you say, Melodie? Shall we *conspire* together?"

"All right." Why the hell not? She knew what she was getting into, at least. "Any particular time frame on this?"

"As soon as possible. But don't cut any corners. Do it right."

She nodded.

"Good. I can't tell you how important that is." He raised his eyebrows and cocked his head, grinned again as he noticed her eyeing the specimen. "Go ahead. Take a closer look."

She turned her attention to the specimen

more closely, her interest aroused. It was a three-, four-hundred-gram chunk of brown rock. Right away she could see what it was, at least in general terms. There was some really unusual structure in there. She felt her pulse quicken, her heart speed up. *New Mexico, specimen #1.* This was going to be fun.

She lowered the baggie and her eyes met his. He was looking at her intently, his pale gray eyes almost colorless in the fluorescent glow of the lab.

"This is amazing," she said. "If I'm not mistaken this is —"

"Ah!" He placed a finger gently against her lips, and winked. "Our little secret." He removed his hand, rose as if to go, then turned back as if on an afterthought. He reached into his jacket pocket and pulled out a long velvet box. He held it out to her. "A little thank you."

Crookshank took it. *TIFFANY* was written on the front.

Yeah right, she thought, taking the box. She snapped it open and was dazzled by the sight of gemstones, blue stars. She blinked, hardly able to see. Star sapphires. A bracelet of star sapphires set in platinum. She peered closely and recognized immediately they were real, not synthetics. Each one was different, each one slightly flawed, each one with its very own nuance of color and hue and personality. She turned the box in the light, seeing the stars on each stone move, the light reflecting off their rutilated depths. She swallowed, feeling a sudden lump in her throat. No one had given her anything like this, ever. Ever. She felt a hot tickling in her eyes, which she instantly blinked away, horrified to discover herself so vulnerable.

She said in an offhand way, "Nice collection of aluminum oxide you got here."

"I was hoping you would like star sapphires, Melodie."

Crookshank swallowed again, keeping her face turned to the bracelet so he couldn't see her eyes. She didn't think she had ever loved anything so much as this bracelet. Sri Lankan star sapphires, her favorite, each one unique, forged in the depths of the earth by immense heat and pressure — mineralogy incarnate. She knew she was being shamelessly and openly manipulated, but at the same time she thought: Why not? Why shouldn't she take it? Wasn't that the way the world worked?

She felt Corvus's hand come to rest on her shoulder, giving it the gentlest of squeezes. It was like an electric shock. To her mortification a tear escaped and ran hotly down her cheek. She blinked rapidly, unable to speak, grateful that he was standing behind her and couldn't see. Another hand took the other shoulder, squeezing just a little in unison, and she could feel the heat of his presence on the nape of her neck. An erotic charge ran through her like a bolt of lightning, and she flushed and tingled all over.

"Melodie, I'm awfully grateful for your help. I know how good you are at what you do. That's why I entrusted this sample to you — and to no one else. That's why I gave you the bracelet. It's not just a bribe — although it *is* a bit of that." He chuckled, patting her shoulder. "It's an expression of my faith in you, Melodie Crookshank."

She nodded, her head still turned away.

The hands squeezed, rubbed, caressed her shoulders. "Thank you, Melodie."

"Okay," she whispered.

8

When Tom's father had died, and he had inherited an ocean of money, his sole indulgence had been buying his truck. It was a 1957 Chevy 3100 pickup with a turquoise body and a white top, chrome grill, three-speed on the floor. It once belonged to a classic car collector in Albuquerque, a real fanatic who had lovingly rebuilt the engine and drive train, machined the parts he couldn't find, and rechromed everything down to the knobs on the radio. As an ultimate touch, he'd upholstered the interior in the finest, creamiest white kid leather. The poor man had died of a heart attack before he could enjoy the fruits of his labor, and Tom had picked it up from an ad in the Thrifty Nickel. He had paid the widow every penny it was worth — fifty-five grand — and still he felt he'd gotten a bargain. It was a work of driveable sculpture.

It was already noon. Tom had driven everywhere, asked around at the Sunset, and had wandered as many of the forest roads that he knew near the high mesas, to no avail. All he learned was that he was merely retracing the footsteps of the Santa Fe Police, who were also trying to find out if anyone had encountered the murdered man before his death.

It seemed the man had been very careful to hide his tracks.

Tom had decided to visit Ben Peek, who lived in the funky hamlet of Cerrillos, New Mexico. A former gold-mining town that had seen better days, Cerrillos lay in a cottonwood-filled hollow off the main road, a cluster of old adobe and wooden buildings scattered along the dry bed of Galisteo Creek. The mines had played out decades ago but Cerrillos had avoided ghost-town status by being revived by hippies in the sixties, who bought up abandoned miners' cabins and installed in them pottery studios, leather shops, and macrame factories. It was now inhabited by a curious mixture of old Spanish families who once worked the mines, aging freaks, and curious eccentrics.

Ben Peek was one of the latter, and his place looked it. The old battenboard house hadn't been painted in a generation. The dirt yard, enclosed by a leaning picket fence, was crowded with rusted mining equipment. In one corner stood a heap of purple and green glass insulators from telephone poles. A sign nailed to the side of the house said,

THE WHAZZIT SHOP
EVERYTHING FOR SALE
including proprietor
no reasonable offers refused

Tom stepped out. Ben Peek had been a professional prospector for forty years until a jack mule broke his hip. He had grudgingly settled down in Cerrillos with a collection of junk and a stock of dubious stories. Despite his eccentric appearance, he had an M.S. in geology from the Colorado School of Mines. He knew his stuff.

Tom mounted the crooked portal and rapped on the door. A moment later the lights went on in the dimness beyond, a face appeared, distorted by the old rippled glass, and then the door opened to the tinkle of a bell.

"Tom Broadbent!" Peek's rough hand grasped Tom's and gave it a bone-crushing squeeze. Peek was no more than five feet five, but he made up for it with vigor and a booming voice. He had a five-day growth of beard, crow's-feet around a pair of lively black eyes, and a brow that wrinkled up so much that it gave him a perpetual look of surprise.

"How are you, Ben?"

"Terrible, just terrible. Come on in."

He led Tom through his shop, the walls covered with shelves groaning under heaps of old rocks, iron tools, and glass bottles. Everything was for sale, but nothing, it seemed, ever sold. The price tags were yellowing antiques themselves. They passed into a back room, which functioned as a kitchen and dining room. Peek's dogs were sleeping on the floor, sighing loudly in their dreams. The old man snagged a battered coffeepot off the stove, poured out two mugs, and gimped over to a wooden table, seating himself on one side and inviting Tom to sit on the other.

"Sugar? Milk?"

"Black."

Tom watched as the old man heaped three tablespoons of sugar into his, followed by three tablespoons of Cremora, stirring the mixture into a kind of sludge. Tom sipped his coffee cautiously. It was surprisingly good — hot, strong, brewed cowboy style the way he liked it.

"How's Sally?"

"Fantastic, as always."

Peek nodded. "Wonderful woman you got there, Tom."

"Don't I know it."

Peek rapped a pipe out on the edge of the fireplace and began filling it with Borkum Riff. "Yesterday morning I read in the *New Mexican* that you found a murdered man up in the high mesas."

"There's more to the story than what

was in the paper. Can I count on you to keep this to yourself?"

"Of course."

Tom told Peek the story — omitting the part about the notebook.

"Any idea who the prospector was?" he asked Peek at the end.

Peek snorted. "Treasure hunters are a pack of credulous half-wits. In the whole history of the West nobody ever found a real honest-to-God buried treasure."

"This man did."

"I'll believe it when I see it. And no, I haven't heard anything about a treasure hunter up there, but that doesn't mean much — they're a secretive lot."

"Any idea what the treasure might be? Assuming it exists."

Peek grunted. "I was a prospector, not a treasure hunter. There's a big difference."

"But you spent time up there."

"Twenty-five years."

"You heard stories."

Peek lit a wooden kitchen match and held it to his pipe. "Sure did."

"Humor me."

"When this was still Spanish territory, they say there was a gold mine up there north of Abiquiú called El Capitán. You know that story?"

"Never heard it."

"They say they took out almost ten thousand ounces, cast it into ingots stamped with the Lion and Castle. The Apaches were tearing up the country, so instead of packing it out they walled it up in a cave waiting for things to settle down. It so happened that one day the Apaches raided the mine. They killed everyone except a fellow named Juan Cabrillo, who'd gone to Abiquiú for supplies. Cabrillo came back and found his companions dead. He took off for Santa Fe and returned with an armed group to collect the gold. But a couple of weeks had passed and there'd been heavy rains and a flash flood. The landmarks had changed. They found the mine all right, the camp, and the skeletons of their murdered friends. But they never could find that cave. Juan spent years looking for it — until he disappeared in those mesas, never to be seen again. Or so the story goes."

"Interesting."

"There's more. Back in the 1930s, a fellow named Ernie Kilpatrick was looking for a maverick bull in one of those canyons back up there. He was camped near English Rocks, just south of the Echo Badlands. As the sun was setting he claimed he saw where a fresh landslide on a nearby rock face — just up Tyrannosaur Canyon — had unseated what looked like a cave. He climbed up and crawled inside. It was a short, narrow tunnel with pick marks in the walls. He followed it until it opened up into a chamber. He just about died when his candle lit up a whole wall of crude gold bars stamped with the Lion and Castle. He pocketed one and rode back to Abiquiú. That night he got drunk in the saloon and like a damned fool started showing the gold bar around. Someone followed him out, shot and robbed him. Of course, the secret died with him and the gold bar was never seen again."

He spit a piece of tobacco off his tongue. "All these treasure stories are the same."

"You don't believe it."

"Not a damned word." Peek leaned back and rewarded himself by lighting his pipe afresh and taking a few puffs, waiting for comment.

"I have to tell you, Ben, I talked to the man. He found something big."

Peek shrugged.

"Is there anything else he might have found of value up there besides the El Capitán hoard?"

"Sure. There's all kinds of possibilities up there in terms of minerals and precious metals. If he was a prospector. Or maybe he was a pot-hunter, digging up Indian ruins. Did you get a look at his equipment?"

"It was all packed on the burro. I didn't see anything unusual."

Peek grunted again. "If he was a *prospector,* he might have found uranium or moly. Uranium is sometimes found in the upper member of the Chinle Formation, which crops out in Tyrannosaur Canyon, Huckbay Canyon, and all around lower Joaquin. I looked for uranium back in the late fifties, didn't find squat. But then again I didn't have the right equipment, scintillation counters and such."

"You mentioned Tyrannosaur Canyon twice."

"Big damn canyon with a million tributaries, cuts all the way across the Echo Bandlands and up into the high mesas. Used to be good for uranium and moly."

"Is uranium worth anything these days?"

"Not unless you have a private buyer on the black market. The feds sure aren't buying — they've got too much as it is."

"Could it be of use to terrorists?"

Peek shook his head. "Doubt it. You'd need a billion-dollar enrichment program."

"How about making a dirty bomb?"

"Yellow cake, even pure uranium, has almost no radioactivity. The idea that uranium is dangerously radioactive is a popular misconception."

"You mentioned moly. What's that?"

"Molybdenum. Up there on the backside of Tyrannosaur Canyon there's some outcroppings of Oligocene trachyandesite porphyry which has been associated with moly. I found some moly up there, but they'd already high-graded the deposit and what I found didn't amount to day-old piss in a chamber pot. There could be more — there's always more, somewhere."

"Why do they call it Tyrannosaur Canyon?"

"There's a big basaltic intrusion right at the mouth, weathered in such a way that the top of it looks like a T. Rex skull. The Apaches wouldn't go up it, claim it's haunted. It's where my mule spooked and threw me. Broke my hip. Three days before they medevacked me out. So yeah — if it isn't haunted, it should be. I never went back."

"What about gold? I heard you found some back there."

Ben chuckled. "Sure I did. Gold is a curse to all who find it. Back in '86 I found a quartz boulder all spun through with wire gold in the bottom of Maze Wash. Sold it to a mineral dealer for nine thousand dollars — and then I spent ten times that amount looking for where it came from. The damn rock had to have come from somewhere but I never did find the mother lode. I figure it somehow rolled all the way out of the Canjilon Mountains, where there's a bunch of played-out gold mines and old mining towns. Like I said, gold is a loser. I never touched the stuff after that." He laughed, drew another cloud of smoke from his pipe.

"Anything else you can think of?"

"This 'treasure' of his might have been an Indian ruin. There are a lot of Anasazi ruins back up in there. Before I knew better I used to dig around some of those old sites, sold the arrowheads and pots I found. Nowadays a nice Chaco black-on-white bowl might fetch five, ten thousand. That's worth troubling about. And then there's the Lost City of the Padres."

"What's that?"

"Tom, my boy, I've told you that story."

"No you haven't."

Peek sucked on his pipe, with a gurgle. "Back around the turn of the century, a French padre named Eusebio Bernard got lost up there somewhere on Mesa de los Viejos on his way from Santa Fe to Chama. While wandering around trying to find his way out, he spied a huge Anasazi cliff dwelling, big as Mesa Verde, hidden in an alcove in the rock below him. It had four towers, hundreds of room blocks, a real lost city. No one ever found it again."

"A true story?"

Peek smiled. "Probably not."

"What about oil or gas? Could he have been looking for that?"

"Doubt it. It's true that the Chama wilderness lies right on the edge of the San Juan Basin, one of the richest natural gas fields in the Southwest. Trouble is, you need a whole team of roughnecks with seismic probes for that game. A lone prospector doesn't stand a chance." Peek stirred the ashes of his pipe with a tool, tamped it down, relit it. "If he was looking for ghosts, well, they say they're quite a few up there. The Apaches claim they've heard the T. Rex roar."

"We're getting off the subject, Ben."

"You said you wanted stories."

Tom held up a hand. "I draw the line at ghost dinosaurs."

"I suppose it's possible this unknown prospector of yours found the El Capitán hoard. Ten thousand ounces of gold would be worth . . ." Peek screwed up his face, "almost four million dollars. But you have to consider the *numismatic* value of those old Spanish bars stamped with the Lion and Castle. Hell, you'd get at least twenty, thirty times the bullion value. Now we're talking money . . . Anyway, you come back and tell me more about this murder. And I'll tell you about the ghost of La Llorona, the Wailing Woman."

"Deal."

9

In the first-class cabin of Continental flight 450 from LaGuardia to Albuquerque, Weed Maddox stretched out. Easing his leather chair back, he cracked his laptop and sipped a Pellegrino while waiting for it to boot up. Funny, he thought, how he was just like the other men around him, wearing expensive suits and tapping away at their laptops. It would be rich, really rich, if the executive vice president or managing partner next to him could see what it was *he* was working on.

Maddox began sorting through the batch of handwritten letters — illiterate letters laboriously written out on cheap lined paper in blunt pencil, many with grease stains and fingerprints. Clipped to each letter was a snapshot of the ugly bastard who had written it. What a bunch of losers.

He pulled the first letter out, smoothed it down on his tray table next to the computer, and began to read.

Dere Mr. Madocks,
   Im Londell Franklin James A 34

year old White Aryan Man from Arundell, Ark. my dick is 9 inchs rock hard all the way and Im looken for a blond lady no fat ass back talking bitches please just a lady who likes 9 inchs right up to the hilt plus im 6 foot two pure pumped up rock hard mussle with a tatoo of a deaths head on my right deltoid and a dragon on my chest Im looken for a slim lady from the Deep South no niggers quadroons or New York femminatzi bitches just an old fashoned White Aryan Southern Girl who knows how to please a man and cook chicken and grits Im doing five to fifteen armed robbery the DA lied about the plea bargin but I got a parole hearing in two yeares 8 months I want a hot lady waiten for me on the outside reddy to take it right up to the hilt.

Maddox grinned. Now there was a mother who was going to spend the rest of his life in prison — parole or no parole. Some people were just naturally born to it.

He started typing into his laptop:

My name is Lonnie F. James and I'm a thirty-four-year-old Caucasian male from Arundell, Arkansas, doing five to fifteen years for armed robbery,

75

with parole expected in less than three years. I am in superb physical condition, six feet two inches tall, 190 pounds, a serious weight lifter and body builder. Ladies, I am very well endowed. My sign is Capricorn. I have a tattoo of a death's head on my right arm and a tattoo of St. George killing the Dragon on my chest. I'm looking for a petite, blond, blue-eyed, old-fashioned Southern Belle for correspondence, romance, and commitment. You should be trim and shapely, twenty-nine or younger, sweet as mint julep — but at the same time a woman who knows a real man when she sees one. I like country music, good country cooking, pro football, and holding hands on long walks down country roads in the misty morning.

Now that was inspired, thought Maddox, reading it over. *Sweet as mint julep.* He read through it again, deleted the "misty morning" bit, saved it on his computer. Then he looked at the photograph that came with the letter. Another ugly mother — this one with a bullet head and eyes set so close together they looked like they'd been squeezed in a vise. He would scan it and post it all the same. In his experience looks didn't count. What counted was that Londell Franklin James was in there and not out here. As such, he offered the right woman a perfect relationship. A woman could write him, exchange sex-letters, make promises, swear undying love, talk about babies and marriage and the future — and none of it would change the fact that he was in there, and she was out here. She had ultimate control. That's what it was all about — control — plus the erotic bang it gave some women to correspond with a chiseled-up guy doing serious time for armed robbery who claimed he had a nine-inch dick. Yeah, and who was to prove otherwise?

He clicked on a fresh screen and moved to the next letter.

Dear Mr. Maddox,
I am looking for a woman to mail my jizum to so as she can have my baby —

Maddox made a face and crumpled that one up, shoving it into the seat pocket in front of him. Christ, he ran a dating service, not a sperm bank. He had started Hard Time while working in the prison library, where there was an old IBM 486 computer being used as a card catalog. His days in the Army as a gunnery sergeant had taught him all he needed to know about computers. In this day and age you could hardly fire a projectile bigger than a .50-caliber round without a computer. Maddox was surprised to find he had a major talent for computers. Unlike people, they were clean, odorless, obedient, and didn't haul around a bullshit attitude. He started off collecting ten bucks from cons for posting their names and addresses at a Web site he had created, soliciting female penpals on the outside. It had really taken off. Maddox soon realized the big money was to be made not from the cons, but from the women. It amazed him how many women wanted to date a man in prison. He charged twenty-nine dollars and ninety-nine cents a month to belong to Hard Time, $199 a year, and for that you got unlimited access to the personals — photos and addresses included — of more than four hundred real cons doing serious time for everything from murder and rape to kidnapping, armed robbery, and assault. There were now three women subscribers to every con, almost twelve hundred ladies, and after deducting expenses he was pulling down three bills a week, free and clear.

A "prepare for landing" announcement came over the intercom and a flight attendant came through, nodding and smiling, murmuring for all the businessmen to shut down their laptops. Maddox stowed his under the seat and looked out the window. The brown landscape of New Mexico was passing by as the jet approached Albuquerque from the east, the land rising to the slopes of the Sandia Mountains, suddenly dark with trees and then white with snow. The plane passed the mountains and they were over the city, banking toward the approach. Maddox had a view of everything, the river, the freeways, the Big I, all the little houses climbing up into the foothills. It depressed him to see so many useless people living such pathetic lives in those ant boxes. It was almost like being in prison.

No, he took that back. Nothing was almost like being in prison.

His mind drifted to the problem at hand, feeling a sudden rush of irritation. Broadbent. The man must have been waiting for his moment up there in the Maze. Just waiting. Maddox had done all the work, popped the guy, and then Broadbent stepped in, helped himself to the notebook, and split. The son of a bitch had wrecked a perfect finish.

Maddox took a deep breath, closed his eyes, said his mantra over a few times in his head, tried to meditate. No sense in getting all worked up. The problem was fairly simple. If Broadbent was keeping the notebook in his house, Maddox would find it. If not, then Maddox would find a way to force it out of him. The man simply had no idea who he was dealing with. And since Broadbent was up to his neck in it, it was unlikely he'd call in the cops. This was going to be settled between them privately.

He owed it to Corvus; Jesus, he owed him his life.

He settled back as the 747 came in for a landing, nice and soft, the plane barely kissing the ground. Maddox took it as a sign.

10

The next morning Tom found his assistant, Shane McBride, at the hot walker, eyeballing a sorrel quarter horse trudging around the circle. Shane was an Irish guy from South Boston who went to Yale, but he'd picked up western ways with a vengeance and now he looked more cowboy than the locals. He stomped around in roping boots and sported a bushy mustache, with a dented Stetson with a scoop-brim jammed on his head, a faded black bandanna tied around his neck, his lower lip packed with chaw. He knew horses, had a sense of humor, was serious about his work, and was loyal to a fault. As far as Tom was concerned he was the perfect partner.

Shane turned to Tom, pulled off his hat, wiped his brow, and screwed up one eye. "What do you think?"

Tom watched the horse move. "How long's he been on there?"

"Ten minutes."

"Pedal osteitis."

Shane unscrewed his eye. "Naw. You're wrong there. Sesamoiditis."

"The fetlock joints aren't swollen. And the injury is too symmetrical."

"Incipient, and sesamoiditis can also be symmetrical."

Tom narrowed his eyes, watched the horse move. "Whose is it?"

"Noble Nix, belongs to the O Bar O. Never had a problem before."

"Cow horse or hunter-jumper?"

"Cutting horse."

Tom frowned. "Maybe you're right."

"*Maybe?* There ain't no *maybe* about it. He just came back from competing in Amarillo, won a saddle. The workout, combined with the long trailering, would do it."

Tom stopped the walker, knelt, felt the horse's fetlocks. Hot. He rose. "I still say it's pedal osteitis, but I'll concede that it might be pedal osteitis in the sesamoid bones."

"You should've been a lawyer."

"In either case, the treatment's the same. Complete rest, periodic hosing with cold water, application of DMSO, full leather pads for the feet."

"Tell me something I don't know."

Tom grasped Shane by the shoulder. "You're getting pretty good at this, eh, Shane?"

"You got it, boss."

"Then you won't mind running the show today, too."

"Things go a lot better when you're not here — cold cerveza, mariachis, bare-assed women."

"Don't burn the place down."

"You still looking for that gal whose daddy was killed in the Maze?"

"I'm not having much luck. The police can't find the body."

"It ain't no surprise to me they can't find the body. That's a big damn country back up there."

Tom nodded. "If I could figure out what he'd written in that journal of his, it would probably tell me who he was."

"It probably would."

Tom had told Shane everything. They had that kind of relationship. And Shane, despite his garrulousness, was implicitly discreet.

"You got it on you?"

Tom pulled the notebook out of his pocket.

"Lemme see." He took it, flipped through it. "What's this? Code?"

"Yes."

He shut it, examined the cover. "That blood?"

Tom nodded.

"Jesus. The poor guy." Shane handed him back the notebook. "If the cops learn you held out on 'em, they'll weld the cell door shut."

"I'll remember that."

Tom walked around behind the clinic to check the horses in the stalls; he went down the line, patting each one, murmuring soothing words, checking them out. He finished up at his desk and sorted through the bills, noting that some were overdue. He hadn't paid them, not through lack of money but through sheer laziness; both he and Shane hated the paperwork end of the business. He dumped them back into the in-box without opening any. He really needed to hire a bookkeeper to handle all this paperwork, except that the extra expense would put them back into the red, after a year of hard work getting themselves to the breakeven point. The fact that he had a hundred million dollars in escrow didn't matter. He wasn't his father. He needed to turn a profit for himself.

He shoved the papers aside and pulled out the notebook, opening it and laying it on the table. The numbers beckoned — in there, he felt sure, was the secret to the man's identity. And of the treasure he found.

Shane poked his head in.

"How's that O Bar O gelding?" Tom asked.

"Doctored and in his stall." Shane hesitated in the door.

"What is it?"

"You remember last year, when that monastery up the Chama River had a sick ewe?"

Tom nodded.

"When we were up there, remember hearing about a monk up there who used to be a code breaker for the CIA, gave it all up to become a monk?"

"Yeah. I remember something like that."

"Why don't you ask him to take a crack at the notebook?"

Tom stared at Shane. "Now that's the best idea you've had all week."

11

Melodie Crookshank adjusted the angle on the diamond wafering blade and upped the rpm. It was a beautiful piece of precision machinery — you could hear it in the clear singing noise it made. She set the sample in the cutting bed, tightening it in place, then turned on the laminar water flow. A gurgling noise rose above the whine of the blade as the water bathed the specimen, bringing out flecks of color in it, yellow, red, deep purple. She made some final adjustments, set the automatic guide speed, and let it rip.

As the specimen encountered the diamond blade there was a note of pure music. In a moment the specimen had been cut in half, the treasure of its interior exposed to view. With the deft experience of years she washed and dried it, flipped it, embedding the other side in epoxy resin on a steel manipulator.

As she waited for the epoxy to harden she examined her sapphire bracelet. She'd told her friends that it was a cheap bit of costume jewelry and they believed her.

Why wouldn't they? Who would have thought, she, Melodie Crookshank, Technical Assistant First Grade, making all of twenty-one thousand dollars a year, living in an airshaft apartment on upper Amsterdam Avenue, with no boyfriend and no money, would be walking around wearing ten carats of Sri Lankan blue star sapphires? She knew very well she was being used by Corvus — such a man would never take a serious romantic interest in her. On the other hand it wasn't coincidence that he had entrusted her with this job. She was good — damn good. The bracelet was part of a strictly impersonal transaction: compensation for her expertise and discretion. Nothing dishonorable in that.

The sample had hardened. She placed it back in the cutting bed and sliced again on the other side. In a moment she had a slender wafer of stone, about half a millimeter thick, perfectly cut with nary a crack or chip. She quickly dissolved the resin, freed the wafer, and cut it into a dozen smaller pieces, each one destined for a different kind of test. Taking one of the chips, she fixed it in epoxy on another manipulator and used the lap wheel and polisher to thin it further, until it was beautifully transparent and about twice the thickness of a human hair. She mounted it on a slide and placed it on the stage of the

Meiji polarizing scope, switched it on, and put her eyes to the oculars.

With a rapid adjustment of the focusing knobs a rainbow of color leapt into her vision, a whole world of crystalline beauty. The sheer splendor of the polarizing scope always took her breath away. Even the dullest rock bared its inner soul. She set the magnification at 30x and began stepping through the polarization angle thirty degrees at a time, each change producing a new shower of color in the specimen. This first run was purely for aesthetics; it was like gazing into a stained-glass window more beautiful than the Rosette in Chartres Cathedral.

As she moved through 360 degrees of polarization, Crookshank felt her heart accelerating with every new angle. This was truly an incredible specimen. After a complete series she upped the magnification to 120x. The structure was so fine, so perfect — astonishing. She could now understand the secrecy. If there were more of this in situ — and there probably was — it would be of the utmost importance to keep it secret. This would be a stunning coup, even for a man as distinguished as Corvus.

She leaned back from the eyepieces, a new thought entering her head. This might be just the thing *she* needed to leverage a tenure-track position for herself, if she played her cards right.

12

Christ in the Desert Monastery lay fifteen
miles up the Chama River, deep in the
Chama wilderness and hard alongside the
enormous cliff-walled bulk of Mesa de los
Viejos, the Mesa of the Ancients, which
marked the beginning of the high mesa
country. Tom drove up the monastery road
with excruciating slowness, hating to subject his precious Chevy to one of the most
notorious roads in New Mexico. The
road had so many potholes it looked
bombed, and there were sections of washboard that threatened to shake loose
every bolt in the vehicle and chip his
teeth down to stubs. The monks, it was
said, liked it that way.

After what seemed like a journey to the
very ends of the earth, Tom spied the
adobe church tower rising above the juni-
pers and chamisa. Gradually the rest of the
Benedictine monastery came into view — a
cluster of brown adobe buildings scattered
helter-skelter on a bench of land above the
floodplain of the river, just below where
Rio Gallina joined the Rio Chama. It was

said to be one of the most remote Christian monasteries in the world.

Tom parked his truck in the dirt lot and walked up the trail to the monastery's shop. He felt awkward, wondering just how he would go about asking for the monk's help. He could hear the faint sound of singing drifting down from the church, mingling with the raucous cries of a flock of piñon jays.

The shop was empty, but the door had tinkled a bell when Tom had opened it, and a young monk came in from the back.

"Hello," said Tom.

"Welcome." The monk took a seat on a high wooden stool behind the shop's counter. Tom stood there indecisively, looking at the humble products of the monastery: honey, dried flowers, hand-printed cards, wood carvings. "I'm Tom Broadbent," he said, offering his hand.

The monk took it. He was small and slight and wore thick glasses. "Pleased to meet you."

Tom cleared his throat. This was damned awkward. "I'm a veterinarian, and last year I doctored a sick ewe up here."

The monk nodded.

"While I was here, I heard mention of a monk who'd been in the CIA."

The monk nodded again.

"Do you know who I'm talking about?"

"Brother Ford."

"Right. I was wondering if I could talk to him."

The monk glanced at his watch, a big sports watch with buttons and dials, which looked out of place on the wrist of a monk, Tom wasn't sure why. Even monks needed to know the time.

"Sext is just over. I'll go get him."

The monk vanished up the trail. Five minutes later Tom was startled to see a gigantic figure marching down, his enormous feet in dusty sandals, a long wooden staff in his hand, his brown robes flapping behind him. A moment later the door was flung open and he came striding into the shop, his robes astir, and without a beat he strode up to Tom and enveloped his hand in a large, but surprisingly gentle, grasp.

"Brother Wyman Ford," he graveled out in a distinctly unmonkish voice.

"Tom Broadbent."

Brother Ford was a strikingly ugly man, with a large head and a craggy face that looked like a cross between Abraham Lincoln and Herman Munster. The man didn't seem particularly pious, at least on the surface, and he certainly didn't look like a typical monk, with his powerful six-foot five-inch frame, beard, and unruly black hair that spilled over his ears.

A silence ensued and Tom once again felt the awkwardness of his visit. "Do you have a moment to talk?"

"Technically, on the grounds we're under a vow of silence," said the monk. "Shall we take a walk?"

"Fine."

The monk set out at high speed along a trail that wound down to the river from the shop and skirted the riverbank, Tom struggling to keep up. It was a beautiful June day, the orange canyon rims standing against the blue sky in a brilliant contrast of color, while above puffy clouds drifted along like tall ships at sea. For ten minutes they hiked, saying nothing. The trail ascended, terminating at the top of a bluff. Brother Wyman tossed back the skirt of his robe and sat down on the trunk of a dead juniper.

Sitting beside the monk, Tom studied the canyon country in rapt silence.

"I hope I haven't taken you from anything important," he said, still unsure how to begin.

"I'm missing a terribly important meeting in the Disputation Chamber. One of the brothers swore at Compline." He chuckled.

"Brother Ford —"

"Please call me Wyman."

"I wonder if you'd heard about the

murder in the Maze two days ago."

"I gave up reading the paper a long time ago."

"You know where the Maze is?"

"I know it well."

"Two nights ago, a treasure hunter was murdered up there." Tom recited the story of the man, finding the body, the notebook, the disappearance.

Ford was silent for a while, looking out over the river. Then he turned his head and asked, "So . . . where do I come in?"

Tom removed the notebook from his pocket.

"You didn't give it to the police?"

"I'd made a promise."

"Surely you gave them a copy."

"No."

"That was unwise."

"The policeman investigating the case didn't inspire much confidence. And I made a *promise*."

He found the monk's steady gray eyes on him. "What can I do for you?"

Tom held out the notebook but the monk made no move to take it.

"I've tried everything I know to identify the man so I can give this to his daughter. Nothing's worked. The police haven't a clue and tell me it may be weeks before they find the body. The answer to the man's identity lies in here — I'm sure of it.

Only problem is, it's written in code."

A pause. The monk continued to gaze steadily at Tom.

"I heard you were a code breaker for the CIA."

"A cryptanalyst, yes."

"Well? How about taking a crack at it?"

Ford eyed the notebook but again made no move to take it.

"Well, take a look," said Tom, holding it out.

Ford hesitated, then said, "No, thank you."

"Why not?"

"Because I choose not to."

Tom felt a surge of irritation at the high-handedness of the answer. "It's for a good cause. This man's daughter probably has no idea he's dead. She may be worried sick about him. I made a promise to a dying man and I'm going to keep that promise — and you're the only man I know who can help me."

"I'm sorry, Tom, but I *can't* help you."

"You can't or you won't?"

"Won't."

"Are you afraid of getting involved because of the police?"

A dry smile creased the man's craggy face. "Not at all."

"Then what is it?"

"I came up here for a reason — to get

away from just that sort of thing."

"I'm not sure I know what you mean."

"In less than a month I'm going to take my vows. Being a monk is more than wearing a habit. It's taking on a new life. That" — he pointed to the book — "would be a throwback to my old life."

"Your old life — ?"

Wyman stared across the river, his craggy brows contracted, his lantern jaw working. "My old life."

"You must've had a pretty rough time of it, to run away to a monastery."

Ford's brow contracted. "Monastic spirituality is not about running away from something, but about running *toward* something — the living God. But yes, it was rough."

"What happened? If you don't mind me asking."

"I do mind. I guess I'm no longer used to the kind of prying inquisitiveness that in the outside world passes for conversation."

Tom was stung by the rebuke. "I'm sorry. I'm out of line."

"Don't be sorry. You're doing what you feel is right. And I think it *is* right. It's just that I'm not the man to help you."

Tom nodded and they both rose, the monk slapping the dust off his robes. "About the book, I don't think you'll have much trouble with that code. Most homemade codes are what we call idiot ciphers — designed by an idiot, decipherable by an idiot. Numbers substituted for letters. All you need is a frequency table of the English language."

"What's that?"

"A list of the most to least common letters in the English language. You match that list up with the most to least common numbers in the code."

"Sounds easy enough."

"It is. You'll crack that code in a jiffy, I bet."

"Thanks."

Ford hesitated. "Let me take a quick look at it. I might be able to crack it on the spot."

"You sure you don't mind?"

"It won't bite me."

Tom handed it to him. Ford leafed through it, taking his time with each page. Five long minutes passed.

"Funny, but this is looking a lot more sophisticated to me than a substitution code." The sun was descending into the canyons, suffusing the arroyos in a bright golden light. Swallows flitted about, the stone walls reverberating with their cries. The river tumbled by below, a whisper of water.

He shut the book with a slap. "I'll keep the book for a few days. These numbers are intriguing — all kinds of weird patterns in there."

"You're going to help me out after all?"

Ford shrugged. "It'll help this girl learn what happened to her father."

"After what you told me I feel a little uncomfortable about this."

He waved a large hand. "Sometimes I get a little too absolutist about things. There's no harm in giving it a quick try." He squinted at the sun. "I better be getting back."

He grasped Tom's hand. "I admire your stubbornness. The monastery doesn't have a telephone, but we do have an Internet connection via satellite dish. I'll drop you a line when I crack it."

13

Weed Maddox remembered the first time he had blown through Abiquiú on a stolen Harley Dyna Wide Glide. Now he was just another asshole in khakis and a Ralph Lauren Polo shirt driving a Range Rover. He was really coming up in the world. Beyond the town of Abiquiú the road followed the river, past green alfalfa fields and groves of cottonwoods, before climbing out of the valley. He took a left on 96, drove over the dam and up along the southern side of the valley, in the shadow of Pedernal Peak. In another few minutes the left-hand turn to the Broadbent place appeared, with a hand-painted sign on a weathered board: *Cañones*.

The road was dirt, not well maintained. It paralleled a small creek. There were some small horse ranches on either side, forty to eighty acres, with cute names like Los Amigos or Buckskin Hollow. The Broadbent place, he'd heard, had a strange name, *Sukia Tara*. Maddox slowed at the gate, passed it, continued on for another quarter of a mile, and parked the car in a thicket of gambel oaks. He got out and eased the door shut. Strolling back to the road, he made sure the car wasn't visible. Three o'clock. Broadbent would probably be gone, at work or out. They said he had a wife, Sally, who ran a riding stable. He wondered what she looked like.

Maddox slung the rucksack over his shoulder. First thing, he thought, was to reconnoiter the land. He was a firm believer in reconnaissance. If no one was home he'd search the place, get the notebook if it was there, and get out. If the little woman was home that would make things easier. He had yet to find the person who wouldn't cooperate with the business end of a gun grinding the back of their mouth.

Leaving the road, he hiked along the bank of the creek. A thread of water appeared, then disappeared among white stones. Cutting to the left, he passed through a grove of cottonwoods and brush oaks before coming up behind Broadbent's barn. Moving slowly, being careful not to leave footprints, he climbed through a triple-strand barbed-wire fence and edged along the back wall of the barn. Crouching at the corner, he parted the rabbitbrush to get a view of the back of the house.

He took it in: a low adobe, some corrals, a couple of horses, a feeding area, a watering trough. He heard a high-pitched shout. Beyond the corrals there was an outdoor riding arena. The wife — Sally — held a lunge line dallied around her elbow, with a kid riding on a horse, going around and around in circles.

He raised his binoculars and she leapt into focus. He watched her body turn with the horse, front, side, back, and around again. A breeze caught her long hair and she raised a hand to brush it from her face. Jesus, she was pretty.

He moved his view to the kid. Some kind of retard, a mongoloid or something.

He turned his attention back to the house. Next to the back door was a picture window opening into the kitchen. They said in town that Broadbent was loaded — big time. He'd heard that Broadbent had grown up in a mansion surrounded by priceless art and servants. His old man had died a year ago and he'd supposedly inherited a hundred million. Looking at the house, you'd never know it. There was no sign of money anywhere, not in the house, the barn, the horses, the dusty yard and gardens, in the old International Scout sitting in the open garage or the Ford 350 dually sitting under a separate car port. If Maddox had a hundred million, he sure as shit wouldn't live in a dump like this.

Maddox set down his pack. Taking out

his sketchbook and a freshly sharpened number two artist's pencil, he began sketching as much as he could of the layout of the house and yard. Ten minutes later, he crawled around behind the barn and through some brush to get a fresh angle to sketch the front and side yards. Through a pair of patio doors he studied a modest living room. Beyond was a flagstone patio with a Smoky Joe barbecue and some chairs, bordered by an herb garden. No swimming pool, nothing. The house looked empty. Broadbent, as he had hoped, was out — at least his '57 Chevy was gone from the garage and Maddox figured he'd never let anyone drive that classic except himself. He'd seen no sign of a handyman or stable hand, and the nearest neighbor was a quarter mile away.

He finished his sketch and examined it. There were three sets of doors to the house: a back door to the kitchen, a front door, and the patio doors leading to the side yard. If all doors were locked — and for planning purposes he assumed they would be — the patio doors would be the easiest to get into. They were old and he'd opened quite a few in his day with the pair of shims he carried in the rucksack. It would take less than a minute.

He heard a car, crouched. A moment later it appeared coming round the back of the house, a Mercedes station wagon, and parked. A woman got out and walked over to the arena, shouting and waving at the kid on the horse. The kid waved back, yelled some unintelligible expression of joy. The horse slowed and Broadbent's wife helped the kid off the horse. The kid ran over to the woman, hugged her. The lesson was finally over. They chatted for a while and then the kid and his mother got in the car and drove off.

The wife, Sally, was left alone.

He watched her every movement through the binoculars as she led the horse to a hitching post, unsaddled it, and groomed it, bending over to brush the belly and legs. When she was done, she led the horse to a corral and turned it loose, threw a few flakes of alfafa into a feeder, and then headed toward the house, slapping bits of alfalfa off her thighs and butt. Was there another lesson in the works? Not likely — not at four o'clock.

She went in the back door to the kitchen, letting the screen door bang. A moment later he saw her pass by the picture window, go to the stove, and start making coffee.

It was time.

He took one last look at the sketch before shoving it into his rucksack. Then he began pulling out his equipment. First he slipped the green surgical booties over his shoes, the hair net over his hair, then the shower cap. Over that he slid a stocking. After that he put on the plastic Wal-Mart raincoat, the kind that came in a small packet and cost four dollars. He slid on a pair of latex gloves and took out his Glock 29, 10mm Auto, 935 grams fully loaded with ten rounds in the magazine — a very slick firearm. He wiped it down and shoved it in his pants pocket. Finally he took out an accordion of condoms, tore off two, and tucked them into his shirt pocket.

He'd leave no DNA at this crime scene.

14

Detective Lieutenant Willer slid out of the cruiser and tossed his cigarette butt onto the asphalt in front of him. Walking over it with a twist of his toe, he entered the back entrance to headquarters, passing through a slate-and-Plexiglas lobby. He swung through the glass doors of homicide, walked down the hall past a potted ficus and into the briefing room.

His timing was good. Everyone had arrived, and the murmur of voices fell as he entered. Willer hated meetings but in his line of work they were unavoidable. He nodded to his deputy, Hernandez, a couple of others, pulled a foam cup out of the stack and filled up on coffee, laid his briefcase on the table, sat down. For a moment he focused on only his coffee, took a sip — freshly made for a change — then set down the cup. He opened the briefcase, took out a sheaf of papers marked maze, and slapped them on the table with just enough vigor to get everyone's attention.

He opened the folder, laid a heavy hand on it, looked around. "We all here?"

"Think so," said Hernandez.

Nods, murmurs all around.

Willer took a noisy sip, set the cup down. "As you know, ladies and gentlemen, we got a killing up in the Chama wilderness, in the Maze, that's attracted a lot of press attention. I want to know where we stand and where we're going. If anyone's got any bright ideas I want to hear them."

He looked around the room.

"First, let's have the M.E.'s report. Dr. Feininger?"

The police pathologist, an elegant-looking, gray-haired woman in a suit who looked out of place in the dingy briefing room, opened a slim leather folder. She did not rise to speak, and her voice was quiet, dry, just a touch ironic.

"Ten and a half quarts of blood-soaked sand containing most of the five point five quarts of blood found in a typical human body were recovered from the site. No other human remains have been found. We did what tests we could — blood type, presence of drugs, and so forth."

"And?"

"Blood group O positive, no drugs or alcohol detected, white blood cell count apparently normal, blood serum proteins, insulin, all normal. The victim was a male in good health."

"Male?"

"Yes. Presence of the Y chromosome."

"You do any DNA testing?"

"Yes."

"And?"

"We ran it against all the databases, no matches."

"What do you mean, no matches?" broke in the D.A.

"We have no national DNA database," the M.E. said patiently, as if talking to an idiot — which, Willer figured, she probably was. "There's usually no way to identify a person from his DNA, at least not yet. It's useful only in comparisons. Until we find a corpse, a relative, or a spot of blood on a suspect's clothing, it's useless."

"Right."

Willer took a swig of coffee. "That all?"

"Give me a body and I'll tell you more."

"We're working on it. K-9?"

A nervous, carrot-haired man hastily squared some papers: Wheatley, from Albuquerque.

"We took six dogs up to the area in question on June fourth —"

Willer interrupted. "Two days later, after there'd been a hard rain that got all the washes running, swept the Maze free of tracks or scent trails." Willer paused, staring aggressively at Wheatley. "I mention that for the record."

"It's a remote area, hard to get to."

Wheatley's voice had ridden up a notch.

"Go on."

"On June fourth, with three handlers from the Albuquerque K-9 tracking division, the dogs picked up a scent . . ." He looked up. "I've got maps here if you want to —"

"Just give the report."

"Picked up a possible ground scent at the scene. They followed it up the canyon and up onto the rim of Mesa de los Viejos, where it was noted that there was insufficient ground cover to hold a good scent —"

"Not to mention that half inch of rain."

Wheatley paused.

"Proceed."

"The dogs were unable to maintain tracking. Three subsequent attempts were made —"

"Thank you, Mr. Wheatley, we get the picture. And now?"

"We've got the dogs on cadaver-sniffing duty. We're working a grid, starting from the crime scene and using GPS to cover the canyon floors. We're working simultaneously deeper into the Maze and down toward the river. Next we'll go up on top."

"Which brings us to the river search. John?"

"The river's low and slow. We've got divers going into all the deep holes and snags, working downstream. So far nothing

— no personal effects or remains. We're almost at Abiquiú lake. It doesn't look likely the perp disposed of the body in the river."

Willer nodded.

"Scene-of-Crime?"

It was Calhoun from Albuquerque, the best guy in the state. At least they'd lucked out on the forensics. Calhoun, unlike the K-9 team, had gotten his ass up to the site at first light.

"We did a complete particle and fiber search, which was a real bear, Lieutenant, given that we're basically working in a dirty sandbox. We picked up anything that looked artificial within a hundred feet of the killing. We also sifted a second site, 220 yards to the northeast, where it appears a burro was standing — we found his droppings. We also looked at a third point on the bluffs above."

"A third point?"

"I'll get to that in a minute, Lieutenant. The killer covered things up pretty good, erased his tracks, but we got a fair amount of hair, artificial fibers, dried foodstuffs. No latents. Two M855 rounds."

"Now we're talking." Willer had heard about the bullets but not the results.

"These are standard NATO rounds, 5.56mm, metal-jacketed, lead alloy core with a steel penetrator, mass of sixty-two grains. Instantly recognizable because of the green tip. Our shooter was probably using an M16 or similar military-type assault weapon."

"Could be ex-military."

"Not necessarily. There are a lot of gun enthusiasts who like these weapons too." He consulted his notes. "One round was embedded in the ground; we found the entry channel — gave us an idea of the angle. The killer was shooting from above, thirty-five degrees off the horizontal. With that we were able to nail the location of the shooter: an ambush point on the rim. That was the third point you asked about. We found some partial boot prints, couple of cotton fibers from what might have been a bandanna or thin shirt. No shells. We had a hell of a time getting up to the shooter's vantage point. The guy knew the country and must've planned the killing ahead of time."

"Suggests a local."

"Or someone who scoped it out pretty carefully."

"Hair?"

"None at point three."

"And the second bullet?"

"Deformed and fragmented by passing through the victim. Traces of blood on it, matched the blood in the sand. Again, no latents."

"Anything else?"

"Wool and cotton fibers at the site of the killing — we're still analyzing — and a human hair with root. Golden brown, straight, Caucasian."

"From the killer?"

"Could be anyone: victim, killer, one of your cops. Maybe even me." He grinned, ran a hand through his thinning hair. "Won't be the first time. We're getting DNA on it, see if it matches the blood. Might need to get some hair from your guys for elimination purposes."

"Broadbent, the guy who found the body? He's got light brown, straight hair."

"Might need a sample from him, too."

Willer thanked Calhoun, turned to his deputy. "Hernandez?"

"I checked out Broadbent's story. Seems he rides around a lot in the high mesas."

"So what was he doing in the Maze?" Willer asked.

"He says he was taking a shortcut up Joaquin Canyon."

"A long cut, you mean."

"Says he likes the ride. Says it's nice country."

Willer grunted. "I thought he was a vet. Vets are supposed to be busy."

"He's got a partner, a guy named Shane McBride."

Willer grunted again. He hadn't liked Broadbent from the beginning and he had a feeling that the guy was holding out on him. It was asking a lot to believe he just happened to be up there when the man was shot. "Hernandez, I want you to ask around, see if Broadbent's shown any recent interest in that area up there — prospecting, pot hunting, that sort of thing."

"Yes, sir."

"You consider him a suspect?" asked the D.A.

"He's what you'd call a 'person of interest.' "

There was a guffaw from the D.A. "Yeah, right."

Willer frowned. No wonder they couldn't convict anyone these days, with guys like that in the D.A's office. He looked around. "Any bright ideas?"

Calhoun said, "This is a bit out of my field, but I'm curious — is there any permanent water up in those canyons?"

"I don't know. Why?"

"It'd be a great place to grow marijuana."

"Noted. Hernandez?"

"I'll look into it, Lieutenant."

15

Weed Maddox was just rising from his hiding place in the chamisa when he heard a sound from the house — the shrill of a telephone.

He hastily crouched back down and raised his binoculars. She had gotten up from the table and was walking toward the phone in the living room, disappearing around the corner. He waited. She must have answered the phone and was talking.

At the corner of the house he could see where the phone lines came in. He had rejected the idea of cutting them, because a lot of houses these days had private alarm systems that notified a firm offsite when the phone lines went down. He cursed softly to himself; he couldn't move on her until she was off the phone. He waited, five minutes . . . Ten. The stocking on his head itched, the latex gloves made his hands hot and sticky. She reappeared in the living room, coffee cup in one hand, holding a cordless to her ear with the other, nodding and talking — still on the phone. He felt a rising impatience, which he tried to quell by closing his eyes and reciting his mantra — to no effect. He was already too keyed up.

He clutched the Glock. The unpleasant smell of latex filled his nostrils. He watched her take two turns around the living room, talking away and laughing, her blond hair swinging. She picked up a brush and began brushing out her long hair, head tilted to one side. Now that was a sight to see, the long golden hair sprung out by static, backlit by the sun as she passed a window. She shifted the phone to the other ear, brushed the other side, her hips swinging with the effort. He felt a tingle of anticipation as she went into the kitchen. From his vantage point he could no longer see her, but he hoped she was hanging up the phone. He was right: she reappeared in the living room without the phone, went toward the front hall, and disappeared again — into a bathroom, it looked like.

Now.

He rose, scurried across the lawn to the patio door, flattened himself against the side of the house. He took a long, flexible shim out of his pocket, began working it in between the door and the frame. He couldn't see into the house now, but he would be inside in less than sixty seconds, before she got out of the john. When she emerged, he'd get her.

The shim was through and he now worked it down, encountered the latch, gave it a sharp downward tug. There was a click and he grasped the handle, getting ready to throw it open.

Suddenly he paused. A door had slammed. The kitchen door to the backyard. He heard footsteps crunching on the gravel of the drive, coming around the corner. He ducked down, crouching behind a bush next to the patio door, and through the screen of leaves he saw her striding to the garage, keys jangling from her hand. She disappeared inside. A moment later came the roar of a car engine and the International Scout nosed out, went down the driveway and out the gate in a swirl of dust.

Maddox felt an impotent fury take hold, a mixture of frustration, disappointment, and anger. The bitch didn't know how lucky she was. And now he'd have to search the house without her help.

He waited five minutes for the dust to settle, then he stood up and slid open the patio door, stepped inside, shut it behind him. The house was cool and smelled of roses. He controlled his breathing, calmed himself down, focusing his mind on the search ahead.

He started in the kitchen, working swiftly and methodically. Before he touched anything he noted where it was, then returned it to its original position. If the notebook was not in the house, it would be a mistake to alarm them. But if the notebook was there, he'd find it.

16

Dr. Iain Corvus strolled to the lone window of his office facing Central Park. He could see the park pond, a bright sheet of metal reflecting the afternoon sunlight. As he watched, a rowboat drifted across the water — a father and his son on an outing together, each manning an oar. Corvus watched the oars slowly dipping as the boat crept across the water. The young son appeared to be struggling with his oar, and finally it hopped out of the oarlock and slipped into the water, floating away. The father rose and gestured in wrath, all of it taking place in silent, distant pantomime.

Father and son. Corvus felt a faint sickness in his gut. The charming little scene reminded him of his own father, late of the British Museum, one the most famous biologists in England. By the time his father was thirty-five, Corvus's present age, he was already a fellow of the Royal Society, winner of the Crippen Medal, and on the Queen's birthday list to receive a K.C.B.E. Corvus felt a shiver of old anger as he recalled his father's mustachioed face, veiny cheeks, and military bearing, his spotted hand perpetually closed around a whiskey-and-soda, his voice offering sarcastic correction. The old bastard had died ten years ago of a stroke, fell over like a dead mackerel, scattering ice cubes on the Aubusson carpet of their town house in Wilton Crescent, London. Sure, Corvus had inherited a bundle, but neither that nor his name had helped him get a job at the British Museum, the only place he'd ever wanted to work.

Now he was thirty-five and still Assistant Curator in the Department of Paleontology, hat in hand, awaiting tenure. Without tenure, he was only half a scientist — half a human being, really. *Assistant Curator.* He could almost smell the odor of failure clinging to it. Corvus had never fit into the American academic perpetual-motion machine; he wasn't a member in good standing of the milling gray herd. He knew he was prickly, sarcastic, and impatient. He hadn't joined in their playground games. He had come up for tenure three years before but the decision had been deferred; his paleontological research trips to Tung Nor Valley in Sinkiang had not borne fruit. For the past three years he'd been running around like a blue-arsed fly with precious little to show for it. Until now.

He glanced at his watch. Time for the bloody meeting.

The office of Dr. W. Cushman Peale, president of the museum, occupied the southwestern tower of the museum, and it commanded a sweeping view of Museum Park and the neoclassical facade of the New-York Historical Society. Peale's secretary ushered Corvus in and announced his name in a hushed voice. Why was it, Corvus wondered, as he stood before the august presence with a genial smile sculpted on his face, that one always whispered in the presence of kings and cretins?

Peale came from behind his desk to greet Corvus, gave him a firm, manly handshake with the second hand grasping his upper arm, salesman-style, then seated him in an antique Shaker chair before a marble fireplace — unlike the one in his own office, this one worked. Only when he was assured Corvus was comfortable did he take his own seat, in a display of old-world courtesy. With his leonine mane of white hair brushed straight back, his charcoal suit, and his slow, old-fashioned way of speaking, Peale looked like he had been born a museum director. It was a show, Corvus knew: underneath the genteel exterior was a man with all the refinement and sensitivity of a ferret.

"Iain, how are you?" Peale settled back into his armchair, making a tent of his fingers.

"Very well, thank you, Cushman," said Corvus, tugging the crease on his pants as he crossed his legs.

"Good, good. Can I offer you anything? Water? Coffee? Sherry?"

"No thank you."

"I myself enjoy a small glass of sherry at five o'clock. It's my one vice."

Right. Peale had a wife thirty years his junior who was making an ass of him with a young archaeology curator, and if playing the doddering old cuckold wasn't exactly a vice, marrying a woman younger than your daughter was.

The secretary brought in on a silver tray a small crystal glass filled with amber liquid. Peale took it, sipped fastidiously. "Graham's '61 tawny. Nectar of the gods."

Corvus waited, maintaining a pleasantly neutral expression on his face.

Peale set down the glass. "I won't beat around the bush, Iain. As you know, you're up for tenure again. The department begins deliberations the first of next month. We all know the drill."

"Naturally."

"This second time around is it, as you know. The department makes a recommendation to me. Technically, I have the final

119

say, although in my ten-year stint as president of the museum I haven't once gone against a departmental tenure decision and I don't intend to change. I don't know which way the department's going to fall on your case. I haven't spoken to them about it and I don't intend to. But I am going to give you some advice."

"Advice from you, Cushman, is always welcome."

"We're a museum. We're researchers. We're lucky we're not at a university, burdened with teaching a gaggle of undergraduates. We can devote ourselves one hundred percent to research and publishing. So there's no excuse for a weak publication record."

He paused, one eyebrow rising slightly as if to signal the subtlety of his point, which as usual was about as subtle as a blunderbuss.

Peale picked up a piece of paper. "I have here your list of publications. You've been here nine years, and I count eleven papers. Roughly one per year."

"What counts is quality, not quantity."

"I'm not in your field, I'm an entomologist, so forgive me if I can't comment on the quality. I've no doubt they're good papers. No one has ever questioned the quality of your work and we all know it was just bad luck that the expedition to

Sinkiang didn't pan out. But eleven? We have curators here who publish eleven papers a *year*."

"Anyone can knock out a paper. Publication for the sake of publication. I prefer to wait until I have something to say."

"Come now, Iain, you know that's not true. Yes, I admit there is some of that publish-or-perish stuff going on here. But we're the Museum of Natural History and most of what we do is world-class. I'm getting off the point. A year has gone by without you publishing anything. The reason I called you in here is because I assume you're working on something important."

The eyebrows went up, indicating it was a question.

Corvus shifted his legs. He could feel the muscles around his mouth straining from the effort to smile. The humiliation was almost unbearable. "As it happens I *am* working on an important project."

"May I ask what?"

"Right now it's at a somewhat delicate juncture, but within a week or two I'll be able to bring it to you and the tenure committee — in confidence, of course. It should answer most satisfactorily."

Peale gazed at him a moment, then smiled. "That's splendid, Iain. The point is, I think you're a fine addition to the museum, and of course your distinguished name, associated as it is with your illustrious father, is also important to us. I'm asking these questions only in the spirit of giving counsel. We take it to heart when a curator fails to make tenure; we look on it more as a failure on our part." Peale rose with a broad smile, extended his hand. "Good luck."

Corvus left the office and walked back down the long, fifth-floor corridor. He was so full of silent rage he could hardly breathe. But he kept his smile, nodding left and right, murmuring greetings to colleagues who were on their way out of the museum at the close of day, the herd heading back to their split-level ranches in faceless American suburbs in Connecticut and New Jersey and Long Island.

17

The whitewashed room behind the sacristy of Christ in the Desert Monastery contained only four things: a hard wooden stool, a rough table, a crucifix, and an Apple PowerBook G4 laptop computer with a printer, running on DC solar power. Wyman Ford sat before the computer, tingling with anticipation. He had just finished downloading two cryptanalysis programs and was about to unleash them on the code he had laboriously typed in from the dead man's notebook. Already he knew that this was no simple code; it had not yielded to any of his usual tricks.

It was something truly special.

He lifted his finger and brought it down smartly: the first program was off and running.

It wasn't exactly a decryption program, but rather pattern analysis software that looked at the code and made a determination, based on number patterns, as to what class of code it belonged to — substitution or transposition, placode or encicode, nomenclator or polyalphabetic. He had determined it wasn't a public-key code based on factoring large primes. But beyond that, he'd struck out.

It was only a matter of five minutes for the program to return a beep, indicating the first analysis was complete. Ford was startled when the conclusion popped up:

UNABLE TO DETERMINE CODE TYPE

He scrolled down through the pattern results, numerical frequency tables, probability assignments. This was no random grouping of numbers — the program had picked out all kinds of patterns and departures from randomness. It proved the numbers contained information. But what information, and how encoded?

Far from being discouraged, Ford felt a shivery thrill. The more sophisticated the code, the more interesting the message. He ran the next program in the module, a frequency analysis on single digits, number pairs, and triplets, matching it against frequency tables of common languages. But that too was a failure: it showed no correlation between the numbers and the English language or with any other common language.

Ford glanced at his watch. He'd missed Terce. He'd been at it now for five hours straight.

Damn.

He went back to the computer screen. The fact that each number had eight digits — a byte — implied a computer-based code. Yet it was written with pencil in a grubby notebook, apparently in the middle of nowhere, with no computer access nearby. On top of that he had already tried translating the eight-digit numbers to binary, hexadecimal, and ASCII, and ran those through the decryption programs, still with no success.

This was getting fun.

Ford paused, picked up the notebook, flipped it open, ruffled through the pages. It was old, the leather cover abraded and worn, and there was sand between the well-thumbed pages. It smelled faintly of woodsmoke. The numbers were written with a sharpened pencil, clean and crisp, in neat rows and columns, forming a kind of grid. The evenness of the writing led him to believe that the journal had been written all at the same time. And in the entire sixty pages of numbers there wasn't a single erasure or mistake. Without a doubt the numbers had been copied.

He shut it and turned it over. There was a stain on the back cover, a smear that was still slightly tacky, and he realized with a start that it was blood. He shivered and quickly put the book down. The blood suddenly reminded him that this was not a game, that a man had been murdered, and that the journal very likely contained directions to a fortune.

Wyman Ford wondered just what he was getting himself into.

He suddenly felt a presence behind him and turned. It was the abbot, hands clasped behind his back, a faint smile on his face, his lively black eyes fixed on him. "We missed you, Brother Wyman."

Wyman rose. "I'm sorry, Father."

The abbot's gaze shifted to the numbers on the screen. "What you're doing must be important."

Wyman said nothing. He wasn't sure it was important in the way the abbot meant. He felt ashamed. This was just the kind of obsessive work habit that had gotten him into trouble in real life, this compulsive focusing on a problem to the exclusion of all else. After Julie's death, he had never been able to forgive himself for all those times he worked late instead of talking to her, eating dinner with her, making love to her.

He could feel the kindly pressure of the abbot's eyes on him, but he couldn't raise his own to meet them.

"*Ora et Labora,* Prayer and Work," said the abbot, his gentle voice with an edge to it. "The two are opposites. Prayer is a way of listening to God, and work is a way of speaking to God. The monastic life seeks a strict balance between the two."

"I understand, Father." Wyman felt himself coloring. The abbot always surprised him with his simple wisdom.

The abbot laid a hand on his shoulder. "I'm glad you do," then turned and left.

Wyman saved his work, backed it up on a CD, and shut down the system. Putting the notebook and CD in his pocket, he returned to his cell and placed them in the drawer of his bedside table. He wondered: had he really gotten the spook trade out of his system? Is that what this was about?

He bowed his head and prayed.

18

Tom Broadbent watched Detective Lieutenant Willer pacing back and forth in his
living room, the policeman's slow, heavy
steps somehow conveying insolence. The
detective wore a plaid sports jacket, gray
slacks, and blue shirt with no tie, and his
arms were short with bony, veined hands
swinging at the end. He was about forty-
five and no more than five-eight, with a
narrow face, bladelike nose, and sagging
black eyes rimmed in red. It was the face
of a true insomniac.

Standing behind him, notebook flopped
open in his hand, was his sidekick,
Hernandez, soft, plump, and agreeable.
They had arrived in the company of a no-
nonsense woman with iron-gray hair who
introduced herself as Dr. Feininger, the
Medical Examiner.

Sally sat on the sofa next to him.

"A human hair was recovered at the
crime scene," Willer was saying as he
slowly turned on his heel. "Dr. Feininger
wants to find out if it came from the
killer, but to do that we need to eliminate

all others who were at the site."

"I understand."

Tom found the black eyes looking at him rather intently. "If you don't have any objection then, sign here."

Tom signed the permission form.

Feininger came around with a little black bag. "May I ask you to take a seat?"

"I didn't know it was going to be dangerous," said Tom, with an attempt at a smile.

"I'll be pulling them out by the roots," came the crisp answer.

Tom sat down, exchanged a glance with Sally. He felt pretty sure there was more to this visit than getting a few hairs. He watched as the M.E. removed a couple of small test tubes from her black bag and some sticky labels.

"In the meantime," said Willer, "there are a couple of points I'd like to clear up. Mind?"

Here we go, thought Tom. "Do I need a lawyer?"

"It's your right."

"Am I a suspect?"

"No."

Tom waved his hand. "Lawyers are expensive. Go ahead."

"You said you were riding along the Chama the night of the killing."

"That's right."

Tom felt the doctor's fingers in his hair, poking around, holding a large pair of tweezers in the other.

"You said you took a shortcut up Joaquin Canyon?"

"It's not really a shortcut."

"That's just what I was thinking. Why'd you go up there?"

"As I said before, I like the route."

Silence. He could hear Hernandez's pen scritching on the paper, then the rustle of a page turned. The M.E. plucked one hair, two, three. "Done," she said.

"How many more miles did you have to ride that night?" Willer asked.

"Ten, twelve."

"How long would that have taken you?"

"Three to four hours."

"So you decided to take a shortcut that was actually a long cut, at sunset, when you would have had at least three hours of riding in the dark."

"It was the night of the full moon and I'd planned it that way. I *wanted* to ride home by moonlight — that was the whole point."

"Your wife doesn't mind you coming home late?"

"No, *his wife* doesn't mind him coming home late," said Sally.

Willer continued, not varying from his

stolid tone. "And you heard the shots, went to investigate?"

"Haven't we already gone through this, Detective?"

Willer pushed on. "You say you found the man, dying. You administered CPR, which is how you got his blood all over your clothes."

"Yes."

"And he spoke to you, told you to find his daughter — Robbie her name was? — to tell her what he'd found. But he died before he could say what it was he found. Am I correct?"

"We've been over all this." Tom had not told, and had no intention of telling, that the prospector had a notebook or had mentioned a treasure. He had no confidence in the police's ability to keep it confidential, and news of a treasure would cause a stampede.

"Did he give you anything?"

"No." Tom swallowed. He was surprised at how much he hated lying.

After a moment Willer grunted, looked down. "You spend a lot of time riding around up in that high mesa country, right?"

"That's right."

"Looking for anything in particular?"

"Yes."

Willer looked up sharply. "What?"

"Peace and quiet."

He frowned. "Where do you go, exactly?"

"All over — the Maze, up over Mesa de los Viejos, English Rocks, La Cuchilla — sometimes as far as the Echo Badlands if it's an overnight trip."

Willer turned to Sally. "You go with him?"

"Sometimes."

"I'm told that yesterday afternoon you went to the monastery up in the wilderness, Christ in the Desert."

Tom rose. "Who told you that? Are you having me followed?"

"Take it easy, Mr. Broadbent. You drive a distinctive truck and I might remind you that most of that road is visible from the top of Mesa de los Viejos, where my men are searching. Now: did you go up to the monastery?"

"Do I have to answer these questions?"

"No. If you don't, I'll subpoena you, and you'll need that lawyer we talked about, and then you'll be required to answer them under oath at police headquarters."

"Is that a threat?"

"It's a statement of fact, Mr. Broadbent."

"Tom," said Sally, "take it easy."

Tom swallowed. "Yes, I went up there."

"What for?"

Tom hesitated. "To see a friend of mine."

"Name?"

132

"Brother Wyman Ford."

Scritch, scritch went the pen. As he wrote, Willer made a sucking noise through his teeth.

"This Brother Ford a monk?"

"Novitiate."

"What you go up there to see him about?"

"I wondered if he'd heard or seen anything related to the killing up in the Maze." He felt terrible lying again. He began to realize that the others may have been right, that he never should have kept back the notebook. But there was that damn promise.

"And had he?"

"No."

"Nothing at all?"

"Nothing at all. He didn't even know about it. He doesn't read the newspapers." If the cops went to see Ford, Tom wondered if he would lie about the notebook. It seemed most unlikely — he was, after all, a monk.

Willer rose. "You going to stick around here for a while? Case we need to talk to you again?"

"I don't have any traveling plans at the present time."

Willer nodded again, glanced at Sally. "Sorry, ma'am, for the interruption."

"Don't ma'am me," said Sally sharply.

"No offense intended, Mrs. Broadbent."

He turned to the M.E. "Got what you needed?"

"Yes."

Tom saw them to the door. As he was leaving, Willer paused, his black eyes fixed on Tom. "Lying to a police officer is obstruction of justice — a felony."

"I'm aware of that."

Willer turned and left. Tom watched them drive out, then came back in and shut the door. Sally was standing in the living room, arms crossed. "Tom —"

"Don't say it."

"I *am* going to say it. You're sinking in quicksand. You've *got* to give them the notebook."

"Too late now."

"No it isn't. You can explain. They'll understand."

"The hell they will. And how many times do I have to repeat it? *I made a promise.*"

She sighed, uncrossed her arms. "Tom, why are you so stubborn?"

"And you're not?"

Sally flopped down on the sofa next to him. "You're impossible."

He put his arm around her. "I'm sorry, but would you have me any other way?"

"I suppose not." She sighed. "On top of all this, when I came home this afternoon, I got the feeling that someone had been in the house."

"How so?" Tom said, alarmed.

"I don't know. Nothing was stolen or moved. It was just a creepy feeling — like I could smell some stranger's B.O."

"You sure?"

"No."

"We should report it."

"Tom, you report a break-in and Willer will be all over you. Anyway, I'm not sure at all — it was just a feeling."

Tom thought for a moment. "Sally, this is serious. We already know the treasure is worth killing for. I'd feel better if you broke out that Smith & Wesson of yours and kept it handy."

"I wouldn't go that far, Tom. I'd feel silly walking around with a gun."

"Humor me. You're lethal with a gun — you proved that in Honduras."

Sally rose, slid open a drawer under the phone, took out a key, and went to unlock a cabinet in the den. A moment later she came back with the gun and a box of .38 cartridges. She opened the cylinder, pushed five rounds into the chambers, snapped it shut, snugged it into the front pocket of her jeans. "Satisfied?"

19

Jimson Maddox handed the car keys and a five-dollar bill to the pimply-faced attendant at the curb and walked into the lobby of the El Dorado Hotel, his new Lucchesi snakeskin boots making a pleasing creaking sound. He paused to look around, giving his jacket a little tug. On one side of the large room was a roaring fire, and on the other an old faggot sat at a grand piano, playing "Misty." At the far end stood a bar done up in blond wood.

He sauntered over to the bar, hung his laptop on the back of the chair, eased himself in.

"Coffee. Black."

The bartender nodded, returned with a cup and a bowl of spicy peanuts.

He took a sip. "Say, this is a bit stale, think you could manage a fresh pot?"

"Of course, sir. My apologies." The bartender whisked away the cup, disappeared in the back.

Maddox dipped his fingers into the peanuts, tossed a few in his mouth, watched the people coming and going. They all looked like him, dressed in Polo shirts and sports jackets and nice corduroy or worsted slacks, people who lived their lives on the straight and narrow, two cars in the garage, two point four kids, living off corporate paychecks. He leaned back, tossed in a few more, and bit down. Funny how many attractive middle-aged women — like that one crossing the lobby with the tan slacks and sweater and pearls with her little black handbag — went all wobbly thinking about a tattooed, pumped-up, prison Jeff doing hard time for rape, murder, or assault. He had a lot of work to do tonight, at least twenty new cons to write up and post. Some of the letters were so illiterate he had to make it all up from scratch. No matter: the subscriptions were still rolling in, the demand for cons growing steadily. It was the easiest money he'd ever made in his life, and what amazed him was that it was legal, all of it handled by credit card through an Internet billing company; they took their cut and the rest was wired to his bank account.

If he'd known how easy it was to make money honestly, he could've saved himself a shitload of grief.

He crunched up a few more peanuts and pushed away the dish, mindful of his waistline, as the bartender arrived with a fresh cup. "Sorry it took so long, and my apologies again."

"No problem." He sipped the coffee — very fresh. "Thanks."

"You're welcome, sir."

Weed Maddox turned his thoughts to the problem at hand. The notebook wasn't in the house. That meant that Broadbent either had it on him or had hidden it off-site, maybe in a safe-deposit box. Wherever it was, Maddox knew he wasn't going to get it now by theft. He felt a swelling of irritation. Broadbent was up to his ass in it in one way or another. Maybe as a rival — maybe even as Weathers's partner.

Maddox could almost hear Corvus's Brit voice ringing in his head — *The note book.* There was only one way: he had to *force* Broadbent to give it up. What he needed was leverage.

What he needed was *her.*

"First time in Santa Fe?" the bartender asked, breaking into his thoughts.

"Yeah."

"Business?"

"What else?" Maddox grinned.

"Are you here for the laproscopic surgery conference?"

Christ, he probably did look like a doctor. A Connecticut doctor on a medical junket, all expenses paid by some pharmaceutical giant. If only the bartender could see the tattoo that covered his back from nape to butt. He'd shit his pants . . .

"No," said Maddox pleasantly, "I'm in human resources."

20

The e-mail Tom received the next morning went:

Tom,
   I "deciphered" the journal. You are not going to believe this. I repeat: you are not going to believe this. Come up to the monastery a.s.a.p. and prepare to have your mind blown.

                                        Wyman

Tom had left the house immediately. Now that his Chevy was approaching the last mile of washboard road to the monastery, his impatience had reached a feverish pitch.

Soon the bell tower of the monastery rose above the chamisa, and Tom pulled into the parking lot, a dust cloud rolling back over him as he got out. In a moment Brother Wyman came flying down from the church, his robes flapping behind him, like a giant bat on the wing.

"How long did it take you to crack the

code?" Tom asked as they climbed the hill. "Twenty minutes?"

"Twenty hours. I never did crack the code."

"I don't get it."

"That was the whole problem. It *wasn't* a code."

"Not a code?"

"That's what threw me. All those numbers in neat rows and columns, I kept assuming it had to be a code. Every test I ran on the numbers indicated they were not random, that they were highly patterned — but to what end? It wasn't a prime number code; it wasn't any kind of substitution and transposition code or any other cipher I could think of. I was stumped — until it occurred to me that it wasn't a code at all."

"Then what is it?"

"Data."

"Data?"

"I was a complete idiot. I should've seen it right off." Wyman broke off as they neared the refectory, putting a finger to his lips. They walked inside, down a hall, and into a small, cool whitewashed room. An Apple laptop sat on a crude wooden table underneath a disturbingly realistic crucifix. Ford peered around guiltily and carefully shut the door.

"We're not really supposed to be talking

in here," he whispered. "I feel like the bad boy at school, smoking in the john."

"So what kind of data was it?"

"You'll see."

"Did it reveal the man's identity?"

"Not exactly, but it will lead you to him. I know that much."

They pulled chairs up on either side of the computer. Brother Wyman raised the screen, turned it on, and they waited while it booted up. As soon as it was running, Ford began typing rapidly. "I'm connecting to the Internet via a broadband satellite connection. Your man was using a remote sensing instrument and copying the data into his notebook."

"What kind of instrument?"

"It took me a while to figure it out. Treasure hunters and prospectors commonly use two devices. The first is a flux gradiometer proton magnetometer, which is basically an incredibly sophisticated metal detector. You walk along the ground and it measures tiny variations in the local magnetic field. But the data output, measured in milligauss, doesn't look like these numbers at all.

"The second device is a ground-penetrating radar or GPR. It's a machine that looks like a perforated dish with a cluster of bow-tie antennae. It basically fires pulses of radar at the ground and records the echo. Depending on the type of ground and how dry it is, the radar can penetrate as deeply as five meters before being reflected back up. You can get a rough 3D image of something hidden in the ground or in certain types of rock. It lets you see voids, caves, old mines, buried treasure chests, metal-bearing veins, ancient walls or graves — that sort of thing."

He paused to catch his breath, and went on in a rapid undertone. "It turns out the numbers in your notebook were the data stream from a very sensitive, custom-built ground-penetrating radar. Luckily it had a standard output mimicking a Dallas Electronics BAND155 Swept FM, so that the imagery could be processed by off-the-shelf software."

"This treasure hunter was serious."

"He certainly was. He knew exactly what he was doing."

"So did he find a treasure?"

"He certainly did."

Tom could hardly stand the suspense. "What was it?"

Wyman smiled, held up his finger. "You're about to see a radar image of it, mapped using the GPR. That's what all those numbers in the notebook were all about: a careful mapping of the treasure in situ in the ground."

Tom watched as Ford connected to a

Web site maintained by the Boston University Department of Geology. He drilled down through a series of highly technical hypertext pages dealing with radar, satellite imagery, and Landsat, before arriving at a page entitled:

BAND 155 Swept-FM GPR Processing and Analysis with TerraPlot®
Enter your ID and password

"Hacked my way in," Ford whispered with a grin, typing in an ID and password. "No harm done, just pretended to be a student at BU."

"This doesn't strike me as very monkish behavior," said Tom.

"I'm not a monk yet." He typed some more and a new screen popped up:

Upload data now

He typed some more, then sat back with a grin, his finger poised above the ENTER key, a smile hovering on his lips. "Are you ready?"

"Don't torture me any longer."

He brought his finger down with a crisp rap, executing the program.

21

Cowboy Country Realty was located in a cutsie pseudo-adobe building on the Paseo de Peralta, strings of red chiles flanking the door and a chipper secretary in a western outfit manning the reception desk. Maddox strolled in, his own boots making a satisfying *clunk-clunk* on the Saltillo tile floors. He raised his hand to remove the Resistol hat he had purchased that morning — 16X beaver, $420 — but then decided against it, seeing as how he was now in the West where real cowboys left their hats on indoors. He went over to reception, leaned on the desk.

"What can I do for you, sir?" the receptionist asked.

"You handle summer rentals, right?" Maddox gave the girl a lopsided grin.

"We sure do."

"Name's Maddox. Jim Maddox." He extended his hand and she took it. Her blue eyes met his.

"Are you here to see anyone in particular?"

"Nope, I'm what you might call a walk-in."

"Let me call an agent for you."

A moment later he was being ushered into a well-appointed office, fully loaded in Santa Fe style.

"Trina Dowling," said the agent, offering her hand and seating him down opposite herself. She was a fright — fifty something, X-ray thin, black dress, blond hair, a voice that scared you with its efficiency. A potential client, thought Maddox. Definitely a potential client.

"I understand you're interested in a summer rental."

"That's right. I'm looking for a place to finish my first novel."

"How interesting! A first novel!"

He crossed his legs. "I was in a dot com business, sold out before the crash, went through a divorce. Now I'm taking a break from making money, hoping to live my dream." He offered her a self-deprecating smile. "I'm looking for something north of Abiquiú, quiet, isolated, no neighbors for miles."

"We manage more than three hundred rental properties and I'm sure we'll be able to find you something."

"Great." Maddox shifted in the chair, recrossed his legs. "I'm not kidding about privacy. Nearest house has to be at least a mile away. Something at the end of the road, in the trees."

146

He paused. Trina was taking notes.

"An old mining cabin would be perfect," he said. "I've always been interested in mines. There's a mine in my novel."

Dowling finishing up her note-taking with a sharp tap of her pen. "Shall we take a look in the database? But first, Mr. Maddox, do you have a price range in mind?"

"Money is no object. And please call me Jim."

"Can you wait a moment, Jim, while I look at our database?"

"Of course."

He recrossed his legs while Trina hammered away on the keyboard.

"Well." She smiled again. "I've got several suitable properties here, but here's one that really pops out. The old CCC Camp up on Perdiz Creek, in the foothills of the Canjilon Mountains."

"CCC Camp?"

"That's right. The Civilian Conservation Corps put a camp up there in the thirties for the men building trails in the national forest — a dozen or so wooden cabins surrounding an old dining hall and lodge. Some years ago a gentleman from Texas bought the whole camp. He renovated the lodge, turned it into a really cute three-bedroom, three-bath house. Left everything else as is. He lived up there for a while, found it a little lonely, and now he rents it out."

"Sounds like there might be tourists."

"It's gated. Sits in the middle of a section of private land surrounded by national forest. It's at the end of an eight-mile dirt road, the last two miles four-wheel drive only." She glanced up. "You *do* have a four-wheel drive vehicle?"

"Range Rover."

She smiled. "A road like that would tend to keep away visitors."

"Right."

"It's got some interesting history here. Before it was a CCC Camp Perdiz Creek was an old gold-mining town. There are some old mines up there and" — she smiled at him — "they say there's a ghost. I wouldn't mention that to everyone, but seeing as how you're a writer . . ."

"My story could use a ghost."

"It says here it's a great place for hiking, mountain biking, horseback riding. Surrounded by national forest. It's not off the grid, though: power and telephone to the site."

"It sounds ideal. Only thing is, I wouldn't want the owner dropping in unannounced."

"He's in Italy and I can tell you he's not that kind of owner. We manage the rental for him and if anyone needed to come up,

148

it would be us — and only then for a good reason and with twenty-four-hour notice. Your privacy would be respected."

"Rent?"

"Quite reasonable. Thirty-eight hundred a month if you take it all summer."

"Sounds perfect. I'd like to see it."

"When?"

"Right now." He tapped his jacket pocket, where his checkbook was. "I'm prepared to conclude the deal today. I'm anxious to get to work on my novel. It's a murder mystery."

22

Tom stared intently at the white screen of the PowerBook. At first nothing happened, and then an image began to crawl down the screen, a blurry first iteration.

"Takes a while to process," murmured Wyman.

The first pass was complete, but the image remained a shadow, a blob. It didn't look at all like a chest of gold or a lost mine, but maybe it was delineating the cavern itself. A second pass began, the image sharpening, line by line. Tom caught his breath as the blob became an object. An unmistakable object. He could hardly believe it, he felt it must be an optical illusion, that it was actually something other than what it seemed. On the third pass he realized it was no optical illusion.

"My God," Tom said. "It's no treasure. It's a dinosaur."

Wyman laughed, his eyes sparkling. "I told you it would blow your mind. Look at the scale bars. It's a T. Rex, and according to some research I did, it's by far the biggest ever found."

"But it's the whole thing, not just the bones."

"Correct."

Tom fell silent, staring. It certainly was a Tyrannosaurus rex — the outline was unmistakable — lying twisted and on its side. But it wasn't just a fossil skeleton — much of the skin, internal organs, and flesh appeared to have been fossilized along with the bones. "It's a mummy," said Tom, "a fossilized dinosaur mummy."

"That's right."

"This is incredible. This must be one of the greatest fossils ever found."

"Right. It's virtually complete, except for a few teeth, a claw, and the last foot of tail, anyway. You see how some of it appears to be emerging from the rock."

"So the murdered man was a *dinosaur* prospector."

"Exactly. This 'treasure' he was talking about may have been an attempt to mislead, or it may have simply been a manner of speaking. That *is* a treasure, only one of the paleontological variety."

Tom gazed at the image. He could still hardly believe it. As a child he had always wanted to be a paleontologist, but while other kids had grown out of dinosaurs, he had never managed to shake his dream. His father had pushed him into becoming a vet. And now here he was, staring at what had to be one of the most stupendous dinosaur fossils of all time.

"There's your motive," said Ford. "That dinosaur's worth a fortune. I did some poking around the Web. You heard about the dinosaur named Sue?"

"The famous tyrannosaur at the Field Museum?"

"That's it. Discovered in 1990 by a professional fossil hunter named Sue Hendrickson in the South Dakota badlands. Largest and most perfect T. Rex ever found. It was auctioned at Sotheby's ten years ago, pulled down $8.36 million."

Tom gave a low whistle. "This one must be worth ten times that."

"At least."

"So where is it?"

Ford smiled and pointed to the screen. "You see that fuzzy outline encasing the dinosaur? That's a cross-section of the rock outcrop the fossil's imbedded in. It's a big formation, more than forty feet in diameter, and it's such an unusual shape that it should be easily recognizable. All the location information you need is right there. It's merely a question of hiking around until you find it."

"Starting with Tyrannosaur Canyon."

"That would be a charming coincidence. The fact is, Tom, it could be anywhere in the high mesas."

"It could take forever to find it."

"I don't think so. I've spent a lot of time hiking around back there and I believe I could find it in less than a week. Not only do you have the shape of the formation, but you can see that part of the dinosaur's head and upper body are exposed along the side. That must be quite a sight, the dinosaur's jaws emerging from the rock like that."

"Like that black monolith that gave Tyrannosaur Canyon its name?" said Tom.

"I know that monolith — it's got nothing to do with the fossil. With this plot, now we know just what to look for — eh, Tom?"

"Wait a minute. Who says we're going to look for it?"

"I do."

Tom shook his head. "I thought you were studying to be a monk. I thought you'd left this sort of thing behind."

Ford looked at him for a while and then dropped his eyes. "Tom — the other day you asked me a question. I'd like to answer it."

"I was out of line. I really don't want to know."

"You weren't out of line and I'm going to answer your question. I've bottled it all up, I've used silence as a kind of crutch, a way to avoid the issue." He paused.

153

Tom said nothing.

"I was an undercover operative. I studied cryptology but I ended up working undercover as a Systems Analyst for a large computer firm. I was, in reality, a CIA hacker."

Tom listened.

"Let's say — theoretically speaking, of course — that the government of, say, Cambodia buys servers and software from, say, a large American firm with a three-letter acronym which I shall not mention. Unbeknownst to the Cambodians, a small logic bomb has been hidden in the software code. The bomb goes off two years later, and the system starts acting funny. The government of Cambodia calls the American company for help. I get sent in as Systems Analyst. Let's say I bring my wife — which helps the cover and she's also a Company employee. I fix the problem, while at the same time burning onto CD-ROMs the entire contents of the Cambodian government's classified personnel files. The CD-ROMs are tarted up to look like bootlegged copies of Verdi's *Requiem*, music and all. You can even play them. Again I'm speaking theoretically. None of this may have actually happened."

He paused, exhaled.

"Sounds like fun," said Tom.

"Yeah, it was fun — until they car-bombed my wife, who happened to be pregnant with our first child."

"Oh, my God —"

"It's all right, Tom," he said quickly. "I've got to tell you. When that happened, I just walked out of that life and into this one. All I had were the clothes on my back, my car keys and wallet. First chance, I dropped the wallet and keys into a bottomless crack up there in Chavez Canyon. My bank accounts, house, stock portfolio — I don't even know what's happened to them. One of these days, like any good monk I'll get around to giving them to the poor."

"No one knows you're here?"

"Everyone knows I'm here. The CIA understood. Believe it or not, Tom, the CIA wasn't a bad place to work. Good people for the most part. Julie — my wife — and I knew the risks. We were recruited together out of MIT. Those personnel files I scooped up exposed a lot of former Khmer Rouge torturers and murderers. That was good work. But for me . . ." His voice trailed off. "The sacrifice was too great."

"My God."

Ford held up a finger. "No taking the Lord's name in vain. Now I've told you."

"I hardly know what to say, Wyman. I'm sorry — I'm really sorry."

"No need to say anything. I'm not the

only hurt person in the world. It's a good life here. When you deny your own needs by fasting, poverty, celibacy, and silence, you get closer to something eternal. Call it God, call it whatever you like. I'm a fortunate man."

There was a long silence. Tom finally asked, "And how does this connect to your idea that we should find the dinosaur? I promised to give the notebook to the man's daughter, Robbie — and that's it. As far as I'm concerned the dinosaur's hers."

Ford tapped the table. "I hate to tell you this, Tom, but all that land out there, the high mesas and all the badlands and mountains beyond, belong to the Bureau of Land Management. In other words, it's all federal land. *Our* land. The American people own that land and everything on it and in it, including the dinosaur. You see, Tom, your man wasn't just a dinosaur prospector. He was a dinosaur *thief*."

23

Dr. Iain Corvus softly turned the handle of the metal door labeled MINERALOGY LAB and stepped quietly into the room. Melodie Crookshank was sitting at a workstation, her back turned, typing. Her short brown hair bobbed as she worked.

He crept up to her, laid his hand softly on her shoulder. She gave a muffled gasp and jumped.

"You didn't forget our little appointment, did you?" asked Corvus.

"No, it's just that you snuck up on me like a cat."

Corvus laughed softly, gave her shoulder a little squeeze, and left his hand there. He could feel her heat through her labcoat. "I'm grateful you were willing to stay late." He was glad to see she was wearing the bracelet. She was pretty but in that athletic and unglamorous American way, as if one of the prerequisites of being a serious woman in science was to wear no makeup and avoid the hairdresser. But she had two important qualities: she was discreet and she was alone. He had quietly inquired into her background; she was a product of the Columbia degree mill that turned out far more Ph.D.s than were actually employable; her parents were both dead, she had no siblings, few friends, no boyfriend, and almost no social life. On top of that, she was competent and *so* eager to please.

His eyes returned to her face, glad to see she was blushing. He wondered if perhaps they might not take their relationship a step or two beyond the professional — but no, that path was always unpredictable.

He dazzled her with his finest smile, and took her hand, which was hot in his. "Melodie, I'm delighted you've made such splendid progress."

"Yes, Dr. Corvus. It's — well, it's incredible. I've burned it all onto CDs."

He lowered himself into a chair before the big flat-panel screen of the Power Mac G5. "Let the show begin," he murmured.

Melodie seated herself next to him, picked up the top CD in a stack, opened the plastic holder, and slid it into the drive bay. She pulled over the keyboard and rapped out a command.

"First, what we've got here," she began, switching into professional speech, "is a piece of the vertebra and fossilized soft tissue and skin of a large tyrannosaurid, probably a T. Rex or maybe a freakishly large Albertosaurus. It's fantastically well preserved."

An image appeared on the screen.

"Look at that. It's an imprint of skin." She paused. "Here it is closer up. You see those fine parallel lines? Here they are again at 30x."

Corvus felt a momentary shiver. This was even better than he had imagined, much better. He felt suspended, light in his chair. "It's the impression of a feather," he managed to say.

"Exactly. There it is: proof that T. Rex was feathered."

It was a theory that had been advanced a few years ago by a group of young paleontologists at the museum. Corvus had derided the theory in the *Journal of Paleontology*, referring to it as a "peculiar American fantasy," which had occasioned much sneering and anti-British comment from his colleagues in the museum. And now, here it was, in his very hands: proof that *they* were right, and *he* was wrong. The unpleasant sensation of being proven wrong quickly gave way to more complex feelings. Here was an opportunity . . . In fact, a rare opportunity. He could steal *their* theory from *them,* while standing up to the world and admitting he had been mistaken. Utter, total preemption — wrapped in a cloak of humility.

That was exactly how he would do it.

With this in hand, they would *have* to give him tenure. But then he wouldn't really need it, would he? He could get a job anywhere — even at the British Museum. Especially at the British Museum.

Corvus found he had been holding his breath, and released it. "Yes, indeed," he murmured. "So the old gentleman was feathered after all."

"It gets better."

Corvus raised his eyebrows.

She rapped a key and another image appeared. "Here's a polarized image at 100x of the fossilized muscle tissue. It's totally petrified, of course, but it has to be the most perfect fossilization on record — you see how fine-grained silicon dioxide has replaced the cell tissue, even the organelles, capturing the image of everything. What we're looking at is an actual image of the muscle cell of a dinosaur."

Corvus found he could not speak.

"Yeah." She rapped again. "Here it is at 500x . . . Look — you can see the *nucleus.*"

Click.

"Mitochondria."

Click.

"And these — Golgi complex."

Click.

"Ribosomes —"

160

Corvus put out his hand. "Stop. Stop a moment." He closed his eyes, took a deep breath. He opened them. "Wait a moment, please."

He stood up, steadied himself with a hand on the back of the chair, and took a deep breath. The moment of dizziness passed, leaving him strangely hyperalert. He looked around the lab. It was as silent as a tomb, with only the faint hiss of air, the hum of the fan in the computer, the smell of epoxy, plastic, and heated electronics. Everything was as it was before — and yet the world had just changed. The future flashed through his mind — the awards, the best-selling book, the lectures, the money, the prestige. Tenure was only the beginning.

He looked at Crookshank. Did she, too, see it? She was no fool. She was thinking the same kinds of things, imagining how her life had now changed — forever.

"Melodie . . ."

"Yeah. It's awesome. And I'm not done. Not by a long shot."

He managed to sit down. Could there really be more?

Crookshank rapped a key. "Let's go to the electron micrographs." A black and white image leapt into sharp focus. "Here's endoplasmic reticulum at 1,000x. You can see now the crystalline structure of the replacement mineral. True, you can't see much — we're at the limit. The structure is breaking down at this magnification — fossilization can't preserve everything. But the fact you can see *anything* at a thousand x is incredible. You're looking at the microbiology of a dinosaur, right there."

It was extraordinary. Even this little sample was a paleontological discovery of the first water. And to think that there was probably a whole dinosaur like that, if his information was correct. The perfectly fossilized carcass of a T. Rex, complete — the stomach, no doubt with its last meal, the brain in all its glory, the skin, the feathers, the blood vessels, the reproductive organs, nasal cavities, liver, kidneys, spleen — the diseases it had, its wounds, its life history, all perfectly duplicated in stone. It was the closest they were going to get to *Jurassic Park* in the real world.

She clicked to the next image. "Here's the bone marrow —"

"Wait." Corvus stayed her. "What are those dark things?"

"What dark things?"

"Back in the last image."

"Oh, those." She backed up to the previous picture. Corvus pointed to a small thing in the image, a small black particle.

"What is it?"

"Probably an artifact of the fossilization process."

"Not a virus?"

"It's way too big. And it's too sharply defined to be part of the original biology anyway. I'm pretty sure it's a microcrystalline growth, probably hornblende."

"Quite right. Sorry. Keep on."

"I could zap it with the alpha particle X-ray spectrometer, see what it's made of."

"Fine."

She clicked through another series of micrographs.

"This is stupendous, Melodie."

She turned to him, her face flushed, radiant. "Can I ask a question?"

He hesitated, collecting himself. He was going to need her help, that much was clear, and doling out a few grains of glory to a female lab assistant would be a lot better than cutting another curator in on the deal. Melodie had no contacts, no power, and no future, just another underemployed Ph.D. grunt. So much the better that she was a woman and wouldn't be taken as seriously.

He put his arm around her, leaned close. "Of course."

"Is there any more of this out there?"

Corvus couldn't help smiling. "I suspect, Melodie, that there's a whole dinosaur like this out there."

24

Sally felt a lot more disturbed than elated at the computer-plotted image Tom had spread out on the kitchen table.

"This just gets worse and worse," she said.

"Better and better, you mean. This is exactly the kind of information I needed to identify the man and find his daughter."

This is Tom all over, Sally thought — stubborn, operating from some kind of deep-seated moral conviction that landed him in trouble. It had nearly gotten him killed in Honduras.

"Look, Tom — this man was illegally prospecting for fossils on public land. He was certainly involved in the fossil black market and maybe with organized crime. He was a bad guy and he got murdered. You don't want to be messing around with this. And even if you *found* his daughter, the fossil wouldn't belong to her. You yourself said it belongs to the feds."

"I made a promise to a dying man and that's the beginning and the end of it."

Sally sighed in exasperation.

Tom circled the table like a panther prowling around a kill. "You haven't said what you think of it yet."

"It's amazing, of course, but that's not the *point*."

"That *is* the point. It's the most important paleontological discovery ever made."

Despite herself, Sally was drawn to the strange image. It was blurry, indistinct, but it was clearly a lot more than just a skeleton. It was a dinosaur, complete, entombed in the rock. It lay on its side, its neck thrown back, jaws open, its two front limbs raised up as if trying to claw its way free.

"How did it fossilize so well?"

"It had to have been an almost unique combination of circumstances, which I don't even begin to understand."

"Could there be any organic material left? DNA?"

"It's at least sixty-five million years old."

"Amazing how fresh it looks, almost as if it should stink."

Tom chuckled. "It's not the first mummified dinosaur found. Back around the turn of the century a dinosaur hunter named Charles Sternberg found a mummified duck-billed dinosaur in Montana. I remember seeing it as a kid at the natural history museum in New York, but it isn't nearly as complete as this one."

She picked up the plot. "Looks like he died in agony, with his neck twisted back and his jaws open like that."

"It's a she."

"You can tell?" She looked closely. "I don't see anything down there but a blur."

"Female tyrannosaurs were probably bigger and more ferocious than the males. And since this is the biggest T. Rex ever found, it's a good guess it was female."

"Big Bertha."

"That twisting of the neck was caused by the tendons drying and contracting. Most dinosaur skeletons are found with contorted necks."

Sally whistled. "What now? You have a plan?"

"I sure do. Very few people realize this, but there's a thriving black market in dinosaur fossils out there. Dinosaur fossils are big business and some dinosaurs are worth millions — like this one."

"Millions?"

"The last T. Rex that came on the market sold for over eight million, and that was ten years ago. This one's worth at least eighty."

"Eighty million?"

"Ballpark."

"Who would pay that kind of money for a dinosaur?"

"Who would pay that kind of money for

a painting? Give me T. Rex over Titian any day."

"Point taken."

"I've been reading up on this. There are a lot of collectors out there, especially in the Far East, who'll pay almost anything for a spectacular dinosaur fossil. So many black market fossils were being smuggled out of China that the country passed a law declaring dinosaurs to be part of their national patrimony. But it hasn't stopped the flow. Everybody wants their own dinosaur these days. The thing is, the biggest and best-preserved dinosaurs still come from the American West — and most of them are found on federal land. If you want one, you have to go steal it."

"Which is just what this man was doing."

"Right. He was a professional dinosaur hunter. There can't be too many of them in the world. He'll be easy to identify if I ask the right people. All I have to do is find the right people."

Sally looked at him suspiciously. "And how do you propose to do that?"

Tom grinned. "Meet Tom Broadbent, agent for Mr. Kim, the reclusive South Korean industrialist and billionaire. Mr. Kim is looking to buy a spectacular dinosaur, money no object."

"Oh, no."

He grinned, stuffing the paper into his pocket. "I've worked it out. Shane will handle the clinic on Saturday while we fly to Tucson, fossil capital of the world."

"We?"

"I'm not leaving you here alone with a murderer roaming around."

"Tom, I've got a whole gymkhana planned on Saturday with the kids. I can't leave."

"I don't care. I'm not leaving you here alone."

"I won't be alone. I'll be surrounded by people all day long. I'll be perfectly safe."

"Not at night."

"At night I've got Mr. Smith & Wesson here — and you know how I handle a gun."

"You could go to the fishing cabin for a few days."

"No way. It's too isolated. I'd feel a lot more nervous up there."

"Then you should check into a hotel."

"Tom, you *know* I'm not some helpless female who needs watching over. You go to Tucson and do your Mr. Kim song and dance. I'll be fine."

"No way."

She gave it one final push. "If you're so worried, go to Tucson for the day. Fly out early Saturday morning, return in the evening. That would give you most of the day.

We're still having our usual picnic lunch on Friday, aren't we?"

"Of course. But as for Saturday —"

"Do you plan to stand guard over me with a shotgun? Give me a break. You go to Tucson and get back before dark. I can take care of myself."

PART TWO

CHICXULUB

The Tyrannosaurus rex was a creature of the jungle. She lived in the deepest forests and swamps of North America, not long after it had broken off from the ancient continent of Laurasia. Her territory encompassed more than five hundred square miles, and it stretched from the shores of the ancient Niobrara inland sea to the foothills of the newly minted Rocky Mountains. It was a subtropical world, with immense forests of prodigious trees the likes of which have never existed since. There were monkey-puzzle trees that reached almost five hundred feet in height, giant magnolias and sycamores, metasequoias, huge palms, and giant tree ferns. The height of the canopy allowed little light to reach the forest floor, which as a result was open and clear, giving plenty of lebensraum to the huge predatory dinosaurs and their prey as they acted out the great drama of life.

She lived during the last great flowering of the Age of the Dinosaurs. It was an age that would have gone on indefinitely had it not been abruptly terminated by the greatest natural disaster ever to befall planet Earth.

She shared the forest with a host of other creatures, including her favorite prey, two species of duckbill dinosaurs, Edmontosaurus and Anatotitian. Occasionally she attacked a lone triceratops, but she avoided their herds, except to follow and pick off a sick or dying member. A huge type of brontosaur, Alamosaurus, roamed the land, but she rarely hunted it, preferring to consume it as a scavenger rather than risk killing it as a predator. She spent a great deal of time hunting along the shores of the ancient seaway. In this body of water lived a predator even bigger than she, the fifty-foot-long crocodilian known as Deinosuchus, the only animal capable of killing a T. Rex unwise enough to venture into the wrong body of water in pursuit of prey.

She hunted leptoceratops, a smaller dinosaur about the size of a deer, with a parrotlike beak and a protective frill on the back of its neck. Another dinosaur she hunted, but warily, was the ankylosaurs, as well as her own cousin, the nanotyrannosaurus, a smaller, faster version of herself. Once in a while she attacked an old and feeble torosaurus, a dinosaur with a viciously horned, eight-

foot-long head, the largest skull that ever evolved on a land mammal. Occasionally she killed an unwary Quezalcoatlus, a flying reptile with a wingspan about the same as an F-111.

The ground and trees swarmed with mammals that she scarcely noticed — fruit-eating rodents, marsupials, the earliest ancestor of the cow (an animal the size of a rat) and the world's first primate — a creature named Purgatorius that ate insects. There were dinosaurs beyond her ability to hunt: the ornithomimus, an ostrich-sized dinosaur that could run more than seventy miles an hour; and the troodon, a fleet-footed carnivore about the size of a human being, with dexterous hands, keen eyesight, and a brain-to-body ratio even greater than that of T. Rex.

She was a creature of habit. During the rainy season, when the rivers and swamps pushed out of their banks, she moved westward to the higher ground of the foothills. During the dry season, after mating, she sometimes traveled to a chain of sandy hills in the lee of an extinct volcano, to build a nest and lay eggs. When the dry season began, she moved back to her haunts in the great forests along the shores of the Niobrara seaway.

The climate was hot, wet, and humid. There were no polar ice caps, no glaciers

— the earth was in the grips of one of its hottest climate cycles in its history. The ocean levels had never been higher. Large parts of the continents lay under inland seas. Great reptiles ruled the air, the land, and the water, and had done so for two hundred million years. Dinosaurs were the most successful class of animal life that had ever evolved on planet Earth. Mammals had coexisted with the dinosaurs for almost one hundred million years, but they had never amounted to much. The largest mammal to live during the Age of Dinosaurs was about the size of a bread box. Reptiles had a hammerlock on all the higher niches.

She occupied the highest niche of all. She ruled the top of the food chain. She was the greatest biological killing machine the earth had ever seen.

1

The morning sun burned over the high mesas, cauterizing the land. Jimmie Willer halted in the shade of a juniper, easing himself down on a rock. Hernandez took a seat beside him, his plump face beaded with sweat. Willer slipped a thermos of coffee out of his rucksack, poured a cup for Hernandez and one for himself, shook out a Marlboro. Wheatley had gone on ahead with the dogs, and he watched them moving slowly across the barren mesa.

"What a scorcher."

"Yeah," said Hernandez.

Willer took a deep drag, looked out over the endless landscape of red and orange canyons, domed rocks, spires, ridges, buttes, and mesas — three hundred thousand acres, frigging hopeless when you stopped to think about it. He squinted into the brilliant light. The body could be buried at the bottom in any one of a hundred canyons or in God knows how many caves and alcoves, walled up in some rock shelter, deep-sixed down some crevasse.

"Too bad Wheatley didn't get on the

trail when it was fresh," said Hernandez.

"You can say that again."

A small plane droned in the sky overhead — DEA, looking for marijuana.

Wheatley appeared beyond the rise in front of them, struggling up a long incline of slickrock shimmering in the heat, four heavy canteens slung over his shoulders. His two unleashed bloodhounds tumbled along ahead of him, tongues lolling, noses to the ground.

"Bet Wheatley's sorry now," said Willer. "He has to carry water for himself and his dogs."

Hernandez chuckled. "So what do you think? Got any theories?"

"At first I figured it was drugs. But now I think it's something bigger. There's something going on out here, and both Broadbent and the monk are in on it."

Willer inhaled again, snapped the butt, and watched it bounce along the naked rock.

"Like what?"

"I dunno. They're looking for something. Think about it. Broadbent claims he spends a lot of time riding around here, for 'pleasure.' Well look out there at that son of a bitch. Would you ride around here for pleasure?"

"No way."

"Then he just happens to come across

this prospector, right after he's shot. It's sunset, eight miles from the road, middle of nowhere . . . Coincidence? Give me a break."

"You think he shot him himself?"

"No. But he's involved. He's holding out on us. Anyway, two days after the shooting, he goes up to visit this monk, Wyman Ford. I've checked up on this guy and it seems he too goes hiking all over the desert, stays out for days at a time."

"Yeah, and what are they looking for?"

"Exactly. And here's something you don't know, Hernandez. I asked Sylvia to see if there was anything in the system about that monk. Guess what? He was CIA."

"You're shitting me."

"I don't know the whole story, but it seems he quit suddenly, showed up at the monastery, they took him in. Three and a half years ago."

"What'd he do for the CIA?"

"Can't find out, you know how it is with the CIA. His wife was in it too and she was killed in the line of duty. He's a hero." Willer took one more drag, tasted the bitter filter, threw the butt down. It gave him a curious feeling of satisfaction to litter this pristine landscape, this place that had been shouting, *"You're nobody, you're nothing,"* into his ear all day long. Suddenly he sat up. He had spied a black dot moving on a low ridge in the middle distance, framed against some high bluffs. He brought his binoculars to his eyes, stared.

"Well, well. Speak of the devil."

"Broadbent?"

"No. That so-called monk. And he's got a pair of binoculars dangling from his neck. It's just what I said: he's looking for something. Hell yeah — and I'd give my left testicle to know what it is."

2

Weed Maddox came out onto the porch of his rented cabin, hitched a thumb in a belt loop, and inhaled the scent of pine needles warmed by the morning sun. He raised the mug of coffee to his lips and took a noisy sip. He'd slept late; it was almost ten o'clock. Beyond the tops of the ponderosa pines he could see the distant peaks of the Canjilon Mountains gilded with silver light. He strolled across the porch, his cowboy boots thunking hollowly on the wood, and stopped beneath a fancy sign that read Saloon. He gave it a little push with his finger, sending it squeaking back and forth on rusty hinges.

He looked down main street. There wasn't much left of the old CCC Camp; most of the buildings had collapsed into pancaked slabs of rotting wood, overgrown with bushes and small trees. He drained his coffee, set the mug on the rail, strolled down the wooden steps and onto the old main street of town. Maddox had to admit, he was really a country boy at heart. He liked being alone, away from roads, traffic,

181

buildings, and crowds. When it was over, he might even buy a place like this. From here, he could continue to run Hard Time, living a life of peace and quiet for a change, with a couple of ladies for company and nothing else.

He began walking down the dusty old main street, hands shoved in his pockets, whistling tunelessly. At the far end of town the road petered out into a weedy trail going up the ravine. He continued on, swishing his boots through the tall grass. He picked up a stick, beheading tall weeds as he went.

Two minutes brought him to a sign planted in the trail that read:

DANGER: UNMARKED MINE SHAFTS
NO TRESPASSING
OWNER NOT RESPONSIBLE FOR
ACCIDENTS

It was quiet in the forest, the wind sighing ever so lightly through the trees. Maddox slipped past the sign. The trail mounted slightly, following the dry bed of a wash. Ten minutes of walking brought him to an old clearing. An open hillside rose on the right, with a trail angling up. He mounted the trail, which ran parallel but below the summit for a quarter of a mile before coming to a decrepit shaft house enclosing the entrance to an old mining tunnel. The shaft-house door sported a fresh padlock and chain, along with another no trespassing sign, both of which Maddox had affixed the day before.

He slipped a key out of his pocket, unlocked the padlock, and stepped into the cool, fragrant interior. A pair of old railroad tracks led into a dark hole in the rock, covered by a heavy iron grate, also padlocked. He unlocked the grate and swung it open on freshly oiled hinges, inhaling the scent of damp stone and mold, then flashed his light around. As he proceeded he was careful to step over rows of old railroad ties and puddles of water. The tunnel had been cut into the living rock, and here and there where the rock was rotten and fractured the ceiling had been shored and cribbed with massive beams.

After a hundred feet the tunnel veered to the left. Maddox turned the corner and his light illuminated a fork in the tunnel. He took the left branch. It soon came to a dead end, across which Maddox had built a wall of timbers bolted into the mine cribbing to create a small prison cell. He walked up to the timber wall and gave it a proud smack. Solid as a rock. He had begun at noon the day before and had worked straight to midnight, twelve hours of nonstop, backbreaking labor.

He slipped through the unfinished opening into a small room built into the dead end of the tunnel. He plucked a kerosene lantern off a hook, raised the glass chimney, lit it, and hung it on a nail. The friendly, yellow glow illuminated the room, perhaps eight by ten feet. It wasn't such a bad place, thought Maddox. He'd laid a mattress in one corner, covered with a fresh sheet, ready to go. Next to it stood an old wooden cable spool serving as a table, a couple of old chairs dug out of a ruined house, a horse bucket for drinking water, another bucket for a toilet. Opposite him, affixed into the stone of the far wall, he had sunk four half-inch-steel eye bolts, each with a case-hardened chain and manacles — two for the hands, two for the feet.

Maddox paused for a moment to admire his handiwork, and he marveled once again at his luck in finding a setup like this. Not only was the tunnel perfect for his purposes, but he had managed to find most of his timber on-site, old beams and boards stacked up in the back of the mine where they had survived the ravages of time.

He broke off this pleasant reverie and glanced at his rough mechanical drawing, which lay on the barrel, curled up by moisture. He flattened it, weighing it down with bolts, and looked it over. A few more beams and he'd be done. Instead of a door, which would be vulnerable, he would bolt three beams over the opening — a simpler, stronger, and more secure solution. He would only need to go in and out at most a few times.

The cave was humid and warm. Maddox stripped off his shirt and tossed it down on the mattress. He gave his well-muscled torso a flexing, ran through a series of stretching exercises, then picked up the heavy-duty Makita cordless and slapped in a fresh battery. He went to the old pile of beams, probed a few with a screwdriver until he had found a good one, measured it off, marked a spot with a pencil, and began drilling. The whine of the Makita echoed in the cave and the smell of old, damp wood reached his nostrils as brown ribbons of oak curled out of the drill hole. Once through, he grasped the beam and hefted it upright, muscling it into position. After tacking it into place with a nail, he drilled a matching hole in the fixed beam behind it, slid through it an eighteen-inch bolt, twirled on a hex nut, and cranked it down so hard with a socket wrench that it bit a good quarter inch into the wood.

Nobody, no matter how desperate, was going to get that nut off.

In an hour Maddox had finished all, leaving only the door opening. The three beams that would bar the opening lay stacked next to it, predrilled and ready to go.

Maddox strolled the length of the finished wall, caressing the beams. Then with a yell he seized a beam between two massive hands, jerked it back and forth as hard as he could, this way and that, stepped back and side-kicked the beams, shouted, screamed, swore, slammed his shoulders into the wall again and again. He spun, picked up the wooden table, and hurled it against the wall of beams, all the while shrieking, "Sons of bitches! Bastards! I'll kill you all, I'll pull your guts out!"

All at once he stopped, breathing heavily. From his knapsack he fished out a hand towel, dried the sweat off his chest and shoulders, patted his face, smoothed back his hair, then combed it back with his fingers. He picked up his shirt, slipped it on, flexed his back muscles.

Maddox allowed himself a grin. Nobody was going to bust out of his jail. Nobody.

3

Wyman Ford shook the dust out of the hem of his robes and sat down on the fallen, corkscrewed trunk of an ancient juniper. He had hiked almost twenty miles from the monastery and had reached the lofty heights of Navajo Rim, a great long mesa running for many miles along the southern boundary of the Echo Badlands. Far behind him lay the vermilion canyons of Ghost Ranch; and the view to the northwest was framed by the snowcapped peaks of the Canjilon Mountains.

Ford removed four 1:24,000 U.S.G.S. topographical maps from his backpack, unfolded them, and laid them side by side on the ground, weighing down the corners with stones. He took a moment to orient himself, visually matching various landmarks to their corresponding outlines on the maps. With his binoculars he began searching the Echo Badlands, looking for a rock formation resembling the one on the computer plot. Whenever he saw something promising, he marked its location on the map in red pencil. After fifteen minutes he lowered the binoculars, encouraged by what he saw. He hadn't found a likely match, but the more he looked into the endless canyons crisscrossing the Echo Badlands, the more he was convinced that the formation containing the T. Rex would be found there. The domelike shape of the rock in the plot seemed to be typical of the badland formations he could see from his vantage point. The problem was that much of his view was blocked by intervening mesas or canyon rims. Adding to his difficulties, the computer plot only showed a two-dimensional slice through the rock. There was no telling what the formation might look like from a different angle.

He raised the binoculars again to his eyes and continued searching, until he had covered all that he could see from that vantage point. It was time to move on to a point he had marked on the map as Vantage Point 2, a small butte at the far end of Navajo Rim that stuck up like an amputated thumb. It would be a long hike, but well worth the trouble. From there, he'd be able to see almost everything in the badlands.

He picked up his canteen, shook it, estimating that it was still more than half full. He had another, completely full, tucked away in his pack. As long as he was careful, he would have no problems with water.

He took a small sip and set off, following the edge of Navajo Rim.

As he hiked, he fell into a pleasant reverie brought on by the physical exertion. He'd told the abbot that he needed some spiritual time by himself in the desert, and he'd promised to be back by Terce the following day. That was now out of the question, and if he went into the badlands it might be two more days before he got back. The abbot wouldn't mind — he was used to Ford going off into the desert on spiritual retreats. Only this time Ford had the vague feeling that he was doing something wrong. He had misled the abbot as to the purpose of this trip; just because he prayed, fasted, and denied himself bodily comforts while in the desert did not mean he was on a spiritual quest. He realized he had allowed himself to become swept up in the intrigue of it, the mystery, the thrill of finding the dinosaur. The monastery had taught him the gift of self-reflection, something he'd never been too keen on before, and now he used that to reflect on his motives. Why *was* he doing this? It wasn't to recover the dinosaur for the American people, as much as he'd like to think he was acting from altruistic motives. It wasn't for money, and certainly not for fame.

He was doing this because of something deeper, a flaw in his character, a craving for excitement and adventure. Three years ago he had made a decision, impulsive at the time but by now well considered and confirmed by prayer, to retreat from the world and devote his life to serving God. Was this little expedition serving God?

Somehow, he didn't think so.

Despite these thoughts, as if in thrall to a power not his own, Brother Wyman Ford continued to hike along the windswept cliffs of Navajo Rim, his eye fixed on the distant butte.

4

Iain Corvus, standing at the window, heard the phone-set chime on his desk and the voice of his secretary announce, "Mr. Warmus from the Bureau of Land Management is on line one."

Corvus slipped quickly around behind his desk, picked up the phone, and assumed his friendliest voice.

"Mr. Warmus, how *are* you? I trust you received my permit application."

"Sure did, Professor. Got it right here in front of me." The western cracker accent grated across Corvus's ear. *Professor.* Where did they find these people?

"Any problems?"

"As a matter of fact there are. I'm sure it was just an oversight, but I don't see any locality data here."

"That wasn't an oversight, Mr. Warmus. I didn't include that information. This is an exceptionally valuable specimen, highly vulnerable to looting."

"I 'preciate that, professor," came the long-distance drawl, "but the high mesas are a big place. We can't issue a museum paleontological collection permit without locality info."

"This specimen is worth millions on the black market. Giving out that information, even to the BLM, is a risk I'm reluctant to take."

"I understand that, sir, but here at the BLM we keep all our permit data under lock and key. It's very simple: no locality, no permit."

Corvus took a deep breath. "We could certainly give you a generalized location —"

"No, sir," the BLM man interrupted. "We specifically require township, range, section, and GPS coordinates. Otherwise we can't process it."

Corvus took a deep breath, tried to moderate his voice. "I'm concerned because, as you may recall, last year up in McCone County, Montana, a first-rate diplodocus was nicked right after the permit was filed."

"Nicked?"

"Stolen."

The nasal voice went on tediously, "I'm not in the Montana district of the BLM, so I wouldn't know about a *nicked* diplodocus. Here in *New Mexico* we require locality coordinates to issue a collecting permit. If we don't know where the specimen is, how are we supposed to give you permission to collect it? Or to prevent someone else from collecting it? Should we put a moratorium on all nonprofit fossil collecting in the high mesas until you get your specimen? I don't think so."

"I understand. I'll get you the locality data as soon as possible."

"See that you do. And another thing."

Corvus waited.

"There aren't any photos or a survey attached to the application. It's supposed to be in Appendix A. It's spelled out right there in the rules and regulations: *'Permittee must attach a scientific survey of the site, showing the fossil in situ, along with any remote-sensing surveys, if existing, as well as photographs of said specimen.'* We've got to have some kind of proof that there's a fossil out there."

"The discovery is recent and the site is remote. We haven't been able to return for a survey. The point is, I wanted to be sure of establishing precedence, on the offchance another application comes in for the same fossil."

A bureaucratic grunt. "Precedence goes to the first 501(c)(3) museum or university in official standing to file a legal permit. I have to tell you, Professor, that there isn't enough in this here permit of yours to qualify for precedence."

Corvus gritted his teeth. *This here permit.* "Surely there must be a way to establish precedence without giving the exact coordinates."

There was a long, superior sniff at the other end. Corvus felt the blood pounding in his temples. "As I said, when you get your paperwork in order, we'll issue the permit. Not before. If someone else submits a permit for the same fossil — well, that's not our problem. First come first served."

"Bloody hell, man, how many complete T. Rex's could there be out there?" Corvus exploded.

"Hold your horses, Professor."

Corvus made a huge effort to control himself. This was the last man in the world he could afford to alienate. He was the bureaucrat who had the power to grant him permission to collect the fossil on federal land. The man could just as easily give it to that bloody bawbag Murchison at the Smithsonian.

"My apologies for speaking precipitously, Mr. Warmus. I'll get you the required information just as soon as I can."

"Next time," the man intoned, "when you're applying for a fossil collecting permit on federal land, take the time to get the application right. Makes our job easier. Just because you're a big New York City museum doesn't mean you don't have to play by the rules."

"Again, my sincerest apologies."

"Have a nice day."

Corvus placed the phone back in its cradle with elaborate care. He took a long breath, smoothed back his hair with a trembling hand. The arrogant little prick. He glanced up: it was just five o'clock, which made it three o'clock in New Mexico. Maddox hadn't called in forty-eight hours, damn him. The last time they talked he seemed to have everything under control, but a lot could happen in two days.

He paced his office, turned at the window, and paused to look out. The evening rowboats were just venturing out into the pond, and he found himself looking for the father and son. But of course they weren't back, why would they? — once was enough.

5

Six o'clock. The sun had fallen below the canyon rim and the heat of the day was going down, but it was still stuffy and dead between the sandstone walls. Willer, trudging up yet another endless canyon, suddenly heard an eruption of baying from the dogs from just around the bend, followed by Wheatley's high-pitched shouting. He glanced at Hernandez, met his partner's eye.

"Looks like they found something."

"Yeah."

"Lieutenant!" he heard Wheatley's panicked voice. "Lieutenant!"

The hysterical baying of the dogs and Wheatley's yelling echoed down to him distorted by the narrow canyon walls, as if they were trapped in a giant trombone. Even though he was fed up with searching, Willer had dreaded this moment.

"About time," said Hernandez, his short legs churning him forward.

"I hope to hell Wheatley's got those dogs under control."

"Remember last year when they ate that geezer's left —"

"Right, right," said Willer hastily. When he rounded the last bend, he saw that Wheatley did not have the dogs under control. He'd lost the leash of one and was unsuccessfully trying to haul back the other, both dogs frantically trying to dig into a patch of sand at the base of a tight curve in the canyon wall. Hernandez and Willer rushed forward and snatched up the leashes, hauling the dogs back and tying them up to a boulder.

Huffing and red-faced, Willer examined the scene. The bed of sand had been disturbed by the dogs, but it was no great loss, considering that the hard rain of the past week had already swept it clean of any traces. As he examined the area he could see nothing that indicated anything lay under the sand — beyond a faint, unpleasant odor that the breeze wafted past his nostrils. Behind him, the dogs whined.

"Let's dig."

"Dig?" Hernandez asked, his round face showing alarm. "Shouldn't we wait for the SOC team and the M.E.?"

"We don't know we've got a body yet. Could be a dead deer. We can't chopper a whole SOC team out here until we know."

"I see your point."

Willer heaved off his backpack and slipped out the two trowels he had brought, tossing one to Hernandez. "I doubt it's very deep. Our killer didn't have a hell of a lot of time."

He knelt and began scraping the trowel across the loose sand, removing one layer at a time. Hernandez did the same at the opposite end of the area, making two careful piles that the forensic team would later sift through. As he swept the sand aside he kept an eye out for clues — clothing or personal articles — but nothing came to light. The hole deepened, moving from dry sand into wet. There was something down there, for sure, Willer thought, as the smell intensified.

At three feet his trowel scraped against something hairy and yielding. A sudden wave of stench, thick as soup, hit his nostrils. He scraped a bit more, breathing through his mouth. It had been buried five days in wet sand in ninety-eight-degree heat and it smelled the part.

"It's not human," said Hernandez.

"I can see that."

"Maybe it is a deer."

Willer scraped some more. The fur was too coarse and matted to be a deer, and as he tried to clear more sand off it to see clearly the fur and skin began coming away in patches, exposing slimy, brownish-pink flesh underneath. This was no deer: it was a burro. The prospector's burro, the one that Broadbent mentioned.

He stood up. "If there's a stiff it'll be next to it. You take that side, I'll take the other."

Once again they began scraping away the sand, piling it carefully to one side. Willer lit a cigarette and held it between his lips, smoking it that way, hoping to chase off some of the stench.

"Got something."

Willer abandoned his side and went over to where Hernandez was crouching. He troweled some more sand away, exposing something as long and swollen as a boiled kielbasa. It took Willer a moment to realize it was a forearm. A second foul wave of odor seemed to strike him bodily, a different and far worse smell. He inhaled a lungful of smoke, but it did no good: he could taste the dead body. He stood up, gagging, and backed off. "Okay. That's good enough. It's a stiff — that's all we need to know."

Hernandez beat a hasty retreat, only too eager to get away from the makeshift grave. Willer moved upwind, smoking furiously, inhaling a lungful of smoke with each breath as if to scour his lungs free of the odor of death. He looked around. The dogs were at their rock, whining and eager. For what? A meal?

"Where's Wheatley?" asked Hernandez, looking around.

"Hell if I know." He saw Wheatley's fresh footprints going farther up-canyon. "Find out what he's doing, will you?"

Hernandez hiked up the canyon and soon disappeared around the corner. He returned a moment later, a smirk on his face. "He's puking."

6

Friday morning dawned a flawless blue, with flocks of jays squawking and fighting in the piñons, the cottonwoods casting long cool shadows across the meadow. Tom had fed the horses that morning, given them an hour to eat, and now he led his favorite horse, Knock, over to the rail to be saddled. Sally joined him with her buckskin gelding, Sierra, and together they worked in silence, brushing out their coats, picking the hooves, saddling and tacking up.

By the time they set off, there was only a memory of coolness in the green cottonwood shadows along the creek. The flanks of Pedernal Peak rose on their right, the steep slopes ending in the chopped-off summit made so famous by the paintings of Georgia O'Keeffe. They rode in their usual silence, preferring not to talk when on horseback — the pleasure of being together was enough. They reached the ford, the horses splashing across the shallow stream, still icy from melting snow in the mountains.

"Where to, cowboy?" Sally asked.

"Barrancones Spring."

"Perfect."

"Shane's got everything under control," Tom said. "I don't have to get back at all this afternoon."

He felt a twinge of guilt. He'd been relying on Shane far too much this past week.

They reached the bluffs and began climbing the narrow trail to the top. A hawk circled above them, whistling. The air smelled of cottonwood trees and dust.

"Damn, I love this country," Sally said.

The trail wound up the side of the mesa into the cool ponderosa pines. In half an hour they reached the top and Tom turned his horse to look at the view. He never got tired of it. To his left was the steep flank of Pedernal, and to his right the sheer orange cliffs of Pueblo Mesa. Below lay the irregular alfalfa fields along Cañones Creek, which opened to the vast Piedra Lumbre Valley, one hundred thousand acres broad. On the far side rose up the stupendous outline of the Mesa of the Ancients, notched by canyons — the beginning of the high mesa country. Somewhere, out there, lay the fossil of a fabulous Tyrannosaurus rex — and a half-crazy monk looking for it. He glanced over at Sally. The wind was blowing her honey hair and her face was turned into the light, her lips slightly parted in pleasure and awe.

"Not a bad view," she said with a laugh.

They continued on, the wind rustling through the sideoats grama grass that edged the trail. He let Sally ride ahead and watched her on her horse. They continued to ride in silence, the only sound the rhythmic creaking of their saddles.

As the country opened up to high grasslands of Mesa Escoba, she touched her heels to Sierra's flank and moved into a trot. Tom followed suit. They abandoned the trail, riding across the windblown grass, dotted with Indian paintbrush and lupines.

"Let's go a little faster," Sally said, giving her horse another nudge with her heel. He broke into an easy lope.

Tom kept pace. At the far end of the meadow Tom could see the cluster of cottonwoods marking Barrancones Spring, at the base of a red cliff.

"All right," cried Sally. "Last one to the spring is a rotten egg! Giddyap!" She gave Sierra one final touch of heel. The horse shot forward, stretching out into a dead run while Sally gave a whoop.

Knock, who always wanted to be in the lead, needed little urging to follow suit, and soon they were tearing across the meadow, neck and neck. Sally began to pull ahead, her hair streaming behind like a golden flame. Tom watched her fly, and he had to admit she was one hell of a rider. The two horses whipped over the grass and into the sudden cool of the trees surrounding the spring. At the last minute, Sally reined in and Tom followed; the horses leaned back and dug in like the well-trained reining horses they were, sliding to a stop. When he looked over, he saw Sally sitting on her horse, her hair wild, her white shirt partly open, having popped a couple of buttons, her face in high color.

"That was fun."

She hopped off the horse.

They were in a small grove of cottonwoods, with an old fire ring in the center and a couple of logs for seats. *Genízaro* cowboys from days gone by had built a line camp here, with tables shaped from rough-hewn logs of ponderosa, a wooden box nailed to a trunk, a broken piece of mirror wedged into the fork of a tree, and a chipped enamel washbowl hung from a nail. The spring itself lay at the bottom of the cliffs, a deep pool hidden behind a screen of desert willows.

Tom collected the two horses, unsaddled them, watered them at the spring, and staked them out to graze. When he returned, Sally had spread out lunch on a thin blanket. In the middle of the table was a bottle of red wine, freshly opened.

"Now that's class," said Tom, picking it up. "Castello di Verrazzano, '97 Riserva."

"I snuck it in my saddlebags. I hope you don't mind."

"It's been dreadfully shaken up, I fear," said Tom in mock disapproval. "Are you sure we should be drinking at lunch? It's against the rules to drink and ride."

"Well now," Sally drawled in imitation of him, "we're just going to have to bend the rules, aren't we?" She tucked into her sandwich, taking two great bites, and then poured some wine into a plastic glass. "Here."

He took it, swirled it around, and sipped, aping a connoisseur. "Berries, vanilla, hints of chocolate."

Sally poured herself a glass and took a good slug. Tom took a bite from his own sandwich and watched her eat. A green light filtered through the foliage, and every time a breeze blew the trees rustled. When he finished his lunch, he lounged back on the blanket they had thrown down over the soft grass. In the distance, through the cottonwoods, he could see the horses grazing out on the flats, dappled in sunlight. Suddenly he felt a cool hand on his temple. He turned and found Sally was bending over him, her blond hair falling like a curtain.

"What are you doing?"

She smiled. "What does it look like?"

She laid her hands on either side of his face.

Tom tried to sit up, but the hands gently pushed him back down into the grass.

"Hey . . ." he said.

"Hey yourself."

One of her hands slid inside his shirt, caressing his chest. She bent down and put her lips to his. Her mouth tasted of peppermint and wine. She leaned over him and her hair fell heavily across his chest.

He reached up to touch her hair, then stroked it and ran his hand down to the strong hollow of her back, where he could feel her back muscles moving. As he drew her down, he felt her slender body and soft breasts glide up against his.

Afterward, they lay next to each other on the blanket. Tom's arm was thrown over her shoulder and he was looking into her amazing turquoise eyes.

"Doesn't get much better than this, does it?" he said.

"No," she murmured. "It's so good it almost makes me afraid."

7

Maddox strolled up Canyon Road and rounded the corner at Camino del Monte Sol. A forest of hand-carved signs greeted his gaze, festooning both sides of the narrow lane, each trying to outdo the other in hand-crafted cuteness. The sidewalks were crowded with tourists decked out as if for a trip across the Sahara Desert, with floppy sun hats, water bottles strapped to their waists, and big-lugged hiking shoes. Most of them looked pale-faced and confused, as if they'd just emerged like grubs from the rain-rotten cities of the East. Maddox himself was going for the rich Texan look today, and he figured he'd gotten it down pretty good with his Resistol, boots, and a bolo tie sporting a manly, golfball-sized chunk of turquoise.

The road passed some old Victorian houses, converted like everything else into gallery space, windows gleaming with Indian jewelry and pots. He checked his watch. Noon. He still had a little more time to kill.

He wandered in and out of the galleries,

amazed at the sheer quantity of silver, turquoise, and pottery there was in the world — not to mention paintings. Art, Maddox felt, was basically a scam, as his eye took in one more window full of Day-Glo-colored canyons, coyotes howling at the moon, and Indians draped in blankets. Another easy way to make money, and all perfectly legal. Why hadn't he seen the opportunities before? He'd wasted half his life trying to make money the hard, illegal way, not realizing that the best moneymaking scams were all legal. When he was finished with this last job, he'd go one hundred percent legit, plow some money back into Hard Time, and maybe even look for investors. He could be the next dot-com millionaire.

One gallery packed with enormous sculptures in bronze and stone caught his eye. The stuff looked expensive — just moving it would cost a fortune. The door chimed as he entered and a young woman came clicking up on high heels, giving him a bright lipsticked smile.

"Can I help you, sir?"

"Sure thing," he said, already hearing a drawl in his voice. "This sculpture here" — he nodded at the biggest one he could see in the store, a life-sized group of Indians carved out of a single piece of stone that weighed three tons if it weighed an ounce. "If you don't mind me asking, how much is it?"

"*Blessingway.* That's one seventy-five."

Maddox stopped himself just in time from asking, *Thousand?* "Do you accept credit cards?"

If she was surprised she didn't show it. "We just have to verify the credit limit, that's all. Most people don't have that kind of credit limit."

"I'm not most people."

Another bright smile. He noticed she had freckles on her chest where her silk shirt was unbuttoned.

"I like to charge things whenever possible and get the frequent flyer miles."

"You could go to China with the miles on that one," she said.

"I'd rather go to Thailand."

"There, too."

He looked at her more closely. She was one good-looking woman, as she'd have to be, working in a place like this. He wondered if she was going to get a commission.

"Well . . ." He smiled, winked. "How about the price on that one?" He pointed to a bronze of an Indian holding an eagle.

"*Freeing the Eagle.* That's one-ten."

"I just bought a ranch out of town and I've got to furnish the damn place. Ten thousand square feet, and that's just the main house."

"I can imagine."

"Name's Maddox. Jim Maddox." He held out his hand.

"Clarissa Provender."

"Good to meet you, Clarissa."

"The artist is Willy Atcitty, an authentic, registered member of the Navajo tribe, one of our foremost Native American sculptors. That first one you were looking at is carved out of a solid block of native New Mexico alabaster from the San Andres Mountains."

"Beautiful. What's it about?"

"It represents a three-day Blessingway sing."

"A what?"

"The Blessingway is a traditional Navajo ceremony which is meant to restore balance and harmony in one's life."

"I need one of those." He was close enough to her now to smell the creme rinse she had used that morning in her glossy black hair.

"Don't we all," said Clarissa Provender, with a laugh, her sly brown eyes looking at him sideways.

"Clarissa, you must get asked this all the time, and if I'm out of line tell me — but how about dinner tonight?"

A bright, phony smile. "I'm not supposed to date potential customers."

Maddox took that as a yes. "I'll be at the Pink Adobe at seven. If you just happen to run into me there, I'd be happy to treat you to a martini and a Steak Dunigan."

She didn't say no, and that encouraged him. He waved a hand at the sculptures. "I think I'm going to take the one in alabaster. Thing is, I have to measure the space first, make sure it fits. If not that one, the other one for sure."

"I have all the specs in the back: dimensions, weights, delivery routine."

She clicked back and he watched her behind twitching in its little black dress. She came back with a sheet, a card, and a brochure about the artist, handing them to him with a smile. He could see a streak of lipstick on her left canine. He slipped them into his inside jacket pocket.

"Mind if I use the phone to make a quick local call?"

"No."

She led him to her desk in the rear of the gallery, punched a line, and handed him the phone. "This'll just be a second. Hello? Dr. Broadbent?"

The voice on the other end said, "No, this is Shane McBride, his associate."

"I just moved to Santa Fe, bought a ranch south of town. I've been looking to buy a reining horse. It's a paint, a beautiful animal, and I need a vet check. Is Dr. Broadbent available?"

"When?"

"Today or Saturday"

"Dr. Broadbent's not here right now, but he can do it Monday."

"Not Saturday?"

"I'm on call Saturday, and let's see . . . I've got a slot at two."

"Sorry, Shane, nothing personal, but Dr. Broadbent came highly recommended and I'd be more comfortable with him."

"If you want him, you'll have to wait 'til Monday."

"I need it done Saturday. If it's a matter of his day off, I'm willing to pay extra."

"He's going to be out of town that day. Sorry. As I said, I'd be happy to do it."

"Nothing personal, Shane, but like I said . . ." He let his voice trail off in disappointment. "Thank you anyway. I'll call on Monday, reschedule."

He replaced the receiver, gave Clarissa a wink.

She looked back at him, her face unreadable.

"See you at the Pink, Clarissa."

For a moment she didn't respond. Then she leaned forward, and with another sly smile said in a low voice, "I've been in this job for five years and I'm very, very good at it. You know why?"

"Why?"

"I know bullshit when it walks in the door. And you're so full of it you're leaving tracks."

8

The helicopter transporting the forensic team had to land almost half a mile down the canyon, and the team was forced to hike their equipment up the wash. They arrived in a ferocious mood, but Calhoun, head of forensics and always the wit, had turned it around with jokes, stories, slaps on the back, and the promise of cold beer all around when it was over.

Calhoun had run it just like an archaeological dig, the site mapped out with a grid, his men troweling down layer by layer, the photographer documenting every step. They ran all the sand through one-millimeter wire mesh and then again through a flotation tank to recover every hair, thread, and foreign object. It was brutal work and they'd been at it since eight that morning. Now it was three o'clock and the temperature had to be close to a hundred. The flies had arrived in force, and their droning sound filled the confined space.

Pretty soon, Willer thought, it would be time for the "scoop" — that moment when a ripe corpse is rolled into a body bag, ideally without falling apart like an overcooked chicken. A lot happened to a body in five days in the heat of summer. Feininger, the police pathologist, stood nearby, supervising this particular operation. She seemed to be the only one who managed to remain cool and elegant in the heat, her gray hair done up in a scarf, not a bead of sweat appearing on her lined but still handsome face.

"I want all three of you on the right side, please," she said, gesturing to the SOC team. "You know how it works, slip your hands under, make sure you've got a good grip, and then, at the count of three, roll it over and onto the plastic sheet, nice and easy. All got on protective covering? Check for tears and holes?" She looked around, her voice ironic, perhaps even half amused. "Are we ready? This is a challenging one, for sure. Let's get it right, fellows. Count of three."

A few grunts as the men got in place. Feininger had long ago banned the SOC boys from smoking cigars, and instead each one had a big smear of Vicks VapoRub under the nose.

"Ready? One . . . two . . . three . . . *roll*."

With a single economical motion they rolled the body onto the open body bag.

Willer noted it as a successful operation, in that nothing came off or was left behind in the process.

"Good work, boys."

One of the SOC team members zipped it up. The body bag had been prepositioned on a stretcher, and all they had to do was pick it up and carry it down to the chopper.

"Put the animal head in that one," directed Feininger.

They duly placed the burro's head in a wet-evidence bag and zipped it shut. At least, thought Willer, they had agreed to leave most of the burro behind, just taking the head with the gaping hole made by a 10mm round fired into the animal at point-blank range. The round had been found imbedded in the soft sandstone of the canyon wall, an excellent piece of evidence. They had uncovered the prospector's equipment, and the only thing they hadn't found, it seemed, was any indication of his identity. But that would come in time.

All in all a good haul of evidence.

He checked his watch. Three-thirty. He wiped his brow, pulled an iced Coke out of the cooler, rolled it against his forehead, his cheek, and the back of his neck.

Hernandez came up beside him, nursing his own Coke. "You think the killer expected us to find the stiff?"

"He sure went to a lot of trouble to hide it. We're, what, two miles from the killing? He had to strap the body on the burro, lug it up here, dig a hole big enough for the burro, the man, and all his shit . . . No, I don't think he figured we'd find it."

"Any theories, Lieutenant?"

"The killer was looking for something on the prospector."

"Why do you say that?"

"Look at the prospector's shit." Willer gestured to the plastic tarp on which all the prospector's gear and supplies had been laid out. One of the SOC boys was lifting each piece of evidence in turn, wrapping it in acid-free paper, labeling it, and packing it away in plastic evidence lockers. "You see how the sheepskin padding on the packsaddles is torn off, the other stuff ripped or slit open? And you see how the guy's pockets were turned inside out? Not only was our man looking for something, but he was pissed that he wasn't finding it." Willer took a last noisy sip, chucked the empty Coke can back into the cooler.

Hernandez grunted, pursed his lips. "So what was he looking for? A treasure map?"

A slow smile spread across Willer's face. "Something like that. And I'll bet you the prospector gave it to his partner before the

216

shooter could hike down from the rim into the canyon."

"Partner?"

"Yeah."

"What partner?"

"Broadbent."

9

It was early Saturday morning. The rising sun clipped tops of the ponderosa pines along the ridgeline above Perdiz Creek and invaded the upper valley, pencils of light shooting into the mists. The trees below were still wrapped in the coolness of night.

Weed Maddox rocked slowly on the porch of his cabin, sipping his coffee, rolling the hot, bitter liquid around in his mouth before swallowing. His mind wandered back to the day before and he remembered the bitch in the art gallery. Rage suddenly swelled his veins. Somebody would pay.

He swallowed the last bit of coffee, put the mug aside, and rose. He went into the living room and brought his knapsack out on the porch, laid it down, and began methodically lining up all the equipment he'd need for the day's work.

First came the Glock 29, with two magazines, ten rounds in each. Next to that he laid his usual kit: a hair net, a shower cap, stocking, two pairs of surgical gloves, plastic raincoat, surgical booties, and condoms; next came pencil and drawing paper, cell phone (fully charged), Ziploc bags, buck knife, bag of gorp to snack on, bottle of mineral water, flashlight, hand-cuffs and key, plastic clothesline, gaffing tape, matches, chloroform and a cloth diaper . . . He laid out the drawing of the Broadbent house and scrutinized it, visualizing all the rooms, doors, windows, locations of telephones, and lines of sight. Finally, he checked all the items off his list as he packed them into the knapsack, one by one, each snug in its own place.

He went back into the cabin, dropped the knapsack by the door, poured himself a second cup of coffee, picked up his laptop, and came back out, easing into the rocking chair. He had most of the day to kill and he might as well make good use of the time. He leaned back, flipped up the laptop screen, and booted it up. While waiting for the start sequence to finish he took a small pack of letters out of his pocket, undid the rubber band, and began with the top one, at random.

He worked through them, one at a time, translating the shit-stupid prison English into acceptable prose. Two hours later he was finished. He uploaded it and sent it as an attachment to the Webmaster who handled his site, a guy he'd never met, never even spoken to on the telephone.

He rose from the rocking chair, tossed the rest of his cold coffee off the railing, and went inside to see what there was to read. The bookshelf was mostly biographies and history, but Maddox passed by those to check out the small section of hardback thrillers. What he needed to kill the time was something he could really sink his teeth into, keep his mind from dwelling too much on his plans for the afternoon, which he had already mapped out in detail. He scanned the titles, his eye arrested by a novel entitled *Death Match*. He pulled it off the shelf, read the flap copy, leafed through it. He carried it out to the porch, settled in the rocking chair, and began reading.

The rocking chair creaked rhythmically, the sun slowly moved higher in the sky, and a pair of crows flapped up from a nearby tree and glided through the ruined town, cutting the air with a rusty cry. Maddox paused momentarily to check his watch. Almost noon.

It was going to be a long, quiet Saturday — but it would end with a bang.

10

Willer sat behind his desk, his feet thrown up, watching Hernandez waddle back from the records department with an accordion file tucked under his arm. With a sigh he plumped himself down in an easy chair in a corner, the folder in his lap.

"That looks promising," said Willer, nodding at the file. Hernandez was a hell of a good researcher.

"It is."

"Coffee?"

"Don't mind if I do."

"I'll get it for you." Willer rose, stepped out to the coffee machine, filled two foam cups, and came back, handing one to Hernandez. "Whaddya got?

"This Broadbent's got a history."

"Let's have it, *Reader's Digest* style."

"Father was Maxwell Broadbent, a big-time collector. Moved to Santa Fe in the seventies, married five times, had three kids by different wives. A ladies' man. His business was buying and selling art and antiquities. He was investigated by the FBI a couple of times for dealing in black market stuff, accused of looting tombs, but the guy was slick and nothing stuck."

"Go on."

"Strange thing happened about a year and a half ago. Seems the family went off to Central America on some kind of extended vacation. Father died down there, kids came back with a fourth brother, half Indian. The four of them divided up about six hundred million."

Willer raised his eyebrows. "Any suspicion of foul play down there?"

"Nothing definite. But the whole story's confused, nobody seems to know anything, it's all rumors. His old mansion is occupied by his Indian son, a guy who writes inspirational books, New Age stuff. They say he has tribal tattoos.

"Broadbent lives modestly, works hard. Married last year, wife's name is Sally, born Sally Colorado. Comes from a working-class background. Broadbent runs a large-animal vet clinic up in Abiquiú with an assistant, Albert McBride — calls himself Shane."

Willer rolled his eyes.

"I talked to some of his clients and he's equally respected among both the fancy-horse crowd and the old-time ranchers. Wife gives horse-riding lessons to kids."

"Record?"

"Other than a few minor scrapes as a juvenile, the guy's clean."

"McBride?"

"Clean too."

"Tell me about these 'minor scrapes.' "

"Records are sealed but you know how that is. Let's see . . . A dumb prank involving a truckload of manure and the high school principal . . ." He flipped through some papers. "Went for a joyride on somebody else's horse . . . broke a guy's nose in a fight."

"The other brothers?"

"Philip, lives in New York City, curator at the Metropolitan Museum of Art, nothing unusual there. Vernon, just married an environmental lawyer, lives in Connecticut as a house husband, stays at home with the baby while the wife goes to work. Got into a couple of financial scrapes a while ago but nothing since the inheritance."

"How much they get?"

"It seems they each got about ninety million after taxes."

Willer pursed his lips. "Kind of makes you wonder — whatever it is that guy is looking for in the high mesas, it can't be just about money, right?"

"I don't know, Lieutenant. You see these CEOs with hundreds of millions risking prison for a few thousand more. It's a disease."

"True." Willer nodded, surprised at Hernandez's insight. "It's just that this Broadbent doesn't seem like the type. He doesn't flash around his money. He works even though he doesn't need to. I mean, here's a guy who'll get up at two in the morning to stick his arm up a cow's ass and make forty bucks. There's a piece missing here, Hernandez."

"You got that right."

"What news on the stiff?"

"No ID yet. It's in the works, dental records, fingerprints. It's going to take a while to work it all through the system."

"The monk? You follow up on him?"

"Yeah. He's got quite a background. Son of Admiral John Mortimer Ford, Under-Secretary of the Navy in the Eisenhower administration. Andover, Harvard, under-graduate major in anthropology, summa cum laude. Went to MIT and pulled down a Ph.D. in cybernetics, whatever the hell that is. Met his wife, got married, both of them joined the CIA — and then nada, just like you said earlier. Those guys are serious about keeping a lid on their own. He did some kind of cloak-and-dagger work with code breaking and computers, wife was murdered in Cambodia. He up and quit to become a monk. The guy just walked away from everything, including a million-dollar house, bank accounts up the wazoo, a garage full of antique Jaguars . . . Unbelievable."

Willer grunted. It just wasn't coming together. He wondered if his suspicions of Broadbent and the monk were justified — they had all the attributes of the straight and narrow. Yet he was sure that somehow, some way, they were in it up to their eyeballs.

11

It was midafternoon by the time Tom drove into the parking lot of the Silver Strike Mall, located in a sea of shabby sprawl on the outskirts of Tucson. He parked his rental car and headed across the sticky asphalt to the mall entrance. Inside, it was air-conditioned to just above arctic conditions. The Fossil Connection was at the unfashionable far end of the mall, where Tom found a surprisingly modest storefront, with a few fossils on display in a window that was mostly whitewashed out. A sign on the door announced: "Wholesale Only. No Walk-Ins."

The door was locked. He buzzed, the door clicked, and he stepped in.

It looked more like a law office than one of the largest fossil wholesalers in the West. The place was carpeted in beige, with inspirational posters on the walls about entrepreneurship and customer service. Two secretaries worked at desks flanking each side of a waiting area with a couple of taupe chairs and a glass and chrome table. Some fossils decorated a shelf on one side and a large ammonite sat in the middle of the coffee table, along with a stack of fossil magazines and brochures advertising the Tucson Gem and Mineral Show.

One of the secretaries looked up, took in his two-thousand-dollar Valentino suit and handmade shoes, and gave an ostentatious raise of her eyebrows. "May I help you, sir?"

"I have an appointment with Robert Beezon."

"Name?"

"Broadbent."

"Please have a seat, Mr. Broadbent. Can I get you anything to drink? Coffee? Tea? Mineral water?"

"No, thank you."

Tom sat, picked up a magazine, flipped through it. He felt a twinge of anticipation thinking about the deception he had planned. The suit had been sitting in his closet, along with a dozen others he never wore, bought for him by his father in Florence and London.

A moment later the phone on the secretary's desk chimed. "Mr. Beezon will see you now." She nodded toward a door with a frosted glass window that said, simply, BEEZON.

Tom rose as the door opened, framing a heavyset man with a combover, in shirtsleeves and a tie. He looked indistinguishable from an overworked, small-town lawyer.

"Mr. Broadbent?" He held out his hand.

The office itself finally betrayed that the man's business was not accounting or law. There were posters on the walls of fossil specimens, and a glass case contained an array of fossilized crabs, jellyfish, spiders — and in the center a curious fossil plaque containing a fossil fish, with a fish in its belly, which in turn had a minnow in its belly.

Tom sat in a chair and Beezon took a seat behind his desk.

"You like my little gem? It reminds me that it's a fish-eat-fish world."

Tom gave the obligatory chuckle to what was obviously Beezon's standard opening line.

"Nice."

"Now, Mr. Broadbent," Beezon went on, "I haven't had the pleasure of working with you before. Are you new to the business? Do you have a shop?"

"I'm a wholesaler."

"We sell to a lot of wholesalers. But it's odd I haven't run into you before. We're a rather small club, you know."

"I'm just getting into the business."

Beezon folded his hands on the desk and looked at Tom, his eyes flickering up and down his suit. "Card?"

"Don't carry one."

"Well then, what can I do for you, Mr. Broadbent?" He cocked his head, as if awaiting an explanation.

"I was hoping to see some samples."

"I'll give you the cook's tour 'round the back."

"Great."

Beezon heaved up from his desk, and Tom followed him through the office suite to an unassuming door in the back. He unlocked it and they stepped into a room as cavernous as a Sam's Club, but instead of merchandise the metal shelves were heaped with fossils, thousands, maybe even millions of them. Here and there, men and women drove about with forklifts or hand-pushed flatbed carts loaded with rocks. A smell of stone dust drifted in the air.

"It used to be a Dillard's," said Beezon, "but this end of the mall never seemed to work for retail, so we got it at a good price. It's a warehouse, showroom, and pick-and-pack operation all rolled up into one. The raw stuff comes in one end, the finished stuff goes out the other."

He took Tom's elbow and led him forward, waving his hand along a wall against which leaned gigantic slabs of buff-colored rock, braced with two-by-fours, padded and shrink-wrapped. "We just got some excellent material from Green River, super stuff, you can buy it from me by the square yard, split and break it down and sell it by the fish, quintuple your money."

They came to bins heaped with fossils that Tom recognized as ammonites.

"We're the largest dealer of ammonites in the world, polished or rough, in matrix or no, sell by weight or by number, prepared or unprepared." He kept walking, passing shelf after shelf covered with boxes of the curious-looking curled-up ammonite shells. He paused, reached into one box, pulled one out. "These are pretty basic at a two bucks the pound unprepared, still in matrix. Got some over there with pyrites, and over here some really nice agatized specimens. Those cost more."

He walked on. "If you're interested in insects, I just got some beaut spiders from the Nkomi Shales of Namibia. New shipment of crabs from Heinigen, Germany — those are hot these days, they're getting two, three hundred dollars apiece. Agatized wood — sell that by the pound. Great for tumbling. Crinoids, concretions with ferns. Coprolites — kids love 'em. We got it all — and no one can beat our prices."

Tom followed. At one point Beezon stopped, pulled out a concretion. "Lot of these haven't even been split. You can sell them that way, let the customer split them. The kids'll buy three or four. Usually there's a fern or leaf inside. Once in a while a bone or jaw — I've heard of mammal skulls even being found in some. It's like gambling. Here —"

He handed Tom a concretion, and then he swiped a rock hammer off an anvil. "Go ahead — split it."

Tom took the hammer and, remembering his cover, fumbled with it a bit before placing the fossil on the anvil.

"Use the chisel end," said Beezon quietly.

"Right, of course." Tom turned the hammer around and gave the concretion a whack. It split open, revealing the single leaf of a fossilized fern.

He found Beezon eyeing him thoughtfully.

"What do you have as far as, er, higher-end material goes?" Tom asked.

Beezon went silently to a locked metal door and led him into a smaller, window-less room. "This is where we keep the good stuff — vertebrate fossils in here, mammoth ivory, dinosaur eggs. In fact, I just got a new shipment of hadrosaur eggs from Hunan, at least sixty percent of the shell intact. I'm letting them go at one-fifty apiece. You can get four, five hundred for them." He unlocked a cabinet, hefted a stone egg out of a nest of crumpled news-paper, held it up. Tom took it, looked it over, gave it back, then fussily dusted off his hand with a silk handkerchief pulled out of his pocket. The little move did not escape Beezon's notice.

"Minimum order a dozen." He moved on, coming to a long, coffin-shaped metal box, unlocked it to reveal an irregular plaster lump about four feet by three. "Here's something really sweet, a Struthiomimus, forty percent complete, lacking the skull. Just came in from South Dakota. Legal, strictly legal, came from a private ranch. Still jacketed and in matrix, needs preparation."

He gave Tom a rather pointed look. "Everything we deal in here is legal, with signed and notarized documents from the private land owner." He paused. "Just what *are* you after, Mr. Broadbent?" He was not smiling now.

"Just what I said." The encounter was going exactly as he had hoped: he had aroused Beezon's suspicions.

Beezon leaned forward and said in a low voice. "You're no fossil dealer." His eyes flicked over the suit again. "What are you, a fed?"

Tom shook his head, putting on a sheepish, guilty smile. "You smoked me out, Mr. Beezon. Congratulations. You're right, I'm no fossil dealer. But I'm also no fed."

Beezon continued to gaze at him, all his

western friendliness gone. "What are you then?"

"I'm an investment banker."

"What the hell do you want with me?"

"I work with a small and exclusive clientele in the Far East — Singapore and South Korea. We invest our clients' money. Sometimes our clients seek eccentric investments — old master paintings, gold mines, racehorses, French wines . . ." Tom paused, and then added, "Dinosaurs."

There was a long silence. Then Beezon echoed, "Dinosaurs?"

Tom nodded. "I guess I didn't cut a convincing figure as a fossil dealer."

Some of Beezon's friendliness returned, combined with a look of a man taking satisfaction in not having been fooled. "No, you didn't. First of all, there was that fancy suit. And then as soon as you held that rock hammer I knew you were no fossil dealer." He chuckled. "So, Mr. Broadbent, who is this client of yours and what kind of dinosaur is he in the market for?"

"May we speak freely?"

"Naturally."

"His name is Mr. Kim, and he is a successful industrialist from South Korea."

"This Struthiomimus here is a pretty good deal, at one hundred and twenty thousand —"

"My client is not interested in junk." Tom had shifted his tone, and he hoped the new persona of crisp, arrogant investment banker would be convincing.

Beezon lost his smile. "This is not junk."

"My client runs a multibillion-dollar industrial empire in South Korea. The last hostile takeover he launched resulted in the suicide of the CEO on the other side, an occurrence which Mr. Kim did not find displeasing. It's a Darwinian world my client inhabits. He wants a dinosaur for the corporate headquarters that will make a statement about who he is and how he does business."

There was a long silence. Then Beezon asked, "And just what kind of dinosaur might that be?"

Tom stretched his lips in a smile. "What else — but a T. Rex?"

Beezon gave a nervous laugh. "I see. Surely you're aware that there are only thirteen tyrannosaur skeletons in the world and every single one is in a museum. The last one that came up for sale went for eight and a half million. We're not talking chump change."

"And I am also aware that there may be one or two others for sale — quietly."

Beezon coughed. "It's possible."

"As for *chump change,* Mr. Kim will not even consider an investment under ten

234

million. It's simply not worth his time."

Beezon spoke slowly. "Ten million?"

"That's the lowest limit. Mr. Kim is expecting to pay up to fifty million, even more." Tom lowered his voice and leaned forward. "You will understand, Mr. Beezon, when I tell you he is none too particular about how or where the specimen might have been found. What is important is that it be *the right specimen.*"

Beezon licked his lips. "Fifty million? That's a bit out of my league."

"Then I am sorry to have wasted your time." Tom turned to leave.

"Now hold on a minute, Mr. Broadbent. I didn't say I couldn't help you."

Tom paused.

"I might be able to introduce you to someone. If . . . well, if my time and effort is compensated, of course."

"In the investment banking business, Mr. Beezon, everyone involved in a deal is remunerated to the extent of his contribution."

"That's exactly what I was hoping to hear. As to the commission —"

"We would be prepared to commission you with one percent, at the time of sale, for an introduction to the appropriate person. Satisfactory?"

The calculation clouded Beezon's brow for only a moment and then a faint smile spread on his round face. "I think we can do business, Mr. Broadbent. Like I said, I know a gentleman —"

"A dinosaur hunter?"

"No, no, not at all. He doesn't like to get his hands dirty. I guess you might call him a dinosaur seller. He lives not far from here, in a little town outside Tucson."

There was a silence.

"Well?" said Tom, pitching his voice to just the right level of impatience. "What are we waiting for?"

12

Weed Maddox crouched behind the barn, watching. Children were riding around the arena in circles, shouts mingling with laughter. He had been there an hour and only now did the gymkhana for retards or whatever it was seem to be winding down. The kids began to dismount, and soon they were helping to unsaddle and brush down the horses, turning them out one by one in a back pasture. Maddox waited, his muscles aching, all keyed up, wishing he had come at five instead of three. Finally the kids were shouting good-bye and the pickup trucks and soccer-mom SUVs were driving out of the parking area behind the house amid a lot of waving and shouting good-byes.

He checked his watch. Four o'clock. Nobody seemed to have stayed on to clean up — Sally was alone. She wouldn't go out like she did last time. It had been a long day and she was tired. She'd go inside and rest, maybe take a bath.

With that interesting thought in mind he watched the last SUV drive out of the driveway with a flourish of dust. The slow cloud drifted off and disappeared into the golden afternoon sunlight and all became quiet. He watched her cross the yard carrying an armload of bridles and halters. She was a knockout, dressed in western riding boots, jeans, and a white shirt, long blond hair streaming behind her. She came toward the barn and entered it, and he could hear her moving around, hanging up stuff, talking to the horses. At one point she was no more than a few feet from him on the other side of the flimsy wooden wall. But this was not the time; he needed to seize her inside the house where the confined space would deaden any noise she might make. Even though the nearest neighbors were a quarter mile away, sound did carry and you never knew who might be walking or riding around within earshot.

He heard more activity in the barn, the horses blowing and pawing, the scraping of a shovel, more murmurings to the animals. Ten minutes later she emerged and went into the house by the back door. He could see her through the kitchen window, moving around, filling a kettle at the faucet and putting it on the stove, bringing out a mug and what looked like a box of tea bags. She sat at the kitchen table, waiting for the water to boil, flipping through a magazine. Tea and then a bath? He couldn't be sure, and it was better not to wait. She was where he wanted her anyway, in the kitchen. The making and drinking of the tea would take at least five minutes, giving him the opportunity he needed.

He worked quickly, slipping on the plastic booties, the plastic raincoat, the hair net, shower cap, and stocking. He checked the Glock 29, popped out the magazine, and slapped it back in place. As a last step he unfolded the map of the house and gave it a final scrutiny. He knew exactly what he wanted to do.

Maddox moved around to the other side of the barn, where she couldn't see him from the kitchen window. Then he straightened up, walked easily across the yard, in through the gate leading to the patio, and then quickly flattened himself against the side of the house, with the patio doors on his right. He peered into the living room and saw it was empty — she was still in the kitchen — and he swiftly inserted a shim into where the door latched, worked it through to the other side, then pulled it down. The door latch released with a loud click; he slid the door open, ducked inside, shut it, and flattened himself behind an angled wall where the hall led from the living room to the kitchen.

He heard the chair scrape in the kitchen. "Who's there?"

He didn't move. A few soft tentative footsteps into the hall to the living room. "Is someone there?"

Maddox waited, controlling his breathing. She would come in and see what made the noise. He heard several more hesitant steps down the hall, which paused as she evidently halted in the entryway to the living room. She was just around the corner, close enough that he could hear her breathing.

"Hello? Is someone there?"

She might turn and go back to the kitchen. She might go for the phone. But she wasn't sure . . . She'd heard a noise, she was standing in the doorway, the living room looked empty . . . it could have been anything — a falling twig hitting the window or a bird flying into the glass. Maddox knew exactly what she was thinking.

A low whistle started from the kitchen, climbing in shrillness. The kettle was boiling.

Son of a bitch.

She turned with a rustle and he heard her footsteps receding down the hall to the kitchen.

Maddox coughed, not loudly, but distinctly, as a way to bring her back.

The footsteps halted. "Who's that?"

The whistle in the kitchen got louder.

240

She suddenly came charging back into the living room. He leapt out at the same time that he saw, to his complete shock, that she had a .38 in her hand. She whirled and he dove at her legs at the same time the gun went off; he hit her hard and dropped her to the carpet. She screamed, rolled, her blond hair all in a tangle, her gun bouncing across the carpeted floor, her fist lashing out and dealing him a stunning blow to the side of the head.

The yellow-haired bitch.

He struck back wildly, connecting with his left somewhere in a soft place, and it was just disabling enough to get himself on top of her, pinning her to the floor. She gasped, struggled, but he lay on her with all his weight and pressed the Glock to her ear.

"You bitch!" His finger almost — *almost* — pulled the trigger.

She struggled, screamed. He pressed down harder, lying on top of her, pinning her flailing legs in a scissor grip between his. He got himself under control. Christ, he'd almost shot her, and maybe he would still have to.

"I'll kill you if I have to. I will."

More struggling, incoherent sounds. She was unbelievably strong, a wildcat.

"I *will* kill you. Don't make me do it, but so help me I *will* if you don't stop."

He meant it and she heard that he meant it and stopped. As soon as she was quiet he slid around with his leg, trying to snag the .38, which lay on the rug about ten feet away.

"Don't move."

He could feel her under him, hiccuping with fear. Good. She should be afraid. He had come so close to killing her he could almost taste it.

He got his foot on the .38, pulled it to him, picked it up, shoved it in his pocket. He pushed the barrel of the Glock into her mouth and said, "We're going to try this again. Now you know I'll kill you. Nod if you understand."

She suddenly twisted hard and gave a vicious kick backward to his shins, but she had no leverage and he checked her struggling with sharp, wrenching constriction of his arm around her neck.

"Don't fight me."

More struggling.

He twisted the barrel hard enough to make her gag. "It's a gun, bitch, get it?"

She stopped struggling.

"Do what I say and nobody'll get hurt. Nod if you understand."

She nodded and he loosened his grip, slightly.

"You're coming with me. Nice and easy. But first, I need you to do something."

No response. He pushed the barrel deeper into her mouth.

A nod.

Her whole body was trembling in his arms.

"Now I'm going to release you. No sound. No screaming. No sudden moves. I'll kill you fast if you don't do just what I tell you."

A nod and a hiccup.

"You know what I want?"

A shake of the head. He was still lying on top of her, his legs entwined around hers, holding her tight.

"I want the notebook. The one your husband got from the prospector. Is it in the house?"

Shake of the head.

"Your husband has it?"

No response.

Her husband had it. That much he was sure of already. "Now listen to me carefully, Sally. I'm not going to screw around. One false step, one scream, one bullshit trick, and I'll kill you. It's that simple."

He meant it and once again she got the message.

"I'm going to get off you and step back. You will go to the telephone answering machine over there on the table. You will record the following message: *'Hi, this is Tom and Sally. Tom's away on business and I'm out of town unexpectedly, so we won't be able to get back to you right away. Sorry about the missed lessons, I'll get back to everyone later. Leave a message, thanks.'* Can you do that in a normal voice?"

No response.

He twisted the barrel.

A nod.

He removed the gun barrel and she coughed.

"Say it. I want to hear your voice."

"I'll do it."

Her voice was all shaky. He got off her and kept the gun trained on her while she slowly got up.

"Do what I said. I'm going to check the message on my cell as soon as you're done, and if it isn't right, if you've pulled some kind of stunt, you're dead."

The woman walked over to the phone machine, pressed a button, and spoke the message.

"Your voice is too stressed. Do it again. Naturally."

She did it again, and a third time, finally getting it right.

"Good. Now we're going to walk outside like two normal people, you first, me five feet behind. You won't forget, even for an instant, that I've got a gun. My car is parked in a grove of scrub oaks about a quarter mile up the road. You know where those trees are?"

She nodded.

"That's where we're going."

As he pushed her across the living room, he became aware of a sensation of wetness on his thigh. He looked down. The plastic raincoat was torn and a tuft of material stood out from the pant leg. There was a dark patch of blood, not a lot, but still it was blood. Maddox was astonished because he had felt nothing, and still felt nothing. He scanned the rug but saw no evidence that any of the blood had dripped to the floor. He reached down with a hand, explored, feeling the sting of the wound for the first time.

Son of a bitch. The blond had winged him.

He marched her out of the house and across a brushy flat and alongside the creek, soon arriving at the hidden car. Once in the cover of the scrub oaks he took a pair of leg cuffs out of his rucksack and tossed them at her feet.

"Put them on."

She bent over, fumbled with them for a while, snapped them on.

"Put your hands behind your back."

She obeyed and he spun her around and snapped on a pair of handcuffs. Then he opened the front passenger door. "Get in."

She managed to sit and swing her feet in.

He took off his knapsack, took out the bottle of chloroform and the diaper, poured a good dose.

"No!" he heard her scream. "No, don't!" She swung her feet up to kick him but she had little room to maneuver, and he had already lunged in on top of her, pinning her manacled arms and mashing the diaper into her face. She struggled, cried out, writhing and kicking, but in a few moments she went limp.

He made sure she had breathed in a good dose, then got in the driver's side and slid behind the wheel. She lay slumped on the seat in an unnatural position. He reached over, hefted her and propped her up against the door, put a pillow behind her head and drew a blanket up around her, until she looked like she was peacefully asleep.

He powered down the windows to get the stench of chloroform out of the car, and then pulled off stocking, shower cap, booties, hair net, and raincoat, balling them up and stuffing them inside a garbage bag.

He started the car, eased out of the grove, and drove down the dirt road to the highway. From there he crossed the dam and drove north on Highway 84. Ten miles up the road, he eased onto the unmarked

Forest Service road that ran up into the Carson national forest, to the CCC Camp at Perdiz Creek.

The woman lay against the door, eyes closed, blond hair all in a mess. He paused, looking at her. Damn, he thought, she was good-looking — a real honey-haired beauty.

13

"They say it used to be a bordello," Beezon said to Tom as they stood in the dirt turnaround in front of a shabby old Victorian mansion, which rose incongruously from a desert sprinkled with palo verde, teddy bear cholla, and ocotillo.

"Looks more like a haunted house than a whorehouse," said Tom.

Beezon chuckled. "I warn you — Harry Dearborn's kind of eccentric. His brusqueness is legendary." He clomped up onto the porch and lifted the ring on the big bronze lion doorknocker. It fell once, with a hollow boom. A moment later a rotund voice inside said, "Come in, the door is unlocked."

They entered. The house was dark with most of the drapes drawn, and it smelled of mustiness and cats. It looked like a traffic jam of dark Victorian furniture. The floors were laid with overlapping Persian carpets, and the walls were lined with oak display cases of rippled glass, mineral specimens crowding their shadowy depths. Standing lamps with tasseled shades stood here and there, throwing pools of feeble yellow light.

"In here," came the deep rumble of the voice. "And don't touch anything."

Beezon led the way into a sitting room. In the middle, a grossly fat man was imbedded in an oversized armchair of flowered chintz, antimacassars resting on the armrests. The light came from behind, leaving the man's face in shadow.

"Hello, Harry," said Beezon, his voice a little nervous. "Long time, eh? This is a friend of mine, Mr. Thomas Broadbent."

A large hand emerged from the darkness of the chair, made a vague flicking motion toward a pair of wing chairs. They both sat down.

Tom studied the man a little closer. He looked remarkably like Sidney Greenstreet, dressed in a white suit with a dark shirt and yellow tie, his thinning hair combed carefully back, a neat and tidy man despite his corpulence. His broad forehead was as smooth and white as a baby's and heavy gold rings winked on his fingers.

"Well, well," Dearborn said, "if it isn't Robert Beezon, the ammonite man. How's business?"

"Couldn't be better. Fossils are going mainstream as office decor."

Another dismissive gesture, a raised hand and a barely perceptible movement of two fingers. "What do you want with me?"

Beezon cleared his throat. "Mr. Broadbent here —"

He stopped Beezon and turned to Tom. "Broadbent? You aren't by chance related to Maxwell Broadbent, the collector?"

Tom was taken aback. "He was my father."

"Maxwell Broadbent." He grunted. "Interesting man. Ran into him a few times. Is he still alive?"

"He passed away last year."

Another grunt. A hand came out holding a huge handkerchief, dabbed away at the fleshy, slabbed face. "I'm sorry to hear that. The world could use a few more like him, larger than life. Everyone's become so . . . *normal.* May I ask how he died? He couldn't have been more than sixty."

Tom hesitated. "He . . . he died in Honduras."

The eyebrows rose. "Is there some mystery here?"

Tom was taken aback by the man's directness. "He died doing what he loved doing," he said with a certain crispness. "He might have asked for better, but he accepted it with dignity. No mystery there."

"I am truly shocked to hear it." A pause. "So, what can I do for you, Thomas?"

"Mr. Broadbent here is interested in purchasing a dinosaur —" Beezon began.

"A dinosaur? What in the world makes you think I sell dinosaurs?"

"Well . . ." Beezon fell silent, a look of consternation on his face.

Dearborn extended a large hand to him. "Robert, I want to thank you most sincerely for introducing Mr. Broadbent to me. Excuse me if I don't rise. It seems Mr. Broadbent and I have some business to discuss, which we should prefer to do in private."

Beezon stood and hesitatingly turned to Broadbent, wanting to say something. Tom guessed what it was.

"About that agreement we made? You can count on it."

"Thank you," said Beezon.

Tom felt a pang of guilt. There wouldn't, of course, be any commission.

Beezon said his good-byes and a moment later they heard the thump of the door, the whine of the car engine starting.

Dearborn turned to Tom, his face creasing into the semblance of a smile. "Now — did I hear the word dinosaur? What I said is true. I don't sell dinosaurs."

"What exactly *is* it that you do, Harry?"

"I'm a dinosaur *broker*." Dearborn leaned back into his chair with a smile, waiting.

Tom gathered his wits. "I'm an investment banker with clients in the Far East, and one of them —"

The fat hand rose up yet again, halting Tom's prepared speech. "That may work with Beezon but it won't wash with me. Tell me what it's really about."

Tom thought for a moment. The shrewd, cynical glitter in Dearborn's eye convinced him that he would be better off telling the truth.

"Perhaps you read about the murder in New Mexico, in the high mesas north of Abiquiú?"

"I did."

"I was the man who found the body. I happened to come across him as he was dying."

"Go on," said Dearborn, in a neutral tone.

"The man pressed a journal into my hand and made me promise to give it to his daughter, named Robbie. I'm trying to keep that promise. The problem is, the police haven't identified him or as far as I know even found his body."

"Did the man tell you anything else before he died?"

"He was lucid for only a moment," Tom said evasively.

"And this journal? What does it say?"

"It's just numbers. Lists of numbers."

"What kind of numbers?"

"Data to a GPR survey."

"Yes, yes, of course, that's how he did it. May I ask what *your* interest is in this, Mr. Broadbent?"

"Mr. Dearborn, I made a promise to a dying man. I keep my promises. That's my interest — no more, no less."

Harry Dearborn seemed amused by the answer. "I do believe, Mr. Broadbent, that if I were Diogenes, I would have to put out my lantern. You are that rarest of things, an honest man. Or you are a consummate liar."

"My wife thinks I'm merely stubborn."

He gave a flabby sigh. "I did indeed follow that murder up in Abiquiú. I wondered if it wasn't a certain dinosaur hunter of my acquaintance. I was aware that the fellow had been prospecting up there and there was a rumor he was on to something big. It seems my worst fears have been realized."

"You know his name?"

The fat man shifted, the chair creaking under the massive redistribution of weight. "Marston Weathers."

"Who's he?"

"Nothing less than the top dinosaur hunter in the country." The fat man gathered his hands together and squeezed. "His friends called him Stem, because he was tall and kind of stringy. Tell me one thing,

Mr. Broadbent: did old Stem find what he was looking for?"

Tom hesitated. Somehow, he felt he could trust this man. "Yes."

Another long, sad sigh. "Poor Stem. He died like he lived: ironically."

"What can you tell me about him?"

"A great deal. And in return, Mr. Broadbent, you will tell me about what he found. Agreed?"

"Agreed."

14

Wyman Ford could see the tapering point of Navajo Rim a few hundred yards ahead, where the mesa ended in a small, thumb-shaped butte. The sun hung low in the sky, a disc of red-hot gold. Ford felt exhilarated. He now understood why the Indians of old went off into the wilderness and fasted in search of a vision quest. He had been on half rations for two days, eating only a slice of bread drizzled with a little olive oil for breakfast, and then for dinner half a cupful of cooked lentils and rice. Hunger did strange and wonderful things to the mind; it gave him a feeling of euphoria and boundless energy. He found it curious that a mere physiological effect could produce such a profoundly spiritual feeling.

He skirted the sandstone butte, looking for a way up. The view was incredible, but from the top he would be able to see even more. He edged along a sandstone ledge no more than three feet wide, plunging a thousand feet down into the blue depths of a canyon. He had never been this deep into the high mesa country before, and he felt like an explorer, a John Wesley Powell. This was, without a doubt, some of the remotest country that existed in the lower forty-eight.

He came around the edge and stopped in surprise and delighted astonishment. There, wedged into the side of the bluff, was a tiny but almost perfect Anasazi cliff dwelling — four small rooms constructed from stacked pieces of sandstone and mortared with mud. He edged around the precipice with great care — how in the world had they raised children here? — and knelt down, peering in the doorway. The tiny room inside was empty, save for a scattering of burned corn cobs and a few potsherds. A single shaft of sunlight penetrating through a broken part of the wall, splashing a brilliant splotch of light on the ground. There were recent footprints in the dust of the floor made by someone wearing hiking boots with chevron-shaped lugs, and Ford wondered if these belonged to the prospector. It seemed likely; if you were going to search this corner of the high mesas, you couldn't find a better lookout.

He stood up and continued along the ledge past the ruin, where he encountered an ancient hand-and-foot trail pecked into the sloping sandstone, going to the top of the butte.

The summit afforded a dazzling vista across the Echo Badlands, almost, it seemed, to the very curve of the earth itself. To his left, the enormous profile of Mesa de los Viejos loomed up, level after level like a great stone staircase, rising to the foothills of the Canjilon Mountains. It was one of the most awesome views it had ever been his privilege to see, as if the Great Creator had blown up and burned the landscape, leaving it an utter wreck.

Ford sorted through his maps and removed one. He traced the quadrants of the map with his eye and then mentally drew those same lines on the badlands in front of him. Having sectioned and numbered the landscape to his satisfaction, he took out his binoculars and began searching the first quadrant, the one farthest to the east. When that was done he moved on to the next one and the next, methodically working his way across the landscape, looking for the peculiar rock formation outlined in the computer plot.

His first sweep yielded too many candidates. Similar formations were often found in groups, having been carved from the same layers of stone by the same action of wind and water. Ford had a growing conviction that he was on the right track, that the T. Rex was somewhere in the Echo Badlands. He just needed to get closer.

He spent the next fifteen minutes examining each quadrant a second time, but while many rock formations looked similar to the one he was after, none were a perfect match. There was always the possibility, of course, that he was looking at the right formation from the wrong angle, or that the formation might be hidden in one of the deep canyons at the far end of the badlands. As his eyes roved about, one canyon in particular captured his attention. Tyrannosaur Canyon. It was the longest canyon in the high mesas, deep and tortuous, cutting more than twenty miles across the Echo Badlands, with hundreds, maybe even thousands, of side canyons and tributaries. He identified the great basalt monolith that marked its opening, and he followed its sinuous length with his binoculars. Deep in the badlands, the canyon petered out in a distant valley jammed with queer, domelike rocks. Some of the domes looked uncannily like the image in the computer plot — broader on top, with narrower necks. They were jumbled together like a crowd of bald men knocking their heads together.

Ford measured the distance from the sun to the horizon with his fingers at arm's length, and decided it was about four o'clock. Being June, the sun wouldn't set until well past eight. If he hustled, he could reach the cluster of sandstone domes before dark. It didn't look like there would be any water down there, but he had recently filled his two canteens at a fast-evaporating pothole left from the recent heavy rain, giving him four liters in reserve. He would camp somewhere down in that impressive canyon, commence his exploration at the crack of dawn tomorrow. Sunday. The day of the Lord.

He pushed that thought out of his mind.

Ford took one last look through his binoculars at the deep, mysterious canyon. Something twisted in his gut. He knew the T. Rex. was down there — in Tyrannosaur Canyon.

The irony of it made Ford smile.

15

Harry Dearborn drew in a long breath of air, his face hidden in shadow. "My goodness, it's four-thirty already. Would you care for tea?"

"If it isn't too much trouble," Tom said, wondering how the enormously fat man would get out of his chair, let alone make tea.

"Not at all." Dearborn moved his foot slightly and pressed a small bump in the floor; a moment later the dim presence of a servant materialized out of the back of the house.

"Tea."

The man withdrew.

"Now where were we? Ah, yes, Stem Weathers's daughter. Roberta's her name."

"Robbie."

"Robbie, that's what her father called her. Unfortunately, she and her father were somewhat estranged. Last I heard she was trying to make it as an artist in Texas — Marfa, I believe. Down there by the Big Bend. A small town — she should be easy to find."

"How did you know Weathers? Did he collect dinosaurs for you?"

A fat finger tapped on the arm of his chair. "Nobody collects *for* me, Thomas, although I might pass on suggestions from some of my clients. I have nothing to do with the collecting — beyond requiring documentary proof that the fossil came from private land." Here, Dearborn paused long enough for an ironic smile to stretch across the lower part of his face. Then he continued.

"Most of the fossil hunters out there are looking for small stuff. I call them the ferns and fishes crowd, like our Mr. Beezon. Crap by the truckload. Once in a while they stumble over something important and that's when they come to me. I have clients who are looking for something quite particular: businessmen, foreign museums, collectors. I match buyers and sellers and take a twenty percent commission. I never see or touch the specimens. I am not a field man."

Tom stifled a smile.

The servant appeared with an enormous silver tray carrying a pot of tea covered in a quilted cozy, plates heaped with scones, cream puffs, small eclairs, and miniature brioches, jars of marmalade, butter, clotted cream, and honey. He placed the tray on a table to the side of Dearborn and vanished as silently as he had come.

"Excellent!" Dearborn pulled the cozy off the pot, filled two china cups, added milk and sugar.

"Your tea." He handed the cup and saucer to Tom.

Tom took his cup, sipped.

"I insist on my tea being prepared English style, not as the barbaric Americans make it." He chuckled and drained his cup in a single smooth motion, placed it down empty, and then reached out with a plump hand and plucked a brioche from the tray, opened it steaming, slathered it in clotted cream, and popped it in his mouth. He next took a hot crumpet, placed a soft dollop of butter on top, and waited for it to melt before eating it.

"Please, help yourself," he said in a muffled voice.

Tom took an eclair and bit into it. Thick whipped cream squirted out the back and dribbled down his hand. He ate it, licking up the cream and wiping off his hand.

Dearborn smacked his lips, dabbed them with a napkin, and went on. "Stem Weathers wasn't a ferns and fishes man. He was after unique specimens. He spent his whole life looking for that one big strike. Big-time dinosaur hunters are all of a type. They're not in it for money. They're obsessed. It's the excitement of the hunt, the thrill of the strike, an obsession with finding something of enormous rarity and value — that's what keeps them going."

He poured a second cup of tea, raised the cup and saucer to his lips, drained it halfway in a single loud sip.

"I handled Stem's finds but otherwise left him alone. He rarely told me what he was doing or where he was looking. This time, however, word got out that he was on to something big in that high mesa country. He talked to too damn many people looking for information — geophysicists, cosmochemists, curators of paleontology at various museums. It was very unwise of him. He was too well known. The rumors were flying thick and fast. Everyone knew how he operated — his homemade GPR and that notebook were both legendary — so it doesn't surprise me someone went in there after him. On top of that, the high mesas is all federal land — overseen by the Bureau of Land Management. He wasn't supposed to be in there. Anything taken off BLM land without a proper federal permit is grand theft — pure and simple. And they only issue permits to a select few museums and universities anyway."

"Why would he take the risk?"

"It's not much of a risk. He's not the

only one doing it. Most BLM land is so remote the chances of getting caught are almost nonexistent."

"What kind of finds did he bring you?"

Dearborn smiled. "I never kiss and tell. Suffice to say, he never bothered me with mediocre stuff. They say he could smell dead dinosaurs even though they'd been buried millions of years."

He expelled an elegiac sigh, prematurely cut off by a marmaladed scone entering his mouth. He chewed, swallowed, and went on.

"His problem wasn't finding the dinosaurs; it was what to do after he found them. The financial side always tripped him up. I tried to help but he was always getting himself into trouble. He was a difficult man, a loner, prickly, easy to take offense. Sure, he might find a dinosaur he could sell for half a million dollars, but just to get that fossil out of the ground and ship it to a lab cost him a hundred grand. It takes about thirty thousand man-hours to clean and prepare a large dinosaur — and that doesn't include mounting it. Weathers cared too much about his dinosaurs and as a result he was always broke. But he sure could find them."

"Do you have any idea who murdered him?"

"No. But it isn't hard to guess what

might have happened. Some of the lesser folks had taken to following him around. As I said, word got out. He asked too many questions of too many geologists, especially those studying the K-T mass extinction. Everyone knew Stem was on the prowl, sniffing up something big. My guess is he was murdered by a claim jumper."

Tom leaned forward. "Anyone in particular?"

Dearborn shook his head, picked up an eclair, and swallowed it. "I know everyone in this business. Black market dinosaur hunters are a rough lot. They get in fistfights at meetings, they rob each other's quarries, they lie, cheat, steal. But murder? I can't see it. I would guess the killer is a newcomer, or perhaps a hired hand who takes his work a little too seriously."

He drained his cup, poured another.

"These rumors you spoke about?"

"For a couple of years Weathers had been trying to trace a layer of sandstone known as the Hell Creek Formation down into New Mexico."

"Hell Creek?"

"Almost all the T. Rexes in existence have come out of this immense sedimentary formation which crops out in various places across the Rocky Mountains, but which has never been found in New Mexico. The layer was first discovered by a paleontologist named Barnum Brown, in Hell Creek, Montana, about a hundred years ago, when he found the world's first T. Rex. But Weathers was in search of more than just Hell Creek rocks. He had an obsession with the K-T boundary itself."

"The Cretaceous-Tertiary boundary?"

"That's right. You see, the Hell Creek Formation is topped by the K-T boundary layer. That layer, which is only half an inch thick, records the event that killed off the dinosaurs — the asteroid strike. There aren't many places in the world where there's an interrupted sequence of rocks at the K-T boundary. I think that's what brought him to the high mesa country of Abiquiú — looking for the K-T boundary layer."

"Why was he looking for the K-T boundary specifically?"

"I'm not sure. In general terms, the K-T boundary is about the most interesting layer of rock ever found. It contains the debris from the asteroid impact along with ash from the burning of the earth's forests. There's a spectacularly clear sequence of K-T boundary layer rocks in the Raton Basin in Colorado. They tell quite a story. The asteroid struck where the Yucatán Peninsula of Mexico is now, coming in at an angle that sprayed molten debris across much of North America. They've named the asteroid Chicxulub, a Mayan word meaning 'The Tail of the Devil' — cute, eh?"

He chuckled and used the opportunity to eat another crumpet.

"Chicxulub struck the earth moving at a speed of Mach forty. It was so large that when the bottom of it was contacting the ground the top was higher than Mount Everest. It vaporized a major chunk of the earth's crust on contact, blasting up a plume of material more than a hundred kilometers wide that punched through the earth's atmosphere and went into orbit, some of it rising halfway to the moon before plunging back at speeds of more than twenty-five thousand miles an hour. The falling material superheated much of the atmosphere, igniting gigantic wildfires that swept the continents, releasing a hundred billion tons of carbon dioxide, a hundred billion tons of methane, and seventy billion tons of soot. The smoke and dust was so thick that the earth became as dark as the darkest cave, all photosynthesis stopped, and food chains collapsed. A kind of nuclear winter set in and the earth froze for months; that was immediately followed by a galloping greenhouse effect caused by the sudden release of carbon dioxide and methane. It took 130,000 years for the earth's atmosphere to cool down and return to normal."

Dearborn smacked his lips, licking off a dribble of crème fraîche with a large pink tongue.

"All this is beautifully recorded in the K-T rocks in the Raton Basin. First you see a layer of debris from the impact itself. This layer is grayish and high in the rare element iridium, found in meteorites. Under a microscope, you see it's packed with tiny spherules, frozen droplets of molten rock. Above that layer is a second layer, dead black, which one geologist described as 'the ashes of the Cretaceous world.' Geologists are the most poetic of scientists, don't you think?"

"I'm still puzzled why Weathers would be interested in the K-T boundary if he was just after dinosaur fossils."

"That's a mystery. Maybe he was using that layer as a way to locate T. Rex fossils. The late Cretaceous, just before the extinction, was when tyrannosaurs ruled the earth."

"What's a good T. Rex worth these days?"

"Someone once said that all the people who have ever found a T. Rex wouldn't even be enough to field a baseball team. They're the rarest of the rare. I've got two dozen customers waiting to bid on the next T. Rex that comes on the private market, and I'd guess some of them would be willing to pay a hundred million or more."

Tom whistled.

Dearborn laid down his teacup, his face taking on a thoughtful look. "I had this feeling . . ."

"Yes?"

"A feeling that Stem Weathers was looking for something more that just a T. Rex. Something to do with the K-T boundary itself. But exactly what, I couldn't say . . ."

His voice trailed off and he poured himself another cup of tea.

"Poor Stem. And poor Robbie. I don't envy you, having to break the news."

He drained the cup, ate one final scone, dabbed his face, and wiped the tips of his fingers with his napkin.

"Now it's your turn to talk, Thomas. Tell me what Stem Weathers found. Naturally, you can count on my discretion." His eyes glowed.

Tom slipped the computer-plotted drawing from his pocket and unfolded it on the tea table.

Slowly, inexorably, but with huge momentum, the great bulk of Harry Dearborn rose from his chair in silent astonishment.

16

Maddox stood above the woman, who lay on the bed, her blond hair spread out on the pillow like a halo. She had just begun to stir, gave a moan — and finally her eyes opened. He said nothing, watching the look in her eyes go from confusion to fear as it all came back.

He raised the gun so she could see it. "No monkey business. You can sit up, but that's it."

She sat up, wincing as she did so, the manacles around her wrists and ankles clinking.

He gestured around. "So . . . what do you think?"

No answer.

"I worked hard making it nice for you."

He had spread a small tablecloth on the cable spool to make a table, put some fresh flowers in a jam jar, and had even hung a signed, limited edition print that he had taken from the cabin. The kerosene lantern threw a yellow glow across the room, which was pleasantly cool compared to the late-afternoon heat outside. The air was fresh, too — no mine vapors or poisonous gases.

"When's Tom coming back?" Maddox said.

No answer. The blond looked away. This was starting to piss him off.

"Look at me."

She ignored him.

"I said, *look at me*." He raised his gun.

She turned her head slowly, insolently, and looked at him. Her green eyes blazed with hatred.

"Like what you see?"

She said nothing. The look on her face was so intense that Maddox found it a little disconcerting. She didn't look afraid. But she was afraid, he knew that. She was terrified. She had to be. And with good reason.

He stood up and gave her his winning, lopsided smile, holding out his arms. "Yeah, take a good look. I'm not so bad, right?"

No reaction.

"You're going to see a lot of me, you know that? I'm going to start off by showing you the tattoo on my back. Can you guess what it is?"

No reaction.

"It took two weeks to make, four hours a day for fourteen days. A prison buddy of mine did it, a real genius with the needle.

You know why I'm telling you this?"

He paused but she said nothing.

"Because that tattoo is the reason I'm here with you today. Now listen carefully. I want that notebook. Your husband has it. When he gives it to me, I let you go — simple. But to do that, I need to get in touch with him. He got a cell phone? Give me the number and you could be out of here in a few hours."

Finally she spoke. "Look him up in the phone book."

"Aw, now why do you have to be a bitch about it?"

She said nothing. Maybe she still thought she had some kind of say in the situation. He would have to show her otherwise. He would break her like a young filly.

"See those shackles on the wall? They're for you, in case you hadn't guessed."

She didn't turn.

"Take a good look at them."

"No."

"Stand up."

She remained seated.

He carefully pointed the gun at her ankle, aimed just to the left, fired. The noise was deafening in the enclosed space, and she jumped like a deer. The bullet had gone through the mattress and tufts of stuffing came drifting down.

"Darn. Missed."

He aimed again. "You'll limp for the rest of your life. Now stand up."

She stood up, her cuffs jingling.

"Shuffle over there where those manacles are set in the wall. You're going to take off your cuffs and put those on."

Now he could see fear leaking through on that arrogant face of hers, despite her efforts to control it. He aimed the gun. "It might even kill you if it nicks an artery."

No answer.

"Are you going to do what I say or do I have to shoot you in the foot? Last warning and I'm not kidding."

Once again, he was serious, and she realized it.

"I'll do it," she said in a smothered voice. Water was leaking out of her eyes.

"Smart girl. Here's how. The same key goes to both sets. Switch off your ankles first, one at a time. Then your right wrist. I'll do your left myself." He tossed her the key. She bent down and picked it up, awkwardly unlocked the manacles around her ankles, and followed his instructions.

"Now drop the key."

He ducked in, retrieved it. "I'm going to do your left wrist." He stepped over to the table, placed the gun down on it, went over, and shackled her left wrist. Then he tested the manacles to make sure they had all latched properly.

He stepped back and picked the gun off the table. "See that?" He pointed to his thigh. "You winged me, you know that?"

"Too bad it wasn't centered and about four inches higher," said Sally.

Maddox laughed harshly. "We got a real comedian here. The sooner you get with the program, the quicker this'll be over. Your husband, Tommy, he's got the notebook. I want it." He aimed the Glock at her foot again. "Give me his number and we can get the ball rolling."

She gave him a cell number.

"Now you're going to get a real treat."

He grinned, stepped back, and began unbuttoning his shirt.

"I'm going to show you my tattoo."

17

The usual hush prevailed in the reading room of the Amsterdam Club. The only sounds were the genteel rustle of newsprint and the occasional clink of ice in a glass. The oak-paneled walls, the dark paintings, and the heavy furniture gave the place a feeling of elegance and timelessness, reinforced by the fragrance of old books and leather.

In one corner, ensconced in a deep chair, illuminated in a pool of yellow light, sat Iain Corvus, sipping a martini and perusing the latest copy of *Scientific American*. He flipped the pages, not really reading, before tossing the magazine on the side table with impatience. At seven o'clock on a Saturday evening the reading room was beginning to empty, with the members going in to dinner. Corvus had no appetite for either food or conversation. It had now been seventy-two hours since Maddox had last been in contact with him. Corvus had no idea where he was or what he was doing, and no way to contact him safely.

He shifted in his chair, recrossed his legs, and took a good belt from the martini. He felt the welcome spread of warmth in his chest, rising to his head, but it gave him no comfort. So much depended on Maddox; *everything* depended on Maddox. His career was at a crisis point, and he was at the mercy of an ex-con.

Melodie was working late in the Mineralogy lab, doing further analysis on the specimen. She had proven to be a phenomenal scientist, achieving far more than he'd anticipated. Indeed, she'd done so well that a small worry had begun to creep into his mind — that she might prove to be a more awkward person to share the glory with than he'd originally assumed. He had perhaps made a mistake turning over such an important and groundbreaking analysis to her alone, without at least involving himself enough to justify seizing the credit.

She had promised to call him at eleven with the latest results. He checked his watch: four hours.

What she had discovered was already more than sufficient to present to the tenure meeting. It was a godsend. It would be impossible to deny him tenure and watch the most important dinosaur specimen of all time walk off with him to another museum. No matter how much they disliked him, no matter how much they felt his publication record was inadequate, they wouldn't let that specimen go. It was a stroke of luck beyond all luck — but no, thought Corvus, it wasn't luck at all. Luck, someone said, was when preparation met opportunity. He had prepared well. He'd heard the rumors more than six months ago that Marston Weathers was on the track of something big. He knew the old gobshite was in northern New Mexico hoping to score an illegal dinosaur on BLM land — *public* land. Corvus had realized that here was a perfect opportunity: to expropriate a dinosaur from a thief and recover it for science. He would be performing a valuable public service — as well as doing himself a good turn.

Corvus had been more than a little disturbed when he learned Maddox had actually killed Weathers, but when he got over the initial shock he realized that it had been the right decision all around — it vastly simplified matters. And it removed from circulation a man who had been responsible for the theft from public land of more irreplaceable scientific specimens than anyone else, living or dead.

Preparation. That fellow Maddox hadn't just fallen into his lap. Maddox had contacted him because of who he was, the world's authority of tyrannosaurid dinosaurs. When Corvus had the idea that

Marston Weathers was the key to getting his hands on a first-rate specimen, he had realized just how useful Maddox could be — if he were out of prison. Corvus had taken a personal risk getting that done, but he was helped by the fact that Maddox's conviction was for aggravated manslaughter instead of murder two — he'd had a bloody good lawyer. Maddox had a record of good behavior in prison. And finally, when Maddox's first shot at parole came up, the dead victim had no relatives or friends to pack the hearing and tell their tale of victimhood. Corvus himself had spoken at the hearing, vouching for Maddox and offering to employ him. It had worked and the parole board had released him.

Over time Corvus realized that Maddox himself was a man with rare qualities, a remarkably charismatic and intelligent individual, a smooth talker, good-looking, presentable. Had he been born under different circumstances he might have made a rather decent scientist himself.

Preparation meeting opportunity. So far Corvus had played this one perfectly. He really should calm down and trust Maddox to carry through on the assignment and get the notebook. The notebook would lead him straight to the fossil. It was the key to everything.

He glanced impatiently at his watch, polished off his martini, and picked up the *Scientific American*. His mind was now calm.

18

In the dim light of the kerosene lantern, Sally Broadbent watched the man take off his shirt. She could feel the cold steel around her wrists and ankles; she could smell the dampness of the air, hear the dripping of water somewhere. She seemed to be in some kind of cave or old mine. With a coppery taste in her mouth and an aching head, she felt as if it were happening to another person.

Sally did not believe that the man would let her go after he got the notebook from Tom. He would kill her — she could see it in his eyes, in the careless way he showed his face and revealed information about himself.

"Hey, what do you think of this?"

He was facing her, now shirtless, a lopsided grin covering his face, slowly popping his pecs and biceps.

"Ready?"

He held his arms forward, his back hunched. Then all in a rush, he swung around and turned his back to her.

She gasped. There, completely covering

his back, was the tattooed image of a charging Tyrannosaurus rex, claws raised, jaws agape, so real it almost seemed to be leaping from his back. As he flexed his muscles the dinosaur actually seemed to move.

"Cool, huh?"

She stared.

"I said something." His back was still turned, and he was popping one set of back muscles after another, making the T. Rex move first one claw, then another, then its head.

"I see it."

"When I was in prison, I decided I needed a tattoo. It's a tradition, know what I mean? It's also a necessity — it says who you are and defines your alliances. Guys without tats usually end up somebody's bitch. But I didn't want the usual death's head, grim reaper crap. I wanted a tattoo that stood for *me*. A tattoo that told everyone I wasn't going to be anyone's bitch, that I was my own man, that I didn't owe allegiance to anyone. That's why I chose a T. Rex. Nothing meaner's ever lived on this planet.

"But then I had to find the design for it. If I turned my back loose on some idiot, I'd end up with Godzilla or some prison Jack's moronic idea of what a T. Rex might look like. I wanted the real thing. I wanted it *scientifically accurate.*"

He gave a massive flex, the back muscles swelling grotesquely, the jaws of the T. Rex seeming to open and close.

"So I wrote to the world's expert on T. Rex. Of course, he didn't answer my letters. Why would a guy like that correspond with a convicted murderer in Pelican Bay?"

He chuckled softly, flexed again. "Take a good look there, Sally. There's never been a more accurate depiction of a T. Rex — not in any book, not in any museum. All the latest scientific research is in there."

Sally swallowed, listened.

"Anyway, after a year of no answer, all of a sudden this dinosaur expert wrote me back. We had quite a correspondence. He sent me all the latest research, even stuff that hadn't been published. He sent me drawings in his own hand. I had a real tattoo expert do it for me. As the T. Rex came to life, whenever I had a question my dino man on the outside would answer it. He made time for me. He was really into it, making sure this T. Rex was the real thing."

Another rolling flex.

"We got to be friends — more like brothers. And then — you know what he did?"

Sally worked her mouth, managed to say, "What?"

"He sprung me from the slam. I was doing ten to fifteen, aggravated manslaughter, but he vouched for me at my hearing, gave me money and a job. So when he asked me for a favor, I wasn't in a position to refuse. You know what that favor was?"

"No."

"To get that notebook."

She swallowed again, fought against a fresh wave of fear. He would never be telling her this unless he planned to kill her.

He stopped flexing, turned back around, picked up his shirt, pulled it on. "You see now why I'm going to so much trouble? But I've got to go make a phone call. I'll be back."

Then he turned and walked out of her little prison-room.

19

As the car neared Tucson, Tom tried his cell phone again and found there was finally coverage. He checked his watch. Half past five. He'd been with Dearborn longer than he thought. He was going to have to hustle to make his six-thirty flight.

He dialed his home number to check in on Sally. The phone rang a few times and the answering machine kicked on. *"Hi, this is Tom and Sally. Tom's away on business and I'm out of town unexpectedly, so we won't be able to get back to you right away. Sorry about the missed lessons, I'll get back to everyone later. Leave a message, thanks."*

The beep followed and Tom hung up the phone, surprised and suddenly concerned. What was this about being out of town unexpectedly? Why hadn't she called him? Maybe she did call — his cell phone was out of range at Dearborn's place. He quickly checked his phone but it had registered no missed calls.

With a growing sense of unease he dialed his home number again, listened to the message more carefully. She didn't sound normal at all. He pulled over to the side of the road and redialed this time listening very closely. Something was terribly wrong. Tom felt his heart suddenly pounding in his chest. He pulled back on the interstate with a screech of rubber. As he accelerated, he dialed the Santa Fe Police and asked for Detective Willer. A frustrating two transfers later the familiar stolid voice answered.

"It's Tom Broadbent."

"Yeah?"

"I'm out of town and I just called home. Something's not right at my house. My wife should be there but she's not, and she left a message on the answering machine that makes no sense. I think she was forced to leave that message. Something's happened."

A silence, and then Willer said, "I'll go out there right now and take a look."

"I want you to do more than that. I want you to pull out all the stops and find her."

"You think she's been kidnapped?"

Tom hesitated. "I don't know."

A pause. "Anything else we should know?"

"I've told you what I know. Just get out there as quickly as possible."

"I'll take care of it personally. Do we have permission to break in, if the door's locked?"

"Yes, of course."

"When are you getting back to town?"

"My flight from Tucson's landing at seven-thirty."

"Give me your number, I'll call you from the house."

Tom gave his cell phone number and hung up. A feeling of powerlessness and self-reproach washed over him. What a fool he'd been, leaving Sally by herself.

He accelerated, laying the pedal to the metal, blasting down the asphalt at over hundred. No way could he miss this flight.

Fifteen minutes later his cell phone rang.

"Am I speaking to Tom Broadbent?"

It wasn't Willer. "Look, I'm waiting for an important —"

"Shut up, Tommy boy, and listen."

"Who the hell is — ?"

"I said shut up."

A pause.

"I got your little lady. Sally. She's safe — for now. All I want is the notebook. You follow? Just answer yes or no."

Tom gripped the phone so hard as if to crush it. "Yes," he finally managed to say.

"When I get the notebook, you get Sally back."

"Listen, if you even so much as —"

"I'm not going to say it again. *Shut the hell up.*"

Tom heard the man breathing heavily into the other end of the phone.

The voice said, "Where are you?"

"I'm in Arizona —"

"When do you get back?"

"Seven-thirty. Listen to me —"

"I want you to listen to *me*. Very carefully. Can you do that?"

"Yes."

"After your flight lands, get in your car and drive to Abiquiú. Go through town and get on Highway 84 north of the dam. Don't stop for anything. You should be there at around nine o'clock. You've got the notebook on you?"

"Yes."

"Good. I want you to take the notebook, put it in a Ziploc bag, and pack it full of trash to make it look like garbage. The trash has to be yellow. You get it? Bright yellow. Drive back and forth on Highway 84 between the dam turnoff and the Ghost Ranch turnoff. Drive at *exactly* sixty miles an hour with your cell phone on. Coverage is pretty good, only a few dead spots. I'll call you then with more instructions. Understand?"

"Yes."

"What's your flight number?"

"Southwest Airlines 662."

"Good. I'm going to check and find out when you actually land, and I'll expect you up by Ghost Ranch one hour and twenty-five minutes later. Don't stop at home, don't do anything but drive straight up to Abiquiú. You understand? Just go back and forth between the dam and Ghost Ranch until you get my call. Keep it at sixty."

"Yes. But if you hurt her —"

"Hurt Sally? She's going to be taken care of real good, provided you do everything I say in exactly the way I say it. And Tom? No cops. Let me tell you why. No kidnapping ever succeeded after the police were called in. You ever hear that statistic? When the cops are called in, the kidnapping fails and the victim usually dies. You call the police and I'm screwed. The cops'll take over, they'll do their own thing, and they won't pay any attention to you or your concerns. You'll lose control, I'll lose control, and Sally will die. You understand what I'm saying? You call the cops, and you'll be kissing your wife goodbye on a stainless-steel gurney in the basement of 1100 West Airport. Clear?"

Silence.

"Have I made myself clear?"

"Yes."

"Good. It'll just be you and me, in total control at all times. I get the notebook, you get your wife. Total control. Understand?"

"Yes."

"I've got a police band radio here and I've got other ways of knowing if you call the cops. And I've got a partner, too."

The man clicked off.

Tom could hardly drive, hardly see the road. Almost immediately, the phone rang again. It was Willer.

"Mr. Broadbent? We're at your place, in the living room, and I'm afraid we've got a problem."

Tom swallowed, unable to find his voice.

"We got a round in the wall here. The SOC boys are on their way to take it out."

Tom realized he was veering all over the highway, his foot to the metal, the car going almost a hundred and ten. He slowed the car and made an enormous effort to concentrate.

"You there?" came Willer's distant voice.

Tom found his voice. "Detective Willer, I want to thank you for your trouble, but everything's fine. I just heard from Sally. She's fine."

"She is?"

"Her mom's sick, she had to go to Albuquerque."

"Jeep's still in the garage."

"She took a cab, that car doesn't work."

"What about the F350?"

"That's only for hauling horses."

"I see. About this round —"

Tom managed an easy laugh. "Right. It's . . . that's an old one."

"Looks fresh to me."

"Couple of days ago. My gun went off accidentally."

"Is that so?" The voice was cold.

"Right."

"Mind telling me what make and caliber?"

"Thirty-eight Smith & Wesson revolver." There was a long silence. "As I said, Detective, I'm sorry to have bothered you, I really am. False alarm."

"Got a spot of blood here on the rug, too. That also 'old'?"

Tom didn't quite find an answer to that. He felt a wave a nausea. If those bastards had hurt her . . . "A lot of blood?"

"Just a spot. It's still wet."

"I don't know what to tell you about that, Detective. Maybe someone . . . cut himself." He swallowed.

"Who? Your wife?"

"I don't know what to tell you."

He listened to the hissing silence in the phone. He had to make that flight and he had to deal with the man himself. He never should have left Sally alone.

"Mr. Broadbent? Are you familiar with the term 'probable cause'?"

"Yes."

"That's what we've got here. We entered the house with your permission, we found probable cause that a crime had been committed — and now we're going to search it.

We don't need a warrant under those circumstances."

Tom swallowed. If the kidnapper was watching the house and saw it full of cops . . .

"Just make it quick."

"You say your plane lands at seven-thirty?" Willer asked.

"Yes."

"I'd like to see you and your wife — sick mother or not — tonight. At the station. Nine o'clock sharp. You also might want to bring that lawyer you mentioned. I have a feeling you're going to need him."

"I can't. Not at nine. It's impossible. And my wife is in Albuquerque —"

"This is not an optional appointment, Broadbent. You be there at nine or I'll get a warrant for your arrest. Is that clear?"

Tom swallowed. "My wife has nothing to do with this."

"You don't produce her and your problem will get worse. And let me tell you, pal, it's bad already."

The phone went dead.

PART THREE

PERDIZ CREEK

She stood twenty feet at the shoulder and was fifty feet long. She weighed about six tons. *Her legs were more than ten feet long and packed with the most powerful muscles that had ever evolved on a vertebrate. When she walked, she carried her tail high and her stride was twelve to fifteen feet. At a run she could attain a speed of thirty miles per hour, but raw speed was less important than agility, flexibility, and lightning reflexes. Her feet were about three and a half feet long, armed with four scimitarlike claws, three in the front and a dewclawlike spur in back. She walked on her toes. A single well-aimed kick could disembowel a hundred-foot-long duckbill dinosaur.*

Her jaws were three feet long and held sixty teeth. She used the four incisorlike teeth in the front for stripping and peeling meat off bone. Her killing teeth were located in a lethal row on the sides, some as long as twelve inches, root included, and as big around as a child's fist. They were serrated on the backside, so that after biting she could hold her prey while sawing and cutting backward. Her bite could remove more than ten cubic feet of meat at a time, weighing several hundred pounds. A warren of windows, holes, and channels in her skull gave it enormous strength and lightness, as well as flexibility. She had two different biting techniques: an overbite that cut through meat like scissors; and a "nutcracker" bite for crushing armor and bone. Her palate was supported by thin struts that allowed the skull to flatten out sideways with the force of a bite, and then stretch to allow massive chunks of meat to be swallowed whole.

With her overlapping jaw muscles, she could deliver a biting force estimated in excess of one hundred thousand pounds per square inch, enough to cut through steel.

Her two arms were small, no larger than a human's, but many times stronger. They were equipped with two recurved claws set at a ninety-degree angle to maximize their gripping and slashing capability. The back vertebrae, where the ribs attach, were as large as coffee cans, to support her belly, which could be carrying more than a quarter ton of freshly consumed meat.

She stank. Her mouth contained bits

and pieces of rotting meat and rancid grease, trapped in special crevices in her teeth, which gave her bite an added lethality. Even if her victim escaped the initial attack, it would likely die in short order of massive infection or blood poisoning. The bones she expelled in her feces were sometimes almost completely dissolved by the potent hydrochloric acids with which she digested her food.

The occipital condyle bone in her neck was the size of a grapefruit, and it allowed her to turn her head almost 180 degrees so that she could snap and bite in all directions. Like a human being, her eyes looked ahead, giving her stereoscopic vision, and she had an excellent sense of smell and of hearing. Her favored prey were the herds of duckbill dinosaurs that moved noisily through the great forests, calling and trumpeting to keep the herd together and the young with their mothers. But she was an opportunist, and would take anything that was meat.

She hunted mostly by ambush: a long, stealthy, upwind approach, followed by a short rush. She was well camouflaged, wearing the colors of the forest, a rich pattern of greens and browns.

As a juvenile she hunted in packs, but when she matured she worked alone. She did not attack her prey and fight it to the *death. Instead, she fell upon her victim and delivered a single, savage bite, her teeth cutting through armor and plate to reach vital organs and pulsing arteries; and at the moment when she had fixed her prey like a worm on a pin, she cocked a leg and gave it a ripping kick. Then she released it and retreated to a safe distance while it futilely roared, slashed, convulsed, and bled to death.*

Like many predators, she also scavenged; she would eat anything as long as it was meat. Sinking her teeth into a suppurating, maggot-packed carcass satisfied her as much as swallowing whole a still beating heart.

1

Wyman Ford paused, looking down the great cleft in the earth named Tyrannosaur Canyon. Ten miles back he had passed the black basaltic dike that gave the canyon its name, and now he was deep within it, farther than he had ever been before. It was a godforsaken place. The canyon walls rose higher the deeper he went, until they pressed in on him claustrophobically from both sides. Boulders the size of houses had spalled off the cliffs and lay tumbled about on the canyon floor amid patches of poisonous alkali flats, the dust lifted by the wind into white veils. Nothing, it seemed to Ford, lived in the canyon beyond a few saltbushes — and, naturally, a plethora of rattlers.

He halted as he saw a slow movement ahead of him and watched a diamondback with a body as thick as his forearm slither across the sand in front of him, flicking its tongue and making a slow scraping noise. This was the time of evening for snakes, Ford thought, as they came out of their holes as the heat abated to get a head start on their nocturnal hunt.

Ford hiked on, getting back into the rhythm of it, his long legs eating up the ground. It was like a maze, with many side canyons peeling off into nowhere. The miles passed quickly. Toward sunset, as the canyon made yet another turn, he could see the great crowd of rocks up ahead, the ones he had seen from Navajo Rim, which he had whimsically named The Bald Ones. The lower part of the canyon was already in shadow, bathed in a warm orange glow of reflected light from high up on the eastern rim.

Ford felt grateful that the day was over. He had been rationing water since the morning and the cooling of the air brought a welcome lessening of his thirst.

When night arrived in the desert, it came fast. He would not have much time to pick out a good campsite. With a jaunty step he continued down the canyon, looking left and right, and soon located what he was looking for: a sheltered spot between a pair of fallen boulders with a soft, level bed of sand. He unshouldered his rucksack and took a swig of water, rolling it about in his mouth to enjoy it as much as possible before swallowing. He still had fifteen, maybe twenty minutes of light left. Why waste it on cooking and unrolling his bedroll? Leaving his gear, he hiked up the canyon to the beginning of the Bald Ones. From the closer vantage point they looked more like gigantic squashed toadstools than skulls; each was about thirty feet in width and maybe twenty feet high, carved from a layer of deep orange sandstone shot through with thinner lenses of wine-colored shale and conglomerate. Some of the large rocks had been undercut and had fallen like Humpty Dumpty, lying in broken pieces.

He walked into the forest of sandstone pillars holding up the round domes of rock. The pillars were formed from a pale pink sandstone and were all about ten feet in height. Ford scrambled between them, intent on seeing how far the formation extended. From his viewpoint none of the rocks looked like the one he was after, but the family resemblance was strong. Once again he had a shiver of excitement, sure that he was getting closer to the dinosaur. He squeezed his way among the rocks, sometimes forced to crawl, uncomfortably aware of the press of stone rising above him. As he reached the far side, he discovered to his surprise that the Bald Ones hid the entrance to another canyon — or what was actually a hidden continuation of Tyrannosaur Canyon. He started up it, hiking briskly along the bottom. The canyon was narrow and showed evidence of violent flash floods, the sides strewn with bashed tree trunks and branches that had been swept down from the mountains beyond. The canyon's lower walls had been polished and hollowed by the action of water.

The canyon made turn after turn, each elbow disclosing alcoves and undercuts. Some of the higher alcoves contained small Anasazi cliff dwellings. A quarter mile on, Ford came to a "pour-over," a high shelf of sandstone across the canyon, which must have formed a waterfall in wetter times, with a cracked bed of silt below attesting to a former pool. He climbed up, using the projecting stone layers as hand- and footholds, and hiked on.

The canyon took a twist and suddenly opened into a stupendous valley where three tributary canyons came together like a train wreck of rock, creating a spectacle of erosional ferocity. Ford halted, awestruck by the frozen violence of it. With a smile, he decided to name it the Devil's Graveyard. As he stood, the last of the sun winked out on the canyon rim and the evening crept across the strange valley, cloaking it in purple shadow. It was truly a land lost in time.

Ford turned back. It was too late to explore farther; he had to get back to camp before dark. The stones had waited millions of years, the monk thought. They could wait one more day.

2

Tom drove northward on Highway 84, making a great effort to keep his mind focused. The plane had been late, it was eight-thirty, and he was still an hour from the stretch of highway the kidnapper had indicated. On the passenger seat sat a Ziploc bag full of yellow trash with the notebook tucked inside. His cell phone was sitting on the seat, charged up and waiting for the call.

He felt furiously helpless, at the mercy of events — an intolerable sensation. He had to find a way to take charge, to act and not just react. But he couldn't just *act:* he needed to work out a plan, and for that he had to push his emotions aside and think as coldly and clearly as possible.

The dark expanse of desert rushed by on either side of the road, the stars clear and stationary in the night sky above. The plane ride from Tucson to Santa Fe had been the most difficult hour Tom had ever passed. It had taken a superhuman effort to control his speculations and focus on the problem at hand. That problem was simple: to get Sally back. Nothing else mattered. Once he had Sally back, he would deal with the kidnapper.

Once again he wondered if he shouldn't have gone to the police, or bypass Willer entirely and go straight to the FBI. But in his heart he knew the kidnapper was right: if he did that, he would lose control. They would take over. No matter what, Willer would get involved. He believed the kidnapper when he said he would kill Sally if the police became involved. It was too big a risk; he had to do this on his own.

He knew the stretch of Highway 84 the kidnapper wanted him to drive back and forth on. It was one of the loneliest stretches of two-lane highway in the state, with a single gas station and convenience store.

Tom tried to think what he would have done if he were the kidnapper, how he would have set things up, how he would pick up the notebook and avoid being followed. That was what Tom had to figure out — the man's plan.

3

Willer glanced up at the clock from a stack of paperwork. Nine-fifteen. He looked over at Hernandez, who looked almost green in the sickly fluorescent glare of the office.

"He blew us off," said Hernandez. "Just like that."

"Just like that . . ." Willer rapped his pen on the stack of papers. It didn't make sense, a guy with so much to lose. Guys like that had a million legal ways of avoiding an interview with the police.

"You think he's jumped the rez?"

"His vehicle — that classic Chevy he drives — was parked at the airport. His plane landed at eight and now it's gone."

Hernandez shrugged. "Engine trouble?"

"He's playing some kind of game with us."

"What's he up to?"

"Hell if I know."

The room became heavy with silence. Willer finally coughed, lit up, felt he needed to do something to reestablish his authority; it surprised and galled him that Broadbent would simply blow him off.

"Here's what we know for a fact: there's fresh blood on his living-room rug and a fresh round in his wall. He missed an interview with the police. Maybe he's in trouble or dead. Maybe he's running scared. Maybe he argued with his wife, things got out of hand . . . and now she's buried in the back forty. Maybe he's just an arrogant bastard who thinks we don't rate. It doesn't matter: we got to track his ass down."

"Right."

"I want an all points for northern New Mexico, checkpoints on 84 at Chama, 96 at Coyote, 285 south of Española, I-40 at Wagon Mound and the Arizona border, I-25 at Belen, and one at Cuba State Police Headquarters on Highway 44." He paused, shuffling through some papers on his desk, pulled one out. "Here it is: he's driving a '57 Chevrolet 3100 pickup, turquoise and white, NM license plate 346 EWE. We got one thing going for us: driving a truck like that, he'll stick out like a sore thumb."

4

Maddox parked the Range Rover in front of the Sunrise Liquor Mart and checked his watch. Nine twenty-one. A half-dozen beer advertisements in the plate-glass window threw a confusion of neon light onto the dusty hood of his car. Save for the guy behind the counter it was empty. The moon had not yet risen. He knew, from earlier research, he would see the head-lights of a southbound car two minutes and forty seconds before it passed.

He got out, shoved his hands in his pockets, leaned on the car, drew in a deep breath of cool desert air, closed his eyes, murmured his mantra, and managed to get his heart rate down to something a little more normal. He opened his eyes. The highway was still dark. Nine twenty-two. He had passed Broadbent in his '57 Chevy eleven minutes ago, and if the man fol-lowed directions, turned around quickly, and maintained his speed, his headlights should appear in the north in just over six minutes.

He walked into the convenience store,

bought a slice of ten-hour-old pizza and a giant cup of burnt coffee, paid with exact change. He went back out to his car, hooked a boot on the fender, glanced up the dark highway. Two more minutes. Another glance into the store told him the kid was absorbed in a comic. He poured the coffee out on the tarmac and slung the piece of pizza into a cholla cactus already festooned with trash. He checked his watch, checked his cell — good signal.

He got in his car, started the engine, and waited.

Nine twenty-six.

Nine twenty-seven.

Nine twenty-eight.

Bingo: a pair of headlights emerged from the sea of blackness in the north. The headlights slowly grew in size and brightness as the car approached on the undivided, single-lane highway — and then the truck passed in a flash of turquoise, the red taillights receding into the blackness to the south. Nine-thirty and forty seconds.

He waited, his eyes on the watch, counting out one minute exactly, then he pressed the speed-dial button on his cell.

"Yes?" The voice answered immediately.

"Listen carefully. Maintain your speed. Do not slow down or speed up. Roll down the right-hand window."

"What about my wife?"

"You'll get her in a moment. Do as I say."

"I've got the window down."

Maddox watched the second hand on his watch. "When I tell you, take your cell phone, hang up but *leave it on.* Put it in the Ziploc bag with the notebook and throw them all out the window. Wait until I give you the signal. After you toss it, don't stop, keep driving."

"Listen, you son of a bitch, I'm not doing anything until you tell me where my wife is."

"Do what I say or she's dead."

"Then you'll never see this notebook."

Maddox checked his watch. Already three and a half minutes had passed. With one hand on the wheel, he pressed the accelerator and turned out on the highway, leaving a line of smoking rubber in the parking lot. "She's in the old campground at Madera Creek, you know the place? Forty miles south of here on the Rio Grande. The bitch resisted me, she got herself hurt, she's bleeding, she's with my partner, if you don't do what I say I'm going to call him and he'll kill her and split. Now put the cell in the bag and toss it, *now.*"

"Know this: if she dies you're a dead man. I'll follow you to the ends of the earth and kill you."

"Stop the grandstanding and *do what I say!*"

"I'm doing it."

Maddox heard a rustling sound and the line went dead. He released his breath in a big rush. He checked his watch, noted the time to the second, looked at his speedometer. The notebook would be at a point about 4.1 miles south of the mart. He shut his cell phone and maintained speed. He had already scouted the highway, timed the distances, and noted the milestones. He knew within a quarter-mile stretch where the notebook must be.

Maddox passed the mile marker and slowed way down, unrolled his windows, and called Broadbent's number. A second later he could hear the faint answering ring: and there it was, lying by the side of the road, a plastic Ziploc bag. He cruised past, at the same time switching on a mounted lamp on his Range Rover and shining it around, to make sure Broadbent wasn't waiting in ambush. But the prairie stretched out empty on all sides. He had little doubt that Broadbent was heading south at high speed toward the Madera Campground. He would probably stop in Abiquiú to call the cops and an ambulance. Maddox didn't have much time to get the notebook and get the hell out.

He pulled a U-turn, drove back to the

bag, hopped out, and scooped it up. As he accelerated back onto the highway he ripped the bag open with his right hand and groped through trash for the notebook.

There it was. He pulled it out, looked at it. It was bound in old leather and there was even a smudge of blood on the back cover. He opened it. Rows of eight-digit numbers, just as Corvus said. This was it. He'd done it.

He wondered how Broadbent would react when he found the Madera Campground empty. *Ends of the earth.*

He had the notebook. Now it was time to get rid of the woman.

5

About a half mile south of where he had tossed the journal, Tom shut his lights off and veered off the highway, bounced over a ditch, and busted through a barbed-wire fence. He drove into the dark prairie until he felt he was far enough away from the road. He shut off the engine and waited, his heart pounding.

When the man had said Sally was in the Madera Campground, Tom knew he was lying. The campground was overrun with small children at that time of year, and the screened-in cabins were too public, too exposed. The Madera Campground story was designed to draw him south.

A few minutes later he saw the headlights of a car far behind him. He had passed a Range Rover earlier and had seen the same car in the liquor mart, and he had no doubt this was the kidnapper's car now, as he saw it slowing down along the stretch of highway where he had thrown the notebook. A side lamp went on, scouring the prairie. Tom had a sudden fear of being seen, but the lamp searched only the immediate area. The car pulled a U-turn, came back; a man jumped out and picked up the notebook — he was tall and lanky but too far away to be identifiable. A moment later the man had hopped back in and the car headed north in a screech of rubber.

Tom waited until the car was well ahead on the highway, then, keeping his headlights off, he started his car and drove back to the road. He had to drive blind: if he turned his headlights on the man would know he was being followed — the Chevy with its round, old-fashioned headlights was too identifiable.

Once on the highway he sped up as much as he dared without lights, his eyes on the receding glow of the taillights, but the car ahead was moving fast, and he realized he had no hope of keeping up without turning on his lights. He had to chance it.

At that moment, he was approaching the liquor mart, and he saw that a pickup truck had pulled in for gas. He braked hard, swerved into the station, pulled up on the opposite side of the pumps. The truck, a shabby Dodge Dakota, was sitting next to the pumps with the keys dangling from the ignition while the driver paid inside. He could just see, in the door pocket, the handle of a gun.

Tom jumped out of his truck, climbed into the Dodge, started the engine, and peeled out with a squeal of rubber. He floored it, heading northward into the darkness where the pair of taillights had vanished.

6

The call came in at 11:00 p.m. Even though Melodie had been waiting for it, she jumped when the phone trilled in the silent, empty lab.

"Melodie? How's the research going?"

"Great, Dr. Corvus, just great." She swallowed, realizing she was breathing hard into the mouthpiece.

"Still working?"

"Yes, yes, I am."

"Those results come in?"

"Yes. They're — incredible."

"Tell me everything."

"The specimen is riddled with iridium — exactly the type of iridium enrichment you find at the K-T boundary, only more so. I mean, this specimen is *saturated* with iridium."

"What type of iridium and how many parts per billion?"

"It's bound up in various isometric hexoctahedral forms in a concentration of over 430 ppb. That, as you know, is the exact type identified with the Chicxulub asteroid strike."

Melodie waited for a response but it didn't come.

"This fossil," she ventured, "it wouldn't happen to be located *at* the Cretaceous-Tertiary boundary . . . would it?"

"It could be."

Another long silence, and Melodie continued.

"In the outer matrix surrounding the specimen, I found a tremendous abundance of microparticles of soot, of the kind you get from forest fires. According to a recent article in the *Journal of Geophysical Research*, more than a third of the earth's forests burned up following the Chicxulub asteroid strike."

"I'm aware of the article," came the quiet voice of Corvus.

"Then you know that the K-T boundary consists of two layers, first the iridium-enriched debris from the strike itself, and then a layer of soot laid down by worldwide forest fires." She stopped, waiting yet again for a reaction, but there was another long silence on the other end of the phone. Corvus didn't seem to get it — or did he?

"It seems to me . . ." She paused, almost afraid to say it. "Or rather, my conclusion is that this dinosaur was actually *killed* by the asteroid strike — or it died in the ecological collapse that followed."

This dynamite conclusion fell into the void. Corvus remained silent.

"I would guess that this would also account for the fossil's extraordinary state of preservation."

"How so?" came the guarded response.

"While reading that article, it struck me that the asteroid impact, the fires, and the heating of the atmosphere created unique conditions for fossilization. For one thing, there'd be no scavengers to tear apart the body and scatter the bones. The strike actually heated up the whole earth, making the atmosphere as hot as the Sahara Desert, and in many areas the air temperature reached two, even three hundred degrees — perfect for flash-drying a carcass. On top of that, all the dust would trigger gigantic weather systems. Immense flash floods would have quickly buried the remains."

Melodie took a deep breath, waited for a reaction — excitement, astonishment, skepticism. Still nothing.

"Anything more?" asked Corvus.

"Well, then they're the Venus particles."

"Venus particles?"

"That's what I call those black particles you noticed, because under a microscope they look sort of like the symbol for Venus — a circle with a cross coming out of it. You know, the feminist symbol."

"The feminist symbol," Corvus repeated.

"I did some tests on them. They're not a microcrystalline formation or an artifact of fossilization. The particle is a sphere of inorganic carbon with a projecting arm; inside are a bunch of trace elements I haven't yet analyzed."

"I see."

"They're all the same size and shape, which would imply a biological origin. They seem to have been present in the dinosaur when it died and just remained in place, unchanged, for sixty-five million years. They're . . . *very* strange. I need to do a lot more work to figure out what they are, but I wonder if they aren't some kind of infectious particle."

There was that strange silence on the other end of the telephone. When Corvus finally spoke, his voice was low. He sounded disturbed. "Anything else, Melodie?"

"That's all." As if that wasn't enough. What was wrong with Corvus? Didn't he believe her?

The Curator's voice was so calm it was almost spooky. "Melodie, this is fine work you've done. I commend you. Now listen carefully: here is what I want you to do. I want you to gather up all your CDs, the pieces of specimen, *everything* in the lab connected with this work, and I want you to lock it all up securely in your specimen cabinet. If there is by chance anything left in the computer, delete it using the utility program that completely wipes files off the hard disk. Then I want you to go home and get some sleep."

She felt incredulous. Was that all he could say, that she needed sleep?

"Can you do that, Melodie?" came the soft voice. "Lock it all up, clean the computer, go home, get some sleep, eat a nourishing meal. We'll talk again in the morning."

"All right."

"Good." A pause. "See you tomorrow."

After hanging up the telephone, Melodie sat in the laboratory, feeling stunned. After all her work, her extraordinary discoveries, Corvus acted as if he hardly cared — or didn't even believe her. *I commend you.* Here she'd made one of the most important paleontological discoveries in history, and all he could do was *commend* her? And tell her to get some sleep?

She looked up at the clock. *Clunk* went the minute hand. Eleven-fifteen. She looked down at her arm, at the bracelet winking on her wrist, her miserably small breasts, her thin hands, her bitten nails, her ugly freckled arms. Here she was, Melodie Crookshank, thirty-three years old, still an assistant without a tenure-track job, a scientific nobody. She felt a growing burn of resentment. Her thoughts flashed back to her stern university-professor father whose oft-stated goal was that she not grow up to be "just another dumb broad." She thought of how much she had tried to please him. And she thought of her mother, who resented having a career as a homemaker and wanted to live vicariously through her daughter's success. Melodie had tried to please her too. She thought about all the teachers she'd tried to please, the professors, her dissertation adviser.

And now Corvus.

And where had all this agreeableness and pleasing gotten her? Her eye roved about the oppressive basement lab.

She wondered, for the first time, just how Corvus planned to handle their discovery. And it was *their* discovery — he couldn't have done it on his own. He didn't know how to work the equipment well, he was practically a computer illiterate, and he was a lousy mineralogist. She had done the analysis, asked the right questions of the specimen, teased out the answers. She had made the connections, extrapolated from the data, developed the theories.

It began to dawn on her why Corvus wanted to keep it all so very secret. A spectacular discovery like this would set off a furor of competition, intrigue, and a rush to get the rest of the fossil. Corvus might easily lose control of the discovery — and with it lose credit. He understood the value of that concept, *credit*. It was the cold cash of the scientific world.

Credit. A slippery concept, when you really thought about it.

Her mind felt clearer than it had in months — maybe years. Maybe it was because she was so tired — tired of pleasing, tired of working for others, tired of this tomblike lab. Her eye fell on the sapphire bracelet. She took it off and let it dangle in front of her eyes, the gems winking seductively. Corvus had driven one of the best bargains of his career, giving her that piece of jewelry, thinking it would buy her silence and a mousy, feminine agreeableness. She shoved it in her pocket in disgust.

Melodie now began to understand why Corvus had reacted the way he had, why he had been so unforthcoming — even disturbed — on the telephone. She had done too well with her assignment. He was worried that she had found out too much, that she might claim the discoveries as her own.

Like a revelation, Melodie Crookshank knew what she had to do.

7

The M-Logos 455 Massively Parallel Processing Object Unit System was the most powerful computer yet constructed by the human race. It sat in a perpetually air-conditioned, dust-free, static-free basement deep beneath the National Security Agency headquarters at Fort Mead, Maryland. It had not been built to predict the weather, simulate a fifteen-megaton thermonuclear explosion, or find the quadrillionth digit of pi. It has been created for a far more mundane purpose: to listen.

Countless nodes distributed across the globe collected a gargantuan stream of digital information. It intercepted more than forty percent of all traffic on the World Wide Web, more than ninety percent of all cellular telephone conversations, virtually all radio and television broadcasts, many landline telephone conversations, and a large portion of the data flows from governmental and corporate LANs and private networks.

This digital torrent was fed in real time into the M455MPP at the rate of sixteen terabits per second.

The computer merely listened.

It listened with almost every known language on earth, every dialect, every protocol, almost every computer algorithm ever written to analyze language. But that was not all: the M455MPP was the first computer to employ a new, highly classified form of data analysis known as Stutterlogic. Stutterlogic had been developed by advanced cybernetic theorists and programmers at the Defense Intelligence Agency as a way of sailing around the great reef of Artificial Intelligence, which had ship-wrecked the hopes of so many computer programmers over the last decades. Stutterlogic was a whole new way of looking at information. Instead of trying to simulate human intelligence, as AI had sought unsuccessfully to do, Stutterlogic operated under a wholly new kind of logic, which was neither machine intelligence nor AI-based.

Even with Stutterlogic, it could not be said that the computer "understood" what it heard. Its role was merely to identify a "communication of interest," or a CI in the jargon of its operators, and forward it to a human for review.

Most of the CIs that emerged from the M455MPP were e-mails and cellular telephone conversations. The latter were parceled out among one hundred and twenty-five human listeners. Their job required an enormous knowledge base, fluency in the language or dialect in question, and an almost magical sense of intuition. Being a good "listener" was an art, not a science.

At 11:04.34.98 EDT, four minutes into an eleven-minute cellular telephone call, module 3656070 of the M455MPP identified the conversation under way as a potential CI. The computer, having captured the conversation from the beginning, rewound it and began analyzing it, even while it was still in progress. When the CI concluded at 11:16.04.58 it had already passed through a series of algorithmic filters that had parsed it linguistically and conceptually, scrutinizing the voice inflections for dozens of psychological markers, including stress, excitement, anger, confidence, and fear. Object programs identified the caller and the receiver and then went out to examine thousands of databases to retrieve every particle of personal information about the two interlocutors that existed in networked electronic form anywhere in the world.

This particular CI "greened" (that is, passed) this first round of tests, and it was assigned a rating of 0.003. It was then passed through a firewall to a subsystem of the M455 where it was subjected to a powerful Stutterlogic analysis. This analysis upgraded its rating to 0.56 and passed it back to the main database module with "questions." The database loops returned the CI to the Stutterlogic module with the "questions" having been "answered." On the basis of those answers, the Stutterlogic module raised the rating of the CI to 1.20.

Any CI rating over 1.0 was forwarded to a human listener.

The time was 11:22.06.31.

Rick Muzinsky had begun his vicariously lived existence as a boy listening for hours at his parents' bedroom door, hearing with sick fascination everything they did. Muzinsky's father had been a career diplomat and Rick had lived all over the world, picking up a fluency in three languages besides English. He had grown up on the outside looking in, a boy with no friends and no place to call home. He was a vicarious human being, and with his job in Homeland Security he had found a way to make a good living at it. The job paid extremely well. He worked a total of four hours a day in an environment that was free from dim-witted bosses, moronic co-workers, incompetent assistants, and deficient secretaries. He did not have to deal with people at the coffee machine or the Xerox machine. He could clock in his four hours in any way he wished during each twenty-four-hour period. Best of all, he worked alone — that was mandatory. He was not allowed to discuss his work with anyone. Anyone. So when someone asked him that inevitable, obnoxious question, *What do you do for a living?* he could tell them anything he liked but the truth.

Some people might consider it crushingly dull, listening to one CI after another, almost all of them asinine exchanges between idiots, full of empty threats, psychotic rants, political outbursts, brainless pronouncements, and wishful thinking — the self-deluded ramblings of some of the saddest, dumbest people Muzinsky had ever heard. But he loved every word of it.

Once in a while a conversation came along that was different. Often it was hard to say why. It could be a certain seriousness, a *gravitas,* to the utterances. It could be a sense that something else was being said behind the words being spoken. After a few listenings, if the feeling didn't go away, he would then call up the information associated with the conversation and see who the interlocutors were. That was usually most revealing.

Muzinsky had no role in following up on the CIs that he identified as threatening. His only role was to forward those CIs to an appropriate agency for further analysis. Sometimes the computer even identified the agency the CI should go to — should

Muzinsky pass it — as certain agencies seemed to be listening for certain cryptic things. But he passed only about one CI in every two or three thousand conversations he listened to. Most got forwarded to various subagencies of the NSA or Homeland Security. Others went to the Pentagon, State Department, FBI, CIA, ATF, INS, and a host of other acronyms, some of whose very existence was classified. Muzinsky had to match each CI with the right agency and do it fast. A CI could not be allowed to bounce around, looking for a home. That was what led to 9/11. The receiving agencies were now primed to handle incoming intelligence immediately, if necessary within minutes of its receipt. That was another lesson from 9/11.

But Muzinsky had nothing to do with that side of things. Once the CI left his cubicle, it was gone forever.

Muzinsky sat at the terminal in his locked cubicle, headphones on, and punched the READY button indicating he was free to receive the next CI. The computer sent him no preliminary data or background information about the call, nothing that might influence his mind about what he was about to hear. It always started with the naked CI.

A hiss and it began. There was the sound of a phone ringing, an answer, a thump, the sound of breathlessness on the other end, and then the conversation began:

"Melodie? How's the research going?"

"Great, Dr. Corvus, just great."

8

Just before the turn on the Forest Service road leading to Perdiz Creek, Maddox slowed and pulled off the highway. A pair of headlights had appeared behind him, and before he actually made the turn he wanted to make sure they didn't belong to Broadbent. He shut off his engine and lights and waited for the vehicle to pass.

A truck rapidly approached going a tremendous clip, slowed only slightly, then sped past. Maddox breathed a sigh of relief — it was just some old, beat-up Dodge. He started the car and made the turn, bumped over the cattle guard, and continued down the rutted dirt road, feeling a huge lifting of his spirits. He rolled down the windows to let in air. It was a cool and fragrant night, the stars shining above the dark rims of the mesas. His plan had worked: he had the notebook. Nothing could stop him now. There would be a certain amount of law enforcement excitement around the area in the coming days after Broadbent reported his wife's abduction, but he'd be safe up at Perdiz Creek working on his novel . . . And when they came by to question him, they'd find nothing — no body, nada. And they never would find her body. He'd already found a perfect place to lose it, a deep water-filled shaft in one of the upper mines. The roof above the shaft was shored with rotting timbers, and after he deep-sixed the corpse down the shaft he'd set off a small charge to bring down the roof — and that would be it. She'd be as gone as Jimmy Hoffa.

He checked his watch: nine-forty. He'd be back at Perdiz Creek in half an hour, and he had something to look forward to.

Tomorrow, he'd call Corvus from a pay phone to tell him the good news. He glanced at his cell phone, tempted to call him right away — but no, there could be no mistakes now, no risks taken.

He accelerated, the car lurching along the potholed dirt road as it climbed through a series of foothills. In ten minutes he had reached the area where the piñon-juniper forest gave way to tall ponderosa pines, dark and restless in a night wind.

He finally reached the gate in the ugly chain-link fence that surrounded the property. He got out, unlocked it, drove through, and locked it behind him. A couple hundred more yards brought him to the cabin. The moon hadn't risen and the old cabin loomed up pitch-black, a stark outline blotting out the stars. Maddox shivered and vowed to leave the porch light on next time.

Then he thought of the woman, waiting for him in the darkness of the mine, and that thought sent a nice, warm feeling through his gut.

9

Sally's legs ached from standing in the same position unable to move, her ankles and wrists chafing under the cold steel. A chill flow of air from the back of the mine penetrated her to the bone. The dim glow from the kerosene lantern wavered and spluttered, filling her with an irrational fear that it would go out. But what got to her most was the silence, broken only by the monotonous drip of water. She found it impossible to tell how much time had passed, whether it was night or day.

Suddenly she stiffened, hearing the rattle of someone unlocking the metal grate at the mouth of the mine. He was coming in. She heard the grate clang shut behind him and the chain rattle as he relocked it. And now she could hear his footsteps approaching, becoming louder by degrees. The beam of a flashlight flickered through the bars and a moment later he arrived. He unbolted the bars over the door frame with a socket wrench and tossed them aside. Then he shoved the flashlight in his back pocket and stepped inside the small stone prison.

Sally sagged in the chains, her eyes half-closed. She moaned softly.

"Hi there, Sally."

She moaned again. Through half-lidded eyes she saw he was unbuttoning his shirt, a grin splitting his face.

"Hang in there," he said. "We're going to have ourselves a good time."

She heard the shirt land on the floor, heard the jingle as he undid his belt buckle.

"No," she moaned weakly.

"Yes. Oh, *yes*. No more waiting, baby. It's now or never."

She heard the pants slide off, drop to the floor. Another rustle and soft plop as he tossed his underwear.

She looked up weakly, her eyes slits. There he was, standing before her, naked, priapic, small key in one hand, gun in the other. She moaned, drooped her head again. "Please, don't." Her body sagged — lifeless, weak, utterly helpless.

"Please *do,* you mean." He advanced toward her, grasped her left wrist, and inserted the key into the manacle. As he did so he leaned close over her bowed head, put his nose in her hair. She could hear him breathe in. He nuzzled down her neck with his lips, scraping her cheek with his unshaved chin. She knew he was about to unlock her left hand. Then he would step back and make her unlock the others. That was his system.

She waited, maintaining her slackness. She heard the little *click* as the key turned the tumbler and she felt the steel bracelet fall away. In that moment, with all the force she could muster, she lashed out with her left hand, striking at his gun. It was a motion she had rehearsed in her mind a hundred times, and it caught him off guard. The gun went flying. Without a pause she whipped her hand around and clawed her fingernails into his face — fingernails she had spent an hour sharpening into points against the rock — just missing his eyes but managing to score deeply into his flesh.

He stumbled back with an inarticulate cry, throwing his hands up to protect his face, his flashlight landing on the mine floor.

Immediately her hand was on the unlocked manacle. *Yes!* The key was still in there, half turned. She pulled it out, unlocked her foot in time to kick him hard in the stomach as he was rising. She unlocked the other foot, unlocked her right hand.

Free!

He was on his knees, coughing, his hand reaching out, already grasping the gun he'd dropped.

In yet another motion she had rehearsed

in her mind countless times over the past hours, she leapt for the table, one hand closing on a book of matches, the other sweeping the kerosene lantern to the floor. It shattered, plunging the cavern into darkness. She dropped to the ground just as he fired in her direction, the shot deafening in the enclosed space.

The shot was following by a raging scream, *"Bitch!"*

Sally crouched, creeping swiftly through the darkness toward where she remembered the door to be. She already knew she couldn't escape the mine through the outer tunnel — she had heard him lock the grate. Her only hope was to go deeper in the mine and find a second exit — or a place to hide.

"I'll kill you!" came the gargled scream, followed by a wild shot in the dark. The muzzle flash burned an image on her retina of a raging, naked man clutching a gun, twisting around wildly, his body distorted — wrapped in the grotesque tattoo of the dinosaur.

The muzzle flash had shown her the way to the door. She scuttled blindly through it and crawled down the tunnel, moving as fast as she dared, feeling ahead. After a moment she chanced lighting a match. Ahead of her, the two tunnels came together. She quickly tossed the match and scuttled into the other fork, hoping, praying, it would take her to a place of safety deep in the mine.

10

Iain Corvus, waiting in an idling cab across from the museum, finally saw Melodie's slim, girlish figure moving up the service drive from the museum's security exit. He glanced at his watch: midnight. She had taken her bloody time about it. He watched her diminutive figure turn left on Central Park West, heading uptown — no doubt she was heading back to some dismal Upper West Side railroad studio.

Corvus cursed yet again his stupidity. Almost from the beginning of their conversation that evening, he'd realized the colossal mistake he'd made. He'd tossed into Melodie's lap one of the most important scientific discoveries of all time, and she had caught it and run with it to a touchdown. Sure, as senior scientist his name would be first on the paper, but the lion's share of the credit would go to her and nobody would be fooled. She would cloud, if not eclipse, his glory.

Fortunately, there was a simple solution to his problem and Corvus congratulated himself on thinking of it before it was too late.

He waited until Melodie had disappeared into the gloom up Central Park West, then he tossed a fifty to the cabbie and stepped out. He strode across the street and down to the security entrance, went through security with a swipe of his card and a terse nod, and in ten minutes he was in the Mineralogy lab, in front of her locked specimen cabinet. He inserted his master key and opened it, relieved to see a stack of CD-ROMs, floppies, and the prepared sections of the specimen arranged neatly in their places. It amazed him how much she had managed to do in just five days, how much information she had extracted from the specimen, information that would have taken a lesser scientist a year to tease out — if at all.

He picked up the CDs, each labeled and categorized. In this case, possession of the CDs and specimens was more than nine-tenths of the law — it was the whole law. Without that she couldn't even begin to claim credit. It was only right he should have the credit. After all, he was the one who was risking everything — even his own freedom — to claim the tyrannosaur fossil for the museum. He was the one who had snatched it from the jaws of a black marketeer. He was the one who handed her the opportunity on a silver platter. Without him taking those risks Melodie would have nothing.

She'd have to go along with his seizure of her research — what was the alternative? To pick a fight with him? If she pulled something like that, no university would ever hire her. It wasn't a question of stealing. It was a question of correcting the parameters of credit, of collecting his due.

Corvus carefully packed all the material in his briefcase. Then he went to the computer, logged on as system administrator, and checked all her files. Nothing. She'd done what he said and wiped them clean. He turned and was about to leave when he suddenly had a thought. He needed to check the equipment logs. Anyone who used the lab's expensive equipment had to keep a log of time in, time out, and purpose, and he wondered how Melodie had handled that requirement. He went back to the SEM room, flipped open the log, perused it. He was relieved to see that even here Melodie had performed exactly as required, recording her name and times but recording false entries under "purpose," listing miscellaneous work for other curators.

Excellent.

In his bold, slanting hand, he added log entries under his own name. Under "Specimen" he put *High Mesas/Chama River*

Wilderness, N.M. T. Rex. He paused, then added under "Comments," *Third examination of remarkable T. Rex. vertebral fragment. Extraordinary! This will make history.* He signed his name, adding the date and time. He flipped back and finding some blank lines at the bottom of previous pages, he added two similar entries at appropriate dates and times. He did the same to the other high-tech equipment logbooks.

As he was about to leave the SEM room he had the sudden urge to look at the specimen himself. He opened his briefcase, removed the box holding the specimen stages, and took one of the etched wafers out. He turned it slowly, letting the light catch the surface that had been mirrored with twenty-four-karat gold. He switched the machine on, waited for it to warm up, and then slotted one of the specimen stages into the vacuum chamber at the base of the scope. A few minutes later he was gazing at an electron micrograph of the dinosaur's cancellous bone tissue, cells, and nuclei clearly visible. It took his breath away. Once again he had to admire Melodie's skill as a technician. The images were crisp, virtually perfect. Corvus upped the magnification to 2000x and a single cell leapt into view, filling the screen. He could see in it one of those black particles, the ones she'd called the Venus particle. What the devil was it? A rather silly-looking thing when you got down to it, a sphere with an awkward tubular arm sticking out with a crosspiece at the end. What surprised him was how very fresh the particle looked, with none of the pitting, cracking, or damage that you might expect to see. It had weathered well those last sixty-five million years.

Corvus shook his head. He was a vertebrate paleontologist, not a microbiologist. The particle was interesting, but it was only a sidebar to the main attraction: the dinosaur itself. A dinosaur that had actually died from the Chicxulub asteroid strike. The thought of it sent tingles up his spine. Once again he tried to temper his enthusiasm. He had a long way to go before the fossil was safely ensconced in the museum. Above all, he needed that bloody notebook — otherwise he might spend a lifetime wandering about those mesas and canyons. With a chill in his heart he removed the specimen stage and powered down the machine. He carefully locked the CDs and specimens in his briefcase and made one more round of the lab, checking that nothing, not the slightest trace, remained. Satisfied, he slipped his suitcoat on and left the laboratory, turning off the lights and locking the door on his way out.

The dim basement corridor stretched ahead of him, lit with a string of forty-watt bulbs and lined with sweating water pipes. Horrible place to work — he wondered how Melodie could stand it. Even the assistant curators had windows in their fifth-floor offices.

At the first dogleg in the hall, Corvus paused. He felt a tickling sensation on the back of his neck, as if someone were watching him. He turned, but the corridor stretching dimly behind him was empty. Bloody hell, he thought, he was getting as jumpy as Melodie.

He strode down the hallway, past the other laboratories, all locked up tight, turned the corner, then hesitated. He could have sworn he'd heard behind him the soft scrape of a shoe on cement. He waited for another footfall, for someone to round the corner, but nothing happened. He swore to himself; it was probably a guard making the rounds.

Clutching his briefcase, he strode on, approaching the double set of doors leading to the vast dinosaur bone storage room. He paused at the doors, thinking he had heard another sound behind him.

"Is that you, Melodie?" His voice sounded loud and unnatural in the echoing hall.

No answer.

He felt a wave of annoyance. It wouldn't be the first time that one of the graduate

342

students or a visiting curator had been caught sneaking around, trying to get their hands on someone's locality data. It might even be *his* data they were after — someone who had heard about the T. Rex. Or perhaps Melodie had talked. He was suddenly glad he had had the foresight to take charge of the specimens and data himself.

He waited, listening.

"Listen, I don't know who you are, but I'm not going to tolerate being followed," he said sharply. He took a step forward, meaning to walk back and around the corner to confront his pursuer, but his nerve faltered. He realized he was afraid.

This was preposterous. He looked around, saw the gleaming metal doors of the dinosaur bone vault. He stepped over to them and as quietly as possible swiped his key card in the magnetic reader. The security light blinked from red to green and the door softly unlatched. He pushed it open, stepped inside, and closed it behind him, hearing the massive electronic bolts reengage.

There was a small window in the door, with wire-mesh glass, through which he could see into the corridor beyond. Now he would be able to identify who was following him. He would lodge a strong complaint against whoever it was; this sort of intrigue was intolerable.

A minute passed and then a sudden shadow fell across the pane. A face appeared in profile, then turned with a snap and looked in the window.

Jolted, Corvus hastily stepped back into the darkness of the storage room, but the man, he knew, had seen him. He waited, wrapped in a cloak of absolute darkness, looking at the man's face. It was lit from behind and partially in shadow; but he could still see the general outline of the man's features, the skin stretched tightly over prominent cheekbones, a thatch of jet-black hair, a small, perfectly formed nose, and a pair of lips that looked like two thin coils of clay. He could not see the eyes: just two pools of shadow under the man's brow. It was not a face he recognized. This was no museum employee, no graduate student. If he was a visiting paleontologist he must be obscure indeed for Corvus not to know him — the field was small.

Corvus hardly breathed. There was something about the utter calmness in the man's expression that frightened him — that, and those gray, dead lips. The man lingered at the window, unmoving. Then there was a soft brushing noise, a scraping, a faint click. The handle on the inside of the door turned slowly a quarter turn, then slowly returned to its initial position.

Corvus couldn't believe it: the bastard

was trying to get in. Fat bloody chance. With millions of dollars of specimens inside only a half-dozen people had access to Dinosaur Storage — and this man certainly wasn't one of them. Corvus knew for a fact that the door was two layers of quarter-inch stainless steel with a titanium honeycomb core, sporting a lock that was technically unpickable.

Another soft brushing noise, a click, another click. The security light on the inside of the door continued to glow red — as Corvus knew it would. He almost felt like laughing out loud, taunting and insulting the blighter, except that the sheer persistence of the man amazed and alarmed him. What the devil did he want?

Corvus suddenly thought of the museum phone in the back of the storage room, where the study tables were. He'd call security to arrest the bugger. He turned but it was so very dark, and the room was so vast and crowded with shelves and freestanding dinosaurs, that he realized he couldn't possible get back there without turning on lights. But if he turned on the lights the man would run. He slipped his cell phone out of his suitcoat — but of course there was no coverage this far underground. The man was still working the knob, making various clicking and scraping noises as he tried to get in. It was unbelievable.

More soft sounds, a sharper click — and then Corvus stared in disbelief.

The security light on the door had just gone green.

11

After passing the kidnapper's car, which had pulled off the highway and shut off its lights, Tom had driven until he was out of sight, and then he made a U-turn. The road behind him remained dark. The man had evidently turned off on one of the many forest roads going up into the Canjilon Mountains.

Tom accelerated southward, and in a few minutes he found the place where the man had pulled off, leaving a clear set of tracks in the sand. Just beyond that was a forest road turnoff, and he saw that the same tracks went up it.

Tom followed in the Dodge, driving slowly, keeping his headlights off. The road climbed into the Canjilon foothills above the Mesa de los Viejos, and as he gained altitude the piñon and juniper scrub gradually gave way to a dark ponderosa forest. He resisted the impulse to turn on the lights and charge ahead; surprise was his only advantage. He knew in his gut that Sally was still alive. She couldn't be dead. He would have felt it.

The road switchbacked up a steep ridge covered with a dense stand of ponderosa, and at the top it skirted a cliff. Here the trees opened up to a broad vista across the high mesas, dominated by the great dark outline of Mesa de los Viejos. The road turned back into the forest and soon a chain-link fence loomed up out of the darkness, gleaming new, with a pair of gates across the road. A weather-beaten sign read:

CCC Camp
Perdiz Creek

And then, a new sign, hung on the fence:

Private Property
No Trespassing
Violators Will Be Prosecuted to the
Full Extent of the Law

It was some kind of inholding in the national forest. Tom pulled off the road, shut off the engine. Now that he had a moment he pulled the gun out of the door pocket. It was a well-used J. C. Higgins "88" revolver, .22 caliber, a real piece of shit. He checked the cylinder — nine chambers, all empty.

He pulled a wad of old maps and an empty pint of Jim Beam out of the door pocket and felt around, but there were no rounds. He yanked open the glove compartment and searched it, scattering more maps and empty bottles, and in the bottom found a single beaten-up round, which he inserted into the cylinder and shoved the gun in his belt. He pocketed a Maglite from the glove compartment and searched the rest of the truck, under the seats, in every crevice, looking for more loose rounds. Nothing.

He exited the truck. There was no sound beyond the whispering of a night breeze in the trees and the hooting of an owl. The gate was padlocked. He peered through. The road curved off and disappeared in the trees, and there, in the far distance, he could see the faintest glimmer of light.

A cabin.

Tom climbed the chain-link fence, dropped down the far side, and then headed down the road at a fast, silent run.

12

Sally crawled down the dark tunnel and, after a moment, stopped to listen. She could hear the man scrabbling about and swearing, evidently looking for his flashlight.

She peered ahead into the darkness. Where did it go? She felt her matches but didn't dare light one, realizing it would only turn her into a silhouetted target. She crawled ahead blind, making as little noise as possible. More shots rang out, but he was firing at random, the shots going wild in the darkness. She crawled as fast as she could, cutting her knees on the rocky floor of the mine, feeling ahead. In a few minutes her hand made contact with something cold — a length of slimy, rotten wood that swayed under her grasp. She could smell a cold exhalation of damp mine air coming from below. She lay on her stomach and felt past the railing, her hand encountering a sharp edge of rock. She inched forward, feeling downward — it was slick and wet, evidently the vertical side of a shaft.

Hoping there might be a way around, she crouched and moved alongside, feeling the railing as she went.

A voice rang out. "You can't get out, bitch. The grate's locked and I got the key." A pause, then he spoke again, making an effort to be calmer. "Look, hey, I'm not going to hurt you. Forget all that. Let's be reasonable. Let's talk."

Sally reached the tunnel wall. The pit, it seemed, stretched all the way across, blocking her way. She paused, her heart pounding in her chest.

"Look, I'm sorry about all that. I got carried away."

She could still hear him rummaging around for the flashlight he had dropped — which might still work. She had to find a way down the shaft, and fast.

She felt her way back along the railing until she came to a gap. Was this where a ladder descended? She lay flat on her stomach again and leaned over the lip of the pit, feeling the wet wall of stone downward — a ladder! The top rung felt soft and spongy from rot.

She had to see it before she began climbing down. She had to risk a match.

"Hey, I know you're there. So be reasonable. I *promise* I'll let you go."

She took out the box of matches, slid it open, took out a match. Then she leaned out over the edge and struck it, keeping the flame below the edge of the shaft. The rising air caused it to flicker and blue, but there was enough light for her to see a rotting wooden ladder descending into a black, seemingly bottomless pit. Many of its rungs were broken or muffled with rot and creeping white fungus. It would be suicide to go down that ladder.

Wham! A shot followed, snipping the rock just to her right and spraying the side of her shoulder with chips of stone.

She dropped the match with an involuntary gasp, and it spiraled into the darkness, flickering for a moment before going out.

"Bitch! I'll kill you!"

She swung herself over the black void and felt downward with her foot, encountering a rotten rung, tested it with her weight, then lowered herself slowly, trying the next rung.

She heard a muffled exclamation of triumph, then a click — and suddenly the beam of a flashlight swung past her head.

She ducked and scrambled down the ladder. Almost immediately one of the rungs snapped and her leg swung out over the pit before she could reestablish her footing. The entire ladder creaked and swayed.

Down she went, rung after rung, slipping and gasping with effort, the ladder shaking, drops of water cascading about her. Another rung snapped under her foot, two in a row, dropping her so she was only holding on by her hands, swinging once again in the darkness. She gasped, laddering down with her hands and feeling ahead with her feet until she could pick up a solid rung again.

The beam of the light suddenly appeared at the lip of the shaft, a bright light fixating her in its glare. She threw herself sideways as the gun went off, the round tearing a hole in the rung, the entire ladder swaying with her violent movement.

A laugh echoed down. "That was just for practice. Now for the real thing."

She looked up again, gasping. He was leaning over the lip, twenty feet above her, flashlight in one hand, aiming the gun with the other. It was a no-miss shot. He knew he had her and was taking his time. She struggled down the groaning ladder. Any second he would pull the trigger. She looked up, saw just the outline of his face etched against the light. She stopped descending — it was pointless.

"No," she gasped. "Please don't."

He extended his arm, the steel muzzle of the gun gleaming in the light. She could see the muscles tightening in his hand as he began to depress the trigger. "Kiss your ass good-bye, bitch."

Sally did the only thing she could do: she launched herself from the ladder, letting herself fall into the dark pit.

13

Corvus stared at the green LED, paralyzed with fear. How could the man have penetrated the museum's security? What the hell did he want?

The door eased open, casting a widening stripe of yellow light across the floor, which cut through the mounted skeleton of an allosaurus, turning it into a Halloween-like monstrosity. The shadow of his pursuer moved into the bar of light, his outline falling strangely on the dinosaur, and as he took a second step forward Corvus saw he was carrying a long-barreled weapon of some kind.

The sight of it broke the spell and spurred Corvus into action. He turned and fled back toward the dark recesses of the storage room, flying down a narrow corridor lined on both sides with massive steel shelves, past stacks of bones and skulls. He came to a jog and turned right, then ran down another aisle and left into another. He stopped, panting and crouching behind a large centrosaurus skull, looking back to see if the man was pursuing. His heart was pounding so hard he could hear the rhythmic whoosh of blood in his ears. He peered through a hole in the monster's bony frill, and he saw that the man had not moved: he remained a black silhouette in the open door. The man finally raised the weapon, stepped away, and allowed the door to reclose, the security locks latching automatically — and darkness once again descended on the storage room.

Corvus's mind raced. This was insane: he was being hunted in his own museum. It must be connected with the T. Rex in New Mexico. This man wanted his data and was willing to kill for it.

The curator heard someone breathing loudly, realized it was himself, and tried to get himself under control. As noiselessly as possible he slipped out of his shoes, and in his stocking feet retreated deeper into the dark rows of fossils, toward the back of the storage room where the biggest mounted specimens were kept, cheek by jowl. That would offer the best possibilities for hiding. But how long could he remain hidden? The storage room was as large as a warehouse, but the man would have most of the night to ferret him out.

A voice came from the darkness, quiet and neutral in tone.

"I should like to speak with you, Professor."

Corvus did not respond. He had to get to a more secure hiding place. He felt his way forward, crawling on his hands and knees, moving carefully so as not to make any noise. There was, he recalled, the massive torso of a triceratops back there under a sheet of plastic; he could hide in the beast's rib cage. Even with the lights on, he would be in deep shadow from the skeleton and the great horned casque of the dinosaur would act like a hood. The triceratops was packed in among several dozen partially mounted dinosaurs and all were sheeted in plastic. He crawled forward through the forest of bones, squirming under hanging sheets of plastic, working his way deeper into the clutter of fossils. At one point he paused and listened, but he could hear nothing — no footfalls, no movement.

Strange that the man hadn't turned on a light.

"Dr. Corvus, we are wasting precious time. Please make yourself known."

Corvus was shaken: the voice was no longer coming from the front of the storeroom, near the door. It had come from a different place — closer and to his right. The man had been moving through the darkness, only so silently that he had made no sound at all.

On his hands and knees, Corvus continued to creep forward with infinite caution, feeling the mounted foot bones of each dinosaur, trying to identify it and then place it within his mental map of the jumbled storeroom.

He bumped something and a bone fell with a rattle.

"This is getting tiresome."

The voice was closer — a lot closer. He wanted to ask: *Who are you?* But he didn't; he knew perfectly well who the man was — a bloody rival, a paleontologist or someone working for a paleontologist, come to steal his discovery. The bloody Americans were all criminals and beasts.

Corvus lifted yet another piece of plastic, which gave out a loud crackle. He paused, holding his breath, then went back to feeling his way forward. If only he could identify one of these bloody dinosaurs, he'd know where he was — *yes,* it was the furcula of the oviraptorid *Ingenia.* He scurried to the right, avoiding plastic sheets, feeling his way, until he encountered a tail vertebra, and another, along with the bent iron rod supporting them. It was the triceratops. He reached up, encountered a thick sheet of plastic, and with infinite care raised it and wriggled underneath. Once inside, he felt a rib and another, crawling toward the front, where he could huddle under the dinosaur's huge tri-horned casque, almost five feet in diameter. He painstakingly inched himself into the hollow where the beast's heart and lungs once sat. Even with the lights on, it would be bloody difficult to see him. It might take the man hours to find him, maybe even all night. He waited, crouching, unmoving, his heart pounding in his own rib cage.

"It is useless to hide. I am coming to you."

The voice was closer, much closer. Corvus felt a hum of terror, like a swarm of bees unloosed in his head. He could not get the image of that long gun barrel out of his mind. This was no joke: the man was going to kill him.

He needed a weapon.

He felt along the rib cage, grabbed a rib, tried to wiggle it free, but it was solidly fixed. He tested several more and finally found one that gave a little when he tugged on it. He felt up the supporting iron armature for the wing nut and screw that held the bone, found it, tried to turn it. Stuck. He felt back to the bottom, found the other wing nut — but it too was frozen.

Bloody hell, he should have picked up a loose bone to use as a weapon when he had the chance.

"Dr. Corvus, I repeat: this is tiresome. I am coming to you."

The voice was even closer. How was he moving so silently through the darkness? How did he know the room so well? It was like the man was floating in the dark. With a surge of desperation he fumbled with the wing nut, grasping it, trying to wrench it loose; he felt the rusted nut cut into his flesh, the warm blood running down — and still it did not budge.

He let go, swallowed, moderated his breathing. His heart was pounding so hard he felt it must be audible — but you couldn't hear a beating heart, could you? If he just stayed tight, didn't move, kept silent, the man would never find him in this darkness. He couldn't. It was impossible.

"Dr. Corvus?" the voice asked. "All I want is a small piece of information about the Tyrannosaurus rex. When I get that, our business will be concluded."

Corvus crouched there, in fetal position, trembling uncontrollably. The voice was not more than ten feet away.

14

Tom sprinted through the forest toward the yellow light shining through the trees. He slowed when he came up behind a cabin, moving forward cautiously and keeping within the darkness. It was a large, two-story cabin with a porch, and in the glow of the porch light he could see the Ranger Rover parked in front.

With a sudden start of recognition, he realized he had been there before, years ago, with some friends who wanted to explore ghost towns in the mountains. That was before there was a fence and a new cabin.

Tom pressed himself against the rough logs of the house, creeping along until he came to a window. He peered in. The view was of a timbered living room with a stone fireplace, Navajo rugs on the floor, an elk head mounted on the wall. Only a single light was on and Tom had the distinct impression the house was empty. He listened. The place was silent and the second-floor windows were dark.

Sally wasn't in the house. He crept up to

the front and gazed across the ghost town, faintly illuminated by the porch light. Keeping low, moving smoothly and pausing every now and then to listen, he crept up next to the car and put his hand on the hood — the engine was still warm. Crouching by the passenger door, he pulled out the flashlight he had found in the Dodge's glove compartment and turned it on. Holding it low, he examined the marks on the ground. In the loose sand he could see a confused muddle of cowboy boot prints. He cast about. There, just beyond the car, he saw what looked like two parallel drag marks made by boot heels. He followed the marks with the beam of the flashlight and saw they headed up the dirt street toward a ravine at the far end of town.

His heart flopped wildly in his chest. Was it Sally being dragged? Was she unconscious? The ravine, if he remembered correctly, led to some abandoned gold mines. He paused, trying to recall the lay of the land. His hand went unconsciously to the butt of the pistol tucked into his belt.

One round.

He followed the drag marks down the dirt track to the far end of the old camp, where they vanished into the woods at the mouth of the ravine. His flashlight disclosed freshly trampled weeds along an overgrown trail. He listened, but could hear nothing beyond the sigh of wind through the pines. He followed the trail, and after a quarter mile came out into an open area, where the valley widened. The trail ran up the hillside and he sprinted up it. It ran below the ridgeline through a stand of ponderosas and ended at an old wooden shaft house.

Sally was imprisoned in the mines. And that's where they were right now.

The door of the shaft house was chained and padlocked. He paused, resisting the impulse to bash it down, and listened. All was silent. He examined the padlock and found it had been left unlocked, dangling in its chain; he switched off his light, eased the door open, and slipped inside.

Cupping his hands around the flashlight, he turned it on just long enough to examine his surroundings. The mine opening lay ahead, a maw cut into the rocky hillside, breathing out a wash of damp, moldy air. The opening was securely barred and covered with a heavy iron grate, locked with a fat, case-hardened steel padlock.

Tom listened, holding his breath. Not a sound came from the mine tunnel. He tested the lock, but this one was fast. He crouched and, taking out the Maglite, examined the dirt floor. The prints were exceptionally clear in the powdery dust and they belonged to a man with a size eleven or twelve boot. To one side he could see where Sally's heels had dragged, and a flattened area where a body had been laid down — her body — which he must have done while he unlocked the grate. She had been unconscious. He quashed a more awful speculation.

Tom tried to sort out his options. He had to get in — or attract the man to the door and shoot him as he approached.

Hearing a faint sound come from the mine, Tom froze. A shout? He hardly dared breathe. After a moment he heard another sound, a faint cry, distorted by its long travel down the throat of stone. It was a man's voice.

He grasped the padlock and shook it, trying to spring it open, but it wouldn't budge. The grate was forged from heavy steel and cemented into the stone. He had no hope of breaking it.

As he was casting about, he heard another angry shout, this one much louder and clearer, in which he could just make out the word *bitch*.

She was in there. She was alive. And then he heard the muffled boom of a gunshot.

15

Bob Biler turned on the radio in the '57 Chevy and spun through the dial, hoping to pick up his favorite golden oldies station out of Albuquerque, but once again all he got was hiss and sputter. He snapped it off and took a consolation hit from the pint of Jim Beam lying on the passenger seat. He smacked and rolled his lips with pleasure, and tossed the bottle back on the seat with a thump, wiped his hand over his stubbled chin, and grinned at his great good fortune.

Biler had given up trying to figure out the bizarre incident up at the Sunrise. Somebody had stolen his Dodge and left him a beaut of a classic Chevy, keys dangling in the ignition, worth at least ten times his old shit box. Maybe he should've called the police, but it was only fair that if someone stole his truck, he should get theirs. And besides, he'd already parked a pint of Jim Beam in his gut and he was in no condition to be calling the cops. It was his truck that had been stolen, and you didn't *have* to report a stolen vehicle if it was your own, did you?

A sudden rumble of his right tires on the shoulder caused Biler to jerk the wheel to the left, almost swerve off the left shoulder, recover with a faint squealing of rubber, and finally get the truck steady on the road again. The dotted yellow line ran straight and true into the blackness and he put the truck right on top of it, the better to follow it. No problem, he'd be able to see the headlights of an oncoming car from a million miles off, plenty of time to move over. He fortified his concentration with another hit of Jim Beam, his lips making a satisfying pop as he removed the bottle from his mouth.

It was already past ten and Biler would be hitting Espanola at ten-thirty. Jesus, he was tired, it had been a long drive down from Dolores, just to visit his daughter and her worthless unemployed husband. If only he could pick up that golden oldies station out of Albuquerque — some Elvis would really lift his spirits. He turned on the radio, dialed it across the spectrum, stopped at one station that seemed to hint at music behind a wash of static and left it there. Maybe as he got closer it would come in stronger.

He saw headlights in the distance and eased over to his side of the road. A police car passed him and he watched it recede, checking it again as the red taillights began to fade into the enormous darkness. Then he saw, with alarm, a sudden brightening of the lights — the cop had braked — followed by a momentary glimmer, and then the brighter white lights of the headlights as he pulled a U-turn.

Holy shit. Biler swept the bottle of Jim Beam off the seat and gave it a sharp kick with the heel of his shoe, scooting it up and under the seat. The truck drifted out of lane again and he quickly snapped his attention back to the road, the truck swaying with the correction. Shit, he had better slow down and drive like a little old lady. His eyes darted from the road to the speedometer to the rearview mirror. He was keeping at a steady fifty-five and he was pretty sure when the cop passed he wasn't doing more than sixty, still five under the speed limit. Biler, like most longtime drinkers-and-drivers, never broke the speed limit. After a few heart-pounding minutes he began to relax. The cop hadn't put on his bubble-gum machine and wasn't accelerating to catch up with him. He was just tooling along at the same speed, maybe a quarter mile back, nice and easy — just some State trooper on patrol. Biler grasped the steering wheel in the ten-two position, eyes straight ahead, keeping it steady at fifty-five.

Hell, nobody could drive any better than that.

16

For a moment Sally lay in a shallow pool of water, stunned by the fall. It hadn't been a long drop after all and she was more frightened than hurt. But she was far from out of danger. Even as she was recovering her thoughts the flashlight beam was probing down from above. A moment later it fixed her and she jumped sideways as the shots came, the bullets striking the water around her with a zipping sound. She thrashed through the water toward where the flashlight beam had revealed a tunnel running off into darkness. In a moment she had turned the corner, beyond the range of his gun.

She leaned against the wall, taking great gulps of breath. Her whole body ached but nothing seemed to be broken. She felt in her breast pocket for the box of matches. Miraculously, while the outside of the box had gotten damp, the inside was still dry. The matches were the long, wooden, "strike anywhere" variety. She struck a match against the rock wall, one scratch, two. It flared on the third try and it cast a faint illumination down the tunnel ahead, a long corridor cribbed with rotting oak beams. A shallow stream flowed along its bottom, running from puddle to puddle. The tunnel's condition looked disastrous; beams had fallen down, while small cave-ins from the walls and ceilings partially obstructed the passage. What hadn't already fallen looked like it was about to go, the rock ceiling gaping with large cracks, the oak beams bowing under the weight of shifted rocks.

She jogged down the tunnel, shielding the match, until it burned down to her fingers and she was forced to drop it. She kept going as long as she dared in the darkness, retaining the memory of what lay ahead. When she feared going farther she stopped and listened. Was he following? It seemed unlikely he would risk going down the ladder she had descended — no sane person would do it and she had broken too many rungs in her descent. He would have to find a rope, and that would at least give her a moment's reprieve. But no more than a moment: she remembered seeing a rope in her cell, coiled up at the foot of the bed.

Sally struggled to focus her mind and think rationally. She remembered reading somewhere that all caves breathed and that the best way to find your way out was to follow the "breath" of the cave — that is, the flow of air. She lit the match. The flame bent back, toward where she had come from. She went in the opposite direction, deeper into the mine, wading through the water, moving as quickly as she could without putting out the match. The tunnel curved right and opened into a large gallery, with pillars of raw rock remaining in place to hold up the ceiling. A second match showed two tunnels leading off. The flow of water went into the left one. She paused, there being just enough flame to see where the air was flowing from, and decided to take the right tunnel, the only one sloping upward.

The match burned down and she dropped it. She took a moment to count by feel the number of matches in the box. Fifteen.

She tried moving forward by feel, but soon realized her progress was too slow. She had to put as much distance between herself and him as possible. Now was the time to use the matches, not later.

She lit another, continued up the tunnel, turned a corner — and found the tunnel was blocked by a cave-in. She stared upward at the dark hole in the ceiling from which an enormous mass of rock had fallen into a disorderly pile below. Several rocks the size of cars still hung from the ceiling in crazy angles, braced and propped up by fallen beams, looking like they would shift at the merest nudge.

Sally retraced her steps and took the left-hand tunnel, the one that sloped downward with the stream. Her panic was rising; at any moment the kidnapper would be down there after her. She followed the running water, hoping it might lead her to an exit, wading through a series of pools. The tunnel sloped downward and leveled out. The water got deeper and she realized it was pooling; soon it was almost up to her waist. Around the next turn she saw the cause: a cave-in that had completely blocked the tunnel and backed up the water. The water managed to escape through the spaces between the jagged rocks, but there was no opening large enough for her to pass.

She swore to herself. Was there a tunnel she had missed? She knew in her heart there wasn't. In five minutes she had explored all of the mine that was still accessible. In short, she was trapped.

She struck another match, her fingers shaking, looking around desperately for a way out, a tunnel or opening she might have overlooked. She burned her fingers, cursed under her breath, and lit another match. Surely there had to be a way out.

She retraced her steps yet again, recklessly lighting match after match, until she came back to the first cave-in. It was a compact mass, offering no obvious holes. Lighting more matches, she searched through the piled boulders anyway, looking for a space she could wedge herself in. But there was nothing.

She counted her matches. Seven left. She lit another, looked up — and saw the hole in the roof. It was insane to think of going up in there. The light from the match was too feeble to penetrate its recesses, but still, it looked like there might be a crawl space up there where she might at least hide — if she were willing to risk the precarious, sloping pile of loose boulders.

It was a crazy risk. As she stood there, trembling and indecisive, the flame dying at the end of the match, a small pebble came rattling out of the hole, bounced like a pinball down through the tangle of beams and rocks, and came to rest at her feet.

So that was it, then. She had two choices: she could either go back and face the kidnapper, or she could risk climbing up into a hole created by the cave-in.

The match went. She had six more. She picked two out of the box and lit them together, hoping to generate enough light to see deeper into the hole. They flared and she peered intently, but it still wasn't enough to see beyond the tangle of rocks and beams.

The matches went out.

No more time. She lit another match, stuck it between her teeth, grasped a rock in the pile, and began to climb. At the same time she heard a sound — a distant voice, echoing raucously through the tunnels of stone.

"Ready or not, bitch, here I come!"

17

Corvus crouched inside the rib cage of the triceratops, blood pounding in his ears. The man was standing no more than ten feet away. He swallowed, tried to get some moisture in his mouth. He heard the brush of a hand on a bone surface, the faint scuff of a shoe on the cement floor, the ever so small crunch of fossil grit under the man's sole as he approached. *How the bloody hell was the man moving around so well in the dark?*

"I can see you," came the soft voice, as if reading his mind, "but you can't see me."

Corvus's heart felt like a bass drum: the voice was right next to him. His throat was so dry he couldn't have spoken if he wanted to.

"You look silly, crouching there."

Another footfall. He could actually smell the man's expensive aftershave.

"All I want is the locality data. Anything will do: GPS coordinates, name of a formation or canyon, that sort of thing. I want to know where the dinosaur is."

Corvus swallowed, shifted. It didn't make sense hiding any longer; the man knew where he was. He was probably wearing some kind of night-vision device.

"I don't have that information," Corvus croaked. "I don't know where the bloody dinosaur is." He sat up, clutching his brief-case.

"If that's the game you want to play, then I'm afraid I'll have to kill you." The man's voice was so quiet, so gentle, that it left Corvus without the slightest doubt that the man meant what he said. He gripped the briefcase, his hands in a cold sweat.

"I don't have it. I really don't." Corvus heard himself pleading.

"Then how did you acquire the specimen?"

"Through a third party."

"Ah. And the name and place of residence of this third party?"

There was a silence. Corvus felt his terror mingling with something else: anger. Furious anger. His whole career, his life, hung on getting that dinosaur. He wasn't going to give up his discovery to some bastard holding him hostage at gunpoint — he'd rather die. The bloody bastard had night-vision goggles or something of the sort, and if he could get to one of the light banks it would eliminate the man's advantage. He could use the hard attaché case as a club —

"The name and place of residence of this third party, please?" the man repeated, his voice as soft as ever.

"I'm coming out."

"A wise decision."

Corvus crawled toward the back of the skeleton and out the back. He slipped under the plastic and stood up. It was still pitch-dark and he had only a vague sense where the man was.

"The name of this third party?"

Corvus lunged at the voice in the darkness, swinging his case by the handle in an arc toward the voice, striking him somewhere; the man grunted and was thrown back in surprise. Corvus turned, groping blindly through the forest of skeletons toward where he remembered the back light switches were. He stumbled against a skeleton and fell, just as he heard a sharp pneumatic hiss followed by the sound of surgical steel striking fossil bone.

The bastard was shooting at him.

He lunged sideways, collided with a skeleton, which creaked in protest, sending a few bones clattering to the ground. Another hiss of air, another metallic ricochet among the bones to his right. He groped forward, scrabbling desperately among bone forest, and then suddenly he was free of the crowd of skeletons and back in the shelves; he ran wildly down the aisle, careening once off the side, falling, and getting up. If only he could reach the lights and neutralize the man's advantage. He sprinted forward, heedless of what might lie in the way, and virtually collided with the bank of electrical switches. With another shout he clawed at the panel, the lights clicking on by the dozen, a humming and *flick-flick* as the aging fluorescent lights blinked on, one by one.

He spun around, at the same time grasping a petrified bone off one of the shelves, wielding it like a club, ready to fight.

The man stood there placidly, not ten feet away, legs apart, not even looking like he'd moved. He was dressed in a blue tracksuit, night-vision goggles raised up on his forehead. A shabby leather briefcase stood on the ground next to his leg. His hands were in firing position and the shiny tube of a strange-looking weapon was aimed straight at Corvus. He stared in astonishment at the ordinariness of the man, the passionless bureaucratic face. He heard the *snap-hiss!* of compressed air, saw the flash of silver, felt the sting in his solar plexus, and looked down in astonishment; there he saw a stainless-steel syringe sticking out of his abdomen. He opened his mouth and reached down to pull it out but already a darkness unlike any other was rushing upon him like a tidal wave, burying him in its roaring undertow.

18

Ford sat with his back against a rock, soaking in the warmth from a meager fire he had built from dead cactus husks. The walls of Tyrannosaur Canyon rose blackly around him, giving way to a deep velvety sky dusted with stars.

Ford had just finished a dinner of lentils and rice. He took the can the lentils had come in, set it among the fire, and heated it until all trace of food had burned out of it — his method of dishwashing when water was too precious to waste. With a stick he fished the can out of the fire, let it cool off, and filled it with water from his canteen. Holding the can by its metal top, he nestled it upright among the burning husks. In a few minutes the water reached a boil. He removed the can, added a tablespoon of coffee grounds, stirred them in, and set the can back in the fire. In five minutes more his coffee was ready.

He sipped it, holding the can by the lid, savoring the bitter, smoky flavor. He smiled ruefully to himself, thinking of the crowded little café he and Julie used to go to around the corner from the Pantheon in Rome, where they drank perfect cups of espresso at a tiny table. What was the name of that place? The Tazza d'Oro.

He was a long way from there.

Coffee finished, he drained the last bit of moisture from the cup, rapped the grounds out into the fire, and set the can aside for making his morning coffee. He leaned back on the rock with a sigh, pulled his robe more tightly about himself, and raised his eyes to the stars. It was almost midnight and a gibbous moon was creeping over the canyon rim. He picked out some of the constellations he knew, Ursa Major, Cassiopeia, the Pleiades. The glowing skein of the Milky Way stretched across the sky; following it with his eyes he located the constellation Cygnus, the Swan, frozen forever in its flight across the galactic center. He had read there was a gigantic black hole in the center of the galaxy, called Cygnus X-1, one hundred million suns swallowed up and compressed into a mathematical point — and he wondered at the audacity of human beings to think they could understand anything at all about the true nature of God.

Ford sighed and stretched out in the sand, wondering if such musings were proper for a soon-to-be Benedictine monk. He sensed that the events of the past few days were propelling him toward some kind of spiritual crisis. The search for the T. Rex had awakened that same old hunger, that longing for the chase that he thought he had purged from his system. God knows, he had had enough adventure for one lifetime already. He spoke four languages, had lived in a dozen exotic countries, and had known many women before finding the great love of his life. He had suffered unbearably for it and still suffered. So why, then, this continued addiction to excitement and danger? Here he was, searching for a dinosaur that didn't belong to him, that would bring him no credit, money, or glory. Why? Was this crazy search the result of some fundamental defect in his character?

Unwillingly, Ford's mind traveled back to that fateful day in Siem Reap, Cambodia. His wife Julie and he had left Phnom Penh the day before on their way to Thailand. They had stopped for a few days in Siem Reap to see the temples of Angkor Wat — a sightseeing detour that was part of their cover. Only a week before they had learned that Julie was pregnant, and to celebrate they booked a suite at the Royal Khampang Hotel. He would never forget his last evening with her, standing on the Naga Balustrade of Angkor Wat, watching the sun set over the temple's five great towers. They could hear, coming faintly from a hidden monastery in the forest on one side of the temple, the mysterious, hummed chanting of Buddhist monks.

Their assignment had gone off without a hitch. That morning they had delivered the CD-ROM with its data to their operative in Phnom Penh. It had been a clean finish — or so they thought. The only hint was that he'd noticed they were being followed by an old Toyota Land Cruiser. He had washed the guy's laundry — shaken him off his tail — in the crowded streets of the capital before leaving town. It didn't seem like a serious thing, and he'd been followed plenty of times before.

After sunset they had a long dinner in one of the cheap open-air restaurants along the Siem Reap River, the frogs hopping about the floor and moths bumbling against the lightbulbs strung on wires. They'd gone back to their obscenely expensive hotel room and passed a good part of the evening cavorting on their bed. They slept until eleven, ate breakfast on their terrace. And then Julie had gone to get the car while he brought down their luggage.

He heard the muffled explosion just as the elevator doors opened into the lobby. He assumed an old land mine had gone off — Cambodia was still plagued with them. He remembered coming through the palm court and seeing, through the lobby doors, a column of smoke rising in front of the hotel. He ran outside. The car lay upside down, almost split in half, billowing acrid smoke, a crater in the pavement. One of the tires lay fifty feet away on an immaculate stretch of lawn, burning furiously.

Even then he didn't recognize it was his car. He figured it was another political killing, all too common in Cambodia. He stood at the top of the steps, looking up and down the street for Julie coming in with the car, worrying that another bomb might go off. As he stood there, he saw a piece of torn fabric caught in a gust of wind; it fluttered up the steps of the hotel and settled almost at his feet — and he recognized it as the collar of the blouse Julie had put on that morning.

With a wrenching mental effort Ford brought himself back to the present, to the campfire, the dark canyons, the sky sparkling with stars. All those terrible memories seemed far away, as if they had happened in another life, to another person.

But that was just it: was this really another life — and he another person?

19

The lights of Espanola twinkled in the night air as Bob Biler approached the town. The cop was still behind him but Biler was no longer worried. He was even sorry he'd kicked the bottle under the seat in his panic, and several times he tried to weasel it out with the toe of his boot, but the truck began swerving so he gave up. He could always pull over and fish it out, but he wasn't sure if it was legal to pull off the highway there and he didn't want to do anything to attract the attention of the cop. At least the golden oldies station was finally beginning to come in. He cranked up the knob, humming tunelessly along with the music.

A quarter mile ahead he saw the first set of traffic lights at the outskirts of the city. If he hit a red light it would give him just enough time to fish out the bottle. Damn if driving didn't make you thirsty.

Biler approached the lights, braking carefully and smoothly, watching the cop car in his rearview mirror. As soon as his car stopped he leaned over and reached under the seat, fumbling around until his greasy hand fastened on the cold glass bottle. He slid it out and — keeping himself well below the level of the seat — unscrewed the cap and fastened it to his lips, sucking down as much as possible in the shortest period of time.

Suddenly he heard the screeching of rubber and the sounds of sirens, a wailing chorus all around him. He jerked up, forgetting he had the bottle in his hand, and was blinded by a blast of white light from a spotlight. He seemed to be surrounded by cop cars, all with their pinball machines flashing. Biler was stunned, unable to comprehend what was happening. He winced, trying to blink away blindness, his mind having moved beyond confusion to utter, total blankness.

He heard a harsh megaphone voice saying something, repeating it. *"Step out of the car with your hands up. Step out of the car with your hands up."*

Were they talking to him? Biler looked around but could see no people, only the glare of flashing lights.

"Step out of the car with your hands up."

They were talking to him. In a blind panic, Biler fumbled with the door handle, but it was one of those handles that you had to push down instead of up, and he struggled with it trying to shoulder the door open. Suddenly the door gave way and flew open, and he tumbled out, the forgotten pint bottle of Jim Beam flying from his hand and shattering on the pavement. He lay all in a heap on the asphalt beside the truck, too stunned and confused to get up.

A figure loomed over him, blocking the light, holding a badge in one hand and a revolver in the other. A voice barked out, "Detective Willer, Santa Fe Police Department, *do not move.*"

There was a momentary pause. Biler could see nothing but the man's black outline against a brilliant backdrop. In the background, he could hear the staticky wail of Elvis's voice coming from the truck, *"You ain't nothin' but a hound dog . . ."*

A beat passed, and then the silhouette holstered the gun and leaned over him, looking intently into his face. He straightened up and Biler heard him speak again, this time to someone offstage. "Who the hell is this?"

20

Sally climbed up the unstable pile of rocks, the match clenched between her teeth, seeking out footholds and handholds. With every step she could feel the rocks shifting underneath her, some dislodging and tumbling to the bottom. The whole pile seemed to creak and move.

Her breathing came so hard that it put the match out.

She felt in the box — one match left. She decided to save it.

"I'm coming!" the hoarse voice echoed down through the tunnels, maniacally distorted. Sally kept climbing, moving upward by feel, more stones rattling down. Then she heard, above her, a deep groan of shifting wood and rock, followed by a cascade of pebbles. Another step, another creaking shift. It was about to go. But she had no choice.

She reached up, fumbled for a handhold, tested it, drew herself up. Another handhold, another foothold. She moved with the utmost care, easing her weight from one foothold to the next.

"Sally, where are youuu?"

She could hear him splashing through the tunnel. She drew herself up farther and grasped a length of beam above her. Leaning her weight on it, she tested it. It groaned and shifted slightly, but seemed to hold. She paused, trying not to think of what it would be like to be buried alive, then she lifted herself up. Another groan, a flurry of falling pebbles, and she was up and over it. Above, her hands encountered a tangle of splintered wood and broken rock.

She would have to light the last match.

It scraped against the side of the box and flared to life. Above, she could see the dark hole she had to go into. She held the matchbox over the flame until it caught fire, casting a much brighter light into the dark space, but it was still not enough to see where it went.

With one hand holding the burning box, she hoisted herself over the next shifting beam. In a moment she was standing on a precarious ledge just inside the dark opening. By the dying light of the burning matchbox she saw the hole ended in a broad, half-moon crack going off at a shallow angle of about thirty degrees. The crack looked just wide enough to fit in.

There was a sudden crash below her as a

large rock from the ceiling fell to the ground. The flame went out.

"There you are!"

The beam of a flashlight lanced through the darkness, scouring the rock pile below her. She reached up, grabbed a handhold, and hoisted herself up. The flashlight beam was probing all around now. She climbed quickly, even recklessly, scrabbling upward toward the two damp faces of stone and crawling into the broad fissure. The crack went up at a shallow angle and it was wide enough so that she could wedge herself in it and move up by wriggling and inching. She had no more matches, no way to see where she was going, no way to know if the crack went anywhere. She crawled on, pushing herself upward with her hands and knees. For a moment she was seized by the claustrophobic panic of being pressed on both sides by stone. She paused, regulated her breathing, mastered her fear, and resumed.

"I'm coming to get youuuu!"

The voice came from directly below. She continued crawling with a growing sense of dread that the crack was narrowing. Soon it was so narrow she had to force her way deeper in, pushing with her feet and knees, exhaling some air from her lungs to fit through. With another surge of panic she understood that this had become a one-way journey — she would not be able to turn around. Without the leverage of being able to push with her feet she could never back out.

"I know you're up there, bitch!"

She heard the rattle of falling rocks as he began to climb the rockfall. She drew up her feet, twisted her torso, and was able to get her arm loose and slide it in front of her, to feel her way forward. The crack didn't seem to narrow farther, and if anything it felt like it might even get wider. If she could push herself past this narrow section, the crack might lead to another tunnel.

She exhaled and, using her feet as a brace, forced herself deeper in, her shirt pocket tearing, the buttons ripping off. She felt ahead. Another push, another exhale to make herself thinner. She paused, taking shallow breaths. It was like being pressed to death. She heard the sound of more rocks falling below her as he climbed.

She braced herself, and with a mighty push shoved herself deeper into the crack. The terror of being squeezed in the darkness was almost overwhelming. Water dripped down and ran over her face. Now she knew she could never back out. It would have been better to be shot than to die in this crack. If she could just push past this constriction, the crack might widen again. She braced, pushed again, her clothes tearing with the effort. Another push — and she felt forward with her hand. The crack narrowed sharply to something less than an inch wide. She felt wildly, moving her hand back and forth, looking for a wider place — but there was none. She felt again, almost crazed with terror, but there could be no doubt: the crack narrowed to a few inches all along its length, with many smaller cracks radiating out. Back and forth she swept her hands, probing and feeling — but it was no use.

Sally felt an unspeakable terror bubbling up, beyond her ability to control. She tried to wriggle back out, struggling violently, hardly able to breathe. But she had no leverage; her arms were not strong enough to force herself back. She was wedged in. There was no going forward. And there was no going back.

21

Tom tried everything to break the lock on the grate. He bashed it with boulders, rammed it with a log, but it was useless. The faint sounds from inside the mine had ceased, and he felt the silence would drive him mad. Anything could be happening to her — a minute might mean the difference between life and death. He had shouted, screamed in the grate, trying to draw off the kidnapper — to no avail.

He stepped outside, trying to think of what to do. The moon was just starting to rise above the fir trees along the ridgeline above him. He controlled his breathing and tried to think. He had explored some of these mines years ago, and he recalled there were others in the area. Perhaps they connected; gold mines often had several entrances.

He hiked up to the top of the ridge and gazed down the other side. Bingo. About two hundred yards below stood another shaft house, at approximately the same level as the other, with a long streak of tailings below it.

Surely they would connect.

He ran down the hill, sliding and leaping boulders, and in a moment had reached it. Pulling out his gun, he kicked down the door and went inside, shining the light around. There was another mine opening, and this one had no metal grate sealing it. He ventured inside and probed the beam down a long, level tunnel. A feeling of urgency almost choked him now. He jogged down the tunnel, and at the first fork stopped to listen. A minute ticked by, then two. He felt he was going mad.

Suddenly he heard it: the faint echo of a yell. The two mines connected.

He dashed down the tunnel the sound had come from and ran on, his light disclosing a series of air shafts on the left-hand side. He turned a corner and his flashlight revealed two other tunnels, one going up, the other down. He stopped to listen, waiting, his impatience soaring — and then came another distorted shout.

The voice of the man again. Angry.

Tom ran down the left-hand shaft, sometimes having to duck because of a low ceiling. More sounds came echoing down the tunnel from ahead, still faint but getting clearer.

The tunnel made a few sharp turns and came to a central chamber, with four tunnels going off in various directions. He skidded to a stop, breathing heavily, and shined his light around, revealing some old railroad ties, a wrecked ore cart, a pile of rusty chain, hemp ropes chewed by rats. He would have to wait for another sound before he could proceed.

Silence. He felt he would go mad. *Make a sound, dammit, any sound.*

And then it came: a faint cry.

In a flash he ran down the tunnel from which it issued, which dead-ended in a vertical shaft surrounded by a railing. The pit was too deep for his light to reach the bottom. There was no way down — no ladders or ropes.

He examined the rough edges of the shaft, and decided to go for it. He tore off his Italian dress shoes and socks and tossed them over the edge, counting the time it took for them to hit the bottom. One and a half seconds: thirty-two feet.

Sticking the gun back in his belt and holding the Maglite between his teeth, he grasped a rail and let himself over the edge, gripping the bare rock with his feet. Slowly, his heart pounding his chest, he crept down the shaft.

Another foot down, another handhold. He lost his footing and for a terrifying moment felt he would fall. The sharp rocks cut into his toes. He climbed down with maddening slowness, and finally, with a sense of relief, felt solid ground. He shined the light around, collected his shoes and socks, and put them back on. He was in yet another mining tunnel going straight back into the mountain. He listened. All was silent.

He jogged down the tunnel, stopped after a hundred yards to listen again. The flashlight was getting feeble — the batteries, which had been none too good to begin with, were dying. He went on, stopped, listened. Coming from behind him he heard what sounded like a muffled shout. He shut off his light, holding his breath. It was a voice, still coming from distance, but much clearer than before. He could just make out the words.

I know you're up there. Come down or I shoot.

Tom listened, his heart pounding.

You hear me?

He felt a rush of relief that fairly staggered him on his feet. Sally was alive — and evidently free. He listened intently, trying to locate the direction of the voice.

You're dead, bitch.

The words filled him with a rage so sudden that he lost his breath for a moment. He moved another twenty feet, walking back and forth, trying to get a fix. The sound seemed to be coming from below, as if through the very rock. But that

395

was impossible. Some ten feet to his left he could see a web of cracks in the stone floor of the tunnel, where it had sagged and broken. He knelt, held his hand over one of the cracks. Cool air flowed out. He put his ear to the crack.

There was the sudden *crack!* of a large-caliber gun, followed by a scream — a scream so close to his ear he jumped.

22

Willer and Hernandez sped northward on Highway 84, the lights of Espanola receding in the distance, the empty blackness of the desert wilderness mounting in front of them. It was almost midnight and Willer was beside himself that a half-wit like Biler had managed to waste so many precious hours of their time.

Willer slid a butt out of his shirt pocket and inserted it between his lips. He wasn't supposed to smoke in the squad car but he was long beyond the point of caring.

"Broadbent could be over Cumbres Pass by now," said Hernandez.

Willer sucked in a lungful. "Not possible. They've logged all the vehicles coming over the pass and Biler's wasn't one of them. It hasn't gone through the roadblock south of Espanola either."

"He could've ditched the car in some back lot in Espanola and gone to ground in a motel."

"He could've, but he didn't." Willer gave the car a little more pedal. The speedometer inched up from 110 to 120, the car rocking back and forth, the darkness rushing past.

"So what do you think he did?"

"I think he went to that so-called monastery, Christ in the Desert, to see that monk. Which is where we're going."

"What makes you think that?"

Willer sucked again. Usually he appreciated Hernandez's persistent questions — they helped him think things through — but this time he felt only irritation. "I don't know why I think it but I think it," he snapped. "Broadbent and his wife are mixed up in it, the monk's in on it, and there's a third party out there — the killer — who's also up to his ass in it. They've found something in those canyons and they're locked in a life or death struggle over it. Whatever it is, it's big — so big that Broadbent blew off the police and stole a truck over it. I mean, Jesus, Hernandez, you got to ask yourself what's so important that a guy like that would risk ten years in Santa Fe Correctional. Here's a guy who's already got everything."

"Yeah."

"Even if Broadbent's not at the monastery, I want to have a little chat with that so-called monk."

23

Tom recognized, with a freezing sense of disbelief, that the scream came from Sally. He pressed his mouth to the crack. "Sally!"

A gasp. "Tom?"

"Sally! What's happening? Are you all right?"

"My God, Tom! It's you —" She could hardly speak. "I'm stuck. He's shooting at me." Another sobbing gasp.

"Sally, I'm here, it's okay." Tom shone the feeble light down and was shocked to see Sally's face wedged in the crack not two feet below him.

Another *boom!* from the gun, and Tom heard the zing and rattle of a bullet in the rocks beneath.

"He's shooting into the crack, but he can't see me. Tom, I'm trapped — !"

"I'm going to get you out of here." He shone the light around. The rock was fractured already and it would just be a matter of breaking up and prying out the pieces. He cast around with the light, shining it up and down the tunnel, looking for a tool. In one corner was a pile of rotting crates and ropes.

"I'll be right back."

Another shot.

Tom ran to the pile, threw off a rotten coil of rope, searched through a heap of rotting sacks of burlap. Underneath was a broken piece of miner's hand-steel. He grabbed it, ran back.

"Tom!"

"I'm here. I'm going to get you out."

Another shot. Sally screamed. "I'm hit! He hit me!"

"My God, where — ?"

"In the leg. Oh, my God, get me out."

"Close your eyes."

Tom jammed the steel wedge into the crack, picked up a loose rock and slammed it down on the wedge, slammed it again and again. The fractured rock began to loosen. He dropped to his knees and began scrabbling and pulling out the pieces with his hands. The rock was rotten and now that one piece had been removed the work went a lot quicker. All the while he talked to Sally, telling her over and over that she was okay, that she'd be out of there momentarily.

Another shot.

"Tom!"

"You bitch! You're dead as soon as I reload."

Tom pried a piece of rock out, threw it aside, pried out another and another, cutting his hands on the sharp edges, working furiously. "Sally, where did he hit you — ?"

"My leg. I don't think it's bad. Just keep going!"

Another shot. Tom hammered the rock, slamming the hand-steel in again and again, prying out more rocks and enlarging the hole. He could see her face.

Now the rock was coming out fast.

Crack! Sally jumped.

"For God's sake keep going!"

The tip broke off the wedge and he swore, turning it around and prying with the other side.

"It's big enough!" Sally cried.

Tom reached down, took her hand, and pulled as she pushed from below, scraping up through the broken rock, more buttons popping off her shirt. It wasn't enough; her hips stuck.

"You're dead meat!"

Tom drove the hand-steel into the rock, splitting off a chunk of brittle quartz. With complete indifference he noted he had exposed a vein of gold the miners had somehow missed. He tossed it away, pried out another.

"Now!"

He grabbed her under the arms and pulled her free. Another shot sounded from below.

She lay on the ground, filthy, wet, her clothes torn.

"Where are you hit?" He searched her frantically.

"My leg."

Tom ripped off his own shirt and wiped away the blood, finding a series of shallow cuts on her calf. He picked out some fragments of stone from a ricochet.

"Sally, it's okay. You'll be fine."

"That's what I thought."

"Bitch!" The scream sounded hysterical, unbalanced.

Another pair of shots. A stray bullet ricocheted through the crack and imbedded itself in the ceiling.

"We've got to block this hole," Sally said.

But Tom was already rolling rocks over. They jammed them into the crack, hammering them down. In five minutes it was blocked.

Suddenly his arms were around her, squeezing tightly.

"God, I thought I'd never see you again," said Sally with a sob. "I can't believe it, I can't believe you found me."

He held her again, hardly believing it himself. He could feel her heart beating wildly. "Let's go."

He helped her up and they ran back down through the tunnels, Tom shaking the flashlight from time to time to keep it alive. They climbed up the shaft and in another five minutes had exited the shaft house.

"He'll be coming out the other shaft," said Sally.

Tom nodded. "We'll go around the long way."

Instead of going back over the ridge, they ran into the darkness of the trees at the bottom of the ravine, and there they stopped to catch their breath.

"How's your leg? Okay with walking?"

"Not bad. Is that a gun in your belt?"

"Yeah. A .22 with one round." Tom looked back over the silvered hillside, his arm supporting Sally.

"My truck's at the gate."

"He'll be ahead of us," said Sally.

They set off down the ravine. It was dark in the tall pines, and the carpet of needles under their feet was soft and crackled only slightly, the sounds of their passage covered up by a night breeze sighing through the treetops. Tom paused from time to time to listen and see if the kidnapper was following, but all was silent.

After ten minutes the gulch leveled out into a broad dry wash. Ahead and slightly below shone the lights of the cabin. All seemed quiet, except that the kidnapper's Range Rover was gone.

They skirted the edge of the old town, but it seemed deserted.

"You think he panicked and took off?" Sally asked.

"I doubt it."

They bypassed the cabin and moved swiftly through the trees, paralleling the dirt road. The truck was now less than a quarter mile ahead. Tom heard something and stopped, his heart pounding. It came again — the low calling of an owl. He pressed her hand and they continued on. In a few more minutes he saw the faint outline of the chain-link fence running through the trees.

He gave her a leg up.

She grasped the chain link and he lifted, the fence rattling in the quiet. In a moment she was over. He followed. They ran along the outside of the fence line and in a few moments Tom saw the gleam of moonlight off his stolen truck, still parked where he had left it near the locked gate. Except now the gate was wide open.

"Where the hell is he?" Sally whispered.

Tom squeezed Sally's shoulder and whispered, "Keep to the shadows, head down at all times, and get in the truck as quietly as possible. Then I'll start the engine and drive like hell."

Sally nodded. She crept around to the passenger side, crouching below the level of the cab; Tom eased open the door and climbed in the driver's side. In a minute they were in the cab. Keeping his head below the level of the windows, Tom fished out the keys, inserted them in the ignition. He pressed down the clutch and turned to Sally.

"Hold on tight."

Tom threw the switch and the truck roared to life. He jammed it into reverse and gunned the engine, the truck backing up while he spun the wheel. In that same moment a pair of bright headlights went on from a turnaround at the edge of the woods. There was a sudden *thwang! thwang!* of heavy-caliber rounds hitting steel, and the interior of the truck exploded in a storm of shattered glass and plastic.

"Down!"

Throwing himself sideways on the seat, he rammed it into first and floored it, the truck fishtailing onto the road, spraying a shower of gravel. Jamming it into second, he accelerated as he heard more rounds hitting the car. The wheels were spinning, and the back of the truck slewed back and forth. He raised his head up but could see nothing: the windshield was a spiderweb of shattered glass. He punched his fist through it, ripped out a hole big enough to see out of, and continued accelerating, the back fishtailing as they tore down the dirt road.

"Stay on the floor!"

He made the first turn and the shooting temporarily stopped, but he could now hear the roar of a car engine behind them and knew the shooter was coming after them — and a moment later the Range Rover skidded around the corner, its headlights stabbing past them.

Thwang! Thwang! more shots came from behind, hitting the roof of the cab, showering him with broken bits of plastic from the roof light. The truck was now moving fast and he jerked the wheel sideways and back, making them a weaving target. He felt the rear suddenly fishtailing and vibrating and he knew that at least one of the rear tires had been shot out.

"Gas!" Sally screamed from the floor. "I smell gas!"

The tank had been hit.

Another *thwang!* followed by a dull shuddering *whoosh*. Tom instantly felt the heat, saw the glow from behind.

"We're on fire!" Sally screamed. She had her hand on the door handle. "Jump!"

"No! Not yet!"

He steered the truck around another curve in the road, and the firing ceased for a moment. Up ahead, Tom saw where the road skirted the edge of the cliff. He gunned the engine, accelerating straight for it.

"Sally, I'm taking it off that cliff. When I

406

say *out,* jump. Roll away from the wheels. Then get up and run. Head downhill toward the high mesas. Can you do it?"

"Got it!"

He gunned the engine, the cliff approaching. He grabbed the door handle and half opened the door, keeping the accelerator floored.

"Get ready!"

A beat.

"Now!"

He threw himself out, hitting the ground and rolling, regained his feet running. He could see Sally's dark figure on the far side, scrambling to her feet, just as the flaming truck disappeared over the cliff, the engine screaming like a diving eagle. There was a muffled roar and a sudden orange glow from the bottom of the cliff.

The Ranger Rover slamming on its brakes just in time, skidding to a stop at the cliff edge. The door opened. Tom had a glimpse of a shirtless man leaping out, a handgun in one hand and a flashlight in the other, with a rifle slung over his shoulder. Tom ran toward the steep slope just beyond the cliff, but the man had spotted Sally and was running after her, gun drawn.

"Hey, you son of a bitch!" Tom screamed, angling toward the man, hoping to draw him off, but the man kept on after

Sally, rapidly gaining ground as she limped from her leg wound. Fifty feet, forty . . . any moment he'd be close enough to put a bullet through her.

Tom pulled his .22. "Hey, you bastard!"

The man coolly dropped to one knee and unshipped the rifle. Tom stopped and braced himself in a three-point stance, aiming with the .22. He'd never hit the man, but the shot might distract him. It was worth his last shot — it was Sally's only chance.

The man snugged the gun against his cheek and took aim. Tom fired. Instinctively, the man dropped to the ground.

Tom ran at him, waving the revolver like a madman. "I'll kill you!"

The man rose back up and took aim, this time at Tom.

"I'm coming for you!" Tom cried, still charging.

The man squeezed the trigger — as Tom threw himself to the ground and rolled sideways.

The man looked back toward where Sally had been — but she was gone. He threw the rifle over his shoulder, drew his handgun, and came running after Tom.

Tom scrambled to his feet and ran downhill, sprinting for all he was worth, leaping over boulders and fallen trees, glad that the man was now chasing him. The beam from the man's flashlight roved crazily over his head, flickering through the low branches of the trees. He heard a double *crack! crack!* of a handgun, the sound of a round smacking a tree to his right. He dove forward, rolled, was back on his feet and leaping diagonally down the hillside. The man was about a hundred feet behind.

The light beam stabbed past him. Two more shots whacked trees on either side. Tom leapt, wove, dodged, zigzagged among the trees. The hill was getting steeper and the trees thicker. The man behind was keeping up, even gaining. He had to keep drawing him off, to get him well clear of Sally.

He deliberately slowed, cutting to the left, farther from Sally. More bullets ripped past him, tearing a piece of bark off a tree to his right.

Tom kept running.

24

Weed Maddox saw he was steadily gaining on Broadbent. He'd stopped three times to fire, but each time he was too far away and the pause only let Broadbent regain the ground he had lost. He had to be careful; Broadbent had some kind of small-caliber weapon, no match for his Glock, but still dangerous. He had to take care of him first, and then do the woman.

The hill got steeper, the trees thicker. Broadbent was now running down a sloping draw with a dry watercourse at the bottom. He was fast, damned fast, but Maddox was gaining. His training in the Army, his exercise regimen, his running and yoga, all this was the payoff. Broadbent wasn't going to escape.

He saw Broadbent veer to the left. Maddox cut the corner with a diagonal, gaining even more ground. Another few minutes and the son of a bitch would be lying at his feet, his head open like a purse. Broadbent kept dodging, trying to put trees between him and his pursuer. The hill was plunging downward ever steeper, the draw becoming a ravine. Maddox was now only seventy, eighty feet behind. The game was almost over; Broadbent in spite of all he could do was being funneled between two ridges, like being closed in a vise. Fifty feet and closing.

Broadbent disappeared behind some thick trees. A moment later Maddox rounded the trees and saw an outcrop looming ahead — a cliff — about two-hundred-yards wide, forming a "V" where the dry wash went over. He had Broadbent trapped.

He halted. The man had vanished.

Maddox swept his light from one end to the other. No Broadbent. The crazy bastard had jumped off the cliff. Or he was climbing down. He stopped at the edge, shining his light down, but he could see almost the entire curving face and Broadbent was nowhere to be seen, not on the cliff or at the bottom. He felt a surge of fury. What had happened? Had Broadbent turned and run back uphill? He swept the light up the hill, but the slopes were empty, no movement at all through the trees. He went back to the cliff face, playing his light across it, searched the rocks below for a body.

About fifteen feet from the cliff stood a tall spruce. He heard the crack of a branch and saw the lower branches on the opposite side moving.

The son of a bitch had jumped into the tree.

Maddox whipped his rifle around and knelt, aiming for the disturbance. He squeezed off one shot, a second, a third, firing at the movement and sound, to no effect. Broadbent was climbing down on the far side of the trunk, using it as cover. Maddox considered the gap. Fifteen feet. He would need a major running start to bridge that gap, which would mean climbing back uphill. And even then it was a hell of a risk. Only a man facing a life or death situation would attempt it.

Maddox sprinted along the edge of the cliff looking for a better shooting angle for when Broadbent exited the base of the tree. He knelt, aimed, held his breath, and waited for him to appear.

Broadbent dropped out of the lowest branch just as Maddox fired. For a moment Maddox thought he'd nailed him — but the bastard had anticipated the shot and had rolled as he hit the ground, then was up and running again.

Shit.

Maddox slung the rifle over his shoulder and looked around for the woman, but she was long gone. He stood at the edge of the cliff, beside himself with fury. They had escaped.

But not completely. They were heading

down toward the Chama River, on a course that would force them to cross the high mesa country, thirty brutal miles. Maddox knew how to track, he'd been at war in the desert, and he knew the high mesas. He'd find them.

To allow them to escape would mean going back to prison for the Big Bitch — life without parole. He had to kill them or die trying.

25

Willer put one foot out of the cruiser onto the dirt parking lot of the monastery, then goosed the siren, just to let them know he was there. He didn't know what time monks went to bed but he was pretty sure that at one thirty in the morning they'd be sawing wood. The place was as dark as a tomb, not even a few outdoor lights to brighten things up. A moon had risen above the canyon rim, casting a spooky light around the place.

Another goose of the siren. Let them come to him. After a ninety-minute drive over what had to be the worst road in the state, he was in no mood to be nice.

"Light just went on."

Willer followed Hernandez's gesture. A yellow rectangle suddenly floated in the sea of darkness.

"You really think Broadbent's here? The parking lot's empty."

Willer felt a fresh wave of irritation at the doubt he heard in Hernandez's voice. He plucked a cigarette from his pocket, stuck it between his lips, lit it. "We know

Broadbent was on Highway 84, driving that stolen Dodge. He hasn't gone through any roadblocks and he's not at Ghost Ranch. Where else would he be?"

"There are plenty of forest roads going off both sides of the highway."

"Yeah. But there's only one road into the high mesa country and this is it. If he's not here, we'll just have to sweat that monk instead."

He sucked in, exhaled. A flashlight was now bobbing down the trail. A hooded figure approached, face hidden in shadow. Willer remained standing at the open door of the car, boot hooked on the threshold.

The monk arrived with his hand outstretched. "Brother Henry, abbot of Christ in the Desert."

The man was small with brisk movements, bright eyes, and close-cropped goatee. Willer shook the monk's hand, feeling nonplussed at the friendly, confident welcome.

"Lieutenant Willer, Santa Fe homicide," he said, removing his shield, "and this is Sergeant Hernandez."

"Fine, fine." The monk examined the badge by the light of his flashlight, returned it. "You wouldn't mind turning off your warning lights, Lieutenant? The brothers are sleeping."

"Right. Sure."

Hernandez ducked into the police car, switched them off.

Willer felt awkward and defensive talking to a monk. Maybe he shouldn't have goosed the siren like that. "We're looking for a man by the name of Thomas Broadbent," he said. "Seems he's friendly with one of your monks, Wyman Ford. We have reason to believe he might be here or along this road somewhere."

"I don't know this Mr. Broadbent," said the abbot. "And Brother Wyman's not here."

"Where is he?"

"He left three days ago for a solitary prayer retreat in the desert."

Solitary prayer retreat, my ass, thought Willer. "And when's he getting back?"

"He was supposed to be back yesterday."

"That so?"

Willer looked closely at the man's face. It was about as sincere a face as you could find. He was telling the truth, at least.

"So you don't know this Broadbent? My information is that he was up here a couple of times. Sandy hair, tall, drives a '57 Chevy pickup."

"Oh yes, the man with the fabulous truck. I know who you mean now. He's been here twice, as far as I'm aware. The last time would have been almost a week ago."

"He was up here four days ago, according to my information. The day before this monk of yours, Ford, went into the desert on his 'prayer retreat.'"

"That sounds correct," said the abbot, mildly.

Willer took out his notebook, jotted down a heading, made a note.

"May I ask, Lieutenant, what this is all about?" asked the abbot. "We're not accustomed to getting visited by the police in the middle of the night."

Willer snapped his notebook shut. "I've got a warrant for Broadbent's arrest."

The abbot looked at Willer for a moment, and his gaze proved unexpectedly disconcerting. "An arrest warrant?"

"What I said."

"On what charge, if I may ask?"

"With all due respect, Father, I can't go into that right now."

A silence.

"Is there some place we can talk?" asked Willer.

"Yes, of course. Normally we're under a vow of silence in the monastery, but we can speak in the Disputation Chamber. If you'll follow me?"

"Lead on," said Willer, glancing at Hernandez.

They followed the monk up the winding path, approaching a small adobe building behind the church. The abbot paused at the door, looking at Willer with a question in his eyes. Willer stared back.

"Excuse me, Lieutenant: your cigarette?"

"Oh, yeah, right." Willer dropped it and ground it under his heel, aware of the monk's disapproving eye, annoyed at feeling he'd already been bested in some way. The monk turned and they followed him inside. The small building consisted of two spare, whitewashed rooms. The larger one contained benches placed up against walls, with a crucifix at the far end. The other room contained nothing but a crude wooden desk, a lamp, a laptop, and printer.

The monk turned on a light and they sat on the hard benches. Willer shifted his ass, trying to get comfortable, taking out his notebook and pen. He was getting more annoyed by the minute, thinking of the absence of Ford and Broadbent and the time they'd wasted driving up there. Why the hell couldn't the monks have a damn phone?

"Abbot, I have to tell you, I have reason to believe this Wyman Ford might be involved."

The abbot had removed his hood and now his eyebrows arched in surprise. "Involved in what?"

"We aren't sure yet — something connected to the murder up in the Maze last week. Something possibly of an illegal nature."

"I find it utterly impossible to believe that Brother Wyman would be involved in anything illegal, let alone murder. He is a man of sterling character."

"Has Ford been out in the mesas a lot lately?"

"No more than usual."

"But he spends a lot of time out there?"

"He always has, ever since he came here, three years ago."

"You aware he was CIA?"

"Lieutenant, I am 'aware' of a lot of things, but that's as far as my knowledge goes. We do not inquire into the past lives of our brothers, beyond what needs to be addressed in the confessional."

"You noticed any differences in Ford's behavior lately, any changes in routine?"

The abbot hesitated. "He was working on the computer quite a lot recently. It seemed to involve numbers. But as I said, I am sure he would never be involved —"

Willer interrupted. "That computer?" He nodded toward the other room.

"It's our only one."

Willer jotted some more notes.

"Brother Ford is a man of God, and I can assure you —"

Willer cut him off with an impatient gesture. "You have any idea where Ford went on this 'spiritual retreat'?"

"No."

"And he's late coming back?"

"I expect he'll be back at any moment. He promised to be here yesterday. He usually keeps his promises."

Willer swore inwardly.

"Is there anything else?"

"Not at the moment."

"Then I'd like to retire. We rise at four."

"Fine."

The monk left.

Willer nodded to Hernandez. "Let's go out for air."

Once outside, he lit up again.

"What do you think?" Hernandez asked.

"The whole thing stinks. I'm going to sweat that monk Ford if it's the last thing I do. 'Spiritual retreat' — give me a break." Willer glanced at his watch. Almost two o'clock. He felt a growing sense of futility and wastage of time. "Go down to the car and call back to Santa Fe for a chopper, and while you're at it, ask for a warrant to seize that laptop back up there."

"A chopper?"

"Yeah. I want it here at first light. We're going in to find those mothers. It's federal land so make sure the SFPD liaises with the BLM and anyone else who might piss and moan about not being in the loop."

"Sure thing, Lieutenant."

Willer watched Hernandez's flashlight bobbing down the trail toward the parking lot. A moment later the police cruiser leapt to life, and he heard the crackle and hiss of the radio. An unintelligible exchange went on for a long time. He had already finished one cigarette and started another by the time Hernandez rejoined him at the door.

Hernandez paused, his plump sides heaving from the walk up the hill.

"Yeah?"

"They just closed the airspace from Espanola to the Colorado border."

"Who's 'they'?"

"The FAA. Nobody knows why, the order came from on high. No commercial aviation, no private, nothing."

"For how long?"

"Open-ended."

"Beautiful. What about the warrant?"

"No dice. They woke up the judge; he's pissed, he's Catholic, and he wants a lot more probable cause before seizing a monastery's computer."

"I'm Catholic too, what the hell's that got to do with it?" Willer furiously sucked the last ounce of smoke from the cigarette, dropped it on the ground, stomped on it with his heel, and ground it back and forth, back and forth, until nothing was left but a shredded tuft of filter. Then he nodded toward the dark mass of canyons and bluffs rising behind the monastery. "Something big's going down in the high mesas. And we don't have the slightest frigging idea what it is."

PART FOUR

DEVIL'S GRAVEYARD

The T. Rex was highly intelligent. She had one of the highest brain-to-body ratios of any reptile, living or dead, and in absolute terms her brain was one of the largest ever to evolve on a terrestrial animal, being almost the size of a human being's. But her cerebrum, the reasoning part, was virtually nonexistent. Her mind was a biological input-output machine that processed instinctual behavior. Its programming was exquisite. She didn't think about what she was doing. She just did it.

She had no long-term memory. Memory was for the weak. There were no predators she had to recognize, no dangers to avoid, nothing that had to be learned. Instinct took care of her needs, which were simple. She needed meat. Lots of it.

To be a creature without memory is to be free. The sand hills where she was born, her mother and siblings, the blazing sunsets of her childhood, the torrential rains that ran the rivers red and sent flash floods careening through the lowlands, the baking droughts that cracked the land —

425

of these she had no memory. She experienced life as it happened, a single stream of sensation and reaction that lost its past like a river losing itself in the ocean.

She watched her fifteen siblings die or be killed and she felt nothing. She knew nothing. She did not notice they were gone, except that once they were dead their carcasses became meat. That was all. After she had parted from her mother, she never recognized her again.

She hunted, she killed, she ate, she slept, and she roamed. She was not aware that she had a "territory" — she moved following swaths of wrecked vegetation and uprooted ferns left by the great herds of duckbills, without recognition or recollection. Their habits were her habits.

Such human emotions of love, hate, compassion, sorrow, regret, or happiness had no equivalent in her brain. She knew only pain and pleasure. She was programmed in such a way that doing what her instinct demanded gave her pleasure, and not doing it was unthinkable.

She did not ponder the meaning of her existence. She was not aware she existed. She just was.

1

The crossed runways at White Sands Missile Range, New Mexico, lay sleeping in the predawn light, two stripes of blacktop on gypsum flats as white as snow. A terminal building stood to one side of the runway, illuminated by yellow sodium lights, next to a row of hangars. The air had an almost crystalline stillness.

A speck appeared against the rising brightness of the eastern sky. It slowly resolved itself into the twin-tailed, swept-wing shape of an F-14 Tomcat, coming in straight for a landing, the rumble of its engines rising to an ear-shattering roar. The fighter touched down, sending up two puffs of rubber smoke, rattling in its wake a row of dead yuccas along the verge of the runway. The F-14 reversed its thrusters, slowed to the end of the runway, turned, and taxied to a stop in front of the terminal building. A pair of ground crew busied themselves about the jet, chocking its wheels and rolling out fueling lines.

The cockpit opened and the thin figure of a man climbed out of the copilot's seat and leapt lightly to the ground. He was dressed in a blue track suit and carried a battered leather briefcase. He strode across the tarmac to the terminal, crisply saluting a pair of soldiers guarding the door, who returned the salute, startled at the sudden formality.

Everything about the man was cold, clean, and symmetrical, like a piece of turned steel. His hair was black and straight and lay across his forehead. His cheekbones were prominent, the two sharp knobs pushing out the smooth skin of his face. His hands were so small and so neat they looked manicured. His lips were thin and gray, the lips of a dead man. He might have been Asian if it weren't for his piercing blue eyes, which seemed to leap from his face, so strongly did they contrast with his black hair and white skin.

J. G. Masago passed through the entryway and entered the cinder-block terminal. He paused in the middle of the room, displeased that no one was there to meet him. Masago had absolutely no time to waste.

The pause allowed him to reflect that, so far, the operation had gone perfectly. He had solved the problem at the museum and sequestered the data. An emergency review and examination of the specimens at the

NSA had produced results exceeding all expectations. This was it: the momentous event that Detachment LS480, the classified agency he headed, had been waiting for ever since the return of the Apollo 17 mission more than thirty years ago. The endgame had begun.

Masago was sorry about what he had done to the Brit in the museum. It was always a tragedy when a human life had to be taken. Soldiers lost their lives in war, civilians in times of peace. Sacrifices had to be made. Others would take care of the laboratory assistant, Crookshank, who was a lower priority now that the data and samples had been fully secured. Another regrettable but necessary discontinuance.

Masago was the child of a Japanese mother and an American father, conceived in the ruins of Hiroshima in the weeks after the bombing. His mother had died several years later, screaming in agony from cancer caused by the Black Rain. His father had, of course, disappeared before he was born. Masago had made his way to America when he was fifteen. Eleven years later, when he was twenty-six, the Apollo 17 landing module touched down at Taurus-Littrow on the edge of the moon's Sea of Serenity. Little did he know then that this Apollo mission had made what was arguably the greatest scientific discovery of all time — and that this secret would eventually be entrusted to him.

By that time, Masago was already a junior officer in the CIA. From there, because of his fluency in Japanese and his brilliance in mathematics, he followed a convoluted and branching career path through various levels of the Defense Intelligence Agency. He succeeded by virtue of ultra-cautious behavior, self-effacing brilliance, and achievement cloaked in diffidence. Eventually he was given the leadership of a small classified detachment known as LS480, and the secret was revealed to him.

The greatest of all secrets.

It was fated, because Masago knew a simple truth that none of his colleagues had the courage to face. He knew that humanity was finished. Mankind had gained the capability of destroying itself, and therefore it would destroy itself. QED. It was as simple and obvious to Masago as two plus two. Was there a time, in all of human history, when humanity had failed to use the weapons at its disposal? The question was not *if,* but *when*. It was the "when" part of the equation that Masago controlled. It was in his power to delay the event. If he performed his duty, he personally might be able to give the human race five years more, maybe ten — perhaps even a generation. This was the noblest of call-ings, but it required moral discipline. If some had to die prematurely, that was a small price. If one death could delay the event by only five minutes . . . what flowers might therefore bloom? We were all doomed anyway.

For ten years he had headed LS480, keeping the lowest possible profile. They were in a holding pattern, a waiting game, an interregnum. He had always known that someday the second shoe would drop.

And now it had.

It had dropped in a most unlikely place and in a most unlikely way. But he had been ready. He had been waiting for this moment for ten years. And he had acted swiftly and with decision.

Masago's sapphire eyes gave the terminal a second sweep, noting the wall of vending machines, the gray polyester carpeting, the rows of plastic chairs bolted to the floor, the counters and offices — cheerless, spare, functional, and typically Army. He had been waiting two minutes; it was close to becoming intolerable. Finally, out of an of-fice stepped a man in rumpled desert cam-ouflage, with two stars on his shoulder and a thatch of iron hair.

Masago waited for the man to reach him before extending his hand. "General Miller?"

The general took the hand in a firm, military squeeze. "And you must be Mr. Masago." He grinned and nodded out toward the Tomcat refueling on the runway. "Navy man once? We don't see many of those around here."

Masago neither smiled nor responded to the question. He asked instead, "Everything is ready as specified, General?"

"Of course."

The general turned and Masago followed him into a spare office at the far end. On the metal desk lay some folders, a badge, and a small device that might have been a classified version of a military satellite phone. The general picked up the badge and phone, and handed them to Masago without a word. He picked up the first folder, which had a number of red stamps on it.

"Here it is."

Masago took a few minutes to scan the folder. It was exactly what he'd requested, the UAV equipped with synthetic aperture radar, multi- and hyper-spectral imagery. He noted with approval the diversion of one SIGINT KH-11 infrared photographic satellite for his mission.

"And the men?"

"A team of ten, previously assigned by the National Command Authority from the Combined Assault Group and DEVGU to a branch of the CIA Operations Directorate. They're ready to roll."

"Were they read in?"

"These men don't need to be read in, they already deal solely in classified ops. They received your Warning Order but it was pretty vague."

"Intentionally so." Masago paused. "There is, shall we say, an unusual psychological component to this mission which has just come to my attention."

"And what might that be?"

"We may be asking these men to kill several American civilians within the borders of the United States."

"What the hell do you mean by that?" the general asked sharply.

"They're bioterrorists, and they've got their hands on something big."

"I see." The general gazed steadily at Masago for a long time. "These men are psychologically prepared for just about anything. But I'd like an explanation —"

"That won't be possible. Suffice to say, it is a matter of the gravest national security."

General Miller swallowed. "When the men are given their patrol order, that should be dealt with up front."

"General, I will deal with these issues in the way I see fit. I am asking you for assurance that these men are capable of handling this unusual assignment. Now your response leads me to believe I might need better men."

"You won't get any better men than these ten. They're the best damn soldiers I've got."

"I will rely on that. And the chopper?"

The general nodded his grizzled head toward the helipad. "Bird's on the tarmac, ready to fly."

"MH 60G Pave Hawk?"

"That's what was requested." The general's voice had grown as cold as ice.

"The chalk leader? Tell me about him."

"Sergeant First Class Anton Hitt, bio in the folder."

Masago flashed an inquiring glance at Miller. *"Sergeant?"*

"You asked for the best, not the highest ranking," responded the general, dryly. He paused. "The mission isn't here in New Mexico, is it? We'd appreciate a heads-up if this op's in our backyard."

"That information falls into the need-to-know category, General." Masago's lips, for the first time, stretched slightly in the semblance of a smile. As they stretched, they whitened.

"My USAF crew needs a briefing —"

"Your aircrew and pilots will be given mission cards and coordinates once in the air. The CAG/DEVGU team will receive the patrol order en route."

The general did not respond, beyond the slight twitch of a muscle in his jawline.

"I want a cargo helo standing by, ready to fly at a moment's notice to pick up a cargo of up to fifteen tons."

"May I ask the range?" the general asked. "We might have a potential fuel problem."

"The bird will fly seventy-two percent fueled." Masago slapped the folder shut, slipped it into his briefcase. "Escort me to the helipad."

He followed the general through the waiting room, out a side door, and across a broad, circular expanse of asphalt, on which sat the sleek black Sikorsky Pave Hawk, rotors whapping. The eastern sky had grown brighter, turning from blue to pale yellow. The planet Venus stood twenty degrees above the horizon, a point of light dying in the brilliance of the approaching sunrise.

Masago strode over, not bothering to shield himself against the backwash of the rotors, his black hair whipped about. He leapt aboard and the sliding door closed. The rotors powered up, the dust rose in sheets, and a moment later the big bird took off, nosed toward the north, and accelerated into the dawn sky.

The general watched the Pave Hawk disappear into the sky, and then he turned back to the terminal with a shake of his head and a muttered curse. "Goddamned civilian bastard."

2

After managing to find each other in the upper canyons, they had hiked all night long, guided by the light of a gibbous moon. Tom Broadbent paused to catch his breath. Sally came up behind him and rested her hand on his shoulder, leaning on him. The badlands stood in silent repose, thousands of small gray hills like heaps of ash. In front of them lay a depression in the sand, with a cracked bed of silt whitened by alkali crystals. The sky had brightened in the east and the sun was about to rise.

Sally gave the silt a kick, sending up a whitish plume that drifted off. "That's the fifth dry waterhole we've passed."

"Seems the rain last week didn't extend out this far."

She eased herself down on a rock and gave Tom a sideways look. "I do believe you've ruined that suit, mister."

"Valentino would weep," said Tom, mustering a smile. "Let's have a look at your cut."

She let him peel off her jeans, and he carefully removed the improvised bandage.

"No sign of infection. Does it hurt?"

"I'm so tired I can't even feel it."

He discarded the bandage and took a clean strip of silk from his pocket, earlier ripped from the lining of his suit. He tied it gently in place, feeling a sudden, almost overwhelming rage against the man who had kidnapped her.

"I'm going up on that ridge to see if that bastard is still following us. You take a rest."

"Gladly."

Tom scrambled up the slope of a nearby hogback, keeping just below the ridgeline. He crawled the last ten feet to the top and peered over the edge. Under other circumstances it would have given Tom a rush to see the magnificent country they had just come through, but this time it only made him weary. In the past five hours they had hiked at least twenty miles, trying to put as much distance as they could between themselves and their pursuer. He didn't believe the man could have tracked them through the night, but he wanted to make damn sure they'd really shaken him.

He settled in for a wait. The landscape behind him looked devoid of human life, but many low areas and canyon bottoms were hidden; it might be a while before the pursuer emerged into the open. Tom lay on his belly scanning the desert, looking

438

for the moving speck of a man, seeing nothing. Five minutes passed, then ten. Tom felt a growing sense of relief. The sun rose, a cauldron of fire, throwing an orange light that nicked the highest peaks and ridges, creeping down their flanks like slow-motion gold. Eventually the light invaded the badlands themselves, and Tom could feel the heat of it on the back of his head. Still he saw no trace of their pursuer. The man was gone. He was probably still up in Daggett Canyon, Tom hoped, staggering around, dying of thirst, the turkey buzzards circling overhead.

With that pleasant thought in mind, Tom descended the ridge. He found Sally with her back against a rock, sleeping. He looked at her for a moment, her long blond hair tangled up, her shirt filthy and torn, her jeans and boots covered with dust. He bent down and gave her a light kiss.

She opened her eyes, like two green jewels suddenly unveiled. Tom felt his throat constrict. He had almost lost her.

"Any sign?" she asked.

Tom shook his head.

"You sure?"

Tom hesitated. "Not totally." He wondered why he had said that, why a doubt lingered in his own mind.

"We've got to keep moving," she said.

She groaned as Tom helped her to her

feet. "I'm as stiff as Norman Bates's mother. I never should have sat down."

They set off hiking down the wash, Tom letting Sally set the pace. The sun climbed in the sky. Tom popped a pebble in his mouth and sucked on it, trying to ignore his growing thirst. They weren't likely to find water until they hit the river, another fifteen miles distant. The night had been cool, but now that the sun was coming up he could already feel the heat.

It was going to be a scorcher.

3

Weed Maddox lay on his belly behind a boulder, looking through the 4x scope of his AR-15, watching Broadbent bend over and kiss his wife. His nose still ached from the kick she'd given him, his cheek was inflamed by her vicious scratch, his legs felt like rubber, and he was getting thirstier by the minute. The sons of bitches had been hiking at an almost superhuman pace, never stopping to rest. He wondered how they managed it. If it hadn't been for the rising of the moon and his flashlight he would surely have lost them. But this was good tracking country, and he had the advantage of knowing where they were headed — to the river. Where else would they go? Every source of water they'd passed had been dry as a bone.

He shifted, his foot having gone to sleep, and watched them set off down the canyon. From where he was he could probably drop Broadbent, but the shot was dicey and the bitch might escape. Now that day had come, he'd be able to cut them off with a quick burst of speed and an oblique approach. He had plenty of country to set up an ambush.

The key here was not to betray his presence. If they believed he was still following, they would be a lot harder to surprise.

With the scope of his rifle he scanned the landscape ahead, being careful to keep the lens out of direct sunlight; nothing would give him away quicker than a flash of light off ground glass. He knew the high mesa country well, both from his own exploration and from having spent hours pouring over the U.S.G.S. maps that Corvus had supplied him. He wished to hell he had one of those maps now. To the southwest he recognized the great ridge known as Navajo Rim, rising eight hundred feet above the surrounding desert. Between here and there, he recalled, lay a broken country called the Echo Badlands, riddled with deep canyons and strange rock formations, cut by the great crack in the earth known as Tyrannosaur Canyon. Perhaps fifteen miles ahead, Weed could just barely see, like a line of haze on the horizon, the termination of the Mesa of the Ancients. Cut into its flanks were a number of canyons, of which Joaquin Canyon was the biggest. That led to the Maze, where he had killed the dinosaur prospector, and from there it was a straight shot to the river.

That was the way they were headed.

It seemed like a century ago when he had capped that prospector — it was hard to believe it had only been, what, eight days? A lot had gotten screwed up since then.

He had the journal and was close to unscrewing up the rest of it. They'd be heading for the one trail across Navajo Rim, which meant they'd be hiking southwest through the badlands, crossing near the head of Tyrannosaur Canyon. That formed a kind of natural choke point where several tributary canyons came together, and they'd have to pass through it.

He could make a loop southward, skirt the base of Navajo Rim, and come back up north to ambush them at the head of that valley. He would have to move fast, but in less than an hour it would be all over.

He crept down from his vantage point, making sure he wasn't seen, and set off at a fast pace southward through the badlands toward the sandstone wall of Navajo Rim.

This time tomorrow he'd be boarding that early flight to New York.

4

As Melodie Crookshank walked east on Seventy-ninth Street, the museum loomed up before her, its upper-story windows flashing in the early morning light. Sleep had been impossible and she had spent most of the night walking up and down a busy stretch of Broadway, unable to keep her mind from racing. She had stopped for a burger at an all-night eatery somewhere near Times Square, and again for tea in a diner near Lincoln Center. It had been a long night.

She turned into the service drive that led down to the employee entrance, and checked her watch. Quarter to eight. She had pulled plenty of all-nighters writing her dissertation, and she was used to it, but this time it seemed different. Her mind was unusually crisp and clear — more than lucid. She rang the buzzer at the night entrance and slotted her museum pass through the card-reader.

She walked through the central rotunda and passed through a succession of grand exhibition halls. It always thrilled her to walk through the empty museum in the early morning, before anyone had arrived, the cases dark and silent, the only sound the echoing of her heels on the marble floors.

She took her usual shortcut through the Education Department, swiped her card to call the elevator, waited while it rumbled its way to her, and used the key a second time to direct it to the basement.

The doors slid open and she stepped into a basement corridor. It was cool and silent in the bowels of the museum, as unchanging as a cave, and it always gave her the creeps. The air was dead and always seemed to carry a faint odor of old meat.

She quickened her step toward the Mineralogy lab, passing door after door of fossil storage: Triassic Dinosaurs, Jurassic Dinosaurs, Cretaceous, Oligocene Mammals, Eocene Mammals — it was like a walk through evolution. Another turn and she was in the laboratory hall, gleaming stainless-steel doors leading to various laboratories — mammalogy, herpetology, entomology. She reached the door marked Mineralogy, inserted her key, pushed open the door, and felt inside the wall for the light switch. The fluorescent lights stuttered on.

She stopped. Through the shelves of specimens she could see Corvus was already in — asleep over the stereozoom, his attaché case at his side. What was he doing here? But the answer came as soon as she had asked the question: he had come early to check on her work himself — on a Sunday morning, no less.

She took a tentative step inside, cleared her throat. He did not stir.

"Dr. Corvus?" She stepped forward more confidently. The curator had fallen asleep on the desk, head laid on his crooked arm. She tiptoed closer. He had been looking at a specimen under the stereozoom — a trilobite.

"Dr. Corvus?" She walked over to the table. Still no response. At this, Melodie felt a faint alarm. Could he have had a heart attack? Unlikely: he was way too young. "Dr. Corvus?" she repeated, not managing to get her voice above a whisper. She moved around to the other side of the table and leaned over to look into his face. She jerked back with an involuntary gasp, her hand over her mouth.

The curator's eyes were wide open, staring, and filmed over.

Corvus *had* had a heart attack. She stumbled back another step. She knew she should reach out and see if there was still a pulse in his wrist, do something, give mouth-to-mouth — but the idea of touching him was repellent. Those eyes

. . . there was no question he was dead. She took a second step back, reached out, picked up the museum phone — then paused.

Something wasn't right. She stared at the dead curator, slumped over the microscope, head on his crooked arm as if he had laid it down in weariness and gone to sleep. She could feel the wrongness of the scene crawling up her spine. And then it came to her: Corvus was looking at a trilobite.

She picked up the fossil and examined it. An ordinary trilobite from the Cenozoic, of the kind you could buy for a few bucks at any rock shop. The museum had thousands of them. Corvus, who was sitting on the most spectacular paleontological discovery of the century, had chosen that very moment to examine a common trilobite?

No way.

A feeling of dread invaded her gut. She walked over to her specimen locker, spun out her combination on the lock, jerked it open.

The CDs and specimens that she had locked up there at midnight were gone.

She looked around, spied Corvus's attaché case. She slipped it away from his dangling hand, laid it on the table, unlatched it, rifled the contents.

Nothing.

All record of the dinosaur was gone. All

her specimens, her CDs, vanished. Like they had never existed. And then she remembered another small fact: the lights had been off when she entered the lab. If Corvus had fallen asleep over his work, who turned off the lights?

This was no heart attack.

It felt like a piece of dry ice had just formed in her stomach. Whoever had killed Corvus might come after her too. She had to handle this situation very, very carefully.

She picked up the museum phone and dialed security. A lazy voice answered.

"This is Dr. Crookshank calling from the Mineralogy lab. I've just arrived. Dr. Iain Corvus is here in the lab and he's dead."

After a moment, in answer to the inevitable question, she said, with great deliberation: "Heart attack, by the looks of it."

5

Lieutenant Willer stood in the doorway of the Disputation Chamber and watched the sun rise over the buttes above the river. The sound of chanting drifted down from the church behind him, rising and falling in the desert air.

He dropped the butt of his second-to-last cigarette, stomped it out, hawked up a gobbet of phlegm, and shot it to one side. Ford hadn't returned and there'd been no sign of Broadbent. Hernandez was down at the cruiser, making one last call. Santa Fe already had a chopper standing by at the police heliport, flown up from Albuquerque and ready to go — and still the airspace was closed with no word on when it would reopen.

He saw Hernandez duck out of the cruiser, heard the door slam. A few minutes later the deputy came toiling up the trail. He caught Willer's eye, shook his head. "No go."

"Any word on Broadbent or the vehicle?"

"None. Seem to have vanished into thin air."

Willer swore. "We're doing nothing here. Let's start searching the Forest Service roads off 84."

"Yeah."

Willer took a last glance up at the church. What a waste of time. When Ford got back, he'd haul that so-called monk downtown by the short hairs and find out just what the hell he'd been doing out there in the high mesas. And when Broadbent surfaced, well, he'd get a kick out of seeing how that millionaire vet liked sharing a basement cell with a crackhead and eating corn dogs for dinner.

Willer headed down the trail, his nightstick and cuffs jangling, Hernandez following. They'd grab some breakfast burritos and a couple of gallons of coffee at Bode's. And a fresh carton of Marlboros. He hated the feeling of being down to his last smoke.

He seized the door handle of the cruiser and was about to jerk it open when he became aware of a distant throbbing in the air. He looked up and saw a black dot materialize in the dawn sky.

"Hey," said Hernandez, squinting, "isn't that a chopper?"

"It sure as hell is."

"Not five minutes ago they told me it was still on the tarmac."

"Idiots."

Willer slid out his last butt and lit it up — Freddie the pilot always carried a couple of packs.

"Now we can get this show on the road."

He watched the helicopter approach, his feeling of frustration evaporating. They'd crash the canyonlands party of those bastards. There was a lot of country out there, but Willer felt pretty sure the action was up in the Maze, and that's where he'd direct the chopper first.

The black speck was beginning to resolve into something larger, and Willer stared with growing puzzlement. This was no police chopper, at least none that he'd ever seen. It was black and a lot bigger, with two pods hanging off either side like pontoons. With a sickening lurch it suddenly occurred to Willer what this was really about. The closing of the airspace, the black helicopter. He turned to Hernandez.

"You thinking what I'm thinking?"

"FBI."

"Exactly."

Willer swore softly. It was just like the feds to say nothing, let local law enforcement stumble along like blind idiots and then arrive just in time for the bust and the press conference.

The chopper banked slightly as it approached, slowed, and hovered for a landing in the parking lot. It leaned back as it settled down, the backwash from its rotors lashing up a blast of stinging dust. With the rotors still whapping, the side slid open, and a man in desert fatigues, holding an M4 carbine and sporting a backpack, hopped out.

"What the hell is this?" Willer said.

Nine more soldiers hopped down, several loaded with packs of electronic and communications gear. Last to jump was a tall man, thin, with black hair and a bony face, wearing a tracksuit. Eight of the men disappeared up the trail toward the church, jogging single file, while the other two stayed with the man in the tracksuit.

Willer sucked on the last of his butt, chucked it on the ground, exhaled, and waited. These weren't even feds — or at least any feds he knew.

The man in the tracksuit strode over, stopped in front of him. "May I ask you to identify yourself, Officer?" he said in the neutral voice of authority.

Willer let a beat pass. "Lieutenant Willer, Santa Fe Police. And this is Sergeant Hernandez." He didn't move.

"May I ask you to please step away from the cruiser?"

Again Willer waited. Then he said, "If you've got a shield, mister, now's the time to show it."

The man's eyes flickered, barely, toward

one of the soldiers. The soldier moved forward — a brawny kid in a crew cut, face painted, all puffed up with a sense of duty. Willer had seen the type before in the Army and he didn't like it.

"Sir, please step away from the vehicle," the soldier said.

"Who the hell are you to tell me that?" He wasn't going to stand for this shit, at least not until he saw some gold. "I'm a detective lieutenant homicide in the Santa Fe Police Department and I'm here on official business, with a warrant, pursuing a fugitive. Who the hell gave you jurisdiction here?"

The man in the tracksuit spoke calmly. "I am Mr. Masago with the National Security Agency of the Government of the United States of America. This area has been declared a special operations zone, closed under a state of military emergency. These men are part of a combined Delta Force commando team here on a mission involving national security. Now, final warning: step away from the vehicle."

"Until I see —"

The next thing Willer knew, he was on the ground, doubled up, desperately trying to suck some air into his lungs, while the soldier deftly relieved him of his service weapon. Finally, with a great gasp, he got some air in, drinking it greedily. He rolled over, managed to get up on his hands and knees, coughed and spat, trying to keep from puking, the muscles in his stomach jumping and cramping like he'd swallowed a jackrabbit. He rode it out, got to his feet, and straightened himself up.

Hernandez was still standing there, dumbfounded. They'd pulled his weapon too.

Willer watched in disbelief as one of the soldiers went into his cruiser — *his cruiser* — with a screwdriver. He emerged a moment later with the radio in one hand, wires dangling. In the other he had the cruiser's keys.

"Surrender your portable radio, Officer," said the man in the tracksuit.

Willer sucked in another lungful of air, unsnapped the keeper, handed over the radio.

"Surrender your nightstick, cuffs, pepper spray, and all other weapons and communication devices. As well as any other keys to the vehicle."

Willer obeyed. He could see Hernandez being put through the same drill.

"Now we will walk up to the church. You and Officer Hernandez will go first."

Willer and Hernandez walked up the trail toward the church. As they passed the Disputation Chamber, Willer noticed the monastery's laptop lying in the dirt outside

454

the door, smashed to pieces; lying near it was a broken satellite dish, trailing wires. Willer got a glimpse of soldiers busy inside, setting up racks of electronics. One was on the roof erecting a much larger dish.

They went into the church. The singing had stopped and all was silent. The monks were huddled at one end in a group, guarded by two of the commandos. One of the soldiers gestured for Willer and Hernandez to join them.

The man in the tracksuit stepped forward in front of the silent group of monks. "I am Mr. Masago from the National Security Agency of the Government of the United States of America. We are conducting a special operation in this area. For your own safety, you will be required to remain here, in this room, with no communication to the outside world, until it is over. Two soldiers will remain here to serve your needs. The operation will take between twelve and twenty-four hours. All the facilities you need are here: bathroom, water, a small kitchenette with food in the refrigerator. I apologize for the inconvenience."

He nodded at Willer, pointed to a side room. Willer followed him in. The man shut the door and turned, speaking quietly, "And now, Lieutenant Detective, I'd like to hear all about why you're here and who this fugitive is."

6

The sun had risen hours ago and the hidden valley had turned into a dead zone, an inferno of boulders reradiating the pounding heat of the sun. Ford hiked along the dry wash at the bottom, musing that Devil's Graveyard seemed an even more appropriate name during the day than it did the previous twilight.

Ford sat down on a rock, unshouldered his canteen, and took a small sip. It was only with considerable effort that he stopped himself from drinking more. He screwed the top back on and hefted the canteen, estimating that about a liter remained. On a flat rock at his feet he carefully spread out his map, which was already beginning to come apart at the folds, and took out a pencil stub. He gave the tip a quick touch-up with his penknife and marked off another quadrangle futilely searched.

His feelings of being close to discovering the fossil had started to fade in the harsh reality of the landscape he had been tramping around in since dawn. Three big canyons and many smaller ones came together in an absolute chaos of stone — a dead land gutted by erosion, ripped by flash floods, scarred by avalanches. It was as if God had used it as a dumping ground of Creation, a trash heap of all the leftover sand and stone he couldn't find a use for elsewhere.

On top of that, Ford had seen no sign of any fossils at all — not even bits and pieces of petrified wood, so common elsewhere in the high mesas. It was a lifeless landscape in every sense of the word.

He shook the canteen again, thought what the hell, took another sip, checked his watch. Ten-thirty. He had searched about half the valley. He still had the other half left to explore, along with any number of side canyons and dead-end ravines — at least another day's work. But he wouldn't be able to finish unless he found water; and it was pretty clear there was no water in this infernal place. If he didn't want to die of thirst, he would have to set off for the river absolutely no later than dawn the next day.

He folded up his map, slung the canteen over his shoulder, and took a quick bearing with his compass, using as a landmark a sandstone needle that had split off from the canyon face and was leaning at a precarious angle. He trudged across the sandy flat, crossing yet another dry watering hole, his sandals kicking up white alkali dust. He got back into the rhythm of his stride and quickened his pace, passing the needle and turning up a fingerlike wash behind it. He had eaten very little that morning — a few tablespoons of rolled oats boiled in a tin cup — and his stomach had that hollow feeling, by now familiar to him, of a hunger beyond mere hungriness. His legs ached, his feet were blistered, his eyes were red from the dust. On a certain level, Ford welcomed these mortifications of the flesh, the denial of bodily comfort. Penitence itself was comforting. On the other hand, there was a point where discomfort, pushed too far, became itself an indulgence. Right now, he was well into the danger zone, a place where there was no room for accident or error. A broken leg, even a sprained ankle, would be a death sentence: with so little water he would die before any rescue effort could find him. But this was nothing new; he had taken far worse risks in his life.

He hiked on, filled with conflicted feelings. The wash turned in a tight curve against a wall of sandstone, forming an undercut some fifteen feet high, creating a half-moon of shade. Ford rested for a moment. A single juniper tree stood nearby, stock-still as if stunned by the heat. He took a couple of deep breaths, fighting the impulse to drink again. Up the canyon he could see where part of the cliff face had collapsed into a gigantic rockslide, a five-hundred-foot pile of car-sized boulders.

In that pile of boulder's he saw something. The smooth face of one of the boulders was turned at just the right angle to receive the raking light of the sun. And there, outlined with perfect clarity, was an exquisite set of dinosaur footprints — a large, three-toed dinosaur with massive claws, which had evidently crossed what had once been an ancient mud flat. Ford slung his canteen back over his shoulder and walked to the base of the slide, feeling an electric surge of energy, all his weariness evaporating. He was on the right trail, literally and figuratively. The T. Rex was here, somewhere in this maze of rocks — and God only knew, these might be its very footprints.

That was when Ford heard the noise, just audible against the vast silence of the desert around him. He paused, looking up, but only part of the sky was visible among the towering rocks. It grew louder and Ford concluded it was the faint buzz of a small plane. The sound faded away before he could pinpoint it in the blue sky above. He shrugged and climbed up the heap of fallen rocks to examine the footprints more closely. The rock had cleaved along the bedding plane, exposing a ripple-marked surface of mudstone, almost black in color, compared to the brick-red of the layers above and below. He followed it with his eye and traced its continuation as a dark stripe running through the surrounding formations, about four inches in thickness. If these were T. Rex footprints — and they certainly looked like them — that dark layer was like a marker — indicating the layer around which the T. Rex would probably be found.

He climbed down and continued working his way up the small canyon, but after a few more turns it boxed up into cliffs and he was forced to turn back. At that point he heard the sound of the small plane again, louder this time. He looked up, squinting against the glare of the hot sky, and saw a flash of sunlight off a small aircraft passing almost directly overhead. He shaded his eyes, but it disappeared in the harsh glare. He pulled out his binoculars and searched the sky, finally locating it.

Ford stared in surprise. It was a small, windowless white aircraft, about twenty five feet long, with a bulbous nose and a rear-mounted engine. He recognized it immediately as an MQ-1A Predator Unmanned Aerial Vehicle.

He tracked it with his binoculars, wondering what the heck the CIA or the Pentagon would be doing flying a highly classified piece of aviation over what was essentially public land. This Predator, Ford knew, was the operational version of something that had only been in the planning stages when Ford was with the CIA; it was a drone using ICCG technology, an Independent Computer-Controlled Guidance system, which allowed the aircraft to operate independently when temporarily out of contact with its remote human pilot. This greatly diminished the personnel requirement necessary to fly the drone, allowing it to be operated by a three-man ground team with a portable ground station instead of the usual thirty-foot trailer and team of twenty. Ford noted that this Predator carried a pair of Hellfire C laser-guided missiles.

He watched it pass by, flying west. Then, perhaps five kilometers from his position, it banked in a lazy turn and came back around toward him. It was losing altitude and gaining speed — fast. What in the world was it doing? He continued watching it through the binoculars, spellbound. It appeared to be engaged in a simulated attack.

There was a faint puff and the Predator seemed to take a small leap upward — it had just launched one of its missiles. This was unbelievable: who or what could possibly be the target? A split second later, with a profound shock, Ford realized who the target was:

Himself.

7

Maddox climbed over the last ridge and paused to survey the canyon below. Here, two canyons joined to become one larger canyon, creating a rock amphitheater with a smooth floor of yellow sand. He was breathing hard, having hiked like a bat out of hell to reach this junction, and he was beginning to feel light-headed — whether from the heat or thirst he couldn't say. He mopped the sweat from his brow and neck, dabbing carefully at the swollen areas where the bitch had kicked and scratched him. The grazing bullet wound on his thigh throbbed painfully, and the sun was burning the hell out of his bare back. But his biggest worry was water: it had to be a hundred degrees and the sun was now almost directly overhead. Everything shimmered in the heat. The ache of his thirst was growing by the minute.

His eyes traced the deep cleft of the central canyon. This was the canyon the Broadbents would be coming down.

He swallowed, his mouth feeling like it was filled with old paste. He should have thrown a canteen into his car before he took off after them — but it was too late now, and besides, he knew Broadbent and the bitch had to be suffering from thirst at least as much as he was.

Maddox cast his eyes around for a good position from which to kill them. The many boulders that had rolled down from the canyon rims gave him plenty of options. His eye roamed the talus slopes, picking out a spot where a couple of giant stones had jammed up — directly opposite the canyon his quarry would walk out of. It was an ideal place for an ambush, even better than the one from which he'd killed Weathers. But he needed an easy shot: he had two kills to make instead of one and Broadbent was armed. On top of that, he didn't feel too good. He wasn't going to screw around anymore; no more talk, no bullshit, just kill the bastards and get out of this hellhole.

He picked his way down the ridge, slipping and sliding as he went, grabbing on to scrub and sagebrush for balance. At one point a coontail rattlesnake, hiding in the shade of a rock, jerked into an S-coil and buzzed. Maddox gave it a wide berth; it was the fifth one he'd seen that morning. He came to the bottom of the wash, hiked across, and scrambled up the talus slope, all the while being careful not to leave tracks. He paused at the cluster of boulders and looked around for more rattlers, seeing none. It was in the direct sun and hotter than hell, although it provided an ideal view of the opposite side. He unslung his .223 AR-15 and sat down Indian style, the gun laid across his knees. He gave the weapon a quick check, and then, satisfied with its operability, moved into shooting position. Two boulders leaned together, forming a V, which made a perfect firing notch. He rested the barrel in it, crouched, and sighted through the 4x scope, panning the rifle back and forth. A better field of fire could not be asked for: he was looking straight down on the canyon they would exit from, two sheer walls of sandstone with nothing but a flat bed of sand in between. There was no cover, no bushes, no place to run except back up the canyon. The scope's built-in digital range finder told him his targets would be 415 yards away when they came around the last bend; he would let them come on for at least another two hundred yards before firing. It would be clean shooting without a breath of wind.

Despite his aches and pains, Maddox smiled as he previsualized the kill, the rounds knocking the bastards back, their blood spraying on the sand behind them. The air smelled of dust and heated rocks, and he felt a momentary dizziness. Jesus Christ. He closed his eyes and repeated his mantra, trying to bring some clarity and focus into his mind, but he was too thirsty to concentrate. He opened his eyes, looked down the canyon again. They would be at least another ten minutes. He reached in his pocket and removed the notebook; greasy, dog-eared, no more than six inches by four. He was amazed at how insignificant it looked. He flipped through the pages. It was numbers, some kind of code — and there, on the last page, two big exclamation points. Whatever it meant, it wasn't his concern; Corvus would know what to do with it. He shoved it back into his pocket, shifted position, and wiped his sweating neck with his handkerchief. Despite his exhaustion, he could feel the buildup of adrenaline, the clean edge of awareness that came before a kill. The colors seemed brighter, the air clearer, sounds most distinct. This was good. This would see him through the next ten minutes.

He gave his rifle a final check, more as a way of keeping himself occupied. The weapon had lightened him by almost two bills but he'd gotten good use out of it. He stroked the barrel and pulled his hand back: it was burning hot. Christ Almighty.

He reminded himself that he wasn't

doing this job for money, like some hired hit man. He was doing it for higher motives. Corvus had sprung him from prison; and he had the power to put him back in. That created a true sense of duty in Maddox.

But the highest motive of all was his own survival. If he didn't kill both of them, no one, not even Corvus, could save him.

8

With every step Tom could feel the intense heat of the sand coming through the soles of his Italian leather shoes. His blisters had long since broken and the raw spots rubbed with each step. But as his thirst grew, the pain seemed to lessen. They'd passed several *tinajas,* potholes in the rock that normally held water. All had been dry.

He paused in a sliver of shade against an overhanging rock. "Take five?"

"God yes."

They sat down, trying to maneuver as much into the shade as possible. Tom took Sally's hand. "How are you doing?"

She shook her head, shivering her long blond hair. "I'm okay, Tom. And you?"

"Surviving."

She fingered the silk pants of his "Mr. Kim" suit and smiled wanly. "Did it work?"

"I should never have left you alone."

"Tom, stop blaming yourself."

"Do you have any idea of who that man is who kidnapped you?"

"He bragged to me all about it. He's a

hired gun, working for a curator at a museum back east. He may not be educated, but he sure isn't stupid." She leaned back, her eyes closed.

"So he killed Weathers to get the notebook and then came after you. Christ, I never should have gone to Tucson, I'm sorry —"

Sally laid a hand on his shoulder. "Let's save the apologies for when we're out of here." She paused and asked, "You think we really lost him?"

Tom didn't answer.

"You're still worrying about him, aren't you?"

He nodded, gazing down the canyon. "I don't like the way he just disappeared. It's just like what happened back at the ghost town."

"It's what you said. He got lost following us."

"He knows if he doesn't kill us, he's finished. That's a pretty good incentive."

Sally nodded slowly. "He's not the type to give up." She laid her head back against the rock and closed her eyes.

"I'm going higher for another look back."

Tom scrambled up a scree slope to a bench. But there was nothing behind them, just an empty wilderness of stone. They were still at least twenty miles from the

469

river, but he had only a vague notion of where they actually were. He cursed under his breath, wishing he had a map; he had never been this deep into the high mesa country before and he had no idea of what lay between them and the river.

He climbed back down and stood over Sally for a moment, looking at her, before touching her. She opened her eyes.

"We'd better keep going."

She groaned while he helped her to her feet. They were just about to set off when a deep rumble, not unlike thunder, rolled across the badlands, echoing strangely through the canyons.

Tom looked up. "Funny. There's not a cloud in the sky."

9

Ford lay huddled in the lee of the cliff, facedown, arms wrapped around his head, as the deafening roar of the missile strike rolled away like a hundred thunderbolts reverberating down the canyons. A rain of sand and gravel continued as the echoes died away. He waited until all was silent, and then raised his head.

He was inside a dull orange cloud. He coughed, covered his mouth with the hem of his robe, and tried to breathe, still half-stunned from the blast wave. The roar had been so powerful that it almost seemed as if the sound itself could have killed him. And yet here he was, alive and unhurt. He could hardly believe it.

He stood up, steadying himself against the canyon wall, his head pounding and his ears ringing. He had taken refuge in the scooped-out undercut in the canyon wall, a lucky decision. Great shattered chunks of stone littered the ground all around him, but the overhang had protected him well. Slowly the dust began settling and the orange fog turned into a haze. He noticed a peculiar smell, a choking mixture of pulverized rock and cordite. The dust, trapped between the walls of the canyon, drifted slowly, taking a long time to dissipate.

The dust . . . The dust was now his protection. It would hide him from the penetrating eyes of the video cameras onboard the Predator drone, which was no doubt still circling overhead doing damage assessment.

He retreated back under the overhang as the dust finally drifted off, pushed away by an imperceptible movement of air. He crouched, remaining motionless, so thickly coated with dust himself that he figured he probably looked like just another rock. He could still hear the drone making a whispery buzz from somewhere in the sky. Ten minutes passed before the sound faded away.

Ford staggered to his feet, coughing up mud and spitting it out, slapping the dust off his robes, shaking it out of his hair, and wiping his face. He was only now beginning to grasp the inexplicability of what had just happened: a Predator drone had deliberately fired a missile at him. Why?

It had to be a mistake, a test gone awry. But even as the thought came into his mind, he discounted it. For one thing, he knew that a classified drone would never be tested over public land, especially not in

New Mexico, which already had White Sands Missile Range, the nation's largest proving ground. Nor could the Predator have somehow escaped from WSMR and ended up there — it didn't have the range. The turn, dive, and fire maneuver the drone had executed was beyond ICCG capability: a remote human pilot had been behind that maneuver — a pilot who could see who he was and what he was doing.

Could they be hunting someone else? Was it a case of mistaken identity? Ford supposed it was possible, but that would be a gross violation of the first rule of engagement: secure visual identification of the target. How could he, in his monk's robes and sandals, be taken for someone else? Was the CIA after him specifically for something he knew or had done? But it was inconceivable the CIA would murder one of its own — it was illegal, of course, but more to the point it was utterly contrary to CIA culture. Even if they did want to kill him, they wouldn't send a forty-million-dollar classified drone after him when it would be much simpler to assassinate him in his own bed in his cell in the unlocked monastery, and dress it up to look like the usual heart attack.

Something else was going on here, something truly strange.

Ford slipped off his robe, shook the rest

473

of the dust out of it, and put it back on. He scoured the sky with his binoculars, but the drone had disappeared. He next turned his attention to the butte the missile had struck. He could see the fresh orange scar in the darker sandstone, a gouged-out hole in the rock still dribbling plumes of sand and dust. If he hadn't thrown himself under that undercut in the canyon wall, he would surely have been killed.

Ford began walking down the canyon, his ears still ringing. What had just happened was still inconceivable, but he began to feel that the attack had something to do with the dinosaur fossil. He couldn't exactly say why; it was more a hunch than a deduction. But nothing else made sense. How did that old Sherlockian saw go? *When all else has been discarded, whatever remains, however improbable, must be the truth.*

For some unfathomable reason, Ford mused, a government agency was so desperate to get their hands on that dinosaur fossil and leave no witnesses that they were willing to kill a U.S. citizen to do it. But that raised the additional question: how did they know he was out hunting the dinosaur? Only Tom Broadbent knew that.

During his CIA years, Ford had sometimes had dealings with various classified sub-agencies, special task forces, and "black detachments." The latter were small, highly classified teams of specialists formed for specific investigative or research purposes, disbanded as soon as the particular problem had been solved. In CIA lingo they called them Black Dets. The Black Dets were supposed to be under the control of the NSA, the DIA, or the Pentagon, but in actuality they didn't play by anybody's rules. Everything about the Black Dets was classified: purpose, budgets, personnel, their very existence. Some of the Black Dets were so highly classified that top CIA brass couldn't get clearance to interface with them. He recalled those few he had dealt with: they all had important sounding acronyms, the TEMP-WG (Thermonuclear Electromagnetic Pulse Working Group; ANDD (Allied Nations Disinformation Detachment); and BDGZD (Bioweapons Defense Ground Zero Detachment).

Ford recalled how much he and his colleagues at the CIA despised the Black Dets: rogue agencies, accountable to no one, run by cowboy types who felt the end justified the means — whatever means and whatever end.

This situation fairly reeked of Black Det.

PART FIVE

THE VENUS PARTICLE

The days came when the bull tyrannosaurs fought for her in ritualized combat. While she watched, they circled each other, roaring, and feinting, the forest shaking from their cries. Then they rushed at each other, slamming their heads together, backing off, tearing up trees, churning the very earth in their furious lust. Their roaring shivered her flanks and heated her loins. When the winning bull mounted her, trumpeting in triumph, she submitted, her synapses firing in a sustained and barely successful effort to suppress her impulse to rip her suitor open from neck to naval.

As soon as it was over, the memory of that, too, was gone.

To lay her eggs, she traveled westward to a chain of sandy hills in the shadow of the mountains. She scooped out and tamped down a nest in the sand. After laying, she covered the clutch with wet, rotting vegetation that supplied heat through fermentation, nosing it to check its temperature and replacing it often. She hardly ever left the nest, forgoing even food in her vigilance. She guarded her off-spring with violence and raised them with gentleness. She was bigger than the males of her species, to protect her young from their mindless lust for meat. The sensations she felt as she did these things did not meet the definition of "love." She was a biological machine running a complex program, whose goal was to perpetuate copies of itself by insuring the packages of meat that carried those copies survived their turn to breed. The very sensation of "caring" was for her neurologically impossible.

When her young reached a certain size, they began to hunt in a cohort pack, gradually extending their territory as their requirement for meat grew. That was when she abandoned them and migrated back to her old range, their existence no longer part of her consciousness.

When she was on the move, fear ran through the forest like poison gas. Her fifteen-foot stride was silent. The ground did not shake when she walked; it did not even stir. She walked on her toes, lightly and silently, her coloring blending into the forest.

She knew hunger, she knew satiety. She knew the choking gush of blood in the mouth. She knew light, she knew dark. She knew sleep, she knew waking.

The biological program ran relentlessly on.

1

Melodie watched the last group of guards leave the Mineralogy lab, keys jingling, voices loud in the corridor. She closed the door after them, locked it, and leaned against it, exhaling. It was almost one o'clock. The coroner had come, signed a bunch of papers; the EMTs had carted off the body; a bored cop had made a perfunctory walk-through with a clipboard jotting notes. Everyone assumed it was a heart attack, and Melodie felt sure the postmortem would confirm it.

Only she suspected it was murder. The killer was after the dinosaur, of that Melodie felt certain — why else would he have stolen all of their research, *her* research? She had to work fast.

Melodie wondered if she had done the right thing, keeping her suspicions to herself. She had no proof, no real evidence of murder beyond the fact that Corvus wouldn't give a trilobite the time of day. If she had voiced her suspicions and gotten embroiled in the case, it would only focus the attention of the killer on her. That was the one thing she could not afford to have happen — especially not now, when the stakes were so high. She had, as they said, bigger fish to fry.

She grabbed a heavy metal chair and carried it to the door, propping it underneath the knob, jamming it in place until she was sure no one could get in, not even with a key. If anyone asked why she had blocked the door, she could always say the death had spooked her. The fact was that few curators deigned to descend from their wood-paneled fifth-floor offices to the basement lab, especially on a Sunday.

She would have plenty of time to work undisturbed.

Melodie hastened into the storage area contiguous with the lab. Here, tens of thousands of mineral and fossil specimens were arranged on shelves upon metal shelves rising from floor to ceiling, numbered and categorized. The smaller specimens were in drawers, the larger ones in boxes on open shelves. A railed library ladder on wheels allowed access to the highest shelves.

Her heart beating with anxiety, Melodie pushed the library ladder around on its rails until it was in the row she wanted. She climbed up. On the top shelf, in the dim space just below the ceiling, sat an old wooden crate with Mongolian script stamped on it. A faded label read:

Protoceratops andrewsii egg clutch
Flaming Cliffs
Access No 1923-5693A
W. Grainger, collector

The wooden lid looked nailed shut, but it wasn't. Melodie lifted it, laid it aside, and then pulled up a layer of straw matting.

Nestled among the eggs of a fossil dinosaur nest were the copies of the CD-ROMs Melodie had burned containing all her data and images. Next to it was a tiny plastic case containing three wafer-thin sections of the original specimen, too small to have been missed.

Leaving the CDs in place, Melodie removed the plastic specimen case, replaced the straw matting, refitted the lid, climbed down the ladder, and rolled it back to where it was before.

She carried the case back to the polisher, removed one sliver, and fixed it to a polishing plug. When the epoxy had dried she began to polish it, aiming for a perfect, microthin section, enough to get some really good images out of the transmission electron microscope. It was exacting work, made all the harder by the shaking of her hands. Several times she had to stop, take a few deep breaths, and tell herself that there was no reason for the killer to come back, that he had gotten what he was after, and that he could have no idea that she had made duplicates of her data. When the specimen was ready she carried it into the TEM room to turn on the machine and let it warm up. As she did so, she noticed the logbook open next to it. The last entry, written in a bold, slanting hand, leapt out at her:

Researcher: *I. Corvus*
Locality/Specimen number: *High Mesas/ Chama River Wilderness, N.M. T. Rex.*
Comments: *Third examination of remarkable T. Rex. vertebral fragment. Extraordinary! This will make history. I.C.*

Third examination? She flipped back in the book and found two other entries, both written at the bottom of the page where Corvus had obviously found some blank lines. She had suspected something like this, but not quite so blatantly. The bastard had planned to rip her off, lock, stock, and barrel. And being the nice, eager technician she was, she'd almost let him. She went into the SEM room and flipped through the logbook there, finding a similar number of phony entries. So that's what he had been doing in the lab late that night: stealing her work and doctoring the logbooks.

She found herself breathing hard. Almost from the time she was in first grade she wanted to be a scientist, and as she got older she had cherished the idea that science was the one field of human endeavor where people were altruistic and worked not for themselves but for the advancement of human knowledge. She had always believed science was a field in which merit was awarded where due.

How naive.

There was only one way to insure credit and protect herself from the killer at the same time: finish up her research and beat the murderer into print. If she submitted her results to the online section of the *Journal of Paleontology*, they would be peer-reviewed and published electronically within three days.

Naturally, she would give due credit to Corvus for his contribution, which was minor enough — he supplied her with the specimen. Where the fossil had come from, who it belonged to, how he had gotten his hands on it — these were questions beyond the scope of her work. Sure, there would be controversy. The specimen might be stolen, or even illegal. But none of that was germain to her work: she'd been given a sample to analyze and that was what she had done. Once her research was in print, there'd no longer be any point in killing her.

And then she could write her own ticket.

2

In position behind the large boulder, Maddox shifted his weight, stretched out his foot, and rotated it, trying to get the stiffness out. The sun felt like a hot anvil to his bare back. The sweat was trickling down his scalp, neck, and face, stinging his cuts. The wound in his thigh throbbed viciously — it was now definitely infected.

He blotted his face, blinked the sweat out of his eyes. His tongue felt coated with rust, his lips cracked. Christ he was thirsty. Twenty minutes had passed and the Broadbents hadn't showed. He took a look through the scope, sweeping it up and down the empty canyon. Had they taken a detour he didn't know about, or found water? If that was the case, they might have turned and headed north toward Llaves. If he had lost them —

And suddenly there they were.

Fitting his eye to the scope and resting his finger on the hot curve of the trigger, he forced himself to relax, waiting until they reached the range of two hundred yards. He could see the butt of the gun in

Broadbent's waistband. He wouldn't even have time to pull it out, let alone fire it. And even if he did, it would be useless at two hundred yards.

In another minute, they were in position.

He squeezed the trigger, firing a protracted burst, full-auto, the weapon kicking. He looked up, and saw them both sprinting back up the canyon. Both of them.

What the hell — ?

He'd missed. He returned to the scope, tracked the woman, fired another burst, another — but the bullets were kicking up sand ahead of them, each round high as his quarry ran zigzagging toward the canyon wall. They were going to escape around the lee of the canyon bend.

He rose with a roar of frustration, putting the gun on semi, scrambling down the talus slope. He stopped, knelt, fired again, but it was a stupid shot — they'd already gotten into the lee of the stone wall.

How could he have missed? What was wrong with him? He stretched out his hand, unclosed the fist — and was shocked by how much it was trembling. He was exhausted, thirsty, injured, probably running a fever — but, still, how could he have missed? Then it hit him. Unaccustomed to shooting at such acutely high angles, he had overcompensated for the bullet's drop-off. He should have fired a practice round and then zeroed in.

Instead, he rushed his shots.

Still, he had a chance. The canyon had sheer walls — they were trapped. He could still kill them — if he could run them down.

Slinging his rifle over his shoulder, he charged down the slope and sprinted after them. In a minute he rounded the bend. He could see them three or four hundred yards ahead, running, the man helping her along. Even at that distance he could see she was weak. Both of them were fading fast. No wonder: she hadn't eaten in thirty-six hours and they must be at least as thirsty as he was. On top of that, she was limping.

He ran after them, not fast, but keeping to a sustainable pace. The sand was soft and it made running difficult, but this worked to his advantage. He loped along, conserving his energy, sure he could wear them down in the long haul. At first, in their panic they ran fast, lengthening their lead, but as Maddox kept up his steady pace they began to falter and lag. One, two, three more bends he pursued them. When he rounded the third bend he could see her struggling, the man supporting her. Maddox had narrowed the gap to less than two hundred yards. Still, he didn't push himself, didn't speed up. He knew now he could outlast them: he would get them after all. They disappeared around another corner. When he rounded it, they were even closer. He could hear the man talking to Sally, encouraging her as he helped her along.

He dropped to one knee, aimed, fired a burst on auto. They threw themselves down, and Maddox seized the opportunity to gain significant ground. They scrambled back to their feet but he'd closed to less than a hundred yards.

She fell and he helped her up. Forty yards now. Even with his shaking hands it was a no-brainer. Broadbent tried to encourage her, but she staggered — and then they just gave up. Turned and faced him defiantly.

He aimed, thought better of it, walked closer. Twenty-five yards. Flicked off the auto, knelt, aimed, and fired.

Click!

Nothing. The full-auto bursts had emptied the magazine. With a roar, both of them were sprinting at him full bore. He fumbled for his pistol and got off a shot, but the woman was on top of him like a wildcat, grabbing his pistol with both hands. They fell together, struggling over the pistol, and then he got the gun and rolled on top of her, pressing it to her head, fumbling to get his finger through the trigger guard.

He felt a gun on the back of his own head. He could see it was Broadbent's .22.

"Count of three," said Broadbent.

"I'll pop her! I will!"

"One."

"I swear, I'll blow out her brains! I'll do it!"

"Two."

Knowing he couldn't get off two shots, he whipped around, going for Broadbent first, and fired wildly but practically into his face, and the man went down; he aimed to follow up with another shot, but the bitch dealt him a stunning kick to the groin, so hard that his hand spasmed and the pistol went off, and it felt as if something had jerked his leg hard, followed by a numbness — and a gush of crimson on the sand.

"My leg!" he shrieked, dropping the gun and tearing at his pants, feeling madly for the wound. "My leg!" The blood was jetting out, *his* blood, and so much of it! "I'm bleeding to death!"

The woman stepped back, covering him with his own Glock. He knew immediately from the way she held the weapon she knew how to use it.

"No! Wait! Please!"

She didn't fire.

There was no need. The blood — geysering out of his severed femoral artery — inundated his pant leg.

She shoved the gun in her belt and hastened to kneel over Broadbent, shot on the ground. Maddox watched her, overwhelmed with relief that she hadn't killed him. He felt tears of gratitude running down his cheeks, but then he began to feel dizzy and the canyon walls started to move around. He tried to rise but he was so weak he couldn't even raise his head, sinking back to the sand under an irresistible weakness, almost as if someone were holding him down.

"My leg . . ." he croaked. He wanted to see it but he couldn't, he was too weak, all he could see now was the flat blue sky overhead. A remoteness crept into his head, as if he had become smoke and was rising, expanding, dissipating into nothing.

And then he was nothing.

3

Wyman Ford halted next to a pillar of rock and listened. He had heard the shots quite distinctly, three bursts from an automatic weapon, quite possibly an M16, followed by a two deeper-sounding shots from what was probably a large-caliber handgun. The sounds seemed to have come from the very far end of Devil's Graveyard, perhaps a mile to the northeast, across what looked like some hellacious country.

He waited, listening for more reports, but after those few quick bursts of shooting all was quiet.

Ford moved deeper into the shadows. Something extraordinary was going on. If there was anything his CIA training had taught him, it was that the guy with the better information survived. Forget the weapons, the commando training, the high-tech gear. Engagements were won, first and foremost, with information. And that was precisely what he lacked.

Ford hefted his canteen, sloshed the water around, uncapped it, and took a small sip. He was down to about half a liter and the nearest reliable source was twenty miles away. He had no business doing anything but going straight for water. Still, the shots had been close and it would be a matter of twenty minutes to hike to the head of the valley where they had come from.

He turned back, determined to find out what was going on. He headed across Devil's Graveyard, toward the mouth of a canyon at the northeast side, passing through an area of low sand dunes. He climbed over a series of flat rocks, crossed some ash hills, dropped down to a dry wash, and continued on.

The far end of Devil's Graveyard was even stranger than he had imagined. The canyon walls on either side stepped back as the sandstone alternated with shale and volcanic tuff. Dead-end side canyons branched out, many containing clusters of bald domes of rock and pockets of badlands. It was a complicated and confusing country. Somewhere in this very area was the dinosaur fossil.

He shook his head. What a fool he was, still thinking about finding the dinosaur. He'd be lucky to get out of there alive.

4

Tom opened his eyes to find Sally bent over him, her blond hair spilling over his face, the smell of her hair in his nostrils. She was dabbing his head with a torn piece of cloth.

"Sally? Are you all right?"

"I'm fine. You, on the other hand, got creased by a bullet." She tried to smile but her voice was shaky. "Knocked you out for a moment."

"What about *him?*"

"Dead — I think."

Tom relaxed. "How long was I — ?"

"Just a few seconds. God, Tom, I thought —" She stopped. "A quarter of an inch to the right and . . . never mind. You're damned lucky."

Tom tried to raise himself up and winced, his head throbbing.

Sally eased him back down. "I'm not finished. It's a crease, maybe a concussion, but it didn't crack the bone. It's that hard head of yours." She finished tying a strip of blue silk around his head. "I think Valentino ought to go into the designer

495

bandage business. You look ravishing."

Tom tried to smile, winced.

"Too tight?"

"Not at all."

"By the way, I owe you thanks. You made good use of that unloaded pistol."

He reached out and took her hand.

"Help me sit up. My head seems to be clearing."

She raised him into a sitting position, then helped him to his feet. He staggered but the dizziness cleared quickly. "You sure you're okay?" she asked.

"I'm a lot more worried about you than me."

"I have an idea: you do my worrying, I'll do yours."

Tom steadied himself, trying to ignore his thirst. His eye fell on the man lying in the sand — the scumbag who had kidnapped, then tried to rape and murder his wife. He lay on his back shirtless, arms by his side, almost as if he'd gone to sleep. Both legs stuck straight out, but the jeans covering his right leg sported a large hole and were soaked black with blood. Underneath, a large puddle sank into the sand.

He knelt. The man had a hollow, thin face, unshaven, his black hair streaked with dust. His mouth was relaxed, almost smiling, his head tilted back, exposing an ugly Adam's apple covered with stubble. A trace of spittle had escaped from one corner of his mouth. His eyes were slits — almost closed, but not quite. His torso had the pumped-up look of a con.

Tom felt his neck for a pulse and was shocked to find it.

"Is he dead?" Sally asked.

"No."

"What do we do?"

Tom tried to tear away the soggy pant leg, but the jeans were too tough. He removed a buck knife from the man's belt, slit up the pant leg, and spread the material apart. The leg and groin were a god-awful mess and he had nothing to wipe away the excess blood to see clearly. The bullet had exited behind the knee, tearing off almost the entire back of it. Blood was still feebly pulsing out.

"Looks like the bullet hit the femoral artery."

Sally looked away.

"Help me pull him into the shade against this rock."

They propped him up. Tom cut a shirt-tail off and fashioned it into a loose tourniquet, tightening it just enough to stem the flow of blood. He rummaged around in the man's pockets and, extracted his wallet. He opened it, pulled out an Ohio driver's license with a photo of the man, cocky look in his eyes, arrogant, lopsided smile — a real psychopath.

"Jimson A. Maddox," he read out loud. He searched the wallet, pulling out a thick wad of cash, credit cards, and receipts. A soiled business card stopped him:

Iain Corvus, D. Phil. Oxon. F.R.P.S.
Assistant Curator
Department of Vertebrate Paleontology
American Museum of Natural History
Central Park West at Seventy-ninth Street
New York, NY 10024

He turned it over. On the back, written in a strong hand, was a club address, cell phone numbers, e-mail addresses. He passed it to Sally.

"That's the guy he was working for," she said. "The guy who got him out of prison."

"I find it hard to believe a scientist from a great museum like that would be involved in kidnapping, theft, and murder."

"When the stakes are high enough, some people will do anything."

She handed the card back and Tom stuck it in his pocket along with the driver's license. He went through the rest of the wallet and then quickly searched the other pockets. He found the notebook, pulled it out, held it up.

"Well, well, what do you know," said Sally.

He stuck it in his own pocket. In a small musette bag buckled around the man's waist he found an extra magazine for the handgun. He glanced around, saw the gun lying on the ground where Sally had dropped it. He shoved it in his belt and buckled the musette bag around his own waist.

"You really think you're going to need that sidearm?" Sally asked.

"The guy might have a partner."

"I don't think so."

"You never know."

There was nothing else of interest on the man. Tom felt his pulse again. Thready, but still there. He wished the man were dead: it would make things simpler. It vaguely shocked him how he couldn't muster even the slightest pity for the man.

The man's rifle was lying on the sand a few feet away, and Tom retrieved it, ejected the empty magazine, and flung it away. There was a second magazine in the musette bag, which he emptied, scattering the bullets in the sand and tossing the magazine.

"Let's go," he said.

"And him?"

"The only thing we can do for him is get out of here and find help. If the truth be told, he's a goner." Tom put his arm around her. "You ready?"

Arm in arm, leaning on each other, they set off limping down the wash. For ten minutes they walked in silence, and then Tom halted in surprise.

A robed figure was striding up the wash toward them, hand raised. It was the monk — Wyman Ford.

"Tom!" the figure called, breaking into a jog. "Tom!" He was gesturing frantically, now running toward them. At the same time Tom heard a faint droning noise and saw a small, windowless plane with a bulbous nose come flying over the rim of the canyon, making a slow turn toward them.

5

Melodie stared at the computer screen on which was scrolling the data from the last run of the microprobe. She blinked her eyes twice, rolled them around one way, then the other, trying to get them to focus. Strange how she felt both exhausted and wired at the same time, with a buzz in her head as bad as if she'd just downed a martini. She glanced up at the big clock in the lab. Four o'clock in the afternoon. As she gazed at the clock, the minute hand jerked a single minute forward with a faint *clunk*. She hadn't slept in over fifty hours.

She rapped a key and stored the data. She had done all the obvious research that could be done on the specimen and she'd answered most of the major questions. The only loose end was the Venus particle. She was determined to tie that one up before submitting her paper for online publication. Otherwise some other scientist would tie it up for her — and she was so close.

She selected the last of the prepared wafers, put it on a slide, and examined it in the polarizing scope. At 500x she could just barely see them, tiny black dots clustered here and there inside the cells. She removed the wafer, slipped it into a micromortar, and carefully broke it up, gently grinding it with water to a fine slurry, which she poured into a plastic beaker.

She went to the locked cabinet and removed a bottle of twelve percent hydrofluoric acid. It was unwise of her to handle such a dangerous chemical — one that would actually dissolve glass — after so much stress and lack of sleep, but it was the only acid capable of doing what she wanted done: completely dissolving the replacement mineral of the fossil without attacking the carbon coating of the Venus particles. She wanted to free the particles so she could take a look at them in the round, so to speak.

She brought the bottle over to the fume hood and placed it in the area marked HF USE ONLY. Then she put on splash goggles, nitrile gloves, a rubber apron, and sleeve protectors. She lowered the fume hood to six inches to protect her face, turned it on, and began work, unscrewing the cap and pouring a small amount of HF into the plastic test tube containing the ground fossil, acutely aware that even a small spill on her skin could be fatal. She watched as it foamed and clouded, timing it to the second. When it was done she quickly diluted it fifty to one to stop the acidic reaction, poured off the excess, and diluted it a second and third time to get rid of the acid.

She held up the result to the light, a thin layer of mineral sediment at the bottom of a test tube, in which she knew must be present at least some particles.

With a micropipette she sucked up most of the sediments, dried them, and then, using a separation funnel and a solution of sodium metatungstate, floated off the lighter sediments from the heavier grit. A further rinse, and then she took up a small quantity of particles with a micropipette to let them drift over a gridded slide, the particles settling into the grids. A quick count at 100x revealed about thirty Venus particles, largely intact, cleaned of miscellaneous grit and junk.

She zeroed in on one particularly well-preserved particle and upped the magnification to 750x. The particle leapt into clarity, filling the objective. Melodie examined it with growing puzzlement. It looked even more like the Venus symbol, a spherule of carbon with a long piece sticking out of it, with a crosspiece at the end tipped with what looked like hairs. She opened her lab notebook and sketched a picture of it.

M.C.

When she was done, she sat back and looked at her drawing. She was deeply surprised. The particle did not resemble any kind of inclusion that might have crystallized naturally in the rock. In fact, it looked like nothing she had ever seen before — except, perhaps, the radiolaria she had once spent a couple of days examining and drawing as part of a high school science project. It was definitely of biological origin — she was sure of that at least.

Melodie removed a half-dozen Venus particles from the gridded slide and transferred them to a SEM stage. She placed it in a vacuum prep chamber, getting it ready for the scanning electron microscope. She pressed the button and a faint humming rose from the machine as the chamber was evacuated.

Time to take a look at this sucker in the round, she thought.

6

F. P. Masago stood in the whitewashed computer room of the monastery, now serving as the Ground Control Station for the Predator. His eyes were fixed on a flat panel video screen displaying the DLTV feed from the Predator's main camera. The rough wooden monastery table was covered with an array of advanced electronics, manned by three operators. The central operator was a Combat Controller from the 615th Special Tactics Group Wing Command, wearing a UAV FlightSim helmet. The console he worked displayed the basic controls a normal aircraft would have: yoke, throttle, airspeed indicator, heading, and altimeter, along with an F-16 style joystick.

Masago's eyes flickered away from the screen for a moment to the two CAG/DEVGU support operators. They were working intently, aware of nothing except the electronic world in which they were immersed. One worked the payload console, an array of screens, switches, keyboards, and digital readouts that controlled the surveillance and reconnaissance capabilities of the Predator. This 450-pound package contained electro-optical and infrared cameras, a synthetic aperture radar for flight in bad weather; a two-color DLTV television with a variable zoom and 955mm Spotter, along with a high-resolution Forward Looking Infrared Radar with six fields of view, 19mm to 560mm.

The D-boys were back with the chopper. Their turn would come later.

Masago's eyes moved to the second controller. He worked the UAV's three Multi-Spectral Targeting Systems with laser designation, range finder, electronic support and countermeasures, and a moving target indicator. The UAV had already expended one of its two Hellfire C missiles killing the monk.

Masago's attention drifted back to the video display. Suddenly he stiffened.

"Got something." The toneless voice of one of the operators murmured in Masago's headset.

Masago could see two people, and a third, approaching the other two, a hundred yards away. A quarter mile up the canyon, a figure lay supine.

"Zoom in to 900mm on the southern-most target," said Masago.

The new image jumped on the screen. A man, lying against the canyon wall. A large stain — blood. A dead man. He had known of the monk and these two from his debriefing of the cop, Willer. But this third man, this dead man, was an unknown.

"Back out to 240mm."

Now he could see the three figures again. The one to the north had broken into a run. He could see his white up-turned face for a moment. It was the CIA meddler, the so-called monk. Masago stared in surprise.

"Looks like we missed the girl in the dress," murmured the MTS controller.

Masago leaned intently over the picture, staring at it as if to suck out its essence.

"Give me a closer look at the middle target."

The camera jumped and the figure of a man filled the screen — Broadbent. The man he was looking for, critical to the plan. Broadbent had found the dying dinosaur prospector and he was therefore the one most likely to know the exact location of the fossil. According to Willer, both the wife and the monk were involved, although how it all fitted together wasn't clear. Nor did it need to be. His goal was simple: obtain the locality of the fossil, clear the area of unauthorized personnel, get the fossil, and get out. Let some paper pusher assemble the details for the ex post facto classified report.

"Back me out to 160mm," he said to the payload console operator.

The image on the screen jumped back. The three had joined up and were running for the shelter of the canyon walls.

"Activating MTI," said the controller.

"No," murmured Masago.

The controller cast him a puzzled glance.

"I need these targets alive."

"Yes, sir."

Masago scanned the canyon. It was eight hundred feet deep with stepped-back walls, narrowing at a bottleneck before opening up to the big valley of stone. The few side canyons all boxed up. It was almost a closed area, and it presented them with an opportunity.

"See that point where the canyon narrows? About two o'clock on your screen."

"Yes, sir."

"That's your target."

"Sir?"

"I want you to hit that canyon wall in such a way to bring down enough material to block their route forward. We've got a chance to trap them."

"Yes, sir."

"Heading one-eighty, descend to two thousand," said the pilot.

"Tracking stationary target. Ready to fire."

"Hold until my signal," Masago murmured into his head set. "Wait." He could already see the drone was going to over-shoot. The canyon rim loomed up and suddenly the targets were gone, hidden behind the thousand-foot wall of stone.

"Son of a bitch," the pilot muttered.

"Come around on a one-sixty heading," said Masago. "Get the vehicle *down,* follow the canyon."

"They'll see —"

"That's the point. Buzz them. Panic them."

The scene shifted as the drone banked.

"Back me out to 50mm."

The scene jumped back farther to a wide-angled field of view. Now Masago could see both rims of the canyon. As the Predator came around, the three targets reappeared: three black ants running along the base of the sheer canyon walls, heading for the valley.

"Target good," murmured the operator.

"Not yet," murmured Masago. On his wide angle view he could see a turn in the canyon, then a straight stretch of at least four hundred yards. It was like running wildebeest from a helicopter. He watched the figures, which from that altitude seemed to be moving as slowly and helplessly as insects. There wasn't much they could do sandwiched between eight-hundred-foot cliffs. They cleared the bend, now running in the flat, still hugging the canyon wall, hoping it would provide cover.

"At firing," Masago murmured, "switch me to video feed from the missile."

"Yes, sir. Still locked on T."

"Wait . . ."

A long silence. They were running, faltering, clearly exhausted. The woman fell, helped up by the man and the monk. They were now four hundred yards from the target. Three fifty. Three twenty-five . . .

"Fire."

The screen jumped again as the video feed switched from the Predator to the camera onboard the missile, first a stretch of empty sky, then the ground swinging up, fixing on the left canyon wall, high up. The wall rapidly grew in size as the missile zeroed in with laser tracking. As the missile made contact the feed automatically switched back to the Predator's television camera, and suddenly they were back above, looking down — at a silent cloud of dust billowing upward along with soaring chunks of rock. The figures had dived to the ground. Masago waited. He wanted them badly shaken up — but not dead.

The movement of air in the canyon began to push the dust cloud away. And then the figures reappeared — running back the way they had come.

"Look at those sons of bitches go," muttered the controller.

Masago smiled. "Bring the UAV back to ceiling and keep tracking them. I'm putting the bird up. We've got them now, three rats in a hot tin can."

7

Tom ran just behind Sally, the roar of the explosion still ringing in his ears, dust from the explosion boiling down the canyon toward them. They rested for a moment in the shelter of the canyon wall. Tom paused, leaning on the rock, breathing hard, as Ford joined them.

"What the *hell* is *going* on — ?" Tom gasped.

The monk shook his head.

"What was that firing at us?"

"A drone. It's still up there, watching us. It's out of missiles, however. They only carry two."

"This is surreal."

"I think the drone fired only to block the canyon. They want to trap us."

"Who's *they?*"

"Later, Tom. We've got to get out of here."

Tom squinted up and down the canyon, examining the walls on both sides. His eye was arrested by a broad, sloping crack, at the bottom of which stood a long pile of talus. The sloping crevasse offered plenty of handholds and footholds, where falling rocks had jammed, creating natural climbing chocks.

"There," Tom said. "We can climb that crack." He turned to Sally. "Can you do it?"

"Hell, yeah."

"You, Wyman?"

"No problem."

"There's a good climbing line up the right-hand side to that ledge."

Ford said, "You lead the way."

"You know what's beyond?"

"I've never been this far into the high mesas."

Tom looked down at his four-hundred-dollar handmade Italian shoes, battered beyond recognition but still holding up. At least he had ordered the ones with rubber soles. As he looked back up, the tail end of dust from the explosion came rolling lazily over them, casting a sulfurous-colored pall across the sky.

"Let's go."

He grabbed the first handhold and hoisted himself up. "Watch where I put my hands and feet and use the same holds. Maintain a ten-foot gap. Sally, you come next."

Tom braced his knee against the stone and worked his way up. He tried to ignore the fact that his mouth felt like it was full of grit. The agony for water had gone beyond thirst; it had become physical pain.

It was hard, vertiginous climbing, but there were plenty of handholds. Tom climbed methodically, checking every minute to see how Sally was doing. She was athletic and got the hang of it quickly. Ford climbed fearlessly, like a monkey — a true natural. As they ascended, space yawned below, vast and terrifying. They were free-climbing with no ropes, no pitons, nothing. It was what climbers euphemistically called a "no-fall pitch" — you fall, you die.

Tom focused his eyes on the rock face in front of him. He had moved beyond tiredness into unknown territory beyond. They came to a small ledge, pulled themselves up, and rested. Ford took out his canteen.

"Oh, my God, is that water?" Sally asked.

"Very little. Take two swallows."

Sally grabbed the canteen and with trembling hands drank. She passed it to Tom, who drank. The water was warm and tasted of plastic, but it seemed the most marvelous fluid Tom had ever drunk in his life and it took a supreme act of will to stop. He passed it to Ford, who put it back in his pack without taking any.

"You aren't drinking?"

"I don't need it," he said tersely.

Tom looked up. He could still hear the

faint, mosquitolike buzz of the drone but he couldn't see it. He pressed himself back against the stone, still trying to wrap his mind around the attack. "What the hell is going on?"

"That thing hunting us is a forty-million-dollar Predator Unmanned Aerial Vehicle, classified tail to wingtip."

"Why?"

Ford shook his head. "I'm not sure."

Heat radiated off the canyon wall. Tom examined the rest of the cliff above, picked out a route, and began climbing. The others followed in silence. They were now two hundred feet up, but the pitches were getting easier. In another five minutes they had scaled the sheer part of the cliff. The rest of the climb consisted of an exhausting scramble up steep talus slopes and benches. At the top, Sally stretched herself out on the flat stone, gasping, Tom next to her. He looked up at the empty sky, which was silent, the plane apparently gone.

Ford slipped a tattered map from his pocket and opened it.

"Where are we?" Tom asked.

"Just off the map." He folded it back up.

Tom looked up, examining the landscape ahead. The mesa top was slickrock, a plateau of naked sandstone hollowed and carved by the action of wind and water. Some of the lower areas had filled with wind-blown sand, rippled by the constant wind. Here and there a wind-blasted juniper clung to a crack. The mesa ended a quarter mile away in blue sky. Tom squinted, peering ahead. "I'd like to see what's beyond that rim. We're sitting ducks up here."

"We're sitting ducks everywhere, with that eye in the sky."

"They're still watching us?" Sally asked.

"You can be sure of it. And I have little doubt they're sending a helicopter after us. I'd say we've got ten to twenty minutes."

"This is truly insane. You've really no idea what's going on?"

Ford shook his head. "The only thing I can think of is that dinosaur."

"What interest could they possibly have in a dinosaur? It seems to me a lot more likely that a bomber accidentally lost an H-bomb, or a classified satellite crashed — something like that."

Ford shook his head. "Somehow, I don't think so."

"But even if it was the dinosaur, why come after us?" Tom asked.

"To get information."

"What information? We've no idea where it is."

"They don't necessarily know that. You've got the notebook and I've got the GPR plot. With either of those, they could find it in a few days."

"And when they get what they want from us?"

"They'll kill us."

"You don't really believe that."

"I don't believe it, Tom. I know it. They already tried to kill me."

Ford climbed to his feet, Tom painfully following suit and helping Sally up. The monk set off across the stone plateau at his usual breakneck pace, his brown robes sweeping the ground with each step, heading toward the rim on the far side.

8

The rotors were already spinning up as Masago hopped into the chopper, shielding his face against dust and gravel. He threaded past the seven members of the CAG/DEVGU chalk that made up the operation and took a rear-facing seat near the front. The crew commander handed him a pair of headphones with a mouthpiece, plugged into the ceiling by a black cord. He fitted it over his head and adjusted the mike as the bird lifted off and peeled out, doors still open, just clearing the upper canyon rim and skimming above the buttes and mesas, once in a while passing the gaping crack of a canyon plunging down into the earth. The sun was almost directly overhead and the landscape below looked red-hot.

On the matted floor of the chopper Masago unrolled a U.S.G.S. 1:24,000 topo of the target area. He still preferred paper maps to GPS electronic maps; somehow, paper gave him a feeling for the landscape that the electronic version didn't. The images from the drone, circling invisibly at twenty-five thousand feet, showed the objectives had managed to climb out of the canyon after all and were heading toward a deep, complex valley beyond. It was a hell of a place to look for someone, but on the other hand it had the advantage of being a defined area whose perimeter could be secured.

When Masago had finished marking up the map with a red pencil he passed it to the chalk leader, Sergeant First Class Anton Hitt. Hitt examined the map in silence and began punching the way points marked on the map into his GPS unit. The men had received their final Patrol Order just before liftoff without comment or apparent difficulty, especially when Masago briefed them on the possible need to kill American civilians. Of course, he'd laid it on about how they were bioterrorists in possession of a doomsday microbe. Most people were not equipped to deal with complex truths — better to simplify.

He watched Hitt work. The chalk leader was an African-American man of few words, in superb physical condition, with a high mahogany brow, clear pale brown eyes, and a demeanor of great calmness. He was dressed in desert multi-cam fatigues and combat boots, carrying an M4 chambered for the 6.8SPC, equipped with Aimpoint electronic sights. As a sidearm he had a Ruger .22 Magnum revolver, an eccentric choice for a special forces soldier, but one that Masago approved of. For a fixed blade he carried a Trace Rinaldi, another choice that spoke well for him. Masago had allowed Hitt to make the decisions regarding equipment: and the sergeant had decided his men should go in light and fast, carrying no extra ammo, one-liter canteens only, no grenades or extra magazines, and without the usual Kevlar body armor. No Squad Automatic Weapons either. This wasn't, after all, an op in downtown Mogadishu with heavily armed bad guys spilling out of every doorway.

When Hitt was finished, he passed the paper map back to Masago.

"The four men we're dropping in won't need to maintain radio silence. We're setting up a perimeter around our objectives and drawing it tight. It's a very simple plan. I like simple."

Masago nodded.

"Any final questions?" Masago asked.

Hitt shook his head.

"Sergeant Hitt," Masago asked slowly, "the time is coming when I will ask you to kill several unarmed American citizens. These individuals are too dangerous to entrust to the courts. Will you have a problem with that"

Hitt slowly turned his clear eyes on Masago. "I'm a soldier, sir. I follow orders."

Masago settled back, arms crossed. General Miller had been right after all: Hitt was good.

The chopper thudded on, and then Hitt, checking his GPS, pointed to one of the men. "Halber, ten-minute warning to drop point Tango."

The man, a twenty-year-old with a shaved head, nodded and began running the final checks on his weapon. They flew on, following a long, deep canyon that ran to the valley where their objectives were headed, the shadow of the bird rippling up and down directly below them. It was a hellish, corroded landscape, an open sore on the face of the earth, and Masago was looking forward to getting back to the muggy greenness of Maryland.

"Five-minute warning," Hitt said.

The Pave Hawk began to bank, coming around the side of a stone butte, and flew below the escarpment, easing down into a hover where a side canyon debouched into badlands. Halber rose, steadying himself in the netting. The rope, which was coiled neatly before the open door, was kicked out. Halber grabbed it and roped down, disappearing from view.

A moment later the rope was pulled up and the chopper lifted.

"Sullivan." Hitt pointed to another man. "Drop point Foxtrot, eight minutes."

Once again the chopper sped over red desert. To the north, Masago could see the irregular black outline of an ancient lava flow; and far to the right some forested foothills rose to meet a line of snow-covered peaks. He had the country pretty well scoped out by now.

"Sullivan, one-minute warning."

Sullivan finished his weapon check, rose, grabbed the netting as the chopper eased into a hover, the rope was kicked out again, the man was gone.

Five minutes later they had done their fourth and last drop — and then the helicopter headed off toward the landing zone in the valley at the head of the great cleft marked "Tyrannosaur Canyon" on his map.

9

Ford reached the rim first, and looked down into a valley. With a shock, he recognized they had circled back around and were at the far end of Devil's Graveyard. It amazed him that even with his wilderness experience and knowledge of the desert, the landscape was so complex it had turned him around. He took out his map, checked it, and saw they had just entered the area from the northwest.

He glanced around, expecting at any minute to see a black dot on the horizon and hear the familiar sound of a rotary aircraft approaching.

He had been in plenty of tough situations in his life, but nothing quite like this. What he always had before was *information;* now he was operating blind. He knew only that his own government had tried to kill him.

Ford paused, waiting for Tom and Sally to catch up. They were amazingly resilient, considering that both of them were injured, exhausted, and severely dehydrated. When they hit the wall, it would pretty much stop them wherever they were. It might even come in the form of heat exhaustion, hyperthermia, in which the body lost control of its ability to maintain body temperature. Ford had seen it once in the jungles of Cambodia; his man had suddenly stopped sweating; his temperature had soared to 107 degrees, he went into convulsions so severe they snapped off his teeth — and in five minutes he was dead.

He squinted into the brilliant light. The mountains were fifteen miles away on one side, the river twenty miles on the other. They had less than a pint of water left and it was over a hundred degrees. Even without pursuers, they would be in serious trouble.

Ford looked at the cliff with a growing feeling of dismay.

"Here's a possible way down," said Tom, from the edge.

Ford paused, looking down on a horrendous vertical crack. A faint throbbing sound impinged on the threshold of his hearing. He stopped, scanned the horizon, and saw the speck, two, maybe three miles away. He didn't even need to check with his binocs: he knew what it was.

"Let's go."

10

Melodie Crookshank stared at the three-dimensional SEM image of the venus particle on the video screen with a sense of awe. It was sixty-five million years old, and yet it looked as perfect as if it had been created yesterday. The SEM image was much clearer than any obtainable with a light microscope, and it showed the particle in great detail — a perfect sphere with a tube sticking out of it, with two crosspieces at the end like spars on a ship. The crosspieces had some complicated structures at their end, bunches of tubules that resembled a dandelion seed-head.

An X-ray diffraction analysis confirmed what she'd suspected, that the sphere of carbon was what chemists call a fullerene or a "buckyball" — a hollow shell of double-bonded carbon atoms arranged like a Buckminster Fuller geodesic dome. Buckyballs had only recently been discovered, and they were rarely found in nature. Normally they were very small; this one was gigantic. The primary feature of a buckyball was that it was almost indestructible — anything inside a buckyball was totally sealed in. Only the most powerful enzymes carefully manipulated in a laboratory setting could split open a buckyball.

Which is exactly what Melodie had done.

Inside the sphere she had found an amazing mix of minerals, including an unusual form of plagioclase feldspar, $Na_{0.5}Ca_{0.5}Si_3AlO_8$ doped with titanium, copper, silver, and alkali metal ions — essentially a complex mix of doped ceramics, metallic oxides, and silicates. The tube extending orthogonally from the buckyball appeared to be a giant carbon nanotube with a crosspiece on which are attached side groups containing a mixture of ceramic compounds and metallic oxides.

Very weird.

She cracked a warm Dr Pepper and leaned back, sipping meditatively. After the removal of Corvus's body it had been quiet as a tomb, even for a Sunday. People were staying away. It reminded her once again of how few friends she had in the museum. Nobody had called to check and see how she was, nobody had invited her to lunch or for a drink later to cheer her up. It was partly her fault, holing herself up in the basement lab like a sequestered nun. But a lot of it had to do with her lowly status and the whiff of failure that clung to her, the poor post-grad who had been sending out résumés for five years.

All that was about to change.

She called up some of the earlier images of the particle she had captured on CD-ROM, looking for more evidence to support a theory that had been developing in her mind. She had noticed that the Venus particles seemed to be clustered most heavily in cell nuclei. As she examined some of the images she had taken earlier for Corvus, she noticed something significant: many of the cells in which the particles appeared were elongated. Not only that, but many of the particles seemed to inhabit pairs of cells side by side. The two observations were directly related, and Melodie quickly put them together. She felt a prickling sensation at the base of her neck. It was amazing she hadn't seen it before. The particles were mostly inside cells that were undergoing mitosis. In other words, the Venus particles had infected the dinosaur's cells and were actually *triggering* cell division. Many modern viruses did the same thing; that was how they eventually killed their host — with viral-induced cancer.

Back in 1925, the paleontologist Henry Fairfield Osborn of her own museum had been the first to propose that the mass extinction of the dinosaurs had been caused by a Black Plague-like epidemic sweeping across the continents. Robert Bakker in his book, *The Dinosaur Heresies*, had elaborated on the theory. He theorized that the mass extinction could be explained by outbreaks of foreign microbes "running amok" among the dinosaurs. These "foreign" microbes had come from the joining of Asia and North America. As species intermixed, they spread new germs. Bakker's book had been published almost twenty years ago, and as the asteroid impact theory of the mass extinction had gained acceptance, Bakker's theory was gradually forgotten.

Now, it seemed Bakker had been right after all. In a way.

The dinosaurs *had* been killed off by a plague, Melodie mused — and she was looking at the guilty microbe right now. But the plagues weren't caused by the slow joining of continents. They were triggered by the impact itself. The asteroid strike had caused worldwide forest fires, darkness, starvation, catastrophic loss of habitats. Calculations showed that the earth was as dark as night for months afterward, the air filled with choking soot and dust, the rain so acidic it dissolved rocks. The asteroid impact had created perfect conditions for the massive spread of disease among the survivors — the landscape would have been littered with dead and dying animals, the rest starving, burned, injured, their immune systems in collapse. Under those conditions, a devastating epidemic wouldn't just be possible . . . it would be *inevitable*. The asteroid killed off most of the dinosaurs; and the plagues that followed killed the rest.

There was another twist to her theory — a big twist. Melodie was still undecided if this twist was too crazy to put in her paper, if it was a product of going fifty hours without sleep. The twist was this: the Venus particle did not look like a terrestrial form of life. It looked, well, *alien*.

Maybe, just maybe, the Venus particle had arrived *with* the asteroid.

11

Masago hopped out of the chopper, the whistle of the rotor blades powering down above his head. He cleared the landing area and looked around the badlands. The Predator drone indicated that the targets had descended from the rim of the plateau above them into this unnamed valley. The chopper had landed in the middle of the valley, in the center point toward which the four men in the perimeter would draw.

Hitt came up beside him, followed by the last two men in the chalk, Pfc. Gowicki and Hirsch. The terrain was difficult and complex, but their targets were more or less trapped in the valley, cut off by cliffs. The four men had been dropped at the only four exit points, and they were tightening the noose. Now all that remained was for Hitt and his two men to go in and flush them out. There was no chance — none — that they could escape.

The chalk leader with his two specialists had already offloaded and shouldered their kits and were now working their GPSs, while murmuring on the chalk frequency to the team members who were executing the pincerlike movement.

"Move out," said Masago.

Hitt nodded and on his hand signal the men moved to adopt a triangular formation, acute point trailing. Masago, as planned, stayed one hundred yards in the rear, carrying his usual sidearm, a Beretta 8000 Cougar, in a shoulder holster. Pfc. Gowicki and Sgt. Hitt took point, Hirsch the "drag," and together they moved cautiously up a dry wash toward the area to which the three had fled, according to the drone. Masago scanned the sandy floor for footprints, but could see none. It was only a matter of time.

They moved up the wash until it broadened out and divided. Here they paused while Hitt climbed and reconnoitered. A few minutes later he came down with a short shake of his head. Another gesture, and they continued on toward a row of mushroomlike standing rocks.

Not a word was spoken. They spread out as the wash leveled and advanced toward the curious forest of standing stones, soon entering the shady confines.

"Got a print here," came the murmured voice of Gowicki. "And another."

Masago knelt. The prints were fresh, made by a man in sandals — the monk. He cast about and found the others — the woman's, a smaller size, six to seven, and the man's, size eleven and a half or twelve. They'd been moving fast. They knew they were being hunted.

Hitt led them deeper into the shadowy stones. Masago was virtually certain they would not be ambushed: it would be suicide, trying to take down a patrol of D-boys with a few handguns, if they even had any. They would go to ground . . . and they would be ferreted out. The first stage of the op would soon be over.

They came to where several enormous rocks leaned together, necessitating a crawl through a gap underneath. Hitt waited while Masago caught up. He pointed to some fresh scuff marks in the hard sand. They had come through, and not long ago at all.

Masago nodded.

Hitt went first, dropping to his hands and knees. Masago went last. As he rose, he saw how the area boxed up, with flaming cliffs mounting like staircases on all sides. He took a moment to check his map. Their quarry seemed to have walked into a box canyon, a dead end, from which not even they could climb out.

Masago murmured into his headset: "I need them alive until I get the information I need."

12

"Wait here," Ford said. "I'm going up there to take a look."

Tom and Sally rested while Ford scrabbled up a boulder and reconnoitered. They were in the middle of badlands with hoodoo rocks all around. They had seen the helicopter land less than a mile away in the middle of the valley, and Ford felt sure their trail had been picked up. He also knew, from his CIA training, that they must have dropped men at potential exit points, who would be moving in to cut them off. Their only chance was to find an unexpected route out of the canyon — or a hiding place.

He looked toward the far end of the canyon. A series of ashy, barren hills gave way to yet another cluster of bald rocks, like serried ranks of cowled monks. Several miles beyond loomed a series of vermilion cliffs, like stairs leading to another plateau. If they could slip out that way, they might just make it, but it didn't look promising. He glanced down at Sally and Tom. They were both weakening fast and he didn't think they would be able to continue much longer. They had to find a place to go to ground.

He climbed down.

"See anything?" Tom asked.

Ford shook his head, not wanting to get into it. "Let's keep going."

They continued up the wash and into the forest of standing rocks. An oppressive heat had collected in the enclosed space. They continued along, scrambling over fallen rocks and squeezing between sandstone boulders, sometimes in sun, sometimes in shade, driving as deeply into the mass of standing rocks as they could. Sometimes the rocks were leaning so close together that they had to crawl on their hands and knees to get through.

Just as suddenly, they came out against the face of a cliff, which curved back on both sides, forming a kind of coliseum. At the far end, about fifty feet above the canyon bottom, a long-gone watercourse had hollowed out a cave. Ford could see a faint series of dimples in the rock, depressions where ancient Anasazi Indians had pecked out a hand-and-toe trail up into the cave.

"Let's check that out," Ford said.

They walked to the base of the cliff, and Tom examined the ancient hand-and-toe trail. He glanced up.

"They'll find us in there, Wyman," Tom said.

"There's no other option. The cave may go somewhere. And it's *possible* they may miss us, if we erase our footprints down here."

Tom turned to Sally. "What do you think?"

"I'm beyond thinking."

"Let's do it."

After erasing their prints as best they could, they climbed the hand-and-toe trail. It was not a difficult climb and in a few minutes they were in the cave. Ford paused, breathing hard. He himself was getting toward the end of his own endurance, and he wondered how Sally and Tom could even walk. They both looked like hell. For better or worse, this cave was the end of the road.

The cave was shaped like a soaring cathedral dome, with a floor of smooth sand and sandstone walls that curved upward. The indirect sunlight from outside filled it with a reddish glow, and it smelled like dust and time. An enormous boulder sat at the far end of the cave, apparently having fallen from the ceiling eons ago, worn and rounded off by the action of water coming through a web of crevasses in the roof.

As they walked deeper into the cave, they disturbed a colony of nesting canyon swallows, which flitted about in the shadows above, making shrill cries.

"The cave may continue on behind that large rock," said Ford.

They walked toward the back of the cave, approaching the displaced rock.

"Look," said Tom. "Footprints."

The sand had been carefully brushed, but in the gap between the rock and the side of the cave they could see marks from a chevron-lugged hiking boot.

They squeezed through the gap and entered the back part of the cave, behind the massive boulder.

Ford turned and there it was, the great T. Rex, its jaws and forelimb, emerging from the rock. No one spoke. It was an extraordinary sight. The beast looked as if it was engaged in a fierce struggle to break out, to tear itself free from the tomb of stone. The dinosaur lay on its side, but the tilt of the fallen rock had set it almost upright, giving it a further grotesque illusion of life. Looking at it, Ford could almost feel the great beast's last raging moment of earthly consciousness.

In silence, they approached the base of the rock. Scattered on the sand underneath lay a few pieces that had weathered from the fossil — including one long, black, scimitar-shaped tooth. Tom picked it up, hefted it, ran his thumb along the viciously serrated inner edge. He gave a low whistle and handed it to Ford.

It was heavy and cool in his hand. "Incredible," he murmured, glancing once again at the great silent monster.

"Look at this," said Tom, pointing to some strange man-made objects partly buried in the sand — several ancient figurines carved in wood. He knelt down and brushed away the sand, uncovering more figurines below and a small pot filled with arrowheads.

"Offerings," said Ford. "That explains the Indian trail up here. They were *worshiping* the monster. And no wonder."

"What's that?"

Tom pointed to a rim of metal that poked from the sand. He swept the sand aside to uncover a burnt tin can, which he extracted and pried up the lid. Inside was a Ziploc bag enclosing a bundle of letters, sealed in envelopes, dated, and addressed to "Robbie Weathers." The first one had written on it: *For my daughter Robbie. I hope you enjoy this story. The T. Rex is all yours. Love, Daddy.*

Without a word, Tom rolled up the letters and put them back in the can.

Sally, standing farther toward the front of the cave, suddenly hissed. "Voices!"

Ford started, as if coming out of a dream. The reality of their situation came back in a rush.

"We've got to hide. Let's see how far back the cave goes."

Tom pulled the feeble flashlight he still carried and shone it into the back of the cave. They all stared in silence. The cave ended in a narrow, water-worn crack, far too narrow to admit a person. He directed the beam up, around, back and forth.

"We've walked into a dead end," Ford said quietly.

"So that's it?" said Sally. "What do we do now? Give up?"

Ford did not answer. He moved swiftly to the mouth of the cave, flattened himself against the wall, and peered down. A moment later he was back. "They're in the canyon below, three soldiers and a civilian."

Tom moved to the opening himself and looked down in the small amphitheater. Two men with assault rifles, dressed in desert camouflage, were moving below. A third appeared, and then a forth. The men were examining the ground where they had brushed out their tracks. One was pointing up to the cave.

"That's it," said Ford quietly.

"Bullshit." Tom pulled the handgun out of the musette bag, popped out the magazine, topped it off with a couple of loose rounds, slid it back into place. He raised his head to see Ford shaking his own.

"You take a pot shot at those D-boys

and you're looking at instant suicide."

"I'm not going down without a fight."

"Neither am I." Ford paused, his craggy face deep in thought. As if absentmindedly he removed the dinosaur tooth from his pocket, hefted it. Then he slipped it back in. "Tom, do you have the notebook?"

Tom pulled it out.

"Give it to me. And the gun."

"What are you —"

"No time to explain."

13

Masago watched from below as Hitt and the two other D-boys edged up the steep sandstone slope and flattened themselves just below the lip of the cave, spreading out to cover the occupants within from three angles. It was a classic maneuver, a bit of overkill, perhaps, considering the targets were probably unarmed.

When they were in place, Hitt's voice sounded, not loud, but carrying a steely authority.

"You in the cave. You're outgunned and outnumbered. We're coming in. Don't move, and keep your hands in sight."

Masago watched, fighting an uncharacteristic feeling of tension.

Hitt rose, exposing himself to the unseen targets inside. The other two remained covering him.

"That's right. Hands above your heads. Nobody's going to get hurt." He gestured to the other two D-boys, who rose from their cover.

It was over. The three objectives were

standing in the open central area of the cave, hands raised.

"Cover me."

Hitt walked over and patted them down, making sure they weren't armed. He spoke into his comm. "Sir, we've secured the cave. You may come up now."

Masago seized the first handhold, hefted himself up, and in a few minutes stood in the mouth of the cave, looking at the three sorriest bastards he'd seen in a long time: the monk, Broadbent, and his wife.

"Unarmed?"

Hitt nodded.

"Search them again. I want to see everything they have on their persons. Everything. Lay it out on the sand here in front of me."

Hitt nodded to one of his boys, who began searching the bedraggled group. Out appeared a flashlight, wallets, keys, a driver's license, all carefully lined up in the sand. The monk's pack contained an empty canteen, matches, a few empty tin cans, and other camping gear.

The last thing to come out had been hidden in the monk's robes.

"What the hell's this?" the D-boy asked, holding it up.

Without changing expression, Masago said, "Bring it to me."

The boy handed it to him. Masago gazed

on the serrated tooth, flipped it over, hefted it.

"You." He pointed to the monk. "You must be Ford."

The monk gave an almost imperceptible nod.

"Step forward."

The monk took one short step forward.

He held up the great tooth. "So you found it. You know where it is."

"That's correct," said the monk.

"You will tell me where it is."

"I'm the only one who has the information you want. And I'm not talking until you answer my questions first."

Masago unholstered his Beretta, pointed the gun at Ford.

"Talk."

"Screw you."

Masago fired, the bullet singing past Ford's ear. The monk didn't even flinch.

Masago lowered the gun. The man wasn't going to be intimidated — he could see that now.

"Kill me and you'll never find the dinosaur. Never."

Masago smiled thinly. "All right then — you get one question."

"Why do you want the dinosaur?"

"It contains highly dangerous infectious particles, which could be transformed into a bioterror weapon." He could see the monk digesting this statement. He wouldn't say more: nothing that would contradict the Patrol Order that had been distributed to the men.

"The name of your detachment?"

"That's two."

"You can go to hell, then," said the monk.

Masago made a quick step forward and sank his fist in the monk's solar plexus; the man went down in the sand like a sack of cement. Masago stepped over him while the monk coughed, rose to his knees, his hands convulsively sinking and digging into the sand in an effort to right himself.

"The dinosaur, Mr. Ford: where is it?"

"Water . . . please . . ."

Masago unhooked his canteen and shook it provocatively. "When I hear the location of the dinosaur." He unscrewed the cap and bent down toward the shaking monk, who was barely able to support himself on his hands and knees.

The monk exploded like a striking snake. His hand came out of the sand — unexpectedly holding a gun. Before Masago could react Ford's left arm had locked around his throat and wrenched him back. Masago felt the gun barrel jammed in his ear, his arms pinned back, unable to reach his Beretta.

"Now," said Ford, using Masago as a

shield as he spoke to the soldiers, "this man's going to tell all of us what's really going on — or he's dead."

PART SIX

THE TAIL OF THE DEVIL

The end came on a normal afternoon in June. Heat lay over the forest like a blanket, the leaves hung limp, and thunderheads piled up in the west.

She moved through the forest, hunting.

She did not notice, through the trees, the sudden brightness in the south. The light bloomed silently, a yellow glow rising into the pale blue sky.

The forest remained silent, watchful.

Six minutes later the ground shook violently, and she crouched to maintain her balance. In less than thirty seconds the tremor subsided, and she resumed the hunt.

Eight minutes later the ground shook again, this time rolling and pitching as if in waves. That was when she noticed the unusual yellow glow that continued to rise along the southern horizon, casting a second set of shadows among the great trunks of the monkey-puzzle trees. The forest brightened and she felt a source of radiant heat on her flanks, coming from the south. She paused in her hunt, watchful but not yet uneasy.

At twelve minutes she heard a rushing sound, like a great wind approaching. It grew to a roar and suddenly the trees bent double, the forest resounding with sharp cracking and exploding of tree trunks. Something that was neither wind nor sound nor pressure, but a combination of all three, pressed over her with immense force, throwing her to the ground, where she was lashed by flying vegetation, sticks, branches, and tree trunks.

She lay there, dazed and in pain, before her instincts came rushing in, telling her to rise, rise and fight. She rolled, righted herself, and crouched, facing the tempest, enraged, snapping and roaring at the hurricane of vegetation that assaulted her.

The storm slowly abated, leaving the forest a wreck. And into the calm a new sound began to grow, a mysterious humming, almost a singing. A bright streak flashed down from the sky, and another, and another, exploding among the wrecked landscape, until it became a rain of fire. The confused and terrified calls and trumpetings of animals arose on all sides like a chorus of fear. Packs of small animals raced this way and that through the wreckage as the fire rain grew in intensity.

A herd of heedless coelophysis ran be-

fore her and she swung her great head into them as they passed, tearing and snapping, leaving the ground strewn with twitching, wriggling limbs, bodies, and tails. She consumed the pieces at her leisure, occasionally snapping in annoyance at the fire rain, which soon subsided into a slow drift of grit from the sky. She finished eating and rested, her mind blank. She did not see that the sun had disappeared and that the sky was changing color from yellow to orange and finally to bloodred, deepening with each passing moment, radiating heat from everywhere and nowhere at once. The air itself grew hotter until it passed any heat she had known before.

The heat goaded her into action, as did the pain of the searing wounds on her back. She rose, moved to the cypress swamp and her habitual wallow, crouched down and rolled, coating herself with cool, black mud.

Gradually it became dark. Her mind relaxed. All was well.

1

Melodie Crookshank finished organizing the data on her computer screen in HTML format, cropping images, writing captions, and doing a few final edits on the short article she had written in a burst of furious activity. She was running on empty — sixty hours with no sleep — but she still felt buoyed up. This was going to be one of the most significant papers in the history of vertebrate paleontology and it was going to cause an uproar. There would be doubters, naysayers, and self-appointed debunkers, and there might even be accusations of fraud — but the data was good. It would hold up. And the images were impeccable. What's more, she still had one raw slice of the specimen that she intended to offer to either the Smithsonian or Harvard for their paleontologists to perform an independent examination.

The pandemonium would begin as soon as she transmitted the article to the *Journal of VP* online. All it would take was one reader, and then everyone would be reading it, and her world would never be the same.

She was done — or almost done. Her finger was poised over the ENTER button, ready to e-mail the article.

A knock came at the door and she jumped, turned. The chair was still up against the knob. She looked at the clock: five.

"Who is it?"

"Maintenance."

She sighed and got up from the table, walked over to the door, and unhooked the chair. She was about to open the door when she paused.

"Maintenance?"

"What I said."

"Frankie?"

"Who else?"

She unlocked the door, noting with relief the ninety-eight-pound Frankie she knew so well, a sack of unshaven bones stinking of bad cigars and worse whiskey. He shuffled in and she locked the door behind him. He began going around the lab, emptying wastebaskets into a huge plastic bag, whistling tunelessly. He ducked under her desk, grabbed the wastebasket overflowing with soda cans and Mars bar wrappings, bumped his head as he pulled it out, scattering some of the empty Dr Pepper cans on the desktop, splattering the stereozoom scope.

"Sorry about that."

"No problem." She waited impatiently for him to finish. He emptied the basket, gave the desk a quick wipe with his sleeve, jostling the fifty-thousand-dollar microscope in the process. Melodie wondered briefly how it was that some human beings could invent the calculus while others couldn't even empty trash. She squashed that thought completely. It was unkind and she would never allow herself to become like the arrogant scientists she had dealt with over the past few years. She would always be kind to lowly technicians, incompetent maintenance men, and graduate students.

"Thank you, Frankie."

"See you." Frankie left, slapping the bag on the door as he went out, and silence reigned again.

With a sigh Melodie examined the stereozoom. Little droplets of Dr Pepper had sprayed the side of the scope and she noted that some had landed on the wet slide.

She glanced through the oculars to make sure no damage had taken place. There was precious little of the specimen left and every bit counted, particularly the six or seven particles she had managed to free from the matrix with such effort.

The slide was fine. The Dr Pepper would make no difference — a few sugar molecules could hardly damage a particle that had survived a sixty-five-million-year burial and a 12 percent hydrofluoric acid bath.

Suddenly she paused. If her eyes weren't playing tricks on her, one of the crosspieces on the arm of a particle had suddenly moved.

She waited, staring through the oculars at the magnified particles, a crawling sensation at the nape of her neck As she watched, another arm of a particle moved, just like a little machine, clicking from one position to the next. As it did so the particle propelled itself forward. She watched, fascinated and alarmed, as the others began to move in the same clicking fashion. All the particles were beginning to move, the arms working like tiny propellers.

The particles were still alive.

It must have been the addition of sugar to the solution. Melodie reached under her desk and pulled out the last Dr Pepper. She opened it and with a micropipette drew out a small amount, which she deposited at one end of the wet slide, forming a sugar gradient.

The particles became more active, the little arms rotating in a way that drove them up the gradient, toward the higher concentration of sugar.

Melodie felt the prickle of apprehension grow. She hadn't even considered that they might still be infectious. And if they were alive, they were certainly infectious — at least to a dinosaur.

In the herpetology lab down the hall, one of the curators had been breeding parthenogenetic lizards as part of a long-running experiment. The lab contained an incubator of in vitro cell cultures. A cell culture would make an excellent testing bed for whether the particle would infect a modern-day lizard.

She exited the lab. The hall was empty — after five o'clock on a Sunday she would be most unlikely to meet anyone. The herp lab was locked but her card key worked, and it was a matter of five minutes to obtain a petri dish full of growing lizard cells. She brought it back to her lab, loosened some cells with a squirt of saline solution, and transferred them onto the slide.

Then she put her eyes to the oculars.

The Venus particles stopped in their move up the sugar gradient. They turned in unison, almost like a pack of wolves on a scent, and headed for the cells. Melodie felt a sudden constriction in her throat. In a moment they reached the group of cells, clustering around them, attaching themselves to the cell membranes by their long appendages; then, with a swift cutting motion, each one entered a cell.

Melodie, riveted, watched to see what would happen next.

2

Ford manhandled the man in the track suit back into an angle of the rock, where he was covered from the back and sides. The three soldiers had trained their weapons on Ford and the man he was holding. The sergeant made a motion with his hand and the other two began moving to either side.

"Stop moving, all of you, and lower your weapons."

The leader motioned them to halt.

"Like I said, this man's going to tell all of us what's going on or I'm going to kill him. Understand? You wouldn't want to report back to base with your handler in a body bag, would you?"

"You'll be in a body bag next to his," said Hitt quietly.

"I'm doing this for you, Sergeant."

"Us?"

"You too need to know what's really going on."

Silence.

Ford pressed the gun to Masago's head. "Talk."

"Release him or I'll open fire," Hitt said quietly. "One . . ."

"Wait," said Tom. "We're American citizens. We've done nothing wrong. Is this why you went into the military — to kill American civilians?"

There was just the faintest of hesitations. Then Hitt said, "Two . . ."

"Listen to me," Tom continued, speaking directly to the sergeant. "You don't know what you're doing. Don't blindly follow orders. *At least wait until you know what's going on."*

Again the sergeant hesitated. The two other soldiers were looking to him. He was the key.

Hitt lowered his weapon.

Ford spoke quietly, remembering what he'd been taught about interrogations years ago. "You lied to these men, didn't you?"

"No." He was already sweating.

"You did. And now you're going to tell them the truth, or I'll kill you — no second chances, no warnings, nothing. A bullet to the brain and then I'll take what's coming to me."

Ford meant it and that was key. The man knew it.

"Okay. First question. Who do you work for?"

"I'm director of Detachment LS480."

"Which is?"

"Established in 1973 after the Apollo 17 mission to the moon. Its purpose was to study a lunar sample known as LS480."

"A moon rock?"

"Yes."

"Go on."

Masago swallowed. He was sweating. "It was a piece of ejecta from a crater known as Van Serg. The rock contained fragments of the meteorite that formed the crater. In those contaminants were particles. Microbes."

"What kind of microbes?"

"Unknown. They appear to be an alien form of life. Biologically active. They could be weaponized."

"And the connection to the dinosaur?"

"The same particles were found in the dinosaur fossil. The dinosaur died of an infection caused by the LS480 particle."

Ford paused. "You're saying the dinosaur was killed by an alien life-form?"

"Yes."

"And the connection with the moon rock again? I'm a little lost."

"Van Serg crater is sixty-five million years old. The dinosaur died 65 million years ago following the Chicxulub impact."

"Chicxulub?"

"The asteroid that caused the mass extinction of the dinosaurs."

"Go on."

"Van Serg crater was made by a fragment from that same asteroid. It appears the asteroid itself was riddled with the LS480 particles."

"What's the purpose of this op?"

"To clear the area, eliminate all knowledge of the dinosaur, and recover the dinosaur for classified research."

"When you say 'clear the area' you're talking about us."

"Correct."

"And when you say 'eliminate all knowledge of the dinosaur,' you're talking about killing us — am I right?"

"I don't take lightly the idea of killing American citizens. But this is an issue of the gravest national security. Our nation's survival is at stake. There's no dishonor in giving up your life for your country — even if it happens to be involuntary. At times it's unavoidable. You were CIA. You understand." He paused, fixing Ford with pinpoint eyes. "Those LS480 particles caused the mass extinction of the dinosaurs. In the wrong hands, those same particles could cause a second mass extinction — of the human race."

Ford released him.

Masago jumped away and backed up, breathing heavily, then unholstered his Beretta. He positioned himself slightly behind Hitt.

"Sergeant Hitt, eliminate these three people. I don't need their information. We'll get it another way."

There was another long silence.

"You're not going to do this," said Sally. "Now you know it's murder."

"I'm waiting for you to carry out my direct orders, soldier," said Masago quietly.

No one spoke. No one moved.

"You're relieved of command, Hitt," said Masago. "Private Gowicki, carry out my order. Eliminate these people."

Another intense silence.

"Gowicki, I didn't hear an acknowledgment of my order."

"Yes, sir."

Gowicki raised his weapon. The seconds ticked by.

"Gowicki?" Masago asked.

"No," said Hitt.

Masago pointed his Beretta at Hitt's head.

"Gowicki? Carry out my order."

Tom hit Masago's knees with a flying tackle, the gun going off harmlessly into the air. Masago spun, recovered, but with an adroit movement Hitt landed a blow to Masago's solar plexus. Masago fell heavily and lay on the ground, doubled up, unable to make a sound.

Hitt kicked the gun away. "Cuff him."

Gowicki and Hirsch came forward and in

a moment had secured his arms behind his back in plastic cuffs. He was gasping and coughing, rolling in the sand, blood trickling from his mouth.

A long silence ensued.

"All right," said Hitt to his soldiers. "I'm taking charge of the op. And it seems to me these three people need some water."

Gowicki unslung his canteen and passed it around. They all drank deeply.

"All right," said Hitt. "Now that we know what's really going on, we've still got an op to finish. Seems to me we're supposed to locate a dinosaur fossil. And you know where it is." He faced Ford.

"What do you plan to do with us?"

"I'm taking you three back to WSMR. General Miller'll decide what to do with you — he's the real commanding officer around here, not this" — his voice trailed off and he cast a glance at Masago — "civilian."

Ford nodded toward the great boulder that dominated the back of the cave. "It's right behind there."

"No shit?" He turned to Gowicki. "You keep an eye on them while I confirm."

Hitt vanished behind the boulder and came back a few moments later.

"Now that," he said, "is one *mean* mother." He turned to his men. "Far as I'm concerned, the first part of the op is accomplished. We've located the fossil. I'm calling in the rest of the chalk. We'll rendezvous at the LZ, return to base, report to General Miller with these three individuals, and await further orders." He turned to Masago. "You'll come quietly, sir, and make no disturbance."

3

The chopper squatted on the alkali flats like a giant black insect about to take flight. They approached in silence, Tom limping on his own, Sally being helped along by a soldier. Hitt came last with Masago in front of him.

The four other members of the chalk, called in by Hitt, lounged in the shade of a nearby rock, smoking cigarettes. Hitt motioned them toward the chopper and they rose, tossing away their butts. Tom followed them into the chopper and the sergeant gestured for them to take seats on the metal benches along the wall.

"Radio base," said Hitt to the copilot. "Report we've accomplished the first part of the operation. Tell 'em I felt compelled to terminate the command of the civilian Masago and disarm him."

"Yes, sir."

"I'll report the details in person to General Miller."

"Yes, sir."

A soldier slid the cargo door shut while the chopper revved up and lifted off. Tom leaned back against the netting next to Sally, feeling more exhausted than he ever had in his life. He glanced over at Masago. The man hadn't said a word. His face looked strangely blank.

The chopper rose out of the steep-walled valley and skimmed southwestward over the mesa tops. The sun was a large drop of blood on the horizon, and as the chopper gained altitude Tom could see Navajo Rim and beyond that the Mesa of the Ancients, its center riddled with the canyon complex known as the Maze. In the far distance, lay the blue curve of the Chama River.

As the chopper made a lazy turn to the southeast, Tom saw a sudden movement out of the corner of his eye — Masago. The man had jumped up and was running for the cockpit. Tom hurled himself at Masago, but the man twisted free, giving him a sharp upward blow with his cuffed hands. He pulled a knife from his pantleg sheath with both hands, spun and bounded through the open cockpit door. The other men had jumped from their seats to pursue him, but the chopper suddenly yawed, throwing them into the netting, while a gargling scream came from the cockpit.

"He's crashing the chopper!" Hitt cried.

The bird took a sickening downward lurch and a deep shudder came from the rotors. Tom staggered to his feet, gripping the netting, fighting against the decceleration as the chopper screamed and spiraled downward. He caught a glimpse through the cockpit door of the copilot, struggling with Masago — and the pilot lying dead on the floor awash with blood.

As the chopper pitched back, Tom used the motion to launch himself into the cockpit. He slammed into the flight console, righted himself on a seat, threw a punch at Masago, clipping his ear. As he staggered backward the copilot seized the man's cuffed wrists and slammed them down on the console, knocking the knife from his hands. The yawing chopper threw them both to the floor and Masago grabbed the copilot, choking him while both slid around on the floor slick with blood. Tom slammed Masago's head against the floor, rolling him off the copilot.

"Take the controls!" Tom screamed at the copilot, who needed no encouragement. The man lurched to his feet and seized the controls, the bird yawing wildly. With a sudden roar from the back rotors and a gut-wrenching deceleration, he righted the chopper. Masago was still thrashing wildly, fighting with almost superhuman strength, but Hitt had now joined Tom and they had him pinned. Above the screaming engines, Tom could hear the copilot calling in an emergency while he fought with the controls.

Suddenly, through the windscreen, the face of a cliff came rushing past; followed by a bone-breaking jolt and a machine-gun-like series of whangs as pieces of rotor tore like shrapnel through the fuselage. The copilot was hammered to one side by the flying debris, his blood splattering against the shattered Plexiglas of the windscreen. The screeching sound of metal tearing on rock was followed by a weightless moment of free-fall, and then a massive crash.

Silence.

Tom felt like he was swimming out of darkness and it took him a moment to remember where he was — in a helicopter wreck. He tried to move and found he was jammed up in a corner on his side, debris piled over him. He could hear screaming as if coming in from a distance, the dripping of hydraulic fluid (or was it blood?), the stench of aviation fuel and burnt electronics. All motion had ceased. He struggled to free himself. A huge gash had ripped open one side of the chopper and through it he could see they had come to rest on a steep slope of broken rock. The helicopter groaned and shifted, metal rivets popping. Smoke began filling the air.

Tom climbed over the debris and found

Sally all tangled up with a heap of netting and plastic tarps. He pulled the netting aside.

"Sally!"

She stirred, opened her eyes.

"I'm getting you out." He grasped her around the shoulders and hauled her free, relieved to see she seemed to be only dazed.

"Tom!" came the voice of Wyman Ford.

He turned. Ford was crawling up the pile of debris, his face running with blood. "Fire," he gasped. "We're on fire." At the same time there was a whooshing sound and the tail section burst into flame, the heat like a glow in their faces.

Tom wrapped his arm around Sally and carried her toward the tear in the fuselage, the only way out. He grasped the netting and struggled up, hooked an arm over the sill and hauled her up to the hole. She grasped the ragged edge and Tom helped her outside, on top of the fuselage where it was an eight-foot drop to the ground. He could see the fire was spreading rapidly along the tail, crawling along fuel and electrical lines, engulfing the chopper.

"Can you jump?"

Sally nodded. He eased her down the side, and she dropped.

"Run!"

"What the hell are you doing staying

there?" she screamed from below. "Get off!"

"Ford's in there!"

"It's going to blow — !"

But Tom had turned his attention back into the chopper, where Ford, injured, was trying to climb up the netting to the opening. One of his arms dangled uselessly.

Tom lay on his stomach, reached through the hole, grasped the man's good arm, and hauled him up. Black smoke billowed out in a great wave just as he pulled Ford free and up on top of the fuselage, then slid him to the ground.

"Tom! Get off there!" Sally screamed from below, helping Ford away from the wreck.

"There's still Hitt!"

Smoke was now pouring through the opening. Tom dropped down into it and crouched, finding a layer of fresh air underneath. He crawled toward where he had last seen Hitt, keeping low. The unconscious soldier lay on his side in the cockpit amid a shower of debris. Waves of heat from the fire scorched his skin. He slid his arms around Hitt's torso and pulled, but the soldier was huge and he couldn't manage it.

There was a muffled thump as something burst into flame inside the fuselage. A wave of heat and smoke rolled over Tom.

"Hitt!" He slapped the man across the face. The man's eyes rolled. He slapped him again, very hard, and the eyes came into focus.

"Get moving! Get out!"

Tom wrapped his arm around the man's neck and heaved him up. Hitt struggled to his knees, shaking his head, droplets of blood dripping from his hair. "Damn . . ."

"Out! We're on fire!"

"Jesus . . ."

Hitt finally seemed to be coming back to reality, ready to move under his own power. The smoke was now so thick that Tom could barely see. He felt along the floor, Hitt crawling behind him. An eternity later they reached where the fuselage of the chopper curved upward. He turned, grabbed Hitt's arm, placed his meaty fist on the netting. "Climb!"

There was no air and the acrid smoke felt like broken glass in his lungs.

"Climb, damn you!"

The man started climbing, almost like a zombie, the blood running down his arms. Tom followed alongside, screaming at him, dizziness filling his head. He was going to pass out, it was too late. It was over. He felt his grip weakening . . .

And then arms reached down, pulling him up and throwing him off the side of the chopper. He fell heavily in the sand,

and a moment later Hitt landed heavily next to him, with a groan. Sally jumped down beside them — she had climbed back up on the chopper to haul them out.

They stumbled and crawled, trying to get as far away from the burning chopper as possible. Tom finally collapsed, gasping and coughing, able to go no more. Half crawling, half lying in the sand, he heard a dull thud and felt the sudden heat as the last of the chopper's tanks blew, engulfing the wreck in flame.

Suddenly a bizarre sight appeared: a man emerged from the fire, sheeted in flame, his arm raised with a gun in his burning fist. With strange deliberation he stopped, aimed, fired a single wild shot — and then the figure slowly toppled like a statue back into the burning inferno and was gone.

Tom passed out.

4

Night had fallen on the Museum of Natural History in Manhattan. A gentle breeze rustled the leaves of the old sycamores in Museum Park, and the stone gargoyles that haunted the rooftops squatted silently against the darkening sky. Deep in the museum's basement a light burned in the Mineralogy laboratory, where Melodie Crookshank sat hunched over the stereozoom microscope, watching a lump of cells divide.

It had been going on for three and a half hours. The Venus particles had triggered an amazing spurt of growth — triggering an orgy of cell division. At first Melodie thought the particles might have somehow set off a cancerous growth, an undifferentiated bunch of malignant cells. But it wasn't long before she realized that these cells were not dividing like cancerous cells, or even normal cells in a culture.

No — these cells were *differentiating*.

The group of cells had begun to take on the characteristics of a blastocyst, the ball of cells that form from a fertilized embryo. As the cells had continued to divide, Melodie had seen a dark streak develop down the middle of the blastocyst. It had begun to look exactly like the so-called primitive streak that developed in all chordate embryos — which would eventually form the spinal cord and backbone of the developing creature.

Creature.

Melodie, at the limit of exhaustion, raised her head. It hadn't occurred to her exactly what this thing that was growing might be, whether a lizard or something else, and it was too early in the ontological process to know.

She shivered. What the hell was she doing? It would be insane to wait around and find out. What she was doing now was not only foolish, it was extremely dangerous. These particles needed to be studied under biosafety level four conditions, not in an open lab like hers.

She glanced toward the clock, hardly able to focus on the dial. She blinked, rubbed her eyes, rolled them to the left and the right. She was so tired she was almost hallucinating.

Melodie had no idea what these particles were, what they did, how they worked. They were an alien life-form that had hitched a ride to Earth on the Chicxulub asteroid. This was over her head — way over her head.

Melodie shoved back the chair and stood up, a little unsteady on her feet, gripping the side of the table for support, her hands trembling. She began to consider what she had to do. She cast around and her eyes lit on a bottle of 80 percent hydrochloric acid in the chemical stores. She unlocked the cabinet, took down the bottle, brought it to under the fume hood, broke the seal, and poured a few ounces of it into a shallow glass tray. With infinite care she removed the slide from the microscope stage, carried it to the fume hood, and slipped it into the hydrochloric acid. There was a faint foaming and hissing noise as the acid instantly destroyed and dissolved the hideous growing blob of cells until nothing was left.

She breathed a deep sigh of relief. That was the first step, to destroy the organism growing on the slide. Now to destroy the loose Venus particles themselves.

She added a strong base to the acid, neutralizing it and causing the precipitation of a layer of salt at the bottom of the dish. Setting up a Bunsen burner under the hood, she put the glass dish on the burner and began boiling away the solution. In a few minutes all the liquid had evaporated, leaving behind a crust of salt. She now turned up the burner as high as it would go. Five minutes passed, then ten minutes, and the salt began to crust up, glowing red-hot as the temperature approached the melting point of glass. No form of carbon, not even a buckyball, could survive that kind of heat. For five minutes she kept the Pyrex dish over the burner while it glowed cherry-red and then she turned off the gas and let it cool down.

She still had one more thing to do: the most important thing of all. And that was to finish the article, adding what she had just discovered. She spent ten minutes writing up two final paragraphs, describing in the driest scientific language she could muster what she had just observed. She saved it, read it over one final time, and was satisfied.

Melodie silently criticized her own lack of caution. Whatever the particles were, she now believed they might be very dangerous. They was no telling what they might do to a live organism, to a human being. She felt a chill, wondering if she was infected. But that was impossible — the particles were too big to become airborne and besides, aside from those she had painstakingly freed from the rock, the rest were securely encased in stone, sixty-five million years old but still functional.

Functional.

That was really the crux of the matter.

What *was* their function? But even as she asked herself the question, she knew the answer would take months, if not years, to answer.

She attached the article to an e-mail and readied it for sending, her finger poised on the ENTER key.

She hit ENTER.

Melodie leaned back in her chair with a great sigh, feeling suddenly drained. With that keystroke her life was changed. Forever.

5

Tom opened his eyes. The sun lay in stripes across his bed, a monitor beeping softly somewhere in the background, a clock on the wall. Through a haze of pain, he managed to locate Sally sitting in a chair opposite.

"You're awake!" She jumped up, taking his hand.

Tom didn't even consider raising his pounding head. "What — ?"

"You're in the hospital."

It all came rushing back; the pursuit in the canyons, the helicopter crash, the fire. "Sally, how are you?"

"A lot better than you."

Tom looked around at himself, shocked to see himself so bandaged up. "So what's wrong with me?"

"Nothing more than a nasty burn, a broken wrist, cracked ribs, concussion, bruised kidney, and a seared lung. That's all."

"How long have I been out?"

"Two days."

"Ford? How's he?"

"He should be coming up to see you at any moment. He had a broken arm and a few cuts, that's all. He's a tough bird. You were hurt worst."

Tom grunted, his head still pounding. As clarity returned, he noticed a heavy presence sitting in the corner. Lieutenant Detective Willer.

"What's he doing here?"

Willer rose, touched his forehead in a greeting before settling down. "Glad to see you awake, Broadbent. Don't worry, you're not in any trouble — although you should be."

Tom didn't quite know what to say.

"I just dropped in to see how you were getting along."

"That's kind of you."

"I figured you'd probably have a few questions you'd want answered. Like what we found out about the killer of Marston Weathers, the same man who abducted your wife."

"I would."

"And in return, when you're ready, I'd like a complete debriefing from you." He raised his eyebrows in query.

"Fair enough."

"Good. The man's name was Maddox, Jimson Alvin Maddox, a convicted murderer who appears to have been working for a fellow named Iain Corvus, a curator

576

at the American Museum of Natural History in New York. He got Maddox an early release from prison. Corvus himself died the same night Sally here was kidnapped, apparently of a heart attack. Given the timing the FBI is looking into it."

Tom nodded. Damn, his head hurt. "So how did this Corvus know about the dinosaur?"

"He heard rumors that Weathers was on to something big, sent Maddox down to follow him. Maddox killed the guy and, it seems, took a sample off him which Corvus had analyzed at the museum. Something just went up on the Web about it and there's been a hullabaloo like nothing you've ever seen before. It's in all the papers." Willer shook his head. "A dinosaur fossil . . . Christ, I considered just about everything, from cocaine to buried gold, but I never would've guessed a T. Rex."

"What's happening to the fossil?"

Sally answered. "The government's sealed off the high mesas and are taking it out. They're talking about building some kind of special lab to study it, maybe right here in New Mexico."

"And Maddox? He's really dead?"

Willer said, "We found his body where you left it, or at least what was left of it after the coyotes worked it over."

"What about the Predator drone, all that business?"

Willer eased back in his chair. "We're still untangling that one. Looks like some kind of rogue government agency."

"Ford will tell you about that when he comes," said Sally.

As if on cue the nurse came in and Tom could see Ford's craggy face behind her, one side of his jaw bandaged, his arm in a cast and sling. He was wearing a checked shirt and jeans.

"Tom! Glad to see you awake." He came and leaned on the footrest of the bed. "How the heck are you?"

"Been better."

He cautiously settled his huge frame down in a cheap plastic hospital chair. "I've been in touch with some of my old pals in the Company. Apparently heads have rolled over the way this whole thing was handled, the callous disregard for human life, not to mention the bungled op. The classified agency that ran the op's been disbanded. A government panel's looking into the whole business, but you know how it is . . ."

"Right."

"There's something else, something incredible. A scientist at the Museum of Natural History in New York got hold of the piece of the dinosaur, studied it, and has released a paper about it. It's explosive stuff. The T. Rex died of an infection — brought in on the asteroid that caused the mass extinction. No kidding — the dinosaur died of an alien infection. At least that's what they say." Ford told him how Apollo 17 brought back some of the particles on a moon rock. "When they saw the rock was impregnated with an alien microbe, they diverted it to the Defense Intelligence Agency, which in turn set up a black detachment to study it. The DIA named the black agency LS480, short for Lunar Sample 480. They've been studying these particles for the last thirty years, all the while keeping their antennae out in case any more showed up."

"But it still doesn't explain how they found out about the dinosaur."

"The NSA has a ferocious eavesdropping capability. We'll never know the details — seems they intercepted a phone call. They jumped on it immediately. They'd been waiting thirty years and they were ready."

Tom nodded. "How's Hitt?"

"Still in bed upstairs. He's doing fine. Pilot and copilot are both dead, though. Along with Masago and several soldiers. A real tragedy."

"And the notebook?"

Willer stood up, took it out of his pocket, laid it on the bed. "This is for you. Sally tells me you always keep your promises."

6

Melodie had never been inside the office of Cushman Peale, the museum's president, and she felt oppressed by its atmosphere of old New York privilege and exclusion. The man behind the antique rosewood desk added to the effect, dressed in Brooks Brothers gray, with a gleaming mane of white hair brushed back. His elaborate courtesies and self-deprecating phraseology did a poor job of concealing an unshakable assumption of superiority.

Peale guided her to a wooden Shaker chair placed to one side of a marble fireplace and seated himself opposite. From the interior of his suit he removed a copy of her article and laid it on the table, carefully spreading it with a heavy veined hand.

"Well, well, Melodie. This is a fine piece of work."

"Thank you, Dr. Peale."

"Please call me Cushman."

"All right. Cushman."

Melodie leaned back in the chair. She could never be comfortable in this chair that would make a Puritan squirm, but at least she could fake it. She had a bad case of imposter syndrome — but she figured she'd get over it, eventually.

"Now let's see . . ." Peale consulted some notes he had jotted on the first page of the article. "You joined the museum five years ago, am I right?"

"That's right."

"With a Ph.D. from Columbia . . . And you've been doing a bang-up job in the Mineralogy lab every since as a . . . Technical Specialist First Grade?" He seemed almost surprised by the lowliness of her position.

Melodie remained silent.

"Well, it certainly seems time for a promotion." Peale leaned back and crossed his legs. "This paper shows great promise, Melodie. Of course, it's controversial, that's to be expected, but the Committee on Science has gone over it carefully and it seems likely the results will withstand scrutiny."

"They will."

"That's the right attitude, Melodie." Peale cleared his throat, delicately. "The committee did feel that the hypothesis that this, ah, Venus particle might be an alien microbe is perhaps a bit premature."

"That doesn't surprise me, Cushman." Melodie paused, finding it difficult to say his first name. *Better get used to it,* she thought. The deferential, eager-to-please Technician First Grade was history. "Any major scientific advance involves going out on a limb. I'm confident the hypothesis will stand up."

"Delighted to hear it. Of course, I'm only a museum president" — and here he gave a self-deprecating chuckle — "so I'm hardly in a position to judge your work. They tell me it's quite good."

Melodie smiled pleasantly.

He leaned back, placed his hands on his knees, flexed them. "I had a talk with the Committee on Science and it seems we'd like to offer you a position as Assistant Curator in the Department of Vertebrate Paleontology. This is a fine, tenure-track position which will lead, in time, if all goes well, to an appointment to the Humboldt Chair, which might have been occupied by the late Dr. Corvus had he lived. Naturally there will be a commensurate increase in salary."

Melodie allowed an uncomfortable amount of time to pass before responding. "That's a generous offer," she said. "I appreciate it."

"We take care of our own," said the president pompously.

"I wish I could accept it."

Peale's hands came apart. Melodie waited.

"You're turning us down, Melodie?" Peale looked incredulous, as if the idea of not wanting to stay at the museum was preposterous, unthinkable.

Melodie kept her voice even. "Cushman, I spent five years in the basement doing first-class work for this museum. Never once did I receive one iota of recognition. Never once was I thanked beyond a perfunctory pat on the back. My salary was less than the maintenance workers who emptied my trash."

"Of course we noticed you . . ." Peale was nonplussed. "And things will change. Let me say our offer to you isn't engraved in stone, either. Perhaps we need to take it back to the Committee on Science and see if there isn't something more we can do for you. An associate curatorship with tenure might even be possible."

"I already turned down a tenured position at Harvard."

Peale's brows shot up in perfect astonishment, quickly concealed. "My, they're quick on the draw." He managed a strained chuckle. "What sort of offer? If I may ask."

"The Montcrieff Chair." She tried to keep from grinning. Damn, she was enjoying this.

"The Montcrieff Chair? Well, now that's . . . quite extraordinary." He cleared his throat, eased back in his chair, gave his tie a quick adjustment. "And you turned it down?"

"Yes. I'm going with the dinosaur . . . to the Smithsonian."

"The Smithsonian?" At the mention of the name of their big rival, his face reddened.

"That's right. To the National Museum of Natural History. The government plans to build a special Biosafety Level four laboratory in the White Sands Missile Range in New Mexico to study the dinosaur and the Venus particles. They've asked me to be the assistant director in charge of research, which comes with a tenured curatorial appointment at the national museum. Being able to continue my work on the specimen means a lot to me. The mystery of the Venus particles has yet to be cracked; I want to be the one to do it."

"That's your final decision?"

"Yes."

Peale rose, extended his hand, and mustered a weak smile. "In that case, Dr. Crookshank, allow me to be the first to congratulate you."

Breeding had produced one fine quality in Peale, thought Melodie: he was a good loser.

7

The house, a small bungalow, sat on a pleasant side lane in the town of Marfa, Texas. A large sycamore tree cast a mottled pool of shade across the lawn, enclosed by a white picket fence. A 1989 Ford Fiesta was parked in the driveway, and a hand-painted sign that read STUDIO hung outside a converted garage.

Tom and Sally parked on the street and rang the doorbell.

"In here," a voice called from the garage.

They walked around and the garage door came up, revealing a pleasant art studio inside. A woman appeared wearing an oversized man's dress shirt flecked with paint, her red hair tied up in a cloth. She was short, brisk, and attractive, with a small upturned nose, boyish face, and a pugnacious air. "What can I do for you?"

"I'm Tom Broadbent. This is my wife, Sally."

She broke into a smile. "Right. Robbie Weathers. Thanks so much for coming."

They followed her into a surprisingly

pleasant studio with a clerestory. The walls were white and hung with landscape paintings. Odd rocks, weathered pieces of wood, old bones, and rusty pieces of iron were arranged like sculpture on tables against the far wall.

"Have a seat. Tea? Coffee?"

"No thanks."

They sat on a futon folded up to be a couch, while Robbie Weathers washed her hands and pulled off her head scarf, shaking out her curly hair. She pulled up a wooden chair and sat opposite them. The sun streamed in. There was an awkward silence.

"So," she said, looking at Tom, "you're the person who found my father."

"That's right."

"I want you to tell me all about it, how you found my father, what he said — everything."

Tom began to tell the story, relating to her how he heard the shots, rode to investigate, found her father dying on the canyon floor.

She nodded, her face clouding. "How had he . . . fallen?"

"On his face. He'd been shot several times in the back. I turned him over, gave him CPR, and his eyes opened."

"Might he have lived if they'd gotten him out in time?"

"The wounds were fatal. He didn't have a chance."

"I see." Her knuckles had whitened where her hand gripped the side of the chair.

"He was clutching a notebook in his hand. He told me to take it and give it to you."

"What were his exact words?"

"He said, *It's for Robbie . . . My daughter . . . Promise to give it to her . . . She'll know how to find the . . . treasure . . .*"

"*Treasure,*" repeated Robbie, with a faint smile. "That's how he used to talk about his fossils. He never used the word 'fossil,' because he was paranoid about someone jumping his claims. Instead he used to pose as a half-crazed treasure hunter. He often carried around a conspicuously fake treasure map, to mislead people into thinking he was a quack."

"That explains one thing I long wondered about. Anyway, I accepted the notebook from him. He was . . . close to death. I did what I could but he didn't have a chance. His only concern was for you."

Robbie swiped a tear out of her eye.

"He said, '*It's for her . . . Robbie. Give it to her . . . No one else . . . No one, especially not the police . . . You must . . . promise me.*' And then he said, '*Tell her I love her.*'"

"He really said that?"

"Yes." He didn't add that he hadn't managed to say the last word — death had come too quickly.

"And then?"

"Those were his last words. His heart stopped and he died."

She nodded, bowing her head.

Tom pulled the notebook from his pocket and offered it to her. She raised her head, wiped away her eyes, and took it.

"Thank you."

She turned to the back, flipped through the blank pages, stopped at the two exclamation points, smiled through her tears.

"I do know this: from the time he found that dinosaur to when he was murdered, he was certainly the happiest man on earth."

She slowly closed the book and looked out the window into the sun-drenched South Texas landscape, and spoke slowly. "Mom left us when I was four. Who could blame her, married to a guy who dragged us all over the West, from Montana to Texas and every state in between? He was always looking for the big one. When I got older he wanted me to go with him, for us to be a team but . . . I didn't want any part of it. I didn't want to go camping in the desert and hunting around for fossils. All I wanted was to stay in one place and have a friend that would last me more than six months. I blamed the dinosaurs. I *hated* dinosaurs."

She took out a handkerchief, wiped her eyes again, folded it up in her lap.

"I couldn't wait to get away to college. Had to work my way through — Dad never had two nickels to rub together. We had a falling out. And then he called a year ago, saying he was on the trail of the big one, the dinosaur to end all dinosaurs, and that he would find it for me. I'd heard that one before. I got mad. I said some things to him I shouldn't have, and now I'll never have the chance to take them back."

The room filled with light and afternoon silence.

"I wish like hell he were still here," she added softly, and fell silent.

"He wrote you something," said Tom, removing the packet. "We found them buried in a tin can in the sand near the dinosaur."

She took them with trembling hands. "Thank you."

Sally said, "The Smithsonian's having an unveiling of the dinosaur in a new lab custom-built for it out in New Mexico. They're going to christen it. Would you like to come? Tom and I are going."

"Well . . . I'm not sure."

"I think you should . . . They're naming it after you."

Robbie looked up sharply. "What?"

"That's right," said Sally. "The Smithsonian wanted to name it after your father but Tom persuaded them that your dad intended to name it 'Robbie,' after you. And besides, it's a female T. Rex — they say the females were bigger and more ferocious than the males."

Robbie smiled. "He would have named it after me, whether I liked it or not."

"Well?" Tom asked. "*Do* you like it?"

There was a silence and then Robbie finally smiled. "Yeah. I guess I do."

EPILOGUE

JORNADA DEL MUERTO

In four hours, the darkness was complete. She crouched in her wallow, eyes half-closed. The only light came from ribbons of fire burning here and there in the cypresses. The swamp had filled with dinosaurs and small mammals, swimming, thrashing, floating, crazed with fear, many dying and drowning.

She awoke, fed easily and well.

The air became hotter. When she breathed it hurt her lungs, and she coughed in pain. She rose from the water to fight the tormenting heat, ripping and tearing at the air with her jaws.

The heat increased. The darkness increased.

She moved to deeper, cooler water. Dead and dying meat floated around her, but she ignored it.

A black, sooty rain began to fall, coating her back with a tarlike sludge. The air became thick with haze. She saw a red light through the trees. A huge wildfire was sweeping the highlands. She watched it move, exploding through the crowns of the great trees, sending down showers of sparks and burning branches.

The fire passed, missing the swampy enclave where she had taken refuge. The superheated air cooled slightly. She remained in the water, surrounded by bloated, rotting death. Days passed. The darkness became absolute. She weakened and began to die.

Death was a new feeling for her, unlike any she had experienced before. She could feel it working inside her. She could feel its insidious, silent assault on her organs. The fine, downy coat of small feathers that covered her body sloughed off. She could barely move. She panted harder now and yet could not satisfy her hunger for oxygen. Her eyes had been scorched by the heat and they clouded and swelled shut.

Dying took days. Her instincts fought it, resisted every moment of it. Day after day, the pain grew. She bit and kicked at her sides, tearing her own flesh, trying to reach the enemy within. As the pain rose, her fury increased. She struggled blindly toward land, heavy on her feet. Freed of the buoying force of water, she staggered and fell in the shallows. There she bellowed, thrashed, kicking and biting the mud, tearing in a fury at the earth itself. Her lungs began to fill with fluid as her *heart strained to pump the blood through her body.*

The hot, black rain fell.

The biological program that had carried her through forty years of life faltered. The dying neurons fired in one last orgiastic blaze of futile activity. There were no more answers, no programming, no solution for the ultimate crisis. Her fruitless bellowing strangled itself in a shudder of wet, groaning flesh. The left hemisphere of her brain crashed in a storm of electrical impulses, her right leg jerking a dozen savage epileptic kicks before falling into a rigid clonus, the claws flexing open, the tendons popping from the bones. Her jaws opened and snapped shut, opened wide and locked in that position, fiercely agape.

A shudder traveled the length of her tail, vibrating it against the ground until only the tip trembled — and then all neural activity ceased.

The program had run its last line. The black rain continued to fall. Gradually, she became coated with slurry. The water rose, pushed by great storms in the mountains, and within a day she had been buried in thick, sterile mud.

Her sixty-five-million-year entombment had begun.

EPILOGUE

The van bounced along the dirt road, running like an arrow across the vast Jornada del Muerto Desert of New Mexico. The landscape was as flat and empty as the ocean, the only landmark being a distant range of black hills. They were deep in the White Sands Missile Range, a three-thousand-square-mile proving ground for the nation's most advanced weaponry. As they approached, the dark hills took shape. The central one, a volcanic cinder cone, was topped with a row of radio towers and microwave horns.

"We're almost there," said Melodie Crookshank, sitting in the front next to the military driver.

They passed a cluster of burned and boarded-up buildings, enclosed by a double perimeter fence; beyond that stood a gleaming, new structure, faced with brushed titanium panels, surrounded by its own high-security fence.

"This area used to host some kind of genetic engineering lab," said Crookshank, "but they closed it down after a fire. The

Smithsonian worked out an arrangement to lease a part of it. Since it had once been a biosafety level four facility, much of what we needed was already in place — at least in terms of isolation and security. It'll be a perfect place to study the dinosaur — protected by the WSMR security umbrella yet still accessible. All in all, an excellent arrangement."

"It looks like a lonely place to live," said Robbie Weathers.

"Not at all!" said Crookshank. "The desert has a Zen-like purity about it. And this is a fascinating area with all kinds of interesting things to see — ancient Indian ruins, lava flows, caves with millions of bats. Even an old Spanish trail. They've got stables, a swimming pool. I've been learning how to ride horses. It sure beats a windowless basement lab in New York City."

The van bounced over a cattle guard. A guard waved it along. They parked in a graveled lot in front of the building, which was already packed with cars, television vans with satellite uplink dishes, humvees, jeeps, and other military vehicles.

"Looks like quite a party," said Ford.

"I'm told the unveiling will have almost as large a live audience as the World Cup — a billion people."

Ford whistled.

They stepped out of the van into the intense July heat of southern New Mexico. Waves of it were rising off the ground, as if the earth itself were evaporating.

They walked across the parking lot toward the titanium building. A guard held open the door and they entered a large atrium, awash in air-conditioning. A man in uniform, with two stars on his shoulder, came over with his hand extended. "General Miller," he said, shaking hands all around. "Commander of White Sands Missile Range. Welcome." He nodded at Tom. "We met before, but you were one pretty banged-up fellow."

"Sorry, can't say I remember you."

The general grinned. "You look a mite better now."

A group of reporters, waiting at one side of the atrium, came rushing over, flashes popping, cameras and booms thrust forward. "Dr. Crookshank! Dr. Crookshank! Is it true that . . . ?" Their individual questions were lost in a sea of noise as they crowded forward.

Crookshank held up her hands. "Ladies and gentlemen, no questions now. There'll be a press conference after the unveiling."

"A question for Miss Weathers!"

"Save it for the press conference!" shouted Robbie, as they passed into the laboratory complex itself — a long, white corridor lined with stainless-steel doors. They turned a corner and headed toward a large set of double doors at the far end of the hall. The room beyond was a kind of conference room, with rows of seats facing a long, white curtain draped across one wall. The place was packed with scientists in labcoats, gray-suited government types, curators, and military officers; the media were roped off to one side and clearly unhappy about it.

"It's behind that?" asked Robbie, nodding to the curtain.

"That's right. The whole lab was designed so we could work under high security and level four biosafety — but openly, not secretly. That's the key. The results will be posted online for all to see. A discovery like this is . . . well . . . momentous, to say the least."

Melodie greeted various people. More dignitaries arrived and then, in response to an announcement, people took their seats.

"I'm on," said Melodie.

A hush fell as she took to the podium and nervously spread out a half-dozen index cards. A bank of TV floods were switched on and she blinked a few times.

Silence descended.

"Welcome," she said, "to the Smithsonian's new Desert Paleontology Research Station."

A burst of applause.

"I'm Dr. Melodie Crookshank, the assistant director, and I guess you all know why we're here." She shuffled her cards a little nervously. "We're gathered to unveil — and christen — what is, without a doubt, the greatest paleontological discovery ever made. Some would call it the greatest scientific discovery of all time.

"But before we proceed, I'd like to take a moment to mention the man who found this incredible specimen: the late Marston Weathers. You all know the story of Weathers's discovery of the fossil and his murder. Few know that Weathers was probably the greatest dinosaur hunter since the days of Barnum Brown and Robert Sternberg, even if he was a bit unorthodox in his methodology. He's represented here by his daughter, Roberta. Robbie? Please stand up."

A thunderous round of applause went up as Robbie stood, blushing and nodding.

"There are a few other people I want to thank. Tom and Sally Broadbent, first of all, along with Wyman Ford, without whom this dinosaur would not have seen the light of day."

More thunderous applause. Tom glanced at Ford. The man was no longer dressed in brown monk's robes and sandals. Now he was wearing a sleek suit, his beard clipped short, his unruly hair combed neatly back. His big-boned face was still tan from the desert and it was just as ugly. And yet he looked in his element, sophisticated and at ease.

Melodie reeled off a list of people to be thanked, and the crowd began to get restless. But then she paused, consulted her cards again, smiled nervously. A hush fell.

"The MIT physicist Philip Morrison once pointed out that either there is life elsewhere in the universe or there isn't — and that either possibility boggles the mind. Today we stand here knowing the answer to that greatest of scientific questions. There is indeed life elsewhere in the universe.

"The discovery of alien life has been the subject of speculation and science fiction imagination for several centuries, written up in innumerable books and movies. And now it has come to pass. But lo and behold, the discovery happened in a way that was totally unexpected — as an alien microbe entombed in a fossil. Science fiction writers have imagined almost every conceivable scenario for this momentous discovery, except this one. One more proof — as if we needed it — that there are still plenty of surprises in this big, beautiful universe of ours.

"Here, at the Smithsonian Desert Paleontology Research Station, we'll be able to study this new life-form in safety and security — but openly, sharing our discoveries with the world for the entire benefit of humankind. There will be no secrets kept back, no chance that this discovery could be misused in any way except for the good of humankind. Not only that, but the fossil itself will tell us volumes about theropod dinosaurs, in particular Tyrannosaurus rex — their anatomy, cellular biology, how they lived, what they ate, how they reproduced. And finally, we will learn a great deal more about that momentous event sixty-five million years ago, when the Chicxulub asteroid struck, causing the greatest natural disaster ever to befall our planet. We already know that these mysterious alien microbes, these Venus particles, were carried to Earth on the asteroid and were spread by the impact, because a fragment of that same asteroid was found on the moon by the Apollo 17 mission.

"These alien microbes were the last nail in the coffin of the dinosaurs. Whatever dinosaurs survived the impact were killed by a deadly pandemic, a plague to end all plagues. Without the complete and total extinction of the dinosaurs, mammals would never have evolved into anything larger than a rat and human beings would never have existed. So you might say that these particles cleared the earth for us. The asteroid and the epidemic started the great chain of evolution that led to the appearance of human beings."

Crookshank paused, breathed deeply. "Thank you."

Applause filled the room. The director of the Smithsonian Institution, Howard Murchison, strode to the podium, a bottle of champagne in one hand, and shook Crookshank's hand. He turned to the audience and the cameras, smiling broadly.

"May I ask Robbie Weathers to come up?"

Robbie flashed a smile at Tom and Sally and walked to the podium. There the director grasped her hand and placed the bottle of champagne in it.

"Lights, please."

A bank of lights snapped on behind him, spotlighting the heavy curtain drawn across the far end of the hall.

"May I introduce Robbie Weathers, daughter of Marston Weathers, the man who found the dinosaur. We've asked her to officiate at the christening."

There was a burst of applause.

"We can't actually break a bottle of champagne over the dinosaur, but we can at least raise our glasses to it. And who better to do the honors?" He turned to Robbie. "Would you like to say a few words?"

Robbie held up the bottle. "This one's for you, Dad."

More applause.

"Drumroll, please," said the director.

A canned drumroll sounded over the PA system, and at the same time the draperies at the end of the hall drew back, exposing a brightly illuminated laboratory behind a thick sheet of glass. On a set of massive steel tables in the laboratory the astonishing fossil had been laid out in pieces, still partly jacketed in matrix. Preparators had already exposed much of the dinosaur's skull and gaping jaws, twisted neck, clawed hands and feet. More than ever it gave the impression of trying to claw its way out of the rock.

The director held up his hand and the drumroll stopped. "Time to pop the cork. Robbie."

Robbie struggled with the cork, twisting it back and forth. With a pop the cork flew over the heads of the crowd, champagne gushing from the mouth of the bottle. There were cheers and clapping. Murchison caught part of the stream with his glass, raised it to the great fossil, and said, "I christen you *Robbie*, the Tyrannosaurus rex."

A huge cheer went up. Waiters appeared from the wings and walked through the crowd, bearing silver trays loaded with flutes of champagne.

"A toast! A toast!"

The hall filled with the sound of talk, laughter, and tinkling glassware as everyone toasted the great beast. Cries of *"To Robbie, the T. Rex!"* sounded in the hall, while John Williams's score to *Jurassic Park* burst over the loudspeakers.

A few minutes later Melodie rejoined Tom and his group. They clinked glasses all around.

"It's going to be such a kick unlocking the mysteries of that fossil," said Melodie.

"It must be the dream of a lifetime," said Ford.

Crookshank laughed. "I was always a dreamer, but in my wildest dreams I never thought of anything quite like this."

"Life is full of surprising turns, isn't it?" said Ford, winking. "When I entered the monastery, I never would have guessed it would lead me here."

"You don't look much like a monk," said Crookshank.

Ford laughed. "I'm not, never was — and now never will be. The hunt for this dinosaur made me realize I'm not cut out for a life of contemplation. The monastery was the right thing at the right time, but not for the rest of my life."

"What're you going to do?" Tom asked. "Rejoin the CIA?"

He shook his head. "I'm going to hang

up my shingle as a private investigator."

"What? A detective? What would the abbot say?"

"Brother Henry heartily approves. He says he knew from the beginning I'd never become a monk, but it was something I'd have to discover for myself. And so I did."

"What kind of detective?" Sally asked. "Chasing cheating husbands with a camera?"

Ford laughed. "Not at all. Corporate and international espionage, cryptography, cryptanalysis, science and technology. Similar to what I did for the CIA. I'm looking for a partner." He winked at Tom. "How about it?"

"Who, me? What do I know about espionage?"

"Nothing. And that's exactly how it should be. I know your character — that's enough."

"I'll think about it."

There were some more cheers as the director opened another bottle and began circulating among the press corps, refilling their glasses and listening to their complaints.

Ford nodded at the dinosaur head with its bared teeth and hollow eyes. "That tyrannosaur did not go gently into that good night."

"Rage, rage, against the dying of the light," murmured Melodie.

Ford sipped his champagne. "While you were giving your speech, Melodie, a rather offbeat idea occurred to me."

"What's that?"

Ford glanced at the beast, then back at Melodie. "Let me ask you this: what makes you think the Venus particle is alive?"

Crookshank smiled, shaking her head. "Well, you're right that technically it doesn't meet our current definition of life, because it isn't DNA-based. But it meets all the other definitions of life in terms of its ability to reproduce, to grow, to adapt, to feed, to process energy, to excrete waste products."

"There's a possibility you don't seem to have considered."

"And what's that?"

"That the Venus particle is a machine."

"A machine? What, like a nanomachine? Built for what purpose?"

"To ensure the extinction of the dinosaurs. Perhaps it is a machine built to manipulate or direct evolution, which was seeded on an asteroid headed toward Earth — perhaps even on an asteroid *pushed* toward Earth."

"But why?"

"You said it yourself. To make way for the evolution of human beings."

There was a brief silence, and then Melodie laughed uncomfortably. "That *is* an offbeat idea. Only an ex-monk could have dreamed up something as crazy as that."

ACKNOWLEDGMENTS

I am greatly indebted to my editor at Tor/ Forge, the inestimable Robert Gleason, for his ideas, brilliance, and excellent editorial guidance. At Tor I'd also like to thank Tom Doherty, Linda Quinton, Elena Stokes, Eric Raab, and Dana Giusio. I would like to thank Lincoln Child, my partner in literary crime, for his many excellent suggestions. I am most grateful to Eric Simonoff, Matthew Snyder, John Javna, Bobby Rotenberg, Niccolò Capponi, Barbara Peters, and Sebastian Pritchard.

For information on dinosaurs, the Chicxulub strike, the K-T boundary, and the extinction of the dinosaurs, I am indebted to a number of sources, the most important being "The Day the World Burned" by David A. Kring and Daniel D. Durda in the December 2003 issue of *Scientific American*, *The Dinosaur Heresies* by Robert T. Bakker, Ph.D., and *The Complete T. Rex* by John R. Horner and Don Lessem. For anyone wishing further reading in the subject, I recommend these sources, as well as my own nonfiction book, *Dinosaurs in the Attic*, which tells the stories of some of the early dinosaur hunters and their finds.

While Abiquiú, the Chama River, Christ in the Desert Monastery, and the Mesa of the Ancients exist, much of the detailed geography in the novel is fictitious or has been shifted to northern New Mexico from other parts of the country. In particular, I have taken the liberty of moving a remote and truly astonishing canyon in the Big Bend of Texas, known as Devil's Graveyard, into the area to serve as the site of the novel's final confrontation. The recently published photography book about the real Devil's Graveyard, entitled *Ribbons of Time*, contains pictures of the actual terrain described in the novel for those who are interested.

ABOUT THE AUTHOR

Douglas Preston, a regular contributor to *The New Yorker*, has worked for the American Museum of Natural History and taught English at Princeton University. With his frequent collaborator, Lincoln Child, he has authored such best-selling thrillers as *Brimstone, Still Life with Crows, The Cabinet of Curiosities, Riptide, Reliquary, Mount Dragon,* and *Relic,* which became a major Hollywood picture. His nonfiction work includes *Dinosaurs in the Attic,* which chronicles the explorers and expeditions of the American Museum of Natural History's early days. His earlier solo novels include *The Codex* and *Jennie.*

The employees of Thorndike Press hope you have enjoyed this Large Print book. All our Thorndike and Wheeler Large Print titles are designed for easy reading, and all our books are made to last. Other Thorndike Press Large Print books are available at your library, through selected bookstores, or directly from us.

For information about titles, please call:

(800) 223-1244

or visit our Web site at:

www.gale.com/thorndike
www.gale.com/wheeler

To share your comments, please write:

Publisher
Thorndike Press
295 Kennedy Memorial Drive
Waterville, ME   04901